Keeper of the Heart

DISCARDED

By Kim Mattson

Keeper of the Heart
All Rights Reserved

All characters in this book are fictitious. Any resemblance to actual persons, living or dead, is purely coincidental.

This book is protected under the copyright laws of the United States of America. Any reproduction or other unauthorized use of the material or artwork contained herein is prohibited without the express written permission of Port Town Publishing, 601 Belknap Street, Superior WI.

Copyright © 2004 by Kim Mattson

Published By
Port Town Publishing
601 Belknap Street
Superior, WI 54880

Web Address:
www.porttownpublishing.bigstep.com

ISBN: 1-59466-022-0

*Sue and Jeri Ann;
two very special people in my life...*

Note from the author:

When I first sat down and penned *Keeper of the Spirit*, I never imagined that the book would lead to a trilogy about three special brothers who lived in my mind. *Keeper of the Dream* soon followed, and, I never imagined that with the release of *Keeper of the Heart*, the final and last book of the series, I would be home dedicating myself to writing full time. But, here I am, knowing full well how fortunate my life is because I have a chance to live my dream.

Keeper of the Heart is set in 1892 northern Minnesota near a small town called Biwabik. The city's name is taken from the Ojibwa language meaning "valuable". The city is still located in the heart of what is called the Mesabi Iron Range and continues to celebrate its mining heritage and ethnic diversity of yesteryear. In 1891, the Merritt brothers—two of whom will make an appearance in *Keeper of the Heart*—accidentally discovered 'red gold' and, even though the first trainloads of ore began being shipped to Duluth two years later, the Merritt family floundered due to a widespread financial panic in 1892.

It will be hard to say goodbye to the Wilkins family. After all, they have lived with me over the last seven years. I hope you enjoy this last installment of the Keeper Trilogy—it definitely was written from the heart!

—**Kim Mattson**

**Other Titles By
Kim Mattson:**

"An Hour on the Porch"
A short story, included in "Fourteen Pieces of Gold"
Out of Print

"Girls' Weekend"
A short story, included in the anthology, "Sixteen Pieces of Gold"

"Keeper of the Spirit"

"Keeper of the Dream"

*Available direct from Port Town Publishing
Or your favorite bookstore*

Keeper of the Heart

By Kim Mattson

Keeper of the Heart

Prologue

July 4, 1919
Minnesota

    Trevor Wilkins pushed the wood-framed screen door open and strolled out onto the porch. The heavy scent of lavender gardens growing around the edges of the house saturated the hot July morning air.
    He strolled across the wooden planking to a shady area, then seated himself on the swing that hung from an overhead beam. A sigh whispered across his lips as he enjoyed the few moments of solitude before family members converged for the annual Fourth of July celebration. It would be the first time in four years that all but one would be in attendance for the family get-together; four long years of worrying through the Great War and wondering when yet another person close to his heart would be affected by the killing in a world gone mad.
    It had been nearly eight months since the end of the worldwide conflict. Not only his children, but those of his brothers' and sister's, had begun to trickle home. Some were broken after experiencing the travesties of war, and some had simply grown older and wiser, their youth having disappeared, never to be found again.
    A white cat jumped onto Trevor's lap, startling him back to the present. The feline rubbed the side of her face along his chin, and then settled comfortably across his upper legs when Trevor scratched the cat behind an offered ear.
    "Cat." He chuckled quietly. "How come you're not out mousing?" The animal purred in response, worked its claws across the cotton pants, and leaned into the strong fingers that continued to scratch

her neck and ears. "Getting old like the rest of us, aren't you..."

Trevor sighed and glanced up at the lush green grass before him—green grass that comprised the front yard of his home. Rose bushes lined the slate sidewalk that led from the drive to the porch he sat on. The warm morning sunshine turned the pine-covered hillside a deep emerald color, which complemented the bright blue of the lake in the distance. He listened to the loons sing from the far end of the water, their steady forlorn voices a reassuring constant in the many years of his life; a song that greeted him daily, reminding him of the many great fortunes with which he had been blessed.

Trevor remembered a time years ago, when his wife, Claire, diligently and lovingly worked the soil to prepare the area for flowers. She always insisted that a proper lady needed to be constantly aware of how visitors perceived a home as they drove up to pay a call...

Snowball prodded Trevor's hand, which had suddenly stilled. The movement urged the man to scratch the feline's ears with a little more enthusiasm. A deep rumble built in his throat and one corner of his mouth titled upward. "You're as bad as your predecessors. You do realize that you're a fifth generation cat that has lived like royalty in this household?"

To Trevor's wife, the cat was not so much a sign of wealth, but, more fittingly, of a happy, secure life. She would be the first to agree that the world was not perfect. She had always aspired though, to exist in a place where one could lay their head on a pillow at night and hurry sleep into the following day; to slumber soundly without heartache or fear of what the waking hours might bring.

Trevor's gaze swung from the landscape before him to the screen door when it creaked open. Claire stepped from the interior of the house, glanced about the porch, and discovered him sitting alone on the swing.

He observed her feminine form cross the small space between them, her gray eyes surprisingly bright with anticipation of the coming day. A smile curved her full lips—a smile meant only for him. She was as slender as the first time he saw her and her beautiful tresses, now turned gray, were piled atop her head. He did not mind, though; he knew that, when they retired at night, she would remove the pins and the soft curls would tumble about her shoulders while they held one another in the darkness.

She stopped before him, her feminine shape lost momentarily in the glory of the morning sun. The bright rays cloaked her from behind, blotting out the edge of clarity. Trevor reached out to clasp her hand, taking in the hazy apparition before him, and his mind returned to the first time he saw this woman—a woman who now held his heart in the palm of her hand...

Chapter One

June, 1892
St. Paul, Minnesota

Trevor Wilkins clicked the button on the silver stopwatch and, immediately, a wide smile creased his face. "Now, that's the sort of time we've been looking for. I think we've finally got ourselves a winner!"

"Way to go, boss!" Dougan O'Malley slapped Trevor on the back with a joyful grin of his own. "You were right to stick with this one."

Trevor slid the timepiece into his pocket and kept an eye on the magnificent black horse as the training jockey hauled back the reins to slow the animal's pace around the track. "Make sure Willy cools him down good. If I don't get a chance, tell him he's doing a great job. I'd let him know myself, but I have to get the hell out of here and get cleaned up. Tyler and Emma are coming down for a short visit. I'm meeting them at the St. Paul Hotel for an early dinner."

"Will do, Trevor. I plan to hit the road, too, just as soon as I settle The Ghost in." He shook his head; amazement still glowed in his eyes when his gaze settled on the horse and jockey cantering down the dusty track. "That horse is gonna be something, all right. Tell Missus Em I'll see her back at the ranch. If I don't get my Irish butt back up north soon, Katy will be tenderin' my hide!"

A chuckle rumbled in Trevor's chest when he pushed himself away from the stark white fencing and adjusted the Stetson that sat atop his thick, wavy hair. "So, that woman of yours still has you jumping through hoops, huh?"

Dougan's curly reddish-gray head bobbed in a nod. "Nothing

wrong with havin' a good woman to keep you in line when you're needin' it, Trevor—and havin' her to warm your bed on a regular basis is just an added bonus."

Trevor lifted an eyebrow as he shook his dark head. "Well, I'll leave the 'jumping through hoops' to men like you and my brothers. It's definitely not for me. As far as warm beds...well, I'll leave that to your imagination. I never kiss and tell. " He reached out a hand with a wry smile shining in his green eyes. "Thanks for taking the time to bring The Ghost down. I just can't seem to get out of the city anymore. And make sure you tell Katy I'd give anything for one of her home cooked meals."

"You should be tellin' her yourself. It's a bloody shame, Trevor, that you possess a fine house in the making up north, yet you never get home to finish it."

At the Irishman's spoken words, Trevor's brain flashed to a few years earlier, when he decided to move out of the main ranch house permanently and build his own place on the northern most edge of their property. The original homestead had filled up quickly; Cole and August had two children. Combine them with Tyler and Emma's brood, and the place was turned upside down more of often than not. There was no longer room for him, at least to his way of thinking, but he could not work up the enthusiasm required to complete his own home, either. Thinking deeply on the matter, it seemed senseless to put time and money into a house when he spent so much time in the city.

The lines deepened around his eyes as he squinted into the sun. "Ah, someday, Dougan, things will calm down and maybe I'll get it finished. Doesn't seem that important right now. Besides, I like St. Paul and all it has to offer."

Trevor shook Dougan's hand, and then turned toward the stable that sat adjacent to the racetrack. His thick chest ballooned before a deep sigh escaped though his lips. Not only did his family continually badger him about his uncompleted home and unmarried status, but now it seemed they had enlisted the hired help to aid in their cause, as well. He shook his head again.

Why should I change my lifestyle to please them? I'm happy, and that's all that should matter—to anybody.

Trevor had long since given up on the idea of marriage. Instead, he found the excitement of breeding race horses, the thrill of discovering a true winner, and the constant trips around the United States to be better bedmates than a woman who would constantly nag at him because he was never home.

Not that a few pretty fetching ladies haven't tried...and my age doesn't seem to be a factor.

They flounced before him with their powdered faces, rouged cheeks and expensive clothes, each doing their best to cajole him into a trip down the aisle. They offered not only themselves, but their homes as part of the deal.

Trevor pursed his lips and shook his dark head again. Sometimes, the efforts to snag him into wedded bliss were downright embarrassing.

Nope...I'm right where I want to be. Thirty-nine years old and too goddamned set in my ways. I'll leave the contracted lovin' to Cole and Tyler and go on my merry way.

He strolled across the familiar racing grounds, subconsciously noting the cleanliness of the exercise arenas. Trevor planned to bring Emma and Tyler back for a visit that afternoon; his sister-in-law would be pleased to know that The Ghost was being well taken care of while absent from his home on the ranch.

The cool air inside the Whitehope Downs' barn enveloped Trevor when he entered the massive structure and headed for the office to assure his future winner would have one of the better stalls during the training session.

It had taken four years, but the Wilkins' had finally managed to breed the right combination of horseflesh. The result was a two-year old Thoroughbred that promised to tear up the track. Cole, Tyler and Emma were more than content to let Trevor handle the demanding details of track life as they added yet another dimension to their partnership. It was a perfect arrangement—and a perfect life for the middle Wilkins son, contrary to the opinions of his immediate family.

Trevor finished up at the office and retraced his path past the long line of immaculate stalls. He stepped into the bright sunlight by way of the front entrance and was nearly knocked to the ground when a whirling ball of flesh and ragged clothes rammed headlong into his legs.

"Hey, slow down, you little ruffian!" Trevor bent, grabbed the straps of worn out bibs, and set a young tow-headed boy back on his feet again. The child immediately tried to scramble away from the tenuous hold, but Trevor tightened his grip and yanked the boy to safety before he darted into the street and oncoming traffic. "Hey, hold it right there! You gotta watch where you're going, or you're going to get hurt. What's the hurry?"

"Let me go!" A pair of fearful, watery gray eyes glanced up at the much larger man, and then shifted quickly to glance over his shoulder in the direction he had just come from. He lunged once more, but Trevor only twisted his fingers around the straps of the boy's bibs for a firmer grip.

Trevor followed the child's wide-eyed gaze to where a shopkeeper ran toward them, his white apron flapping in the wind and his beefy fist waving in the air.

Wise green eyes narrowed as Trevor glanced down at the boy again. "That merchant isn't perhaps looking for you, is he?" He reached out a free hand and patted the bulging pocket at the boy's waist, immediately figuring out what had transpired just before he was nearly knocked to the ground. "What do you have in there?"

The fight left the lad, his shoulders slumped and, a split-second later, a single tear escaped down a dirty cheek. "It's just a old apple. Mr. Timmons said he was gonna throw out a whole pile of rotten ones anyway."

"This Mr. Timmons must be the man running in our direction, correct?" The small boy trembled again at the mention of the shopkeeper. Instantly, the child's fear pricked at Trevor's own conscience. He relaxed his grip slightly, hunched down, and then smiled to ease the kid's tension. "What's your name?"

The boy wiped at his runny nose with a ragged sleeve and shuffled his feet, but could not find the courage to look up. "Jonah," he muttered to the ground.

"So, Jonah, why did you steal that apple?" Trevor leaned closer, but still missed the mumbled response. "I didn't hear you."

"I said I was hungry," the boy spouted back when he glanced up. "That old man wasn't gonna sell them old apples anyway, so it wasn't really stealin'."

Trevor heaved a sigh. The kid had a point. "That doesn't matter. The apples still belonged to the shopkeeper. If you're hungry, go home and eat. I'm sure your pa wouldn't be happy to hear that you stole something from the shop."

"I ain't got no pa."

"Do you live in this area—"

"Hey—hold onto that kid!" an angry voice shouted.

Trevor and Jonah looked up at the same time—just as the shopkeeper crossed the street.

"I've had enough of you pilfering little brats helping yourselves to anything you want in my store!" Mr. Lucas Timmons skidded to a halt, his face red from exertion. Beads of perspiration ran in rivulets down around his chin, evidencing his wrath—and his lengthy chase. He lifted a hefty opened fist, ready to box Jonah's ears, but his downward swing was halted in mid-air by Trevor's restraining hand.

"Stop right there, mister. I don't think stealing a rotten apple is reason enough to beat this boy." Trevor rose to his full height with a stern frown furrowing his brow.

"The hell it ain't. It's the only thing these urchins understand," the enraged man spewed. "Someone has to put the fear of God into him." He raised his palm again.

Jonah cringed, raced behind Trevor, and grabbed onto the leg of his newfound protector. Timmons launched forward just as quickly to make a grab for the boy. Jonah released a high-pitched shriek and clutched Trevor's leg tighter.

"That's just about enough," Trevor ground out. He grabbed Timmons and muscled him against the bricked stable wall, then held the shopkeeper in place with a bent elbow as he reached behind him to pick the clinging boy free of his leg. It was a useless endeavor. Every time he managed to loosen the boy's arm, the kid wrapped a scrawny leg around his protector's longer limb.

Trevor shook his leg again and watched the boy's head bounce like a puppet; the death grip only tightened. His lips thinned into a straight line. "You know, I'm just about out of goddamned patience..."

"Jonah!"

Trevor swung his head to the right when he heard the raised female voice. A slender, middle-aged woman stood on the curb. A toddler perched on her jutting hip, another held her hand, and two young girls—with heavy burlap sacks in tow—stood behind her. The woman's

Keeper of the Heart

gray eyes held a frazzled, rather desperate look, but the uncommon color complimented the wispy strands of curly sun-bleached hair that fluttered in the wind about her high cheekbones. She tipped her head upward, and the faded brim of her floppy hat flapped in the breeze. She squinted against the glaring sun, deepening the lines about her eyes.

"Ma!" Jonah let go of his savior's leg and ran to her side, then slipped behind the faded folds of her cotton dress. He peeked around the back of the girl straddling her mother's hip—one whom Trevor assumed to be his little sister.

The woman glanced down at her son. "Jonah? Mr. Timmons ran out of his store hollering that you had stolen an apple from him? Did you steal an apple?"

"Ma..."

"Don't 'Ma' me. Answer my question, young man." Her gentle, but firm voice brooked no obstinacy on her son's part.

Jonah trudged from behind her skirts, dug into his pocket, and pulled the rotten fruit into view. He held it out to his mother.

"Don't be giving that thing to me," she admonished. "Give it back to Mr. Timmons, along with an apology."

Trevor withdrew his arm from the shopkeeper's chest and let the man catch his breath. Lucas Timmons glared up at him, straightened his collar, and snatched the apple from the small boy's clutches. He then lifted his nose to peer at Jonah through round spectacles for a moment before turning his gaze back to the boy's mother. "I don't want an apology, Mrs. Holcomb." He cleared his throat and stared into the weary woman's eyes. "I want five cents, and you'd better be glad that's all I'll charge you. As for your son, I intend to call the sheriff and have him handle the matter for me; so, you can march yourself and your passel of dirty little hooligans back to the store."

Her long, thick, lashes fluttered shut with annoyance upon the man's insult to her children, and the bodice of her worn dress swelled when she drew in a deep breath to control her anger. "Mr. Timmons, I will be more than happy to pay you double for the apple, but at the moment I have no money on me. I'll go—"

"Wait a minute." Trevor stepped forward, dug into his pocket, and pulled out a silver coin. He dropped it into Timmons' outstretched palm. "There's no need to harass this woman over a nickel or to bring the law into this simple matter. Take the nickel and consider it done."

The woman bristled unexpectedly upon his interference into her personal matters. "Excuse me, sir." She eyed Trevor's expensive clothes, right down to his shiny black boots, and finally brought her condescending gaze back to his. "I don't need you to be a knight in shining armor, coming to my rescue."

"I just—"

"You just what?" She cut him off again as her gray eyes turned to steel. "Just because you have more money in your wallet at present than I'll probably have in a lifetime means nothing. I can take care of my own—I've managed so far."

Trevor's mouth sagged open in stunned amazement. The petite, feminine, and extremely needy person from a moment before was a sham. The present woman standing in the hot sun looked ready to chew him up and spit him out. "Now listen, Ma'am—"

"You listen! I don't know who you think you are, but you can take your shiny boots and mind your own business while I take care of mine." She raised her quivering chin another notch and looked at Mr. Timmons, but spoke to her son. "Jonah? You apologize this minute for stealing from the store."

Jonah shuffled his feet on the wooden walk, sighed heavily, and shoved his hands into the pockets of his bibs. "Sorry, Mr. Timmons. You won't have to worry about it happening again."

His mother pierced the shopkeeper with a darkened glare. "I hope you won't bring the sheriff into this small matter. As soon as we get home, I'll send Jonah back with your nickel." She hiked the wiggling toddler more securely onto her slender hip and glanced at her silent offspring. "Come, children. If Jonah needs to come back to town, we must be on our way or he'll be traveling in the dark." She turned then and stomped away with her brood.

The tilt of her head and the scrambling children who trailed out behind her reminded Trevor of a mother duck and her babies, out for an afternoon stroll. He blinked, shook his head, and turned to the shopkeeper. "Who in the hell was that?"

The merchant adjusted his glasses on his thin nose and flipped Trevor's nickel through the air, watching as the other man caught it. "That, sir, is Claire Holcomb; one of the toughest one-hundred pound

Keeper of the Heart

bundles I've ever met. Normally, she's a soft-spoken woman, but you don't want to get her dander up—like I did today. I've finally had enough of her brats, though. I have to keep an eye on them every time they come into the store or they'd steal me blind."

Trevor eyed the rotten apple in the man's palm. "You would begrudge a small child a rotted piece of fruit when he's hungry?" His green gaze shifted back to the woman who strode away from them. "She doesn't look like she's got much money."

"Hell, they're always hungry. Claire's old man died two years ago—got drunker than a skunk one night, fell into the river, and drowned. Wouldn't have blamed Claire if she pushed him in herself, though. He was mean as they come when on the liquor. She's trying to make a go of it at her small farm by selling milk and eggs to some of the restaurants in town. Hand to mouth, that one." He shook his head. "She'd be better off givin' those youngins away, but she refuses to do so." With a suddenly disinterested shrug, Timmons nonchalantly pitched the decaying piece of fruit into the street, turned, and headed for his store.

Trevor watched the apple roll to a stop in the middle of the busy lane. A moment later, it was flattened when the wheel of a passing buggy smashed it into the dirt. He shook his head with the ridiculousness of the situation.

He turned, placed his hands in his pockets, and contemplated Jonah's mother as she hustled the children across the street only a half-block away. As though feeling his gaze upon her, she turned and the light breeze pressed her thin cotton dress against her slender body. Beneath the faded material, long legs and a flat stomach were outlined against the brightness of the day.

Claire brushed a wayward strand of hair back from her face and met his gaze again, no matter how hesitantly. Another deep breath followed, leaving no doubt in Trevor's mind as to the fullness of Mrs. Claire Holcomb's chest.

His stomach muscles tightened at the sight, and his green eyes narrowed as he considered his own powerful physical reaction to a middle-aged widow with five scraggily urchins.

Trevor shrugged the incident from his mind a moment later, then mounted his horse and headed in the other direction.

Kim Mattson

* * *

Claire Holcomb perched on an old wooden bench placed on what was left of her rickety front porch and stared numbly across the yard toward the barn. Even in the fading light of day, it was easy to see that the building actually leaned heavily to the right. Her intense gray gaze followed the sloping line of the roof, and then moved to the large logs that shored up the ceiling—logs that were visible through a slatted door that hung open on bent hinges.

One small wind storm and it's going to fall over like a pile of matchsticks... Her chin quivered.

She blinked and allowed one lone tear to escape down her cheek before squaring her shoulders against the pain of losing everything that was hers. Not that it amounted to much.

Claire rose wearily and crossed to the railing, mindlessly testing the sturdiness to assure she would not be flung to the dusty ground, and leaned her slim forearms across the sun-bleached wood. Her brain raced as her gaze darted about the yard. The place had definitely seen better days, but where possible, it was as neat as a pin. With the light from the kitchen lamp casting its hue through the window, she could just make out the small flower patch; the garden was filled with blossoms that reached to the sky—an out of place scrap of colorful loveliness surrounded by a weathered house and barn that slowly disintegrated as each season passed. Her fingers wearily rubbed her smooth forehead.

I have to make a decision—something she had put off until that very moment. *I've got to come up with a way to scratch out some sort of living to feed and clothe all of us...* They could not survive long on twelve dollars and fifty-five cents; correction—fifty cents. She had sent Jonah packing, back to the general store with a silver nickel clutched in his fingers.

A tremulous sigh left her full lips. In only three weeks, Claire and her children would be forced off their property; she had missed yet another payment to the bank. She was already delinquent by six months and the taxes were due again. She straightened, hugged herself, and rubbed away the goose bumps on her arms, even though the night heat enveloped her.

Three weeks... In her frazzled mind, it felt more like three hours.

Claire had wracked her brain over the past few days to think of a solution, but no earth-shattering revelation was forthcoming.

"You'll figure out something," she muttered to the night, and then swatted at a mosquito—anything to take her mind from the frightening future that loomed in the near distance.

A huge lump of fear began to build in her throat, forcing her off the porch and out into the yard. She automatically crossed to the scattered pieces of tree trunk that lay haphazardly around a large stump with an ax imbedded in its center.

Claire grasped the wooden handle and yanked it from its resting spot and, little by little, the growing dread was chipped away along with the oak. Her husband left her vulnerable to the world when he drowned in that river; he left her without any money; and he left her totally alone.

She bent, steadied another chunk of wood on the stump, and raised the ax with a steady hand. Flexing the muscles in her slender arms, she swung with a vengeance. Two pieces of firewood lay on the ground a split second later.

She ignored the sting in her hands as her fingers tightened around the wooden handle. *What would I do if Frank was standing before me right now?* she wondered. *Hell, I'd probably crack the ax over his head.* Had she ever really loved him? Her life with Frank was, for the most part, miserable.

She swallowed to control the emotions that pricked at her heart—emotions that caused her to dwell on what she had missed in the last ten years. *My life should have been so different...*

Claire worked mechanically. One piece after another became a growing pile of wood—wood she would use for fuel to bake bread, using the little bit of flour she had left—or to heat the house from the cold Minnesota winter only months away. Would she even be there to see it?

The dam burst. Tears flooded down her cheeks as the ax slipped from lifeless fingers. It hit the ground with a thud. Claire collapsed beside the stump, unable to fight the panic-born sobs any longer. A terror-filled shriek rose in her throat, but she clasped shaking hands over mouth, muffling her desperation as she rocked in the familiar darkness.

"Damn you, Frank, you miserable..." she sobbed into her hands. He had done this to her. He had put her in this position. The first year of their marriage was bearable; then he took to the bottle like a pig to mud.

His constant tardiness had gotten him fired from one job after another. She never dared to object much as the years moved on; she would only receive the back of his hand in reply. The only good things that came from her marriage to the drunkard were the beautiful children they shared. She had endured him grunting on top of her night after night, and her reward was the five lives she would die for now. She had closed her heart to everything but them.

"Mama?"

Claire spun away from the sound of Jonah's voice and quickly swiped the wetness from her face.

"What's wrong, Mama?"

"Nothing..." Claire breathed deeply to clear her head. She rose with her back to her son and brushed wood chips from her faded dress. "Did your sisters get the little ones to sleep?"

"Everyone's gone to bed." Jonah stepped closer. Even though Claire tried to hide her face, he knew she had been crying. He heard the weeping when he left the house. He stretched out his freshly washed hand and laid it on his mother's arm.

Claire slammed her eyes shut at the warm touch and took another calming breath.

"I heard you crying. Did you hurt yourself?"

"No, honey."

"Then why are you crying?"

Claire filled her lungs again, grappling for the serenity her son needed to see. "Sometimes...Mamas cry for no reason." She turned and a tremulous smile curved her lips. "My goodness, I don't know what I was thinking to carry on so."

Jonah gazed up at her, unconvinced that his mother's lapse from her normal firm, but cheery self was simply nothing. He squared his shoulders and tried to make his thin body appear larger. "I saw the letter from the bank. Are we leaving? Is that why you were crying?" He stood before her, a nine-year old boy ready to take the weight from his mother's shoulders.

She melted at the sight. No matter the stolen apple—Jonah was a good boy who worked hard beside her. She reached out her hand and fondly tousled his blond head. "Can I talk to you about something?"

His head bobbed with importance.

She wiped her eyes with the edge of the sun-bleached apron around her waist. "We're almost out of money, Jonah. I tried. I really did, but I don't think the bank is going to let us live here anymore. We can't sell enough eggs and milk to live off of or to pay the back taxes we owe."

The little boy batted away instant tears and never took his gaze from the one that was so much like his own. "I'm sorry I stole that apple. I didn't mean for you to have to pay that ol' Timmons."

"Oh, honey." Claire sank to her knees and pulled him into her embrace. Jonah went willingly, tucked his head into the crook of her neck, and wrapped his arms around her. The tears burned in her eyes once more. "One little nickel isn't going to make a difference," she mumbled close to his ear.

Jonah leaned back in her embrace and searched her gentle features. "Maybe you should've let that nice man pay for the apple."

Until that moment, Claire had not given the rich gentleman another thought. Her mind was filled, instead, with finding a way out of the situation she and her children were in. Now, the sight of shiny boots and an expensive, immaculate suit flashed in her mind's eye. Immediately, anger and jealously raced through her blood. He had probably never wanted for a thing in his life.

Jonah's eyes widened with a sudden thought. "Maybe we can find him and ask him to give us some money. That way we can stay at the farm." His quick little mind instantly shifted to another worry. "Where will our cat go if we have to leave?" His eyes widened with alarm, and he blurted the last. "We have to ask him, Ma."

"Don't be foolish. Imagine what that man would think if we knocked on his door asking for a handout?" No, the one thing that Claire Holcomb was fully sure of was that she would never depend on a man to take care of her again—even if he had pockets full of money. "People don't ask complete strangers for a handout. And, don't worry about the cat. If we have to leave, we'll take Snowball with us."

She stood, took his hand in hers, and led him in the direction of the house.

"Mama?"

"Yes, dear?"

"How much time do we have?"

She squeezed his little hand, then placed her arm around his shoulders. *Not enough...* "You let me worry about that. No matter what, we'll get through this together. You and me, we're a tough breed, Jonah. And no matter where we lay our heads, it'll be our home as long as we're together."

Chapter Two

Trevor entered the grand foyer of the St. Paul Hotel and immediately headed for the dining room. His excitement increased when he spotted his older brother and sister-in-law already sitting at a table with two other gentlemen. He had not seen Tyler and Emma since the previous fall and was excited to catch up on family news.

As he strode between the tables filled with hotel patrons, his eyes noted Tyler's graying temples and it hit him that twelve years had passed since Emma and his brother were married. Tyler turned his head at the same moment and noted Trevor approach the table. A smile widened across his rugged features as he rose from his chair and extended a palm.

"Trevor! It's damn good to see you!"

Trevor grinned widely in return and squeezed his brother's shoulder before he turned to his sister-in-law. Gently clasping Emma's slender hand, he bent and kissed the back of it. "It's so good to see you, Em."

She rose and was welcomed into his arms. "It's been too long, Trevor. It seems that we must forever travel to St. Paul to find you. We've missed you at the ranch."

Trevor smiled across the top of her auburn head at his brother, who simply shrugged, and then he squeezed Emma's still trim waist. "You get more beautiful as each year passes."

He received a playful punch for his compliment.

"You always were a sweet talker when you know I'm going to take you to task!"

Trevor chuckled as he held the back of her chair and waited until she was seated once more. "And you love every minute of it. How are the kids?"

Emma eyed him closely. "Go ahead, change the subject. The children are busy and doing wonderfully. We just heard from Janie. She loves her art studies in Europe. Thomas is growing like a weed, and Sara spends her days dogging her father and Cole in the horse barns. If I didn't know better, I'd think she was your daughter for how she's always scheming in regard to which animals will breed faster horses. Oh, and Trevor," she retorted with pert, raised eyebrows, "you might think that you've managed to get me off track, but you haven't. We'll simply discuss your continued absence later on." Her chagrin, however, was tempered with an upward curve of her lips.

Lovingly, he patted her shoulder and turned to the two gentlemen seated across the table. "Good afternoon. I'm Tyler's brother, Trevor."

Both gentleman rose. The elder, who was closer, clasped the newcomer's hand. "Hello. I'm Leonidas Merritt and this is my brother, Cassius. I'm sorry. I didn't realize that Tyler and his wife were waiting for a family member. If I'd known, we would have set up a meeting for another time."

Trevor's eyebrows immediately rose as he glanced at his brother. The two gentlemen before him had fast become a commercial name in northern Minnesota. Mining men. *What the hell is Tyler doing meeting with them?*

Tyler spied his silent question, but waited until everyone was settled into their chairs again, and then leaned forward to address Trevor. "Leonidas and his brother have asked to meet with us regarding the sale of some of our land holdings. It wasn't anything I felt I should discuss without you in attendance, since the property in question is the outer northern border of the ranch."

Leaning against the back of his chair, Trevor crossed his arms over his broad chest and glanced from one Merritt brother to the next. Tyler wanted him involved in the conversation for one reason and one reason only. Trevor had begun to build his home on the northernmost edge of the Wilkins' property—property that rested along the edges of the Merritt's Mt. Iron and Biwabik mine holdings. "Your request surprises me. From what I've heard, which I'm sure is no secret to you, people are talking that your Mt. Iron Mine needs capital to stay afloat.

Keeper of the Heart

With the investment money you sank into your rail lines to Biwabik, it's being said that you're now short of funds." His sharp gaze pierced each of the surprised men. He might not reside on his property, but he always made it a point to keep abreast of the mining activities that were quickly escalating to the north. "I guess before we go any further, I'd like you to convince me of how you think you can afford to purchase more land—especially mine?"

The elder Merritt's jaw clenched slightly as he worked to maintain his air of calm. "That land is heavy with virgin timber."

Aha! Now I know where this is going. Trevor remained silent, however, to see how desperate the man actually was.

"We would like to discuss a bargain of sorts. You have access to the gentlemen who took over ownership of your lumber business a few years back. Once you give them permission to clear-cut that particular plot of land, they would receive their fair share of the stumpage profit from the timber sale. The Wilkins' estate would receive the rest of the revenue in its entirety, plus stock options in not only the Mt. Iron and Biwabik mines, but also the Duluth, Missabe and Northern Railroad—which we own. We feel this is a very generous offer. Everyone involved would profit heavily."

Trevor sifted the information through his mind. "Yes, that is a good offer, but what makes you think I want part of your railroad company? Or for that matter, stock in mine holdings?" He straightened in his chair, clasped his hands together on the table, and reflected a moment longer before he continued. "Let's be honest here, Mr. Merritt. You need to dump quite a bit of money into your mining ventures in order for them to remain viable. I, on the other hand, hold a piece of property that not only includes a huge amount of natural ore just beneath the surface, but is covered with virgin timber—one of the last plots in this area to make that claim. Have you seen what the last remaining lumber companies have done to northern Minnesota? They've stripped the land, leaving it totally bare and open to erosion."

Leonidas sipped his brandy after sending a quick glance at the very quiet Tyler. "Strange words from a former lumber baron."

Trevor simply shrugged.

Tyler cleared his throat and finally spoke up. "Not so strange when you consider how we ran Northern Pines Lumber when it was under our ownership. Of the thousands of acres we logged, we never left an area stripped clean. Conservation for the future was always at the forefront. The area you would like us to relinquish now was set aside years ago by our father. He, too, had the foresight to keep part of the land as it was."

Leonidas shook his head, twirling the stem of his crystal glass between his fingers. "Gentlemen, the offer I presented will make you rich beyond your wildest dreams."

"By raping all the land in northern Minnesota? A man can only be so greedy." Trevor's eyes were wide with amazement. "I'm building a home in that area. In fact, I'm close enough to the Biwabik Mine to hear the drilling at night, and the hiss of a steam shovel can be heard at times during the day. Do you actually think I want to look out my window someday and see treeless land surrounding a gaping hole in the earth?"

"It's the future," the other man returned. "Minnesota's Iron Range will be a piece of history someday. Your family owns most of the private land left in the northeastern part of the state. By relinquishing some of your property, you could be a part of that history."

Trevor stifled the snort that threatened to erupt. "I will be—by retaining an untouched section for future generations. That's what you can take to the bank."

Anger blazed in Leonidas' eyes. As he opened his mouth to respond, Cassius reached across to silently grasp his brother's arm and stay his words. Once he was certain he had quieted any further retorts, he cleared his throat and met Trevor's steady gaze. "As much as we'd like to continue this discussion, we have another appointment to attend to." He stood and urged Leonidas from the chair with his eyes. "We'll be in St. Paul until the end of the week. Take a few days and think about our offer. You can either reach us at our office in the city or wire us in Duluth if you should change your minds." His gaze rested on Emma. "It was very pleasant meeting you, Mrs. Wilkins. Best wishes to you and your family."

Emma tipped her chin in recognition and watched the two men weave their way through the dining room and exit into the foyer. A soft breath escaped through her lips as they rounded the corner and disappeared from sight. Immediately, she squeezed Trevor's hand. "I can't tell you how happy I am that you wouldn't even consider their offer."

Trevor smiled into her green eyes. "My father would roll in his grave if we agreed to sell that piece of property." His next words were of a more serious vent, however. "That plot of land will be the only thing left that even resembles the past. I understand that mining is here to stay. I'd be a fool not to believe that, but I want no industrial encroachment on our property. I hope you agree with me, Tyler. If you think, however, that we should give credence to a sale, just let me know. I want to do what you, Cole, and Carrie feel is best, also."

Tyler set his drink glass on the surface of the table. "I spoke with both of them before leaving the ranch. Carrie and Cole feel as you do. So do I. If we don't take a stand now, there'll be nothing left but huge holes in the ground one hundred years from now."

Trevor's sharp brain suddenly shifted to the previous discussion. He was surprised that Leonidas was so easily upset about his refusal to sell. "Don't you think the Merritts seemed rather desperate?"

"They are. Financially, they're running into huge deficits. You've read the papers. John Rockefeller from out east is securing financing and has been buying up their options under the guise of other companies. Personally, the man is close to owning a bigger share of the pie. The writing is on the wall—and the Merritts know it. It's just a matter of time before their years of hard work and exploration are handed over. Already, small mines are springing up faster than you can blink all over northern Minnesota."

Trevor's jaw hardened. "Well, they won't be springing up on Wilkins property. I know there's no way to halt progress, but I'll be damned if it'll be in my own back yard."

"You sound like you plan to continue with the house—and possibly move home someday." Hope shone in Emma's eyes as she spoke the words.

"Someday, maybe. I can't see it being in the near future, however. I've got too much going on here in the city."

Emma's chin came up. "You, quite possibly, are the most stubborn man I've ever met. You know what, Trevor? You need to find a woman, bring her north, and get that house finished."

Trevor threw back his head and laughed. "I don't how you put up with her, Tyler." His laughing eyes settled on his sister-in-law's feminine form. "Emma, dear, I think I've long since passed the time of settling down."

"Hah! You're never too old. Stranger things have happened."

"Yeah? Well, that's neither here nor there at the moment. Now, how about you fill me in on the goings-on at the ranch? How's Cole and August doing?"

"Wonderfully. August is expecting again. Her and Cole are forced to stay within the boundaries, but are two of the happiest people I've ever come across. August has adjusted well. It's as if she's lived on the ranch forever. She even asked me to teach her to read. Cole told me to let you know he expects you to visit at least once this summer." Emma reached across the table, squeezed her brother-in-law's large hand, and lowered her voice. "He misses you, Trevor. And Mamie is getting up there in age. She worries about you all the time. Please, come home and visit."

"All right, all right," he consented. "I'll free up some time at the end of summer and plan to come up for a few weeks. How does that sound?"

Emma clapped her hands together like a small child. "Perfect!"

* * *

The following afternoon, Trevor had again returned to Whitehope Downs to observe The Ghost's midday training, this time with Emma and Tyler in tow. The late June afternoon was filled with sunshine as the small group approached the open doors of the stable. A light, warm breeze filtered through the building, carrying along with it the fresh scent of hay and clean, healthy animals.

Emma eagerly glanced into each stall as they made their way to the far end of individual paddocks, inspecting the many different racing animals with a practiced eye. "I can't wait to see The Ghost. I have to congratulate you on finding Whitehope, Trevor. This place is spotless and it's easy to see they house some wonderful bloodlines! Even though that may be, however, I still think our horses outshine all of them."

Tyler grabbed her hand as she nearly skipped beside him. "You've always thought our livestock surpassed every other four legged creature you've ever come across."

Trevor smiled inwardly at his brother's comment. He would be amiss if he did not agree with his sister-in-law. He felt the same way. Stopping before a whitewashed wooden gate, he turned and swept his arm outward. Before Emma reached the slatted stall entrance, a magnificent black head appeared over the top.

"Ghost!" she squealed with delight. The horse instantly lowered his whiskered snout, nuzzled her cheek, and nickered softly in remembrance. Emma scratched him gently behind his big ears. "Hi, sweet baby. Do you miss your friends from the ranch?"

Tyler and Trevor both rolled their eyes behind her back at the affectionate display.

"It's a racing horse, Em. A big, tough stallion bred to run at top speed. He's not some Shetland pony waiting for a treat." As the words left Trevor's mouth, The Ghost dropped his head and snuffled at Emma's pocket. An instant later, she withdrew a carrot she had secreted away and giggled when the animal gently took it from her outstretched palm and made quick work of the vegetable. The horse then rested his forehead quietly against her chest, as docile as a kitten.

Emma turned her head with a wry smile on her lips and eyed her brother-in-law as she scratched the animal's forehead. "Excuse me? What were you just saying? Oh, yes. The Ghost is a big, mean stallion." She dropped a kiss between his ears. "He seems quite wild, don't you think?"

"You know," Trevor stated with a shake of his head, "he probably gets that from you tucking him in every night at the ranch. It's a damn good thing I had him sent down here before he turned into a carthorse. All right, I stand corrected."

Another bubble of a giggle escaped from Emma's throat as she stroked the horse's thick neck. Just as quickly, however, the laughter was gone when she spotted a movement out of the corner of her eye. Glancing around Trevor's broad chest, she spied a small boy. The child stood by hesitantly, closely watching the trio of adults. "Well, hello there," she stated quietly with a gentle smile on her face.

The men turned to discover whom she spoke to. Trevor's eyebrows rose when he recognized the young lad from the day before.

Jonah shuffled his bare feet against the straw-covered floor and plunged his hands into his faded bibs. He had waited most of the day for the rich gentleman to appear again and had almost given up hope that he would ever return to the stables. Now that he had finally arrived, Jonah was slightly intimidated at the presence of the other two finely clothed adults.

"Jonah, isn't it?" Trevor stated as he took a few steps closer. A small round chin nodded in response when the boy peeked up. The sight of the child's gray eyes reminded Trevor of a pair of glittering ones beneath a floppy brim. "Is there something I can do for you?"

Jonah's toes traced another circle through the straw before he tilted his blond head further. "I been waitin' for you all day..."

"And?"

"I...I wanted to thank you, sir, for helpin' me out yesterday."

Trevor hunkered down to the boy's level, but not before glancing up at the couple who stood in the barn with him. Tyler and Emma's eyes both held a question.

"Jonah had a...let's say a small altercation with a shopkeeper yesterday. I helped him to iron it out." He turned back to face the youngster. "Did you ever get back to town to pay the man his nickel?"

"Yes, sir. My ma wouldn't have it no other way."

"Your ma must be a fine honest lady then." Thinking back on her stiff spine and glaring eyes, however, Trevor imagined that the last thing Jonah would want to do is butt heads with his mother. Claire Holcomb nearly tore his own head off when he offered to help.

Trevor straightened to his full height and held out his hand to accept Jonah's. "All right, son, your thanks has been duly accepted." He waited until the boy's dirt-stained hand clasped his before speaking again. "Remember, no more rotten apples—even if they are going to be thrown out." With a last gentle smile, he turned his attention back to Emma and Tyler, thinking his discussion with the boy was over.

Not so.

"Sir?"

Trevor turned back and waited to see what else the child had to say.

"Sir, I don't even know your name."

"You can call me Trevor. And as long as we're making introductions here, this is my brother, Tyler—" he nodded in the other man's direction "—and his wife, Emma. This here young lad's name is

Jonah."

Jonah's eyes bulged in their sockets. No adult had ever given him permission to use first names. He swallowed and stepped closer, then quickly spit in the palm of one hand and wiped it across the leg of his bibs before he took the lady's extended hand in his. "Nice to meet you, ma'am. You're about the prettiest lady I ever did see."

Emma ignored his damp palm and smiled. "It's very nice to meet you, Jonah. Thank you very much for the compliment."

"You're welcome." The boy's cheeks flushed a bright red hue.

"Hey! Is that kid bothering you?" Before any of the Wilkins adults could answer, Clarence Pettibone, the stable manager, stalked down the center aisle with his fist slightly raised in the air. "You, kid, how many times today have I told you to stay out of the barn? Now, git!"

Before anyone could say a word, Jonah spun in the straw, raced to the end of the aisle, and leapt through the open door. His small form was gone an instant later.

"He botherin' you?" Pettibone finally reached the small group. "I'll take a strap to him the next time he comes skulking around if he is."

Emma's eyes glittered dangerously. Tyler and Trevor simply clamped their mouths shut and let her proceed.

She stepped forward. "I beg your pardon. Were you speaking about that young boy?"

"Dang street kids. They're nothing but trouble. Excuse me, ma'am. Be assured I'll go after the little beggar and give him a what for if he shows up again." Clarence turned to leave.

Emma's eyes blazed. "Stop right there. For your information, he wasn't bothering us, and he certainly wasn't skulking around. The young boy was simply thanking my brother-in-law, Trevor, for a good deed bestowed on him yesterday." She placed one fist on her hip and took a huge breath before continuing. "And, I certainly hope that this little error of yours, in thinking that he might be bothering us, isn't the way you speak to most strangers, whether they be a child or an adult. Because if it is, there's every possibility that I may need to find new housing for one of my horses, namely The Ghost."

She took another pace forward as Pettibone stepped back quickly, and then stopped abruptly when his back flattened against a wooden gate. Astonishment was carved across his weathered face. The realization of who Emma actually was flickered in his bloodshot eyes. "No...no, Missus Wilkins. You are Missus Wilkins, aren't you?" Emma's reputation for being a distinct player in the Wilkins' partnership had reached the stable office months before The Ghost arrived. He swallowed and awaited his doom.

Tyler and Trevor both bit their tongues to hide their amusement. No one messed with Emma's horses and no one got away with picking on someone who couldn't defend himself or herself when she was around.

"Yes. Be assured that's *who* I am. I will be checking with my brother-in-law, Mr. Trevor Wilkins, on a regular basis to assure that my horse is being taken care of properly and that the people who pass through this building are accorded respect—no matter their age or social status. I'll rest easier if I know you'll remember that."

"Yes, ma'am, I sure will—I sure will remember that." Pettibone was not about to further fuel the fire with the words he would like to have said. The Wilkins' connection—and money—was too good to pass up. "I'll leave you now to enjoy your animal. It won't happen again, ma'am." He spun as quickly as the young boy did earlier and headed out of the barn with a quick step.

As the stable manager rounded the corner, an amused laugh busted through Trevor's lips. Tyler joined him a second later.

Emma's slim brows arched over her eyes as she watched the offending man disappear. "I suppose he thinks I'm a real shrew." Her hand suddenly clamped over her rounded mouth when she turned back. "Oh, my God! I am! The words were out of my mouth before I realized it. I just got so angry when I saw how frightened that little boy was."

"They'll both be fine—the kid and Pettibone," Trevor responded. "Come on, you've managed to awe one little boy with your lovely face and scare the hell out of the stable manager, plus prove to me that a stallion can be as gentle as a puppy. You've done enough damage for one afternoon. I've got a few more places I'd like you to see while in the city." He glanced at his brother. "Tyler, are you ready to go?"

"Lead the way."

As they strolled from the barn, Jonah peered from his hiding spot behind a bale of hay and watched as the men helped the pretty lady up onto the carriage seat. Yesterday, the man named Trevor helped him out of a pickle. He was also kind today. The pretty lady hollered at ol' Pettibone; she almost sounded like his Ma when she was mad because someone was being unfair.

Jonah scratched his head and wiped his nose on a dirty sleeve as the carriage moved down the street. *Maybe rich people aren't so bad after all.* Glancing around to check on the whereabouts of Pettibone, Jonah found the coast to be clear and bounded from behind the bale. He raced down the street, headed home, but would return tomorrow and wait for the rich man to appear again.

Chapter Three

Jonah waited two full days before he spotted Trevor dismounting his horse one afternoon at the back door of the stable. He observed the gentleman with shiny boots loop the reins around a post and enter the building. As soon as the man disappeared inside, the boy raced across the paddock, his gray eyes darting from side to side in a constant lookout for Pettibone. He had managed to avoid the stable manager on three separate occasions that morning, but was nearly caught the fourth time. Jonah was beginning to wonder if Trevor would ever return to the stable, and the boy was not about to chance missing the opportunity to talk to his savior now. He slipped inside the stable and saw the man leaning against the stall gate and stroking his stallion's forehead.

Trevor's intuition forewarned him that someone approached. He turned his head, and his gaze found the little urchin from a few days earlier nervously shuffling his bare feet in the straw. "You again."

"Yes, sir. I bin watchin' for you."

Trevor hooked his elbow over the edge of the stall door as a smile curved his mouth upwards. "You live around here or something? I seem to recall your ma saying something about getting home so you could get back to the city before nightfall."

"We live outta town a bit. Not too far."

"So," Trevor stated as he crossed his arms before him, "what did you need to speak to me about this time?"

Gray eyes darted at The Ghost's massive head, which hung over the gate, and then back to the tall gentleman. Jonah swallowed once for courage. "You've got a nice horse. He runs pretty fast."

"Racing man are you?" *The kid must've watched a few*

practices.

"No, sir, but I know a good horse when I see one and I'm a hard worker. I'm lookin' for a job. I could keep his stall clean and do some groomin'." He forged on with more confidence when Trevor remained surprisingly silent. "I could do anything you need me to do. You just give the orders and it'll be done." Hope shone in his gray eyes.

"Well, Jonah, that's a nice offer, but I've already hired someone to take care of him. Have you spoken to anyone else who boards their horses here?"

The young boy's chin dropped with a small shake of his head. "No one else will even talk to me."

Trevor sighed, and then straightened, feeling bad for the kid, but needing to get on his way. "St. Paul is a good sized city, Jonah. I'm sure you could find work with one of the merchants." He watched the boy drag his toe across the ground. The child's chin drooped even lower when he mumbled something beneath his breath.

"What did you say?"

"I said I don't want to work for anyone else." His gray eyes came up. "You've gotta lot of money, and I gotta find work. My ma can't make enough for us to live on."

Trevor straightened further and peered down at his small visitor. "Did your mother send you here?"

"No, sir." His head wagged with the response. "I came up with the idea all by myself. If I don't help her out, we're gonna lose our place. She works hard, but since my pa died, the bankman has been comin' out and scarin' her. I saw a paper. I...I'm not too sure what it said, but it made my ma cry and Ma never cries."

"Someone is threatening you and your family?"

Jonah shrugged. "We ain't got no money. Will you hire me?" He stood before Trevor, bearing the weight of the world on his youthful shoulders, and waited. "I need to help pay for our place. My ma can't do it on her own anymore."

A vision of Claire Holcomb in her faded, worn dress with children clinging to its folds prodded at his conscience. If things were as bad as Jonah stated, the mere pittance he would make working for Trevor would not make a difference. But could he really turn the kid away, especially when he could easily afford having him around?

"All right, I'll tell you what. Why don't you take a walk with me to the office? We'll let them know that I've decided to hire you on a trial basis." He could not help but see the excitement that leaped from Jonah's eyes. A smile broke across his own face at the boy's reaction. "When can you start?"

"I don't have to be home until supper. I can clean out the stall right now!"

Trevor ruffled the boy's blond head as he headed down the center aisle. "Let's go get things straightened away first. I don't want any of the stable's employees chasing you out of here." Jonah fell into step beside him with a skip in his stride. Trevor smiled wider. "Then we'll come back and introduce you to The Ghost."

* * *

The front door to Claire Holcomb's home squeaked open behind her.

"Jonah, that had better be you." She stated firmly over her shoulder as she placed a platter of fried chicken onto the table. She observed the sparkling eyes and flushed face of her oldest child as she turned to settle her hands on her hips with a stern look in her eyes. "Where have you been, young man? You're panting like the devil has been chasing you. I finally decided not to wait dinner for you any longer."

Jonah silently raced to a wooden pail, scooped out some water with the dipper, and poured the liquid into a ceramic bowl. As he splashed water on his face, he was near bursting. A crisp one-dollar bill lay folded in the bottom of his bib pocket. It was the most money he had ever had in his short life. "Sit down, Ma. I got somethin' to tell you!"

"I don't need to be told to sit down. Sofie and Sue Ellen did your chores today. I told you that I wanted the fence fixed. I can't take care of this place all by myself, Jonah. You just can't be going off without letting me know where you are."

Grabbing a towel to wipe his clean hands, Jonah grinned across the room to where she stood by the table admonishing him. He ignored his sisters' scowls and, a moment later, his hand fished out the bill—the one that he had rubbed his fingers across a hundred times to assure himself it was still safely tucked away while he raced home from the stable. He grabbed Claire's hand and proudly placed the dollar in her upturned palm.

Her demanding glare instantly changed to a confused frown. "Where did you get this?" She watched him bounce into a chair and reach for a fried chicken leg. As he brought it to his mouth, Claire pointed a stern finger at him. "Wait until we say grace, young man. Now, I want to know where you got this from?" She took her own seat as she held the dollar with a question in her gray eyes.

"I got a job." Jonah's smile beamed.

"A job?" Her gaze dropped to where her hand clutched the bill. "And you made this much money for only one day's work?" She shook her blonde head. "I want the truth."

"That is the truth, Ma! I got myself a job cleaning out a stall at the practice track. I'm working for a rich man that has a racehorse. You know him. He's the man who wanted to give ol' man Timmons a nickel the other day."

Mr. Shiny Boots... The hair on Claire's neck immediately stood on end, but before she could say anything, one of younger girls began to whine.

"Mommy, can we eat? Please?"

Claire sighed and set the dollar beside her plate. "All right." She eyed her son. "Supper is already late and it's not fair that they have to wait because of you. You can do the blessing, Jonah." She folded her hands, closed her eyes, and ducked her head.

"Thank you, God, for the food we're eating." He hesitated before he peeked up at his mother. "Did you have to kill the chicken by yourself?"

"Continue, Jonah. Don't be worrying about the chicken."

"Thank you for letting us all be together, thank you for Snowball, and thank you for my new job with Mr. Wilkins."

Claire's gaze shot across the table.

"Amen," he ended.

"Amen," sounded the chorus.

Claire reached for the potatoes and began to fill Hannah and Ruth's plates, her two youngest of the brood. A slim eyebrow rose as she watched Jonah slop food onto his dish and eat with gusto as if his explanations were finished. "Didn't I tell you that we don't go around begging rich people for money?"

"I didn't beg for money," her son mumbled through a mouthful of chicken.

"Please chew your food before you talk...then how did you end up with a dollar?"

Jonah swallowed twice, then wiped his mouth with the back of a sleeve. "I told you, I went back to the training center and waited until Trevor showed up again."

"You're on a first name basis with this Mr. Wilkins?"

"He's a nice man. He told me to call him Trevor." The words tumbled from his mouth. "I asked him for a job taking care of his horse. Trevor says I can give it a try. I can work every day if I want. I have to make sure the stall always has clean straw, and I get to feed The Ghost his oats. Trevor says when The Ghost—that's the horse's name—gets to know me a little better, I can brush him. Someday I might even get to lead him around to cool him down when he's done training. Trevor said so. Trevor says he used to live north of here. I can help, Ma. I'll get up early from here on out and get my chores done before I leave. Trevor says..."

Claire picked at the meager food on her plate, batted away the instant tears that burned behind her lids, and listened to her son rattle about all the things this Trevor—correction—Mr. Wilkins had relayed to him throughout the day. Jonah was only nine years old, but had decided to take part of the financial burden from her shoulders. How could she be angry? *Thank you, Lord, for this wonderful boy...*

"Ma?"

Claire shook her head and looked up. "Yes?"

"I know you want me here helping, but maybe if I can work, we can keep the farm and we won't have to move."

His sister Sofie's eyes rounded in surprise and her chin shot up. She stared at her brother, and then back at Claire. "We have to move, Ma?"

Claire's fingers tentatively brushed a stray wisp of blonde hair from her cheek. Her tired gaze moved around the table, where her three oldest children waited silently for her response. "That's...that's nothing to worry about now. Let's eat our dinner. It's getting late."

"But—"

A knock sounded on the wooden door. She glanced at the clock on the fireplace mantel. It was seven-thirty. "Well, it's rather late for company." Jonah rose, but her words halted him. "Sit and eat your dinner, son. I'll get it."

Brushing her hands across the front of her apron, Claire rose and walked to the door, opened it, and stared into the face of her nemesis. "Mr. Stone?"

Judd Prentice Stone, from the St. Paul Bank, stood on her doorstep. "Good evening, Mrs. Holcomb."

"It's rather late to be serving me more papers, isn't it? My children and I are finishing up our supper." She reached out her hand and lifted her chin. "Go ahead and give me whatever you have, and then I'll thank you to leave."

Judd Stone withdrew his arm from where it was hidden behind his back and presented her with a small bouquet of flowers instead. The thin strip of a mustache over his top lip twitched when she withdrew her hand and refused to take the peace offering.

"What...what is this?" Claire glared her dislike. The man had been on her doorstep weekly for the last three months, hounding her about the overdue payments to the bank, and now he had the gall to offer her flowers!

"Mrs. Holcomb, I thought you and I could have a talk." He bowed slightly, and then glanced over her shoulder at the wary faces of her brood. One of the little girls, who sat next to an empty chair, stuck out her tongue. He dragged his gaze back to the widow, whose expression had changed from surprise to dislike, and then to caution.

"If you're not here on bank business, then I'll have to say goodnight." Claire made to close the door, but Judd's hand shot out and forestalled the action. She glared at him again. "I'll thank you to take your hand from the door."

"Mrs. Holcomb...Claire...I thought we could start over."

Jonah slithered from his chair and stepped closer to hear what the man had to say.

"Start over with what?"

Judd shifted uneasily when he discovered that her son now eyed him closely. "I've felt horrible about having to come out here every week, but it's my job. My bank investors depend on me to collect what's due. Knowing the type of financial trouble you're in, however, I thought you and I could have a discussion on how to...to discover a way for you to keep your homestead."

Claire chewed nervously on her bottom lip, wondering just what he proposed. His offer, whatever it was, provided the proverbial light at the end of the tunnel—a glimmer of hope she had not seen since her husband died. Even Jonah, with his job working for the rich man, would never be able to help her in time. She closed her eyes momentarily and made a decision. The door opened wider. "If you'd like to come in for a short time, I'd be interested in what you have to say." She stepped back, surprised that Judd stayed rooted to the front porch. "Mr. Stone?" she questioned.

Judd eyed her children again. *Little heathens*...and then fixed a smile on his lips. "How would you like to discuss this matter on your front porch? That way your children can continue with their supper."

"I...I guess that would be fine. Let me grab my shawl." Claire turned and bumped into Jonah, where he stood behind her, and moved to retrieve her wrap from where it was draped across the back of a rocking chair. "Make sure the girls finish their meal, Jonah. I'm going to go outside with Mr. Stone for a bit. I won't be long."

Jonah's mouth drew in a straight line as he tramped back to the table and plopped disgustedly onto his chair. He did not like Mr. Stone much, either. It made him nervous that the man was on their doorstep at such a late hour. He watched his mother smile hesitantly as she picked up a lantern from a small table beside the front entrance, walked onto the porch, and closed the door behind her.

Sue Ellen's scowl turned from surprise to fright. "What's that man doing here? He always makes Ma cry when he leaves. Is it true, Jonah? Do we have to move away?"

"Hush, and eat your dinner."

* * *

Claire hung the gas lantern on a hook screwed into one of the support beams on the porch. Pulling the shawl tightly around her slim shoulders, she turned to face Judd. "Now, what is this idea you've come up with?"

His lips thinned with his smile. "I know how hard you've worked to keep this place since Frank died. It must be hard, well, with the children being so small and this place being quite a handful for even a man to take care of."

"I'm managing the work. As I've told you before, I just need some time to come up with the payments. I've got some hogs that will be ready for market this fall. I'm also taking in sewing, but that doesn't answer my question. What is this plan you've come up with?" Her heart pounded in her chest. Somehow, she would have to scratch out the time necessary to take on more jobs—if there was even a possibility of staying in her home. Claire squared her shoulders. She would put on the false bravado for him. What she really wanted to do was cry inside, knowing that there was only a slim chance that she would ever be able to make enough money.

Judd set the bouquet of flowers on the top rail of the rickety balustrade. *This place isn't worth anything with these ramshackle buildings. Yet, she thinks it is...* "You and I have come to know each other rather well with my constant visits out here."

Claire simply stared at him—and hid her wariness.

"I thought maybe we could start over." Judd stepped closer, and Claire backed away until her slender hips rested against the railing.

"You've taken on quite a load since Frank died," he continued. "Trying to keep this place going is a monumental task. I can see how tired you are."

Claire nervously patted her stray wisps of blonde hair and adjusted the shawl on her shoulders. It was true. She yearned to lay her head down and find the blessed numbness of sleep—for days. She felt like she had aged fifty years over the last two.

"It's too much for one woman, Claire. I can call you Claire, can't I?" He did not wait for her permission. "Let me help you. I've got the financial resources to get you out of this mess."

She was stunned. He had nipped at her heels for months and caused her countless sleepless nights. Now, he stood before her and offered salvation, but at what cost? "I can't believe that you'd be willing to help me—especially in light of our past."

Judd took another step, bringing himself to within inches of her.

His breath fanned Claire's face, and she struggled to not wrinkle her nose at the fetid smell that touched her nostrils. For some odd reason, the hair rose on the back of her neck.

"Well, Claire, that's not so surprising given the fact that even though the elements have tested you out here, you're still a fetching woman." He chose to misunderstand her words and evade the real issue.

"I think this discussion is over." Claire dipped to the right, intending to skirt around him, but stopped short when his hand snaked out to capture her upper arm.

"Now, don't be going off in a huff."

She tried to shake off his grasp, but to no avail. "Let go of my arm, Mr. Stone. I don't know what you're insinuating, but be assured I'll figure out my problems on my own." The firm conviction in her words belied the true fear that invaded Claire's body to the core.

Judd gently shoved her back against the rail and fitted his body against hers. "Listen now. You're still young enough." His knuckles grazed her cheek as his eyes narrowed. "You can still make a man happy, if you know what I mean. I want to be that man. You give me what I want and, in return, I'll give you the money you need. No one has to know of our little arrangement."

"Get off my land." She shoved at his chest in an attempt to escape, but he refused to budge.

Judd continued to hold her prisoner, clutched the soft skin of her jaw in his beefy hand, and dropped his mouth to hers.

Claire squirmed against his hold, then began to struggle with a vengeance when his other hand groped her breast and pawed at her upper chest in an attempt to work its way inside her buttoned bodice. "Stop it!" she ground against his mouth.

His right hand freed her jaw and worked its way down to encircle her slim waist. He yanked her against him, then the hand moved to her buttocks and pushed her hips against his—and against the bulge at the front of his pants. "Stop it, Claire. Just give me a little lovin' and your problems are over."

Light flooded the porch as the door was yanked open. Jonah appeared a second later, a shotgun pressed to his shoulder. "Let go of my ma!"

Judd ignored the boy and pierced Claire with his angry eyes.

"Tell that kid of yours to go back inside."

Claire's knee came up and, instantly, Judd stumbled back, then doubled over, clutching his groin. Claire, in turn, darted to her son's side. She wrenched the gun from the boy's shaking hands. "Now get off my land!" She clicked back the hammer.

Judd stumbled forward, still holding his crotch, and winced as he leaned heavily against the support beam on the porch. His deep breaths lessened to small, quick pants as he turned his head and glared across the space between them. "You stupid bitch. You almost maimed me."

Claire hiked the gun higher, squared her jaw, and took better aim. "You've got five seconds to get out of my sight or I'll pull the trigger."

Judd lurched to the top of the stairs and slowly made his way down the rotting wooden steps. When he reached the bottom, he turned to glare up at her. His watery gaze sent out a warning. "You've got ten days to make your payment." He stumbled into the darkness then, mounted his horse, and rode out of sight.

Claire dropped the gun and sank onto a nearby bench. Her face dropped into her suddenly shaky, upturned palms, and tears streamed down her face.

Jonah tentatively stroked her back as she rocked forward. "Ma? Did he hurt you?"

Claire shook her head before she raised her eyes and swiped at the tears. "No, Jonah." She inhaled the night air deeply. "Thank you for helping me when you did. It was the right thing to do."

He swallowed the lump in his throat. "Does this mean we have to leave?"

She reached out, pulled him into her embrace, and was surprised at the sudden strength that flowed through her blood when she held her son's small body. Her fingers trailed through his thick hair as she worked to compose herself. "I'm afraid it does. I'm afraid it does."

Chapter Four

Trevor swung a long leg over the saddle, dismounted, and tied the reins to the hitching post in front of the training center barn. Pulling a brown paper-wrapped parcel from his saddlebag, he mentally shook his head at his own eagerness. Inside the crinkled package was a pair of brand new children's boots. He was tired of watching Jonah race around the stable in bare feet. Trevor asked him the day before if he ever wore shoes, and the boy simply stated that he did not own a pair because his ma was sure he grew like a weed. They would wait for a time closer to winter before figuring out what size he would need.

The poverty Jonah and his family lived in amazed Trevor. He had never had to worry about where his next dime was coming from. He had worked hard his entire life, but was always assured of a secure future because of his father's financial legacy. His step quickened in anticipation of the boy's reaction to his gift.

Seeing Jonah at the track had already become an integral part of Trevor's day. Within the last week, the youngster had regaled Trevor with stories of a boy's life—things the older man had forgotten over the years; things as simple as enjoying the heat of the sun on his face as he lay in sweet-smelling grass waiting for a fish to tug on his line.

Simple pleasures. Jonah lived for those times and never bemused the fact that his life was about as underprivileged as one could be.

As Trevor entered the barn, he spied Jonah entering The Ghost's stall with a pitchfork. A smile split the older man's face as he strolled down the center aisle. The boy was an exemplary employee. He was never late and worked harder than most of the grown men who were employed at the track.

Keeper of the Heart

Trevor reached the stall, rested his elbows on the gate, and watched his new young friend stab at the fresh bale of straw he used to spread about the floor. The boy's stiff back forewarned him that all was not right with the world. "You look like your angry about something today."

Jonah spun to face his boss. A smile that did not quite reach his eyes cut across his face. "Hi, Trevor." He immediately turned back to his current work.

"Something wrong, bud?"

"No, sir. Just trying to get my work done." He stabbed again at the pile of straw with rounded shoulders. Jonah was terribly out of character.

"Hey, come on out here minute. I have something for you." He watched the lad carefully stand the pitchfork against the slatted wall, and then waited for him to exit the enclosure. Trevor led the way to a bench, clutching the package beneath his arm. Once Jonah was quietly settled beside him, he patted the boy's back.

"You seem pretty down in the mouth today. Did something happen that you want to talk about?" Trevor received a shrug for his efforts. "Well, when you're ready to talk, just know that I'm here to listen." He held out the package. "Here, take this. It's a small thank you for how hard you've worked this week."

Jonah's chin snapped up. "Somethin' for me?"

The big man next to him nodded.

"But you pay me good for my work. I don't need anything else."

"If only most men had your work ethics... Well, this is what you call a bonus. Go ahead, open it up."

Trembling hands untied the string that bound the package, and Jonah peeled back the paper. He stared down in confusion, and then lifted his gaze to meet Trevor's happy one. "These boots are for me?"

Trevor ruffled his hair. "That they are. A hard working man needs a good pair of boots." He dug into his jacket pocket, pulled out a pair of socks, and stuffed them into the boy's hand. "Why don't you run over to the trough, wash your feet, and give 'em a try."

The boy hugged his new possessions close before his thin shoulders sagged with a disheartened sigh. "Thanks, Trevor. I've never had a new pair of boots before." He set them on the bench beside his employer. "But, I can't take them."

"What do you mean you can't take them?"

Jonah shrugged his shoulders before he lifted his gaze. Trevor had never encountered such despair in the boy's eyes. "I have somethin' to tell you. I can only work for another week or so. I don't think it would be right to take the boots when I'm leavin'."

"Leaving? That comes as a surprise. Where are you going?" Trevor watched the boy's struggle to get the words out.

"My ma got a job up north."

A picture of Claire flashed across Trevor's brain. "Does this have to do with losing your home to the bank?" He watched the blond head nod sadly. Trevor had never seen the Holcomb homestead, so he was not quite sure what it would take to keep the bank from breathing down their necks. He felt the boy's sorrow, however—especially after the last week of excitement—and the possibility of helping his ma out. Trevor made an instant decision. "Listen. Do you think your ma would talk to me? Maybe I can help in some way."

The quick flash of enthusiasm soon dimmed in the gray eyes. "Thanks, Trevor, but I don't think so. My ma has made up her mind. She's tired of fightin' the bank man. I guess her new boss will give us a roof over our heads. Us kids will help her when we can." He wiggled off the bench, scooped up the new boots, and held them out. "So, I don't think it would be right to take these if I'm not staying."

Trevor also rose from the bench, and then placed a firm hand on the boy's small, thin shoulder. "You keep them. If you're going north, you'll need a pair of boots with winter not far off. I want you to have them. Think of them as a gift from one good friend to another."

Jonah blinked back the tears in his eyes before he looked up. "I'm going to miss you, Trevor." Without warning, he grabbed the big man about the waist, hugged him tightly, and raced off to the water trough to clean his feet.

Trevor watched him go, knowing that he would miss the boy terribly. He did not know his mother well, but guessed that Claire Holcomb must be a hard-working woman who instilled goodness in her children. Jonah was living proof.

Having little to do for the rest of the day, he decided he would spend some time with his young friend before the boy left for good.

Keeper of the Heart

* * *

Later that afternoon found both Jonah and Trevor inside The Ghost's stall, grooming the large animal after it had been exercised. It took some doing, but Trevor finally had the boy laughing again.

"Jonah! Jonah!"

The boy ducked past Trevor and exited the stall, nearly knocking his sister to the ground as she raced down the center aisle of the stable on her way past.

"What are you doin' here, Sofie?" Jonah scanned the stable entrance in search of his mother. She rarely ever let the girls leave the farm without her.

Sofie clutched his arm. Now that she had finally found her brother, tears of fright streamed down her cheeks. "Come quick, Jonah! The bank man is at our house! Him and ma are fightin' and he locked us out of the house. Ma's in there with him! Please, hurry!"

The boy spun where he stood to look back into the stall. "I gotta go, Trevor—"

"Who's at your house?"

Jonah's eyes darkened in fear. "Mr. Stone from the bank. He might be hurting my ma!"

Trevor darted from the interior of the stall, firmly grasped each child's arm, and dragged the siblings down the aisle toward the open door. "I'll bring you home. We can get there faster by horse."

They raced to his mount outside. Trevor lifted both children into the saddle and leapt up behind them. "Which way?"

Jonah pointed east. Trevor dug in his heels and the horse bolted forward, leaving a dust cloud in their wake.

* * *

The muffled cries of Claire's daughters filtered into the house as she stood with white knuckles curled around the back of the chair on the far side of the kitchen table. She was careful to keep some piece of furniture between her the increasingly angry Judd Stone. The two had been arguing for the last twenty minutes and, still, the man refused to leave her home. Each minute that passed in the presence of the banker caused her heart to beat quicker.

Her gray eyes chanced another glance at the door behind him. Somehow, she had to get out of the house. Deciding to change her demeanor, she visibly relaxed her shoulders and forced a sick smile to her lips. "My girls are upset, Mr. Stone. Why don't we continue this discussion tomorrow, so I can assure them that everything is all right?"

Judd's gaze slithered across the wooden surface, then back to Claire. The woman was a bit worn, but would serve his needs. He was not leaving until he got what he came for. "Let's cut to the chase, Claire. I locked them outside for one reason." He pulled out a chair on the opposite side of the table and casually seated himself. "The other night I offered you a proposition. I think it would behoove you to simply admit that you can't take care of this place without money at your disposal. I can provide you with cash—in exchange for some 'special favors'."

Claire struggled to keep her breathing even and calm. *They're all the same. Frank, Judd, all of them...* "Mr. Stone, all I've asked for is a little more time—"

Judd's fist banged against the surface of the table, startling Claire to near tears. "There is no more time! You've just received your final offer." He pulled his timepiece from a front pocket and flipped open the silver cover. A thin eyebrow raised over one eye. "I have another engagement of sorts to attend in a few hours. I'd like to get our 'business' concluded. I want an answer." He slid the watch back inside his pocket and met her eyes. His fingers smoothed a gray goatee. "You seem determined to keep this rundown place going for some odd reason. I find it hard to believe that you would so callously throw all your chances to the wind, when there is a solution. Now, what will it be?"

Claire swallowed, hesitated for Judd's benefit, and let go of the back of the chair. Her farm was gone. Even with all the energy she had put forth, she had failed miserably. She had no choice but to take the cook's job up north. Her hands smoothed the front of her dress when she looked up. "You leave me no choice."

An instant jolt of excitement raced through Judd's blood. It had only taken a mere half hour to get her to finally reach a decision that definitely leaned in his behalf—one better than having her put up a fight. He was glad he had the foresight to lock the door. It would keep Claire's whining brood outside while he satisfied himself on top of their mother.

The slender woman would do fine in the future, better than most of the oversized widows who dotted the countryside. He pushed his chair further from the table. "Good. Now that we've made our pact, why don't you come over here and sit on my lap. When we're finished, I'll go back to the bank and get your money."

Claire tentatively stepped from behind the chair and slowly rounded the table. She wanted to slap the complacent smile from Judd's face as the man crossed his arms over his chest, thinking that he had won the day.

Over my dead body will I lay with you... She took a step closer, braced herself, then shoved at his shoulders, sending him and the chair flying backwards to the floor. The surprise in his eyes was the last thing she saw before she raced for the door.

Claire fumbled with the heavy metal latch. Her chest heaved in fear when the sound of wooden legs scraped against the floor. She yanked on the door, then a sob escaped her throat when she realized the hasp was not clear of the metal ring.

Pain shot across her shoulders when Judd's cruel hands hauled her back against his flabby stomach. He secured an arm around her waist, spun her away from the door, and dropped the latch more securely into place. Claire screamed. The wailing outside grew louder, piercing through the door when the children heard their mother's shriek.

"Please..." Claire begged as she was dragged across the floor. Her arms flailed, her legs kicked and her fingers pried at the clawing arm of her offender.

Judd tightened his grip about her waist and threaded his fingers through her blonde hair, pulling the neat bun from its pins. Claire shrieked when she was shoved to the surface of her son's bed, and then gasped in pain when her head banged against the headboard.

Judd took advantage of the woman's momentary daze and dropped on top of her motionless body. Claire was shocked from her stupor by his sudden weight and began her battle in earnest. His mouth captured hers, however, silencing her terrified screams as his hand snaked between their bodies.

Flashes of Frank and the times he took advantage of her body when he stumbled home in a drunken stupor fueled her strength. She tore her mouth from Judd's. "Stop!" Her nails raked his face, instantly drawing blood. "Get off me, you pig!"

Judd roared in pain, raised himself up on one hand and smacked her across the cheek with the other. Claire's head snapped to the side.

"You bitch!" He battled with her flailing arms until he had her hands clasped above her head.

A choked sob escaped Claire's throat at the sound of ripping material. She opened her eyes, batting away the tears that blurred her vision, and struggled desperately to jerk her wrists free of his tight hold. Finally, she let her body go limp.

Judd's breath fanned her face, and an evil smile touched his lips when he recognized the defeat in her eyes.

* * *

Trevor's horse rounded a corner in the road, revealing a ramshackle farm that sat in a small meadow in the distance. He tightened his arm around Jonah and his sister as he yanked on a rein and forced his mount to clear a small ditch instead of taking the driveway.

As the horse galloped up to the house, he saw the other three siblings jumping up and down on the porch. The horse skidded to a stop in a cloud of dust, and Jonah swung his leg over the saddle and jumped to the ground. Trevor quickly followed suit and lifted Sofie down.

Jonah was on the porch by this time and banging his fists against the sturdiness of the door. Fear blazed in his eyes as he turned to Trevor for help. "It's locked. Sue Ellen says ol' man Stone is still inside with my ma!"

Trevor tested the lock, and then heard a muffled scream from somewhere inside. "Stand back. Keep your sisters out here, Jonah." The children scuttled out of the way as he lifted his boot and rammed it against the door. The rusted hinges splintered away from the jamb and the barrier banged against an interior wall.

Trevor charged inside and his own eyes blazed at the sight before him. A sobbing Claire lay on a bed, her slender body all but invisible beneath the girth of the man who held her down. Trevor was across the room in an instant and, through a thick red haze of anger, yanked the reprobate upwards by the collar. He swung him around and slammed his fist into the surprised man's jaw. Judd's head snapped back as he crumpled to his knees.

Claire scrambled to a sitting position on the small bed and, holding her ripped bodice together over her naked breasts, swiped at the tears that ran down her tanned cheeks.

Trevor's dark green gaze quickly swung away from Claire's tattered dress to the man who struggled to a sitting position on the floor; a sagging belly hung over the open fly of his pants. Trevor moved to tower over the other man and, somewhere in the back of his enraged mind, enjoyed when the attacker on the floor cringed. "You spineless son of a bitch," he muttered as he dragged Judd to his feet and effortlessly hauled him to the open doorway.

He shoved the banker onto the porch, the sheer force of the movement sending the ingrate stumbling down the rickety steps and into the dirt. The children huddled on the porch to Trevor's left, their frightened faces being the only thing that kept him from following the piece of dung from the porch and pummeling him to within an inch of his life. Instead, he balled his fists, moved to the top step, and pinned the man to the ground with a scathing glare.

Judd rolled onto his side, dirt caking in the blood that poured from his nose. His palm came up to ward off further any attack. "Don't hit me again!" he pleaded. He struggled to stand, then pulled a hanky from his pocket to stop the flow of blood.

"Get your ass out off this property and, if you ever come near anything that belongs to Mrs. Holcomb again, I guarantee you won't be breathing after your next beating." Trevor's threat blazed in his smoldering green eyes.

Judd dabbed at his nose and sneered back, thinking himself out of harm's way with the distance between him and his attacker. "You won't have to worry about that. The bank's foreclosing on her. She'll be out of here within the week."

Trevor's hand doubled into an even tighter fist as he started down the steps. Judd, in turn, whirled and hobbled toward his horse, all the while sending fearful glances over his shoulder. A moment later, he sat astride the mount and the animal galloped toward town.

Trevor retraced his steps to the house. The porch was void of children now. "I should've beat the hell out of him," he muttered as he hurried back up the steps and into the house.

Claire still sat on the bed, surrounded by all five of her frightened children. The youngest sobbed against her breast; the shaken woman held the little girl close with one arm. Her other hand still clutched the bodice of her torn dress. She lifted a watery gaze to the silent man who now straightened overturned chairs.

"Thank...thank you." Those were the only words she could manage.

Trevor looked at her. Claire's complexion rivaled the color of paste, and her hand shook as she bunched the edges of the ripped material more firmly in her fist.

She was not the woman Trevor remembered; the woman who gave him a dressing down on the streets of St. Paul. She was also not the mother who ruled her children with strength of purpose as purported by Jonah. At the moment, Claire Holcomb looked ready to collapse.

Trevor looked at Jonah, where the boy sat beside his mother on the bed and fought his tears. "Why don't we take your sisters outside, Jonah?" No response. "Jonah?" He waited for the boy to look up. "Your mother will be fine, but I think she needs a few minutes by herself. How about you help me find some wood and nails, so we can get that door fixed. It won't take long. When we're done, you can come right back inside."

Jonah shook his head in stubborn resistance. "I'm stayin' here."

Claire winced when she tried to smile at her son. Her bruised jaw was quickly turning a shade resembling purple. "Go on, Jonah. I need to change my dress. Could you draw me a cold bucket of water from the well? I can feel my face swelling."

Her son continued to battle his tears of fright. "I'm sorry I wasn't here, ma. I would've got the gun again."

Trevor's jaw clenched in anger upon the boy's words. What the hell had transpired before this most recent episode?

Claire smoothed her son's hair off his forehead with a hand that still shook slightly. "It's done with. You came before he hit me again. You did good."

Trevor cleared his throat to gain their attention and held out his hand. "Come on, Jonah. Your mother's right. It's done with and he's gone. I need your help outside. Let's give your mother a few moments to collect herself."

His soft, calm voice did the trick. Jonah reached for his younger sister, who still clung to his mother, and hiked her onto his hip. His other three sisters followed in single file behind him through the splintered doorway and out onto the porch.

Trevor glanced at Claire.

A silent, if bewildered, thank you shined in her teary eyes. "Thank you for getting here in time."

He simply nodded and, without another word, followed the children outside.

Chapter Five

Trevor hammered a last nail and swung the door closed to test his handiwork. The doorjamb was back in place with its repaired hinges. Swinging the hasp over the metal hook, he turned with a comforting grin. "Looks like it'll hold."

Claire perched on a rocking chair with a cold compress pressed to her swollen cheek. She stared at him with wary gray eyes, trying to figure out why this rich man had not tossed her troubles away and left for his own home. Instead, he quite easily oversaw the fixing of the door as if he had been at her farm many times. She was baffled, but he did deserve her thanks. Finally, she broke her silence. "Thank you, but Jonah and I could have fixed it."

"It was no problem, ma'am. I was happy to do it."

Claire continued to stare at his glittering green depths, and then forced her nervous gaze across the room. Jonah had the girls lined up at the table, helping him to prepare sandwiches for a cold supper.

Her son caught her eye when he glanced over his shoulder. "We got plenty of sandwiches, Ma, and Sofie boiled some eggs. Can Trevor stay for supper?"

Instant panic treaded its way through her aching body. She simply wanted to be alone with her children. Only then could she recoup her inner strength after the harrowing experience with Judd and face the world once more. Over the last few hours, it had been so easy to let someone else—mainly Mr. Wilkins—shoulder her responsibilities. He had calmed the children after the bank man was hustled away, given her time to change and cleanup, and even repaired the door with a laughing Jonah by his side. She was ashamed of herself for momentarily losing control and, once again, letting a man rule her life—it was something she had sworn to never let happen again.

Her eyes shifted back to the quick dinner her children prepared. The fare was not much, but it would be unchristian like to send Mr. Wilkins away after what the man had done for her. "I...I guess if you made enough for everyone, Jonah, then we should share." Her tentative gaze met Trevor's when he looked up from where he knelt cleaning up splinters of wood from the floor. "You're welcome to stay, Mr. Wilkins. Jonah's supper isn't fancy, but what is there can easily be shared."

Trevor stood, dropped an armful of wood into the burning box, and then brushed the dust from his palms. "Thank you, but it's not necessary that you provide me with a meal. I was happy to help."

"You gotta stay, Trevor," Jonah exclaimed from across the room as he plopped two pieces of bread onto the table. "I made a sandwich for you. Please?"

Trevor had just given Claire her out and she was definitely going to reinforce his departure. "Mr. Wilkins has made his decision, son. He's probably used to a higher quality supper than the one we'll be eating tonight anyway." The waspish words were out of Claire's mouth before she could stop them.

Trevor's dark head snapped in her direction. He was no fool—it was easy to see that Claire would be much more comfortable if he was not in the room. *Is that the real reason she doesn't want me here? She thinks I'm above eating a sandwich...?* He fixed a smile on his mouth, leaned against the door, and crossed one ankle over the other. Never taking his eyes from the woman who bore a hole in his chest with her gaze, Trevor clenched his jaw and decided to call her bluff. "On the contrary. I love sandwiches. I'd be honored to share your meal with you, Jonah."

* * *

The cold chicken between the slices of bread tasted like sawdust in Claire's throat as she listened to the squeals of laughter coming from her children. At their insistent urgings, Trevor began yet another story.

She swallowed a small sip of milk and carefully set the mostly uneaten sandwich on the plate before her. Everybody else had finished eating. Her surprised gaze trailed the big man when he rose to help the children clean off the table. He needed to be gone, and she needed to take control.

This was her kitchen and her life and no man was going to simply walk in and take away the forced independence she had cultivated over the last two years. She rose from her chair, grabbed her plate, and carried it to the sideboard. "I'll take care of cleaning the dishes, children, since you were so good to prepare our meal tonight. You can see to Mr. Wilkins' horse. I'm sure he needs to be leaving."

Amidst squeals of delight as her brood returned to the table, Claire used the edges of her apron to lift a pot of hot water from the stove and pour it into the wash bucket, declining Trevor's help when he offered to carry the pot.

Trevor stood uncomfortably in the center of the room. Should he say his farewell and leave? Jonah's mother did not act like she wanted any more company.

Sue Ellen tugged on his hand to get his attention, her actions making the final decision for him. "Come on, Mr. Wilkins. Tell us another story until Jonah comes back."

The boy hesitated at the door, thinking his boss was going to follow him out. "Trevor's comin' with me, Sue Ellen. He doesn't have time to be jawin' with a bunch of girls."

Claire's four-year-old, Ruth, slid from her chair and skipped across the room. She stopped before their guest and looked up with round gray eyes. "Can you stay? Jonah allus gets ta see you at work." She took his large hand in her small one. "I can count. My ma says I'm smart."

"Well, then, I bet she knows what she's talking about." He let himself be drawn back to the table.

Sue Ellen stuck her tongue out at her brother before he stomped out the door.

Claire stifled a frazzled sigh when Trevor strolled across the room to join the girls again and refused to look at him as she dropped silverware into the hot water; she listened closely though, to the conversation flowing around her.

Finally, however, the novelty of having a man sitting in her kitchen and the boisterous laughter coming from her children made her turn slightly so as to see the goings on at the table in her peripheral vision. *Why won't he leave?* Her hand fluttered to poke stray strands of hair behind her ear. *I can't very well kick Jonah's employer from our home...*

Claire slid another sidelong glance, intent upon inspecting Mr. Trevor Wilkins more fully while his head was turned away. To her surprise, her youngest, Hannah, perched on the man's knee and Mr. Wilkins actually gave her his utmost attention as she showed him her favorite blanket. With a shake of her head, Claire's eyes moved back to the man.

Not an ounce of fat extended over his expensive leather belt. Thick muscular thighs dwarfed the wooden seat he perched on, and the backs of his large hands were sun-darkened, a stark contrast to the white cuffs of his shirt. His smile showed off an even row of white teeth. Bright green eyes sparkled with childlike humor when he ruffled Jonah's hair when the boy returned to the house. The man absolutely looked like he was having the time of his life. She found the notion hard to believe when they were all from such different worlds.

It was easy to see that the girls were already under Mr. Wilkins' spell. Now her son beamed and moved his chair as close as he could get to the man. Trevor sat regaling yet another story of his youth, his broad shoulders relaxed against the back of the seat. His dark hair waved over his ears, and his eyes twinkled once again when he laughed.

And why do I feel the way I do? He doesn't seem the least bit intimidating, yet he makes me nervous... The man rankled her insides with his handsome dark features, smiling emerald eyes and calm assurance. That was it. He was in a class all his own. Never in her life had Claire been around a man such as this one—one that easily took control of a situation when needed; one that could most likely be depended upon if his earlier actions were any clue. Trevor Wilkins encompassed the uniqueness of the nameless man who lived in the girlish dreams of her youth; the one who assured her that she would always be taken care of; the sort of man that, at one time, she might have been able to open her heart to without fear of losing herself as an individual.

Absolutely not—I will never be fooled by a man again!

Claire spun back to the pan containing dishwater and, in her haste, dropped the glass in her fingers to the floor with a shattering crash. She sank quickly to her knees to scoop up the pieces, embarrassed when the room became suddenly silent. A second later, she yelped in quick pain when a sliver of thick glass sliced across the outside of her palm.

Trevor leapt from his chair and was across the floor in a flash. Seeing what had happened, he grabbed a clean towel from a hook and crouched beside Claire, where she clutched her injured palm as blood oozed out between her fingers and pooled on the floor.

Checking to assure that no shards of glass were hidden in the cut, he quickly wrapped the wound and applied pressure with one hand, while the fingers of the other gently wrapped about Claire's upper arm as he helped her to a chair.

"I'm fine," she stated—anything to get him to loosen his gentle hold. Her skin burned beneath his touch. "It's not that bad."

"You let me be the judge of that. Here—" he took her hand and wrapped her fingers over the towel "—keep pressure on this and I'll fetch some fresh water to clean it up."

As he moved about the room, pouring warm water into a bucket, he gently but firmly issued orders to her children. "Okay, Jonah, you find a broom and sweep up this broken glass. Sofie and Sue Ellen? How about you get your little sisters ready for bed, but first, find me some bandages. Your ma's going to be fine once we get that cut cleaned up."

The children scuttled about doing as Trevor bid. Claire sat holding her injured hand, amazed at their instant obedience. It was not long before he returned with the bucket of warm water, clean towels, and bandages that Sofie easily procured for him.

A chair scraped over the wooden floor when Trevor seated himself beside the quiet woman. His large thighs extended out on either side of her, leaving Claire huddled as tightly to the back of her chair as possible to make sure her knees did not touch him.

"Okay, let's see what we have here. Hopefully, you won't need stitches." He took her hand and gently unwrapped the towel soaked with blood, pulled the gas lamp closer to the edge of the table, and inspected the cut. "You know, my sister is married to a doctor. She was always the one to take charge when someone was injured on our ranch. Either my brothers or myself helped her out."

Claire yearned to yank her hand away from his gentle hold to hide the chipped nails and raised calluses. Mr. Wilkins most likely had never seen the hands of a woman who labored as hard, if not harder, than a man, but it was too late. Already, he was gently washing the blood from around the wound.

Trevor hid his surprise as he tended Claire's injury. Gone was the softness of womanly hands he had always taken for granted; in its place was a testimony to the hard, driven life she must lead on a daily basis. His earlier antagonism also disappeared. Jonah's mother had much to contend with, and she was doing the best job she could. His respect for her elevated another notch. He would be willing to guess that even the loggers' wives from back home did not work as hard as the woman who wiggled on the chair. "You know, Mrs. Holcomb, I think this is your lucky day. You're not going to need stitches."

"Is that your professional opinion?" she snapped.

His head came up and their eyes locked. Trevor was lost for a second in the steely colored depths of Claire's unknown anger. Tearing his gaze away, he reached for bandages and carefully and expertly wrapped her hand. "Can I ask you something?"

"Could I stop you?"

His cheek tightened with a slight tick as he instantly doubted his recently raised esteem, but he tossed his slight bit of annoyance away. "Did I do something to you? More than once tonight, it seemed like you were ready to take the head off of my shoulders. And, for some reason again, I feel like you're angry at me."

She continued to stare at the thick waves running through his hair as he continued to look down at her hand, and then tried to ignore the instant roll of her stomach and the flush of heat that reddened her cheeks. *Yes, you did something! You walked into my home and gave me a glimpse of what my life could have been like!* She nearly gasped out loud at the notion, totally mystified that her train of thought would even go in that direction.

Claire ducked her head, took the bandage from him, and finished wrapping her hand. "I'm sorry if I gave you that impression. It's just..." Suddenly, it took all her might to stay upright in the chair as a wave of weariness washed through her body. The incident with Mr. Stone, Trevor's calming presence in her home and the emotions he caused to swirl in her belly, combined with the knowledge that she had truly lost her homestead, finally took its toll. Her pink cheeks turned ashen before his eyes and her thin shoulders slumped. "It's just...it's just that I've had a long, unsettling day."

Trevor spotted what he was sure were forbidden tears in the corners of her eyes before she turned her face away. He quickly rose, crossed to where Jonah was finishing up the few dishes, and gave Claire the time she needed to gather her wits. He ruffled the smiling boy's blond head. "It looks like you have things pretty well under control."

"Yes, sir! And I can hear Sofie and Sue Ellen tucking in the little ones."

Trevor shook his head. This kid was only nine years old, yet he talked about his siblings as if he were twenty. A flash of his own brother, Tyler, creased his face with a smile. "You know what, Jonah? You remind me of my older brother. I think when he was around nine, I was close to Sofie's age. I always looked up to him. He's still my hero."

Jonah beamed beneath the praise.

Trevor lowered his voice. "I think I'm going to head for home. Why don't you give me a minute to say goodbye to your ma, and then walk outside with me. You and I need to have a man-to-man talk."

Jonah nearly burst with excitement and pride. "Sure! I'll go check on your horse." He quickly wiped his hands and whirled out the door.

Trevor turned to see a slightly more composed Claire cleaning up the mess on the table, but her slim back was still stiff and unyielding. His shoulders dropped with the sigh that left his mouth. She had erected her invisible walls once more. "Well, Mrs. Holcomb, I guess I'll be heading back to St. Paul." Trevor settled his Stetson on his dark head. "I don't think you'll have to worry about Mr. Stone coming back, but keep your door locked just the same. If there's anything you—"

"Thank you, Mr. Wilkins," she cut him off, "for your help today. I'll be sure to lock the door." Her dismissal was quick and clean.

He tipped his hat when she finally glanced at him. "Take care of that hand."

"I will."

He silently crossed to the door.

"Bye, Trevor!" Sofie, Sue Ellen, Ruth, and Hannah all peeked down through the slats of the wooden ladder leading to the loft.

He hesitated, looked around until he spotted the girls, and then smiled up. "Night girls. You take care of your ma and don't let her use her hand tomorrow."

"We won't," came the chorus followed by giggles.

Trevor turned one last time. "Ma'am. Thank you for supper." He nodded, and then disappeared through the doorway. The latch clicked shut behind him.

Claire sank onto a chair, her body trembling with emotions she had not experienced in years. At that moment, she was almost happy to be moving north.

* * *

The following afternoon found Trevor filling his saddlebags with staples from the general goods store. He had slept restlessly the previous night and all because of Claire and her children. Trevor was a man of the world, had experienced most of what life could meet out, and had seen poverty at its worst while living in St. Paul. But nothing had prepared him to deal with the intense emotions of helplessness when it came to the Holcomb family.

He had told Jonah the night before not to come to work that day, but to stay home and help his mother, and now Trevor tried to keep himself busy in the boy's absence. The Ghost required a lot of care, and it surprised him to learn how much stable work the boy was actually responsible for—there were a lot of jobs left undone. Trevor quickly discovered, however, how much he missed Jonah's usual ramblings. He finally gave in to his own yearnings and headed for the market. Buying a few staples for the family would give him an excuse to see the boy. "And his mother..." he finished his thoughts out loud. "Admit it, Wilkins, she piques your interest."

Pulling the last strap tight, Trevor adjusted the bag across the saddle, and then found himself staring blankly at the horizon. What was it about Claire Holcomb that ate at him as he tried to sleep? He was certain the tough exterior she portrayed was a front to cover the real woman inside. From the conversations he had with her son, it was not too difficult to put together a hard life for the willowy woman who performed the work of two men. Knowing that she was at one time married to a man who was basically a drunk put the final touch on what was already a miserable existence. *No wonder I haven't seen her smile yet...not much to be joyful about.*

Trevor unwrapped the reins from the hitching post, mounted his horse, and hoped like hell that Claire would not be too irate when he showed up at their broken-down homestead.

* * *

Claire stepped from the entrance to the barn, shielded her eyes with her bandaged hand, and searched the main road. Weary as she was from a sleepless night, the thought of the loathsome banker returning to hound her set her nerves on edge. Someone on horseback rounded the last corner. Who else but Judd would be coming back to torment her?

Her gaze swung to her daughters, where they played on the porch. "Girls! Get in the house now. Lock the door!" She raced inside the barn, grabbed an old rifle leaning against the door, and hefted the gun clumsily to her shoulder. "Jonah!" she called to her son in the hayloft. "Come quickly. Someone is riding down the lane."

Her son slid down the ladder from the loft and into a pile of straw. Bounding up, he ran to her side. "Give me the gun, Ma."

"No, you just stay by my side if it's Mr. Stone. We're not even going to let him get off his horse this time."

Jonah watched her balance the gun on her hip with her right arm and wince painfully as she used her bandaged left hand to pull back the hammer. "Trevor warned him about coming back."

"Men like Judd Stone are too ignorant to know what's good for them." Her chin lifted when the sound of slowing hooves entered the yard. She drew in a deep breath to help settle her trembling hands and stepped back into the sunlight with her son by her side.

"Trevor!" Jonah lit out across the dusty yard, waving his arms wildly to greet his friend.

Claire snapped back the hammer and lowered the rifle. Leaning the gun against the barn wall, she used the edge of her apron to dab the frightened perspiration from her brow, and then marched in the direction of the house.

Why is he here? The thought of Trevor visiting both annoyed and excited her. At least she would not have to deal with Judd, but as her gaze took in Trevor's neat, expensive attire and those damned shiny boots, the excitement dimmed.

The girls flowed out of the open doorway and raced to where the tall man now stood beside his horse. They surrounded Trevor, who was in the process of pulling packages from the saddlebags and passing them out.

"Look Ma! Trevor brought some food from the store." Jonah dug deeper into one bag and pulled out a paper sack of sweets. "And candy! He brought us candy!" The girls squealed with delight when Jonah instantly distributed peppermint sticks to their waiting palms.

Claire approached slowly and finally met Trevor's gaze as her anger built. He shuffled his feet in the dust, apparently waiting for her to speak first. "What is all this?"

He shrugged his broad shoulders. "Just thought I'd bring out a few things. You all treated me so well yesterday that I wanted to say thank you."

She crossed her arms and tapped her foot beneath the hem of her faded dress. "You said thank you before you left last night. That was plenty sufficient."

"I enjoy seeing the kids smile."

"Ma, try a stick!" Claire's daughter held out her small hand and offered her mother a piece of the candy.

"No, thank you, Sofie."

"Can I have yours then?"

"Share it with your sisters." Claire's glare deepened as she spoke the words; she never took her eyes from Trevor's green ones. She wanted to throw the candy back in his face, but how could she take such obvious enjoyment from her children? They had not had a piece of candy in months. There was never money for such frivolities.

The helplessness she felt at not being able to afford even the smallest of luxuries deepened her rage. She directed it at Trevor in the form of another cold, steely glare. "You can take back whatever you have in the bags. We don't need it."

Trevor was astounded at the anger that glittered in her eyes. He could also see it in the tense set of her thin shoulders, her stiff jaw, and her raised chin. He grappled for the right words. "It's not much, Mrs.

Holcomb. Just some staples I realized were missing in your house last night. The treats for the children were an afterthought. I know how much my nieces and nephews enjoy candy."

"Are you saying I can't provide for my children?"

Jonah had another bag wide open on the ground. "Look, Ma! There's sugar and flour. And—" he dug further inside the bag and pulled out a tin can "—and tea! Remember how you said you'd give up all your chickens for just one cup of tea?"

Claire could have smacked Jonah for his revelation. Now, Mr. Wilkins knew just how bad off they were. Her face flushed red with embarrassment at the poverty they lived with daily.

Trevor looped the reins of his mount around a fencepost. "Why don't you take those goods into the house and put them away, Jonah. I'd like to have a little talk with your mother in private."

If the statement had been from Judd Stone's mouth, Claire would have shook in her shoes. She would never leave herself open for that sort of abuse again. For some reason though, Mr. Wilkins did not frighten her—he only had the ability to raise the hair on the nape of her neck. Before she had a chance to think about it further, her children dragged the saddlebags up the rickety steps and into the house.

"Now," Trevor stated as he turned to her, "can we sit somewhere and talk?"

"I don't know what we have to say to each other. If it's a thank you that you desire, Mr. Wilkins, then thank you for the stores. It wasn't necessary, however."

Trevor closed his eyes momentarily to check his frustration. It would have been easier to dump the flour in her driveway, and then run like hell in the face of her obstinacy.

"All right, let's start over." He took off his Stetson, ran a hand through his wavy hair, and settled the hat back on his head. "We've established that you don't accept gifts readily. I didn't come looking for a thank you, but the kids have already taken everything into the house. They're enjoying the candy, so let's move on. How is your hand today?"

Claire's jaw sagged open. It was infuriating how the man so easily took over a situation, but as he stood in the afternoon sunlight, he looked so damned handsome that she suddenly realized she wanted to know what he had to say. Without another word, she rounded his horse, stalked to a bench by the woodpile, and plopped down in a huff as she struggled to keep her anger at the forefront.

Trevor followed her and sat on the opposite end of the bench, careful not to get to close.

Claire crossed her arms and sent him a withering stare. "You said you wanted to talk. I've got a lot of work to finish today, so let's get this over with." The sound of her children's laughter in the house filtered across the yard. Claire's gaze pierced him one more time, and then she turned her head in the direction of the sound.

Trevor rolled his eyes before he could stop himself and was immediately thankful she continued to stare out across the yard and missed his reaction. "So, has your hand given you any trouble today?"

"It seems to be fine."

He nodded. "Good. Mrs. Holcomb—"

"You might as well call me Claire. Being Mrs. Holcomb is something I'd like to distance myself from."

Her permission surprised him. "All right—Claire it is. When I rode in, I couldn't help but notice you waving the barrel of a rifle at me. Were you expecting someone else?"

"I thought maybe you were Mr. Stone from the bank. After yesterday...I wasn't going to let him get off his horse."

"Has that man ever attempted to hurt you before?"

Claire blinked the instant tears away before he realized how upsetting the entire incident actually was. She could have kicked herself. Lately, it seemed that the harder she struggled to stay strong, the more she felt like crying. She swallowed and gained control of her emotions. "He was here a few nights back. It didn't take much to convince him he'd made an error in judgment. It was my mistake to let my guard down when he came back. I should have known he was up to no good." She stood, stepped away from the bench, and hugged her arms around her midriff.

Trevor shifted his body and studied her from behind narrowed eyes. "I just want to understand what's going on here. Jonah has said you're going to move because you don't have enough money to stay. I know Stone owns a bank in St. Paul. I don't mean to pry, Claire, but is it because of taxes...missed loan payments...what?"

She turned and observed him momentarily. "Why? Why do you

think it's any of your business?"

"Maybe I can help you."

"Listen here, *Mr.* Wilkins, if you think you'll get special favors in exchange for money to catch up—"

"Hey!" Trevor shot up from the bench. "I never..." The words died in his throat. "Is that what Stone was trying to do? Was he forcing you to..."

"You can say it. I'm way past the age to...to have vapors—isn't that what the women in your world refer to it as? Out here, I have to be much tougher. Judd's proposition was that if I agreed to go to bed with him, he would pay up the back taxes and missed payments. Apparently, I'm not the only widow he's tried it with, either. Judd doesn't seem to mind broken down women as long as he gets what he wants. I absolutely refused. He showed up here yesterday, determined to get his way no matter my decision." Her eyes closed for a second. Why had she told Trevor all the facts?

She knew why... There was something about his gentle nature and overall goodness that tugged at her heart. She squared her shoulders and shook off the urge to sit beside him, rest her head on his big shoulder, and simply cry about the life she never asked for.

"I can help, Claire."

"I told you, I don't need your help."

"Why are you being so damned stubborn about this?"

"Why are you? Why would you want to help a complete stranger? No. I've made my decision. I can't do this anymore. This farm is too much. The bank can have it. Good day, Mr. Wilkins. I won't take up anymore of your time." She turned and strode toward the house, the proud set of her shoulders informing him she would speak of her situation no more.

Trevor observed her departure, totally confused as to how to deal with the likes of Claire Holcomb. He had never met a woman so proud and bent on having her own way—or one who had all the confidence in the world to raise five children on her own, but none when it came to looking in the mirror. She had purposely portrayed herself as "broken down" and in a class of woman much lower than he was accustomed to—or so she thought. He rose and walked to his horse with a shake of the head when the door to the house slammed shut.

A second later, it swung back open and Jonah skipped across the porch and down the steps with a happy glow in his eyes. No matter how rocky his world, having Trevor within eyesight did much for his youthful self-assurance. "Are you leavin'?"

"Yup, I think I better get back to St. Paul."

"Can I come to work tomorrow? I promise to have all my chores done so Ma doesn't have to do 'em."

"Sure thing," Trevor replied before he mounted. He glanced at the dilapidated house to make sure no one stood in the window, and then motioned for Jonah to come close. "If Mr. Stone shows up here, you make sure you come and find me. Don't tell your ma, just light out as fast as you can." He held out his hand. "Deal?"

Jonah raised his arm to receive the shake. "Deal."

Chapter Six

The next morning, Trevor entered the St. Paul Bank through a set of ornate doors and strode across the marbled floors to the receptionist's desk. His calm manner belied his anger.

A young man with his hair parted down the middle and thick spectacles perched on the bridge of his nose glanced up absently. "Can I help you?"

"Mr. J.P. Stone, please."

"May I tell him who is calling?"

A smile tugged at the corner of Trevor's mouth. Now that he was only minutes away from speaking with Claire's tormentor, his anger began to recede. "Tell him it's an old friend."

The clerk shuffled off his chair, down a hallway behind him, and disappeared through a doorway. Trevor plopped into a chair and glanced around the interior of the bank. Claire would have his head if she knew about this, but it was too damned bad. She would accept no help, of that he was certain, but it would not hurt to assure Stone kept his distance from here on out.

"Excuse me, sir."

Trevor glanced up.

"Mr. Stone will see you now."

Trevor hauled himself from the chair, hesitated as the directions to Judd's office were given, and headed down a marbled hallway. He was completely inside Stone's office before the man even glanced up to see who had entered. Trevor would have given anything to have a photograph of the fear and astonishment that flashed in the other man's eyes.

"You!" he spouted as he pushed himself away from the desk. "Get out of my office right now."

"I see you're a little braver when there are so many people within shouting distance."

"What do you want?" Judd clutched the arms of his chair.

"For myself? Nothing." Trevor seated himself casually in a chair opposite Judd, pulled a cigar from his jacket pocket, and lit the stogie. He enjoyed how Stone squirmed on his seat with fearful eyes that darted constantly at the open door to the hallway. Trevor casually glanced over his shoulder. "Maybe I should close the door so we can conduct our business in private."

"State what you have to say, and then I'll thank you to leave." Judd tugged at the collar of his suddenly tight shirt. Perspiration beaded across his flabby forehead. The banker's body still held the marks of Trevor's beating—one that had left him aching into the previous night.

"I want to discuss Claire Holcomb." Trevor flicked the ashes from his cigar, not the least bit concerned when they floated to the clean floor. Stone's lips thinned in exasperation. "I understand she's being forced into foreclosure."

"Your trip here was a waste of time. I'm not allowed to discuss our patrons financial problems—or lack there of—with anyone other than the holder of the note."

Trevor drew a long puff from his cigar, blew the smoke from his lungs, and watched the blue cloud float across the top of Stone's desk and right past the obstinate man's nose. "Do you have any objections to discussing your little side deal with her? Or maybe you'd like a witness to this conversation. I'm sure your investors would love to hear how hard you work at helping the widows around the countryside to...let's see, how would you describe it? Discover a way to hold onto their property?"

Judd's skin paled to a pasty shade of white.

"Ah, now I see I have your attention." Trevor leaned forward and stubbed out the lit cigar in an ornate well of writing ink, thoroughly enjoying being a bully for what may have been the first time in his life. "I came to warn you again, Mr. Stone. The ruse is up. If I ever find out that you've been out to the Holcomb place, no matter what the reason, I will hunt you down and beat you within an inch of your life." Trevor's gaze rested on the man's still-swollen nose. "That little bruise on your nose is nothing compared to how you'll feel when I'm done with you the next time. You can also apply this warning to the rest of the widows I'm sure you're hassling. Do we understand each other?"

Judd's hands trembled in his lap. "Who the hell are you?"

"My name is Trevor Wilkins."

The other man's eyes bulged wide.

"I see you know that name. You should. I've got quite a large amount of money sitting in this bank's coffers. If I decide to withdraw all of it, I'll be sure to let the board know it was because of your inability to follow directions. Now—" Trevor stood and buttoned his leather jacket "—I'll be leaving, because *I've* decided to go—not because you'd like me out of your sight. Remember our little bargain." He turned on his heel and left the office without another word.

* * *

Jonah and Trevor relaxed across the top of two large bales of hay at the back of the training center building, eating the lunch the older man supplied. The relationship seemed odd to most of the employees at the track. The two had constantly been in one another's company over the course of the last few days. Trevor Wilkins had become a permanent fixture whenever the young boy worked with The Ghost.

A cool wind whistled through the open stable doorway, the first telltale sign that the endlessly humid late June days would finally be broken by the summer's first storm. A strong gust of wind grabbed one of the large paneled doors and banged it against an interior stall, drawing attention to the tempest building on the horizon.

Trevor glanced up and took real notice of the weather for the first time. "It looks like we're in for a storm, Jonah." He pushed himself up from the bale of hay and crossed to the doorway to check the sky. The boy joined him at the entrance, more concerned about finishing his sandwich than the darkening sky. "I think we'll call it a day and get you home. If it starts to rain, The Ghost won't be training this afternoon anyway."

"I ain't afraid to get wet." Jonah continued to munch his sandwich, unconcerned about the weather.

An amused smile curved Trevor's mouth when he glanced down.

"I'm sure you're not. But your ma will want you close by. How about I give you a ride? We'll leave now so I can get back before the sky opens up." The older man was almost thankful for the storm. It gave him the opportunity to visit Claire with an excuse even she could not argue against. He was tired of asking Jonah subtle questions simply to gain information about the boy's mother. Claire was never far from Trevor's mind as the imminent departure of the Holcomb family loomed in the future.

Jonah rolled his shoulders and popped the last bit of bread between his lips. He swallowed and his stance mimicked his older friend's before he glanced up at the sky. "I'd rather sit here with you than be stuck with my sisters when it's raining."

A chuckle left Trevor's throat. "Well, I'd rather be nice and dry in my hotel suite than stuck in the middle of a storm. You run and get my horse from the paddock. I'll let the office clerk know we'll be gone the rest of the day."

* * *

By the time they reached Jonah's home, the wind had risen considerably and thunder rumbled in the distance. An ominous squall line of thick rolling clouds advanced from the southwest.

Claire stood in the yard, yanking dry linens from a rope strung across the yard. She spotted her son on the back of Trevor's horse, picked up the filled basket, and hurried to the porch. "Did you girls pen up the chickens?" Her daughters, Sofie and Sue Ellen, nodded as they sat playing with their ragged dolls. "Then take the sheets inside. Get them folded and put away. I'll be in shortly. Take Hannah and Ruth with you."

She hurried to the driveway. The last thing she wanted was for the man with her son to stay for a visit. It seemed as if every time he showed up in her life, Claire became a bumbling insecure mess.

She had listened to her son sing Trevor's praises for the past week and, consequently each night when Claire retired, thoughts of her son's wonderful boss were the last thing to cross her mind before drifting into a restless slumber. She had only met with the man twice—actually three times if she counted his interference on the street over a rotten apple—but she was hard pressed to force him from her thoughts. After countless sleepless nights, Claire had finally given up and began to imagine what a fantasy life would be like with someone as rich and handsome as he. It was the only way she could find slumber. Now, the nemesis that haunted her dreams had materialized once more.

Trevor observed her as she hurried toward them. Wisps of curly blonde hair danced about her face in the escalating wind. The top three buttons of her dress were undone, most likely to allow a hint of humid air inside before the weather turned cool. Creamy white skin rested below her collarbone. The dress's skirt hugged her slender legs as the hem flapped around slim, bare feet. This was the Claire he had waited to someday see—the one who did not seem so angry at the world.

The gray eyes that were normally a steely, angry color were bright with relief when she reached them. Jonah jumped from the saddle with the help of Trevor's arm, and she pulled him into her embrace. "Thank goodness you're home. I hoped you'd get here before the storm hit."

"Trevor gave me a ride."

Claire glanced up at the man in the saddle as she cuddled her son. "I see that. Go in the house now and help Sofie with your sisters. Bring some wood inside, just incase the weather turns damp. I'll be right in shortly."

"See ya, Trevor. I'll be back in the morning!"

"If it's raining, stay home!" Trevor called out as the boy loped to the house.

"I told you, I ain't afraid of gettin' wet!" Jonah hollered over his shoulder, and then disappeared a second later.

Trevor simply shook his head at Jonah's tenacity.

Claire nervously smoothed the flapping faded material around her hips. "Thank you for bringing him home."

Trevor's glance lingered on her face. The softness of her rounded chin now devoid of the constant scowl mesmerized him. "He's a great kid. You should be proud of him."

To his amazement, a gentle smile curved her mouth upward. It was the first time he had ever seen her lips in anything but a straight line of disapproval.

"I am. I can't imagine my days without him." Claire glanced about the yard, shuffled her bare feet in the dust, and finally glanced up again. "Mr. Wilkins—"

"Trevor."

"Trevor...I owe you an apology for being so rude last week. Especially after you chased Mr. Stone from my doorstep."

"It was my pleasure, Claire. If that man ever bothers you again, you just send for me." His gaze dropped to her naked wrist, then slid to the tips of her fingers. "I see your hand is healed. Jonah said it wasn't bothering you anymore."

"I'm fine. I should have been paying closer attention that night." Her eyes danced about, her mind acknowledging how handsome he was before she found the courage to look him straight in the eye. "One more thing. Thank you for being so kind to Jonah. He's the happiest I've seen him in a long time." The wind whipped up the dirt around them and sent Claire's loose curls into a riotous swirl around her face. She shielded her eyes from the dust momentarily.

Trevor grabbed his hat before it sailed across the yard on the wind. His mount danced beneath his weight. He hated to leave, but the alternative was a good soaking. "I'd best be on my way before this storm breaks over my head."

Claire stepped back when he reined the horse around. Trevor tipped his hat, firmly set it atop his head, and urged the horse into a gallop. She stood in the building wind until he disappeared around a bend in the road, and then raced for the house as a crack of lightening lit the darkened sky above her.

***

The storm raged on, and the thunder and lightening crashed above their heads as the fierce winds rattled the windowpanes. Three-year-old Hannah clutched at her mother's arm and whined loudly as Claire rocked her in the chair. "Shh, honey, it's all right."

Another thunderous crack brought both Ruth and Sue Ellen running for their mother's side.

"Ma, make the noise go away," Ruth pleaded.

"Hush, it'll be over soon," Claire murmured as her fingers threaded their way through her daughter's soft, fine hair. Her children's fear was the only thing that kept her rooted and calm. Claire hated storms with a passion.

Sofie looked up from where she sat at the kitchen table; she and her brother took turns using a chalkboard as they practiced their letters. "Don't cry, Ruth. Remember what Ma said? The angels are moving furniture around in heaven. That's why it's so loud."

The corner of Claire's mouth lifted. Sofie was forever repeating the things she said throughout the day. Now her oldest daughter looked at her mother for confirmation.

"Ain't that right, Ma. It's the angels. And Daddy and Grandma and Grandpa are helping them."

"That's right, honey." *Well, partially right. Your grandparents are probably helping them, but I'm sure your father is rotting in hell...*

Frank's transgressions reared up inside her mind once more. Claire's gaze skimmed over the shabby wooden furniture and makeshift ladder that led to the second floor, then moved to the few chipped dishes that were piled inside a cabinet with no door. Her deceased husband, in a drunken fit one night, ripped the cupboard door from its hinges and purposely broke one piece of her mother's fine china after another. *No one would want to live in a house like this.* It was clean, but it was nothing.

It is too something! Her gentler side argued.

No, it's not. It's not worth fighting for anymore.

It's the only thing that you can call yours...

That voice was back—the one that could bring her to her knees and make her weep forever. Thankfully, Jonah's excited voice brought her back to the moment before the fear of the future overwhelmed her once again. He had his face pressed against the glass and used his hands to shield the view from the lantern's reflection.

"Ma! Part of the barn is wrecked! The rain is lettin' up, and I can see it from here!"

Claire and the other children rushed to the window. Her heart sank as she peered through the glass. She could care less about the barn; it was the few hogs and a milk cow inside that had her worried. She had not told Jonah yet, but she planned to leave for good the day after tomorrow, so the barn was no loss. The animals were irreplaceable, however. She had planned to sell them to the neighbors. The money would be a slight cushion until the first paychecks started to come in from her new job up north.

"Stay with the girls, Jonah. I'm going to take a lantern and make sure Maisy is all right."

"I'll go check, Ma. That old cow will come to me if I call."

"No you won't. I don't want to be worrying about that building caving in on you. Let me check it first. You stay here." Claire wrapped her shoulders in a heavy shawl and pulled on an old pair of Frank's work boots, suddenly aware that thunder rumbled in the distance once more. Hopefully, the storm was near done. She grabbed a lantern, lit it, and headed out of the house.

Cool, moist air hit her in the face when she opened the door. Her eyes darted about the yard in the muted light of early evening. The storm had done more damage than she realized. Four trees lay toppled between the house and the barn. Another rested across the roof of the garden shed. The building was a total wreck.

She picked her way through the mud and ignored the cold drizzle that dampened her head and the still-fierce wind that blew stray curls around her forehead. Slogging through the muck to the back of the barn, she could not tell if the caved in outer wall was propped against something inside or if it was truly ready to fall in completely, which would bring the entire building crashing down. She turned back and headed for the front of the barn to check the damage from the inside.

Claire set the lantern down and used both hands to tug at the barn door, praying the entire time that she would find the cow and six hogs alive. Once the entrance stood open, she lifted the lantern higher to cast its illumination about the dark interior as she stepped inside. Miraculously, as she walked through the front area of the barn, she saw that nothing in that area had been disturbed. The backside of the barn though, was another story.

"Maisy?" Only silence greeted her. Claire's step slowed when she spotted the animal lying beneath the rubble a short distance away. "Oh, Maisy..."

Testing the sturdiness of a support beam, she hooked the lantern on a rusted peg. Stepping carefully over the debris, she worked her way to the back of the barn. Claire shoved a few boards out of the way, battling the growing lump in her throat as Maisy's motionless body came into better view.

Kim Mattson

The cow was dead—along with the little bit of money she would have made from the sale. Her eyes darted about in the fatal silence as she battled to remain calm. She spotted two of the hogs crushed beneath large timbers. If the others were alive, they had either escaped or were buried deeper in the rubble.

"It'll be all right," Claire murmured to no one as she ran a trembling hand through her wet hair. "You'll figure something else out." She had to keep talking to herself, bolstering herself—or suffer a breakdown. Her life continually got worse, no matter how hard she tried. Claire sank to her knees and her fingers traveled over the cow's cold, wet hide. Just that morning, the animal had given them milk—life-sustaining milk—and now it was dead. How quickly life changed. Her chin trembled. "Don't cry. Just be thankful it wasn't the house that collapsed. You've got the kids and they're all fine. You're a survivor, Claire..."

She inhaled deeply to control the continued trembling of her chin. The action actually helped to keep the tears at bay. "I'm not going to cry. I refuse to cry. Whoever heard of crying over a dead cow..." She stood and began to pick her way back over the debris, but paused when she caught something out of the corner of her eye. Her hand froze midway to the lantern, then moved to cover her mouth. "Please...no..."

Claire forced herself to look again. A small white paw poked out from beneath a pile of timbers formerly belonging to the roof. She moved in a trance-like state to stand beside the heap of broken beams, and then suddenly leapt forward. Ignoring the splinters of wood that cut into her hands, Claire bellowed her rage as she yanked one timber after another and sent them flying behind her, on top of the dead cow. "It's not fair! I didn't ask for this! Frank, you rotten bastard..."

Her chest heaved with the exertion of her tirade. She labored like a mad woman to push aside the affects of the devastating storm. The tears did not begin to flow, however, until the dead cat was completely uncovered. Claire sank slowly to her knees, felt the first sob tighten her throat, and dropped her face into her hands. Once she started to weep, there was nothing she could do but let the past weeks of fear and weariness shake her shoulders with despair. The tears continued to flow as she wrapped the inert body of the animal within her shawl and crawled across the straw-covered floor to rest against a bale of hay.

Painful sobs clogged her throat, making it hard to catch a breath as the next onslaught of despondency wound its way through her heart. Her slender arms cradled the animal as she rocked forward.

Claire's one last symbol of hope had been the white, fluffy cat. Its lighthearted presence had filled her with childish optimism that life could be good again one day; the feline was a constant that could always be depended upon—and now it was gone.

She continued to weep one choking sob after another, and her head lolled weakly to the side as tears flooded her cheeks. "I can't do it any more..." She could not be strong when so many adversities constantly pulled her down. The defeat weighed heavily in her heart as her shoulders shook in rhythm with the tumult of her tears.

* * *

Jonah cautiously approached the barn. He had waited nearly an hour for Claire to return to the house and finally decided to run the risk of disobedience and seek her out. Absolute inky darkness was cut only by the illumination of his lantern. His heart thudded against his tiny ribcage as he crossed the storm-ravaged yard.

The boy's small blond head poked through the doorway, afraid of what he might find. Spying his mother sitting in the straw with something in her arms, he edged forward. "Ma? Are you coming in the house?"

She lifted her chin in his direction, and Jonah's mouth rounded in shock at the sight of her face. Claire's swollen eyes gleamed red in the flickering light of the lantern, but that was not what frightened the boy the most. His mother looked right through him, as if he was not there.

Cautiously, he sidled forward, knowing something was horribly wrong. Jonah sank slowly to his knees and, seeing the cat, reached out to touch the animal. "I didn't know that Snowball was outside. I'm sorry, Ma."

"I'm sorry, too." Claire's raspy voice was barely a whisper.

"Come in the house." His fingers touched the clammy skin of her arms. "You're freezin'."

"You go on. I'm going to sit out here."

"But you can't. The girl's are cryin'."

"So am I."

Jonah's eyes widened. This was not the mother he knew; this was not the person who continually looked for the good in everything for her children's benefit. He did not want to leave her side—he did not dare. Not knowing what else to say, he glanced at the dead cat first, and then back to his mother's flat gaze. "Do you want me to bury her?"

Claire tightened her grip on the cat and her head shook slowly. "Jonah, go. I want to be alone. I'm not coming in tonight. I just want to be alone to cry." The tears began to trickle down her cheeks again from dull, lifeless eyes. "You kids will have to fend for yourselves tonight. I don't have anything left to give. Do you understand that? I've tried so hard, but I've failed."

"You're scarin' me."

"Just go."

"Ma—"

"I said go!" she screamed. "Just leave me alone!"

Jonah scrambled to his feet and raced from the barn. Splashing through the mud, he ran to the house. Yanking the door open and sprinting inside, he grabbed his heavy jacket and slid his arms into the sleeves.

"Where's Ma, Jonah?" Sofie questioned from where she and Sue Ellen sat huddled at the table. The two smaller girls were already in bed.

"She's in the barn and says to leave her alone. You girls stay here. I'm going to town."

Sue Ellen gasped. "You're gonna get it, Jonah. Ma said you can't be in town after dark."

"Just be quiet. I gotta find Trevor."

Chapter Seven

Trevor sat at the desk in his room, trying to concentrate on the daily newspaper, but after reading the same line for the tenth time, he tossed the paper angrily to the floor. The remains of his supper filled a silver tray that was shoved out of the way. He had found it difficult to enjoy such a sumptuous meal when Claire, Jonah, and the girls hardly had anything to fill their bellies.

He rose and peered out the window, agitated because the storm had blown for nearly three hours. If not for the weather, he would have gone back to the farm. Now that the squall had passed, it was too late to be visiting.

Leaning his shoulder against the wooden frame of the window, his gaze took in the sporadic flickers of lightening to the north and, at that moment, he was surprised to realize just how badly he wanted to see Claire again. In his mind, he kept comparing the picture of the first time he saw her standing on the street, admonishing Jonah, to the vision of her standing barefoot in the yard earlier that day with a luminescent smile lighting up her face.

So, what's changed? Nothing...and yet, she was like a different woman earlier. And her smile...

As he stared through the droplets of rain trickling down the windowpane, he remembered how, for a split second, he had wanted to bend down and capture those lips with his. He ran his hand across his bristly cheek and adjusted his shoulder against the window cove. Claire had awakened emotions in him that he had never experienced before. No other woman had created such a desire to protect and care for another person's well being. And Jonah? Trevor could not get out of bed fast enough in the morning in order to get to the training center to see him. The young lad filled a fatherly need that he had never realized lay dormant somewhere inside him.

His thoughts drifted back to the boy's mother. No other woman had ever made him recognize how empty his life actually was...how shallow his existence had been up to now. Trevor had only himself to worry about before and, up to this moment, he always thought it was enough. He straightened with purpose. *Tomorrow...I'm going back out there tomorrow with supplies and food. I'm going to make her take my help. I don't want her and her kids to disappear from my life...*

Three raps against the door startled him back to the present. Trevor crossed the suite to find the concierge standing on the other side of the entryway. "Can I help you?"

The uptight little man wrung his hands. "Sir, I'm sorry to bother you, but you have a guest waiting in the lobby."

"Why didn't you send him up?"

"Well—" his eyes darted around in quiet conspiracy "—this young man is not someone we wanted running through the hotel. We tried to escort him out, but he was rather insistent. He says he knows you. My supervisor finally asked that I come up and give you the choice to speak to your guest or not. If you'd like, we can notify the sheriff and have him removed."

Trevor's brow furrowed. "Just how young is this man?"

The concierge snorted. "That's the thing, sir. He isn't even adult. He's a young boy."

Jonah! Trevor grabbed his jacket from the back of a nearby chair, nearly knocked the man over who stood in the doorway, and took the steps two at time.

Jonah spotted Trevor before the older man reached the last step. The boy flew across the lobby and yanked on his friend's hand. "You've got to come with me! I don't know what to do!"

"Calm down, Jonah, and tell me what happened." Trevor took in the child's disheveled appearance, grasped his hand tighter, and headed across the marble floor to the exit.

"It's my ma. Our place is really wrecked from the storm."

Trevor's heart sank to his stomach. "Is she hurt? Is anyone hurt?" He had originally thought that Stone had shown up at the homestead."

The boy wagged his head. "No, but somethin' ain't right." He tugged on the older man's hand and stopped Trevor's headlong flight as he tried to explain. "The barn caved in on one side and killed our cow. Ma went out to check on things. I don't know what happened, but she must have found our cat. It's dead. Now she's sittin' on the floor and crying and won't come in. She hollered at me to go away and leave her alone. Ma never does that." Jonah tugged at Trevor's hand. "Please, I don't know what to do. She's shiverin' and freezin' cold cuz she got all wet."

Trevor grasped Jonah's hand more firmly in his and headed for the lobby door.

* * *

The inky black night cloaked the landscape when they reached the farm. Only random flashes of lightening now illuminated the sky far to the northeast. The only light to be seen was the glow of the lantern spilling onto the porch through the front window. Both Sofie and Sue Ellen could be seen peering out from the other side of the glass pane.

Trevor and Jonah went into the house first to see if Claire had finally decided to come in from the night. They never had to ask the question. The older girls began to cry when they saw Trevor, and Sofie flung her little body into his comforting embrace.

"Ma is still out there. We've been watching, and the lantern must have gone out—there's no more light inside the barn."

Trevor smoothed her blonde hair with his large palm as he held her quaking body. "She'll be fine, Sofie. Why don't you get me a blanket while Jonah fetches a lantern? I'll go keep her company and bring her back in a little while. She probably just needed some time to herself. You kids can get some water heating so she can warm up in a bath." There, that ought to keep them busy. Trevor had absolutely no idea what he was going to encounter. Something had happened to Claire that she was not willing to share with her children. Hopefully, the reason was not Judd Stone. That thought, and that thought alone, had plagued his mind on the ride out.

Trevor tucked the acquired blanket under his arm, took the

lantern from Jonah, and headed for the barn, sidestepping one of the big trees in the yard that had fallen during the storm. The slight drizzle that started on the way to the farm now turned heavier. After the horrendous heat of the day, it surprised him how the damp air sent a shiver down his spine.

Stepping inside the barn, he lifted the lantern and scanned the damage. His breath whistled across his teeth when his gaze rested on a huddled Claire. Silently, she lifted her head and sent him a vacant stare.

"Claire?"

Receiving no response, he crossed the short space. Still cradling the dead cat, slight shudders made her shoulders tremble. Dampened hair curled down past her shoulders. "Claire? Jonah came to my hotel. He was worried about you."

She tightened her hold on the animal and turned her face away. "He shouldn't have bothered you." Her words were barely a whisper.

"He was frightened. He said you wouldn't come in." Trevor's eyes drifted to the stiff cat. Hunkering down, he reached out a hand and stroked the soft fur with his fingers. "The storm has done a lot of damage out here." His gaze scanned the corner where the wall was opened to the night, and then darted back to Claire when she shuddered violently beside him. "Why don't you let me take the cat, and then you can wrap yourself in this blanket. You don't have to go in until you're ready."

His soothing voice reached her as he set the lantern on the floor and waited. "The rain has started again, but I think the worst is over. The wind is hardly even a breeze any longer. Whenever you're ready, I'll take Snowball so you can warm up."

Surprisingly, she hugged the cat once more and haltingly let Trevor take the animal from her clutches. He rose, crossed the dampened floor of the barn, and laid the dead animal on a bench just outside the door. Returning to her side, he dropped lightly to sit beside her.

Claire hugged her knees to her chest. Her swollen eyes blinked, causing a tear on each side of her face to trickle down.

Trevor shook open the blanket and, without permission, draped it around her trembling shoulders. "Are you sure you don't want go in the house and warm up?"

Her head shook as she clutched the blanket. "I can't," she whispered hoarsely. Claire could not face the responsibilities she would find there.

"Well, then we'll sit out here together until you're ready to go in." Trevor leaned against the wooden slats behind him, rested his forearms across his knees, and watched the lantern's reflection shimmer across the straw-covered floor. Hearing another quiet hiccup of despair come from her throat, he turned his head and hoped he was not pushing her too soon. "You want to talk about it?"

Claire's face dropped to her raised knees. A sudden, hoarse sob echoed in the barn. Trevor waited patiently by her side, stunned though by the complete despair he witnessed as the sob turned into one wretched moan after another. Without thought, he lifted his arm, wrapped it around her heaving shoulders, and pressed her head against his side.

Claire came willingly as her frazzled mind searched for some small beacon of solace that would make the horrible pain in her life disappear. She was only vaguely aware of the strong, warm hand that stroked the outline of her arm beneath the woolen blanket as she sobbed against his broad chest.

Trevor's free arm reached out to coax her into his embrace, and his fingers caressed the soft hair at her temple. Resting his cheek against the top of Claire's head, he closed his eyes and kissed the damp, blonde tresses. "You cry as long as you want. I'll be ready to listen when you're done."

Her cold fingers curled into the material of his cotton shirt, holding him close, numbly absorbing the warmth of his big body and the sheltering comfort he provided. Years had passed since anyone put her needs first and did not force her to stand and be strong. With each reassuring caress of his gentle hands, Claire clutched her fingers tighter and wept harder.

Trevor held her shivering body in the dim light, with the sudden understanding that there was no other place on earth he would rather be. The thought shocked his brain. Claire's immediate emotional dependence affected him like nothing ever had. It felt so right to hold her and share her pain.

Time passed. How much, he was not quite sure, but finally her sobs slowed to small hiccups. Her body ceased to tremble with cold except for random small shudders.

Claire kept her head pressed close to his chest, not yet ready to face the world. To silently share her pain, to dwell in the security of comforting strong arms, and to know that he did not judge her for having fallen apart lessened the horrible ache that resided in her soul. Another tender kiss pressed against her hair filled her body with warmth. Her lids fluttered shut; she would remember every warm breath against her cheek and the sound of his heart beating beneath her ear in the trying days to come. Claire knew she should go back to the house, but she could not force her physical body to leave the safe haven of the reassuring presence he provided—not yet. She needed to stay for a while longer.

"Tell me, Claire. What happened?" The soft plea whispered past her ear. "If it's something I can fix, then let me help."

She rubbed her cheek against his shirt, somehow trusting that she could tell him the truth and he would not think less of her. "I've tried so hard to make a life for myself and the children. I've worked from sun up to sun down. I've prayed that life would become easier. I worked for it, I deserved it, but it never happened." Her head shook against his chest. "I made such a mess of my life."

"Why do you say that? There are a lot of outside forces you're dealing with, Claire. It's not your fault."

She breathed in the light scent of tobacco that clung to his shirt, finding great comfort in the fact that the smell was familiar and she had not even realized it. How could she explain her emotions when she could not put the details together herself?

"I remember a time when I laughed and looked forward to the following day with such anticipation. Good choices always came readily. When I married Frank, I was so excited to be his wife, so thrilled at beginning a life with a new husband. We were going to make this farm profitable."

Trevor wondered at her sudden silence, but remained quiet. He would let Claire continue when she was ready.

"Everything went so wrong," she finally whispered. "When I tried to save money, he stole it to buy liquor. He became a different person. As drunk as he always was, somehow he knew when there was money around." Claire stopped. She could not tell Trevor about the times he forced her to their bed, how she cowered in fear, begging him not to beat her. She hated Frank then, and she hated him now. "I should have left, but I stayed. I stayed for Jonah and Sofie, because they weren't able to see what their father was like. They loved him. And after each of the other children were born, I was too frightened to leave. I didn't know what he would do to me if he found us." Her head lifted slightly from his chest as she glanced around the barn. "So, this is what I stayed for—a broken down farm that never amounted to anything no matter how hard I tried. I look in the mirror, and—" she shuddered with a quiet sob in her throat "—I can't find *me* anymore. Somewhere along the way, I disappeared, and a tired, older, weathered stranger took my place."

Trevor used a finger to tip her chin up so she could see the truth in his eyes. "You've worked hard, Claire. Whether it was the right thing to do or not, you hung in there. You tried to be both parents to those five great kids of yours. And don't think you ever disappeared. When I look at you, I see a mature, wise woman; someone who possesses a great deal more strength than most men. I also see a woman who doesn't even realize the beauty she possesses."

Her lips parted at his statement, and her eyes widened as she stared up in wonder. *Is that how the world sees me? Is that how he sees me?*

Light, gray eyes met green ones.

Trevor cupped her cheek, lowered his mouth before thinking further on it, and pressed his warm lips against hers.

Claire's eyelids wavered shut as she relished the warm softness of his lips against her mouth. She did not respond, but rather marveled at the reverence in his kiss. Breaking the contact of their mouths, she stared into his gentle gaze. In their depths she saw a rare honesty, never encountered before. He actually believed what he had just stated.

Claire waited for the fear to build in her blood. Frank had taken advantage of her many times. If not for Trevor, Judd would have demanded the same. Her fingers trembled as she lightly touched the course stubble that darkened his cheek and jaw; strangely, she could not find the fear anywhere. Nothing was more important at that moment than feeling the safety of this man's tender embrace or the intense heat that built in her blood.

Trevor saw the question in her gray eyes, dipped his head, and captured her mouth once more.

Hesitantly, Claire slid her hand up and around to the back of his head and pulled his lips closer. She needed the reaffirmation that, yes, she was someone with worth—and Trevor was the man to throw her the lifeline.

He tightened his gentle embrace and, at the same time, fought an internal battle. Trevor had kissed her for two reasons. One, to show Claire that she was not the undesirable woman she thought she was and, two, because he could not help himself. Now he wanted to feel the softness of her skin beneath his fingers. He yearned to discover the dips and valleys of her body, to memorize the damp scent that clung to her hair...

He drew back and tucked an errant tress behind her ear. "I'm sorry, Claire. I shouldn't have done that." He cleared his throat uncomfortably. "Are you ready to go back inside?"

She continued to stare up at him in wonder. "Why did you kiss me?"

A gentle smile widened across his face. "Because I think you're one beautiful lady. Because I haven't been able to get you off my mind since the day we met. Because I couldn't help myself."

Her fingers skimmed his cheek once more. "Then kiss me again."

"Claire..."

"Kiss me. Tell me that I'm beautiful," she breathed. "It's been so long since someone said that. It's been so long since I felt like a woman. I...I can't face another night alone." Her fingers curled around the bunched material of his shirt as she tipped her chin upward. "Keep me warm, Trevor. Keep me safe...just for now...just for this minute..."

He searched inside her gaze. The dim light of the lantern turned her eyes to the color of soft pewter. Her lips trembled as she waited.

Trevor lowered his mouth. The initial kiss was tentative, another light touching of lips; exploring, wondering; but it quickly grew passionate as Claire's breathless whisper of his name demanded more. Her arms clung to him tightly now, capturing his innate strength and transforming it into her own long dormant passion.

Her desire to be held warmed his heart and, as he gently laid her willing body beside his on the straw, he continued to kiss her, fascinated by the fact that, for the first time in his life, he wanted to give more than he received. Holding Claire in his arms made his heart pound wildly. The rush of heat in his body was more than a simple physical excitement.

This first real embrace was a sharing of souls.

One last thread of conscience forced Trevor to lift his lips from hers. "Are you sure, Claire? I don't want you to be sorry."

She lay in the straw now, and her body had ceased its trembling—and it had nothing to do with the blanket that was still wrapped around her. Where was the huge streak of responsibility that continually ruled her world? For the first time in her life, Claire no longer cared what would happen come morning. She knew only that she needed to forget her past life, to rediscover the young and happy woman hiding inside and, somehow, she also knew that only Trevor could help her to accomplish that goal.

Claire unfastened the top three buttons of his shirt, slowly slipped a hand inside the opening, and rested her palm over his heart. Her silent, steady gaze met his, and she waited.

Trevor slid an arm beneath her waist and pulled her willing body with him as he rolled onto his back. Stretched full length on top of him now, Claire dipped her head to initiate the kiss as his hands ran a slow path down the trim line of her back. The soft moan emanating from the back of her throat urged him on.

Opening his lips, his tongue sought the warmth of her mouth. Claire was there to meet him, to draw him in as she rolled to her side, taking Trevor with her.

His hand rested against her hip, and then kneaded its way upward to a covered, firm breast that fit perfectly into his palm. Her body arched against him in involuntary response.

"Claire..."

"Don't stop...it's all right. I want this...I need this. Don't leave me alone in the dark..."

Trevor slowly unbuttoned the front of her dress, gently pushed aside the open bodice, and touched his lips to the velvet softness of a bare, round breast. Claire's slight gasp echoed past his ear, and her hands urged his mouth to the other twin mound. He followed her lead with a path of soft nibbles until he captured a peaked tip with his teeth.

He dragged the hem of her dress up an endlessly long limb, then released an audible groan when Claire wrapped her naked leg around his muscular thigh. His hand trembled upon discovering the smooth silkiness of her thigh. He felt like a schoolboy making love for the first time.

He...Trevor Wilkins...the most sought after bachelor in St. Paul, was having second thoughts.

Instinctively, Claire understood that, at any moment, he might walk away from her when she needed him so desperately. Her hand drifted back inside his shirt. "Trevor...stay with me..." she breathed as she pressed small kisses against his throat. "Trevor...Trevor..."

The sound of his name on her warm lips was his undoing and, with no further conscious thought, he gently tugged the pantaloons down past her knees and over her slim ankles, taking her boots with them. He tossed everything aside. A moment later, Trevor had freed his hard length, then his mouth plummeted to capture the swollen lips that now sought his; lips that demanded he share his body with hers.

His hand slid beneath the bunched material at her waist to discover the exquisite flatness of her stomach. Masculine fingers trailed over the curve of one hip, and then moved on to explore the feminine heat surrounded by trim thighs.

Claire tugged at his shoulders, gasping breathlessly each time he stroked her hot feminine core. She writhed against his palm, finding herself lost in the heated, yet tender assault.

Trevor covered her body with his, drawing the sweetness from her mouth as he slid slowly into her warmth. He held her safely in his arms, then lay motionless, relishing the sensations that churned through his belly along with the desire to protect, to shelter; the emotions stirred in his breast. He deepened the kiss.

Claire's lids fluttered open to be greeted by the gentle sea of green above her. A security like she had never known rested quietly in her chest. His warm eyes beckoned her heart to join with his as he began to move inside her.

Claire's eyes drifted shut again when he pressed a soft kiss against her mouth, then she moved in unison with the slow, sensuous rhythm Trevor set. The skin on her arms goose bumped, in contrast to the warmth that built in her blood. She held her breath as he took her further into the heat, higher and higher, reaching for a place she had never been before. The flames licked hotter against her womb, and Claire groaned against his lips when suddenly, passionately, one tremor after another shook her to the soul. It was the first time—the only time—she had experienced such magic when a man held her in his arms.

Trevor's breath caught in his throat upon his own release. Never had he known such explosive ecstasy and somehow he knew he never would again—except with the woman who lay in his arms. She clung to his neck, keeping him with her for a while longer as their lips mingled and they waited for their hearts to slow.

* * *

Claire fastened the last button at her throat and pulled the blanket tightly around her body. They were fully dressed once more, and the awkwardness of the situation hit her.

My God...what does he think? What came over me? She huddled deeper into the warmth of the wool blanket, instinctively knowing that life would never be the same again. Trevor's gentle and worshipful caresses had opened a small door to a world she was unaware of; he had shown her what it was like to be loved, as a woman should be. She was not quite sure, however, what the lovemaking meant to him now that it was over and they both prepared to leave the barn. Most likely, now that sanity had once again set in, he would consider their tryst a simple dalliance. After all, she had blatantly offered him her body...

Her heart jumped when his fingers touched her shoulder.

"I think we should get you in the house."

She did not respond and heard Trevor's deep sigh behind her.

"Claire...I..."

Her hand shot into the air. "No words, Trevor."

Claire's breath caught in her throat when another more frustrated sigh left his lips. His touch remained gentle though, as he helped her stand and silently secured the blanket around her shoulders. Wordlessly, she walked beside him and into the night.

Trevor led Claire to the house, but hesitated when she took the first step up onto the porch. Realizing that she would silently disappear into the dwelling if he did not say something, he gently snatched her arm and halted her progress up the stairs. She turned and halfheartedly tried to shrug off his hold, but his grip only tightened. He looked up at her, his eyes dark with remorse. "We need to talk about what happened back there."

Claire ducked her head and embarrassment colored her cheeks.

She had so completely fallen apart and he had witnessed it. She had begged him to hold her in the dark. His earlier kisses still burned her mouth, and her body still tingled from his tender touch as she finally found the courage to meet his questioning eyes. What did he intend the time in the barn to mean? He had cradled her, kissed her warmly, and treated her gently when he could have roughly and quickly taken what he needed as a man. Now, however, guilt rested in his sorrowful gaze.

"I'm sorry for losing control." Her fingers clasped the edges of the blanket and her gaze searched the yard simply so she did not have to look into his eyes. "Everything that has happened over the last few months finally came to a head when I found the...the cat." Her gray eyes glittered once more with unshed tears. "I just..." She shrugged. "I don't know. I just needed to be held. I needed to let someone else shoulder my responsibilities for a short time until..." Her chin dropped. "I needed to make the numbness go away so I could feel again."

Trevor squeezed her hand. "I wanted to be there for you. I was so scared when Jonah came to find me. I didn't know what had happened." His hand moved to lift her chin again. "You need to know something. I didn't plan to come here tonight and...have the evening end the way it did. That was never my intention."

A soft smile curved her mouth—one that made his heart jump inside his chest. "I know you didn't. I'm not a young girl, Trevor. I knew exactly what I was doing. What you gave me tonight was wonderful. In fact, it was probably the one thing that kept me from completely losing my mind."

"You've got a lot of decisions to make. I want to sit down and discuss how I can help you...and I don't mean in the way Judd Stone wanted to help."

"But—"

"No buts. You've got five children in there who need you to make some correct decisions. I can help, Claire. I don't want to hear another word. Go inside and sleep on it. Things will look better in the morning. I promise." He placed his hands around her waist, took two steps up, and pressed a chaste kiss to her forehead. "I'll come out tomorrow, probably sometime in the afternoon, and we can survey the damage. This is your place, not mine, so you make the final decisions. Whatever you do though, don't shut me out because of what happened between us."

She finally met his eyes. "Why are you being so kind to me? Especially after I've been so rude—" Her gaze dropped again, and her cheeks colored. "Especially after how I acted tonight?"

Trevor chuckled lightly. "You're an enigma to me, Claire. I've found myself thinking about you constantly since the first time we met. I feel a connection with you that I can't quite figure out." He tipped his dark head toward the house. "Go inside. I'll be back out tomorrow. I promise."

She left him standing on the bottom step and continued up to the porch, hesitated, and then turned to face him. "Thank you. Thank you for saving me from drowning tonight."

Trevor recognized the soft gratitude in her eyes. There was nothing dishonest about Claire Holcomb. He suddenly understood that the wall she erected between herself and others was meant to keep her safe, whether she realized she had built it or not. When it crumbled for a short time tonight, Trevor glimpsed the real woman within. "Don't give up. Things will work out."

"I better go inside. I'm sure the children are waiting for me." Still finding it hard to believe that someone of his stature would even be remotely interested in an older, weathered woman, Claire offered him one more chance to bow out of her life. "I'll understand if you can't come back. What happened in the barn? It doesn't mean you owe me anything."

His smile widened and his eyes twinkled when he reached up to take her hand once more. He pressed a kiss against her fingertips. "Good night, Claire. I promise you I'll be back tomorrow. That's a guarantee."

A light breeze swirled around them as they stood frozen, staring at one another, then Claire broke the spell when she took a step back, turned, and silently entered the house.

Trevor waited until he heard the click of the lock, and then forced himself to mount his horse, swing the animal around, and canter down the wet drive. Morning would not come soon enough.

Chapter Eight

Claire rolled onto her back the next morning and stared out the window. Rays of bright sunshine streamed past the faded curtains that hung neatly on either side of the window, promising a beautiful summer day after the tempest of the evening before. Immediately, she tossed away the vision of Trevor making love to her, not yet able to face emotions that had been buried for years.

Dragging her legs over the edge of the mattress, she grabbed a shabby robe from the foot of the bed and tossed the garment over the back of a chair. It was already much too warm to don a second layer.

Forcing herself to leave the comfort of her bed, she crossed to the window, totally unprepared for the storm's aftermath. Her gaze traveled over the yard that now resembled a war zone. Trees had been uprooted, their limbs smashed beneath massive trunks that lay scattered about as far as the eye could see. Pressing her cheek against the windowpane, she was able to survey the damaged barn. Trevor had taken the dead cat from the shelter, and her eyes searched for the forgotten shawl and the poor animal that, up until yesterday, had been her last lifeline. She would have to go outside and find Snowball before one of the girls did.

Claire lifted a clean, if rather ragged, skirt from the peg attached to her bedroom door. As she crossed the small room to retrieve a cotton shirt from a dresser drawer, the reflection in the mirror stopped her dead in her tracks.

Normally, she braided her long hair into a thick plate before retiring for the evening. Last night, however, she was too exhausted to do more than slip off her dress, don a nightgown, and fall into bed. Claire shuffled closer to the mirror, shocked by the woman who stared back. Sun-bleached blonde hair wrapped around her shoulders and hung past her shoulders in a riotous mess. Her fingers lightly touched the curls around her face before they moved to her full lips—the ones that Trevor kissed the night before. A shiver trickled down her spine.

Am I really beautiful? That's what he said... The face in the mirror was a stranger. Her mouth was not turned down in a prominent frown of constant worry. Her long hair was not pulled back into a tight bun to keep it away from her face as she lifted bales of hay into the barn or milked the cow. Last night, Claire had felt like a woman for the first time in more years than she cared to think about. And last night, she had acted like one. This morning, her eyes sparkled to a shade near silver because of it.

When Trevor first arrived, he gave her a shoulder to lean on with no strings attached. He simply and quietly provided succor when she needed it most. No one had ever done that for her. Not her parents and certainly not Frank. After the first kiss, however, the need to be held, the need to be loved washed through her blood, refusing to be ignored. She had craved his strength. Feminine emotions suppressed for so many years had surfaced from somewhere deep inside. Even now, she remembered the textured wave of his hair as she ran her fingers through the dark thickness. The scent of his clean male body surrounded her, providing comfort when she needed it most.

Her lids fluttered shut as she relived the tempest in the barn. Claire was the one who desired that the kiss last forever. Even now, she knew with certainty that, if she had not urged him on, Trevor would never have made love to her—she would never have known what it felt like to be held by a real and honest man. He could have left the farm the night before with a final goodbye. Instead, he rode away with a gentle promise to return and discover a way for her to keep her home.

She hurried back to the bed and perched on the edge, cupping her flushed cheeks with shaking hands, and actually let her heart warm to the fact that it might be possible. Her last thought before falling asleep the night before was the dim glimmer of hope he gave her—the hope that she might be able to stay near St. Paul. But how could she accept Trevor's help? For all intents and purposes, he was a stranger.

She awakened in the middle night though, and ran his offer over and over in her mind. Finally, a small beacon of promising light shined in the distance. Trevor did not intend just to help her stay near St. Paul—he intended to help her find a way to keep her home.

And what about the lovemaking they shared? Her heart thudded in a new rhythm. *Does it mean anything?* The last time she saw him, Trevor promised he would be back. Surely his return would not be for the simple purpose of helping her out. He had spoken of a connection between the two of them...

Did she dare risk being hurt again? He was unlike any other man she had ever known in her life. They were from two different worlds, but he insisted he would be there for her and the children.

Her spirit renewed and, with hope in her heart, she dressed quickly, ready to face the world again. Claire had come to a decision—one that surprised even her. Jonah would stay with the girls while she walked to town. She planned to find Trevor, thrash out any options he might have come up with, and discuss the incident in the barn. She was not a young girl anymore, one who giggled childishly because a boy paid attention to her and tried to steal a kiss. She was a mature woman long past playing the flirting game. Claire needed to know exactly what Trevor wanted—and if what he wanted was her.

* * *

Trevor rested his forearms across the stall gate and observed the track's veterinarian inspect The Ghost. The racehorse was down in the straw and had been since early morning. Labored breaths sounded in the small paddock area as the animal struggled for air.

"What do you think, Doc?"

The graying vet gently patted the horse's neck, picked up his black medical bag, and straightened with a shake of his head. "I don't think he's going to be doing any training for awhile. My guess is some kind of lung infection. I hate to tell you this, but if you don't put him down, he'll have to go into quarantine. We need to get this animal out of here before he has any more contact with the others."

Trevor's shoulders fell with a troubled sigh. "I can't believe he's in the shape he is. He had some great runs yesterday morning. I won't put him down—not yet. I want the best care possible for him, but I can't bring him north to the ranch. If whatever he's got is contagious, I don't dare run the risk of infecting any of the livestock up there."

The veterinarian nodded in agreement. "Taking a long trip would probably do him in anyway. I've got a quarantine area behind my house, but you'll have to figure out a way to get him there. It's going to take you a couple of hours to settle all the details if that's what you want to do. In the meantime, I'll head out and get things ready at my place."

"I guess I have no other choice."

The older man stepped from the enclosure and Trevor clasped his offered hand. "Thanks, Doc. Leave your address when you file your report at the office. Hopefully, I'll have him at your place by noon."

"Sorry about this, Trevor."

"So am I. He was slated to run his first big race in four weeks."

The vet shuffled down the aisle to file his report.

Trevor stood alone by the stall. He rested his arms on the gate again and stared at the horse. Checking his frustration at the turn of events, he mentally listed the things that would need to be done over the next few hours.

He had spent a restless night, tossing and turning until finally he threw the covers aside and rose to pace his bedroom suite until early that morning. Not once did the picture of Claire's tear-stained cheeks leave his mind. The woman had let her guard down for a short time, giving him a glimpse of the real person beneath the hostile exterior. During the long night, he also relived them making love inside the shattered barn; he remembered her smile and the soft feel of her skin beneath his fingers. Those images faded though, and were replaced by a picture of Claire cradling the dead cat and sobbing like a lost child. The visions piled one on top of the other until, finally, he had to escape the room.

He had planned to be at Claire's by this time. Before he could leave, however, he had to tend to the necessary details regarding The Ghost. A visit to the market, where he would buy food and supplies for the Holcomb's, would have to be put on hold until later in the day.

Pushing himself away from the gate with a frustrated sigh, Trevor turned and stopped short. *Just what I need...* He forced a pained smile to his lips.

"Well, hello, Trevor." Regina Simpson, lately a widow, posed with the sunlight at her back, knowing full well the effect it created when the sun glinted off her perfectly coiffed brunette curls. She twirled the dainty sun umbrella in her hands one last time for effect, then snapped it closed before looping it over her wrist. Regina strolled toward the handsome Minnesotan, her heart pounding wildly at the mere sight of him. Her rouged smile widened when she came to a halt beside the stall gate. "Aren't you going to say hello?"

"Good morning, Regina. What brings you down here?"

Her arched brows lifted slightly at his curt response, but she let it go. She had come to the stable for one reason and was not about to let his attitude deter her. "I haven't seen you at any of the clubs or private parties for a while. Knowing how precious your horses are, I decided that if Mohammed wouldn't come to the mountain..." She left the rest unsaid as her lower lip drooped in a pout.

"It's been a busy time for me."

"Too busy to contact a good friend and see how she's doing?" Regina stepped forward and ran a perfectly manicured fingernail over the expensive material of his shirt, batted her long dark lashes, and nibbled on her bottom lip. "I've really missed you. A widow gets lonely at night. I've waited every day for the last two weeks for St. Paul's most eligible bachelor to come calling."

Trevor stared at her with disbelief evident in his green eyes. *Why in hell did I ever think this woman was worth spending time with?* For some reason, her flirting advances, lush body, and full lips served only to agitate his frazzled mind further. The last thing he wanted to do was stand and exchange veiled innuendos, but he had nobody to blame but himself; he was the one stupid enough to dabble with her when she offered herself to him in the past. His eyes followed the taut skin that stretched over her cheekbones, pausing on the fake mole pressed beside her smiling red lips. He could not help but wonder if she had ever worked a day in her life.

Regina swayed toward him, stopping just short of brushing her breasts against his chest. Her perfume wafted up to assault his nostrils, the strong cloying odor nearly making Trevor gag. Strangely, the fresh, clean scent of Claire's hair wavered through his mind.

"I thought that, since I came all the way down here, you could buy a hungry girl lunch, and then maybe we could go back to my house for some...let's say...dessert." She laid both hands flat against his chest, needing to feel the physical strength of the handsome man before her.

Trevor forced the smile back into place, then grasped her elbows with both hands to keep her fingers from wandering inside his jacket. "I'm sorry that you took time from your busy day, Regina, but I'll have to pass."

"Why?" she pouted. "I've really missed you."

"I have to make arrangements for a sick animal. Really, Regina, I need to get going." Somewhere in the back of his mind, Trevor wondered if her heavy perfume would make him physically sick. Why had he never noticed it before?

Regina peeked up from beneath fluttering, heavy lashes. "Will you promise to come calling soon?"

"I'll see how the week goes." It was not an outright lie, but the response kept him from spouting what he really wanted to say.

"Well, I guess I'll have to be happy with that," she pouted again. "I absolutely refuse to leave, however, until you seal your promise with a kiss."

"Regina..."

"I won't take no for an answer. Please, Trevor, I've been so lonely." She lifted her mouth and waited.

Trevor stifled the exasperated sigh that threatened to escape his lips and lowered his mouth—anything to rid the barn of her presence.

Regina's hands instantly slithered up his chest and circled his neck. Her mouth opened, and she forced her tongue past his lips as she molded herself tightly against the long firm line of his body.

It took a second for Trevor's surprised brain to register what was happening. Stifling a curse, he reached up to grasp her clinging arms and force them to her sides.

Regina would have none of it. "Kiss me again," she breathed against his lips as she locked her arms tighter around his neck.

Trevor rolled his eyes as he reached up to pry her fingers free without making too much of a scene. "Hey, this isn't the time or place, Regina. I've really got to get some arrangements made for this horse. I'll see you to your carriage and call on you next week." His bluff finally worked. She stepped out of his arms.

* * *

Claire raced down the busy sidewalk, clutching at her faded bonnet. Thinking back on the long walk, she realized that the closer she got to town, the more excited she became. She had paid her dues over the last ten years. So much time had passed since she felt any kind of hope for the future, and now enthusiasm glowed in her bright eyes and produced a flush across her sun-kissed cheeks. Maybe by accepting Trevor's offer of help, she would be able to care for her children the way they deserved.

And what about Trevor Wilkins? The evening before might have been both horrible and heart wrenching, but he did offer his support. It was almost unbelievable. A fairytale. A rich, handsome man who was kind by nature had, because of his friendship with Jonah, offered to help. And, maybe, just maybe, he also felt a growing attraction to the boy's mother.

As fate would have it, something had changed between herself and Trevor. Yes, something had definitely changed. Claire's smile widened. Something happened to her in that barn. For the first time in years, she had opened her heart and let someone peek in—and discovered that the effort had not left her heartbroken as in the past.

She reached the open door of the training center and stopped on the wooden sidewalk to catch her breath. With any luck, Jonah was right when he said Trevor would be with his horse at this time of the morning. Smoothing her worn skirt around her thighs, Claire adjusted her bonnet, swallowed to gain courage, and took a step through the doorway.

The bright, hopeful smile of anticipation flattened.

Trevor was locked in a sensual embrace with a beautiful woman who had just curled her arms around his broad shoulders in order to pull his lips closer to hers.

Claire was so stunned that she could not move. Her stomach heaved when he gently took hold of the woman's arms, apparently to draw her nearer. Whoever the woman was, she shamelessly rubbed her body against the front of his long torso, and Trevor did not seem to mind in the least.

Claire stumbled backward into the bright sunlight before her presence was noticed and collapsed against the side of the building. Several onlookers paused to stare at her as they walked by. Her knees shook, but not as violently as the hands that swept tears from her cheeks and held back the despondent sob that threatened to escape. She spun to face the wall before calling any more attention to herself. Claire gasped for air to clear her head and pressed her palm against the physical ache in her chest.

Never...never again...

Her hopes shriveled to nothing and suddenly she was old, frumpy, and alone in the world once again. She had unwisely believed every word that came out of his mouth the evening before...

He's like every other man in my life...you are such a fool, such an idiotic woman who will never have anything...

Claire held her forehead with a trembling hand, fearing she would faint, and waited for the waves of nausea to subside. Not until she heard Trevor's voice, as he calmly stated that he would call on the woman the following week, was she startled out of her crushing pain.

Run! her mind screamed. The gentle swishing of straw beneath boots as the couple approached the open doorway whipped her into motion. Claire raced to the end of the building and ducked into a small ally. She flattened her back against the cool brick wall and gulped for air until her head quit spinning. Still she could not stop herself from poking her head around the corner.

Claire froze in the middle of a horrible nightmare. Her aching heart sank further as she studied the woman who posed for the man before her. The bright sunshine rippled through her dark, luxurious hair. Try as she might, Claire could not tear her eyes from the obviously expensive attire, the porcelain skin of her high cheekbones, and the ruby red lips spread wide with a seductive smile meant only for Trevor.

Claire's callused hand clapped over her mouth. Why did she think Trevor would ever be interested in a farm wife when he could easily have a beauty like the woman who stood before him? She ducked closer to the wall when the socialite stepped carefully into the empty carriage and Trevor returned to the stable.

Claire waited for him to disappear into the building before racing back the way she had come.

* * *

The bells of the St. Paul's Cathedral clanged six times as Trevor left the city with a wagonload of supplies for Claire and her family. His patience was ready to snap after the constant delays. The day had quickly been eaten up with details regarding the sick horse, as well as buying goods for the Holcomb's.

Trevor kept a watchful eye for Jonah the entire day; he was surprised that, at some point, the boy did not show up with his eager smile. *Maybe Claire kept him busy cleaning up after the storm.*

It was not too much longer before the farm came into view. Trevor pulled on the reins and turned the wagon onto the Holcomb's drive. It took some maneuvering to skirt the fallen trees and finally reach the front of the house, but eventually, he engaged the break, jumped down from the high seat, and glanced around the silent yard.

"Claire?" he hollered out before looking around again. "Jonah! Are you here?"

Nothing. He crossed to the rickety porch and knocked on the door. It swung open against his light touch.

"What the hell..." He stepped through the doorway. "Claire? Are you in here?" Trevor took another hesitant step and knew immediately that she was gone. Not just gone for an hour or two, but gone permanently. The cabinets were bare, and the mattresses on the shabby beds void of blankets. Even the small figurines he had seen placed about on tables were absent.

Finding it hard to believe that she would light out after the hope he saw in her eyes the night before, Trevor shouldered the door out of his way and headed for the barn. The wagon he saw the night before was also absent. Not so much as a chicken scurried about in the waning light of day. The only noise was a fat mouse that scampered across the straw floor in search of a hiding place.

"Son of a bitch." He nearly ripped the hanging barn door from its hinges as he stomped back to the buckboard. *Where in hell did she go? Why did she go?* The questions bounced around in his brain as he climbed back onto the wagon seat, grabbed the reins, and slapped them across the backside of the horse.

The return ride to St. Paul was a frustrating one. Every question Trevor asked himself went unanswered. He could not imagine what would have sent Claire and her children fleeing from the farm—no reason other than Judd Stone.

He might not have the mother quite figured out, but Jonah? Yes. The boy would have moved heaven and earth to say goodbye to his friend—unless Claire was gripped by such urgency that she would not allow it. Trevor chewed on his lower lip as he worked out a plan. After the events of the night before, there was no way he could callously allow the Holcombs to face their fate alone—nor could he ignore the beginnings of something felt deep in his heart. Claire was running, and he was damned well going to find out why.

After returning the goods he purchased to the grocer and the wagon to the livery, Trevor hurried to the hotel to pack. Claire never said anything, but Jonah talked constantly about the family going north so Claire could work at some other job.

Well, dammit, I've got a family who lives north of here, too. I know that area like the back of my hand. I'll find her no matter where she goes.

He dropped another pressed and folded shirt into his valise and clenched his jaw when a knock sounded on the door. He wanted to leave for home that night and did not have time to be bothered with whoever stood on the other side of the entry. The thought stopped him in his tracks. Home? He had not thought of the ranch as home for a long time. Before he could ponder the revelation any further, someone rapped their knuckles against the door once more.

Trevor quickly crossed the room and yanked it open. "Yes?"

The same concierge from the day before handed him an envelope. "A telegram arrived for you this afternoon."

Trevor fished a coin out of his breast pocket, dropped it into the man's outstretched hand, and slammed the door. Crossing back to the bed, he sat on the edge of the mattress and ripped open the missive, wondering if it was a message from Claire. His eyes quickly scanned the words. A moment later, he ran a hand through the thick dark waves at his temple. Mamie had taken ill. Emma wanted him to come home immediately. A sliver of dread settled in his stomach before he bounded up and continued packing.

Chapter Nine

Trevor reined his mount to a halt, sat quietly atop the animal on a grassy hilltop, and let his gaze follow the dusty road that led to the ranch. A wistful smile appeared on his whiskered face. The comforting site of the homestead welcomed him as it had when he was a young boy.

The same towering pine trees still surrounded the sprawling log home of his youth. The only changes to the panoramic landscape were two large barn structures and a handful of gated back pastures that were added a few years earlier. The new buildings housed the many horses that were now a portion of the ranch's income, a portion of Trevor's income, and the inheritance for the children he could see playing in the front yard. Ignoring the twinge of guilt at being absent for so long, he kneed the horse down the path. By the time he guided his mount through the immense log gate, his sisters-in-law raced down the porch staircase to greet him.

"Trevor! We never heard back from you that you were coming! It's so good to have you home," Emma exclaimed as she threw herself into his waiting arms once he dismounted.

He hugged her tightly with a laugh. "Hell, I figured it would only take a couple of days to get here if I pushed it hard, so I just packed and headed north."

Emma stepped back to allow August a welcoming hug from her brother-in-law. The petite Indian woman was swept into Trevor's arms before she could say a word and squealed with delight when he spun her in the air.

As quickly as he picked her up, Trevor set her back down; instant concern darkened his eyes. "Sorry, August. I didn't mean to spin you like that. I hear you and Cole are going to have another baby. You're okay, aren't you?"

She reached up and squeezed his arm. "I am fine. It is good to see you, Trevor. Cole will be so happy when he discovers you are home. Too much time has passed."

He gave her another quick hug while eyeing the small faces of his niece and nephews. Another twinge of guilt pierced his stomach when he smiled down at them. Giving August's hand a quick squeeze, he rounded her and stretched out his palm to the lanky boy who was the mirror image of Emma, but possessed the same dark features as his brother, Tyler.

"Thomas. I hardly recognize you. You must have grown a foot since the last time I was home."

The boy shook his hand, and then was pulled into his uncle's embrace. "Hi, Uncle Trevor. Are you going to stay awhile? We can get some fishing and hunting in before school starts again."

"If I have something to say about it, yes he will," Emma replied before the boy's uncle had a chance to do the same.

Trevor laughed out loud when he moved to hug a petite auburn-haired girl. "Sara. You are the mirror image of your mother."

The young girl wrapped her arms around Trevor's neck and pressed a kiss against his cheek. "Daddy says I'm also just as sassy."

He chuckled and his head shook at her sweet impudence. "Well, you just tell him that we wouldn't have it any other way. Are you getting too big for me to tell you a bedtime story?"

Her round green eyes twinkled with happiness to think he remembered the special bond the two of them had always shared. She leaned forward and whispered into his ear so no one else would hear. "I get to stay up later now. Come to my room at nine o'clock."

Trevor winked in response and hunkered down before a dark-haired toddler that clung to August's skirt. Cole's firstborn son, Daniel Hawk Wilkins, wanted nothing to do with the strange man and hid his face in the folds of material. Trevor glanced up at his mother. "I guess he's too little to remember me. He's a fine boy, August. You must be very proud of him."

"I am. He is the light of my life, and his father's. His sister is napping right now. Cole and I will be pleased that you will finally meet her."

Trevor straightened and handed the reins of his horse to Thomas. "Would you take Buck down to the paddock? I'm going to run in and see Mamie."

Thomas hustled to do his bidding as the adults headed for the house.

Stepping inside the foyer, a wave of pleasure warmed Trevor's blood. He paused for a moment to look around and take in the welcoming coziness of familiar furniture and expansive log walls. A good year had passed since he last visited, but the months melted away as he breathed in the scent of beeswax and fresh flowers. It hit him that he had missed this place more than he was ever willing to admit. It felt good to be home.

"Where's Tyler and Cole?" he asked as he set his bags down on a bench.

"They took some supplies to Carrie and Steve's. I expect them back before supper." Emma sighed with pleasure. "They'll be so surprised you're here already. Why don't you visit with Mamie? She's in her room. August and I were just going to help Katy get supper ready."

"How is Mamie doing?"

August nestled her hand in Trevor's bent elbow as they walked across the shiny planks of the living room floor. "She is very old, Trevor. Her legs will not do what she asks of them any longer. It is rare that she can get around the house anymore without the chair that Steve brought her. But she always smiles and her mind is sharp, even though her body fails. Seeing you will brighten her day."

He left the women and strolled down the hallway, his eyes scanning the many family photographs that adorned the walls. Three generations posed atop gigantic felled pines, stood beside beautiful horses, or smiled at the camera with newborn babies in their arms. Yes, it was good to be home to cherish the instant memories the pictures evoked.

He hesitated in the open doorway of Mamie's room and silently studied the woman who was more a mother to him than a housekeeper. Her black cheeks, lined by the many years of smiles, shined in the afternoon light. Mamie's hair was the color of snow and still cropped closely to her head to manage the tight curls of her race. Always having been a sturdy, round woman, Trevor could easily tell that her eighty-three years had taken their toll. Now, she was a smaller version of her robust self as she lay beneath the light blankets and stared longingly out the window.

"Mamie?"

Her curly head turned weakly on the pillow and a smile widened her thick dark lips when she recognized him. "My Trevah!" Her arms stretched out to him. "Come to this ol' woman and gives me a hug."

He hastened across the room, sat on the edge of the bed, and tenderly enveloped her in his embrace. "Ah, it's so good to see you."

"Mah boy, mah boy," she crooned as they rocked. "Where you bin? If I had the strength, I'd take a strap to yer backside for leavin' us here to reside without yer stories. Yessiree, you'd be offn' your horse for a week with the ache."

A chuckle rumbled in his throat as he sat back, took her wrinkled hand in his, and ignored the quiet pain in his heart. At one time, Mamie used to boom out her questions and orders. Now, her voice possessed a weak, fragile quality to it as it floated across the surface of the bed. "I see some things haven't changed around here. Still making threats and running the show, aren't you?"

"Somebody got ta do it. Emma and August got them kids and this big house to tend to. The boys, well, they's busy doin' what boys do."

He laughed again, knowing how much the old woman loved a response to her humor. "You mean Tyler and Cole?"

"Yessiree, my other boys. Now—" she smiled as she leaned into her pillow "—you bring a wife back with you?"

Claire's face popped into his brain. He did not dare to stop and consider why. "I just got here. Are you going to start on me right away?"

"Never know how much time I got left to be conjolin' you." Mamie's sudden grin disappeared. She reached up a trembling hand and touched his cheek. "Can I talk to you, boy?" She continued when Trevor nodded. "I allus could talk to you. I'm honest when I say I don't know how long this poor ol' lady has. Ma body hurts fierce all da time. I tries to hide it, but sometimes it be a horrendous task. I'll be meetin' mah Lord soon."

Trevor patted her hand. "Is there anything I can do for you?"

"Only one thing I gots left to see. I bin thinkin' about you all these hours in this bed. It ain't right for a man to be alone. Mah heart would love to see you hitched to a woman like belong to yur brothers before I go. Emma and August. They's two fine women, yessiree."

Trevor squeezed her hand. "Don't you be worrying about me, Mamie. I'll be fine. You just need to concentrate on getting yourself better, so you can continue to abuse us."

Her head rolled on the pillow. "Don't you be changin' no subjects, you hear? You gots to promise me. Iffn there's someone out there, you grab her and never let go. Just make sure she ain't no piece of fluff from that big city. This country's hard. She gotta be strong. You know someone like that?"

Trevor's chin lowered for a moment. Of course he did. *If I didn't know better, I'd swear Mamie knows her, too. Claire...* His head shook slightly. The notion was totally ridiculous.

"Trevah...I's waitin' for an answer."

He glanced up with a wry grin. "St. Paul isn't noted for their strong women, Mamie. Most are what you call 'fluff'."

"Then you get your arse outta here and go lookin' around the countryside. She's out there waitin'."

A huge sigh of relief left Trevor's mouth when August came through the door carrying Mamie's supper on a tray. His sister-in-law's sudden appearance presented him with the perfect opportunity to escape the old woman's loving harassment.

* * *

Trevor was back in his old room. He had just finished unpacking his belongings when a tap on the door brought his head around. The sight of his younger brother leaning against the doorjamb flooded his face with a huge grin. "Cole!"

They met halfway across the room. The welcoming handshake quickly turned into an embrace of brotherly love.

"It's about damned time you come back. Christ, Trevor, it's been almost a year since I've seen you."

Trevor stood back and studied his brother's face. Gone were the lines of weariness and distrust that were permanent features a few years earlier. After what he and August had been through, it took months before Cole quit watching over his shoulder every time he moved about the ranch. Cole's biggest fear was the dreaded idea that someone from the horrible days of Wounded Knee would recognize him or August, and the woman he loved so passionately would be torn from his life again. Somewhere over the last year and the birth of their second child, Cole must have finally found peace and true happiness. The two emotions rested easily in his eyes now as he grinned at Trevor.

"You're looking good, Cole. Life must be agreeing with you."

Cole nodded as he took a seat, stretched out his long legs, and crossed one ankle over the other. "Things couldn't be better. I've got August and the kids. What else could a man like me want? She loves the ranch and everyone on it. We've decided not to mourn the past, but rather make a new future for our kids."

Trevor closed his valise as he thought about everything Cole and August suffered, yet they always looked hopefully to the future. "When Tyler was in St. Paul, he told me Beau has moved to Washington on a permanent basis. I didn't think he'd ever leave Minnesota again."

"I miss Beau, but he felt he could do more for August and her people in the Capital. He still has the ability to rile up those damned politicians, because he's such a free spirit. Say, I don't know if you heard, but Michael and Anna visited last fall. It was wonderful to see them."

Trevor heaved the case to the floor and shoved it beneath the bed. "Emma told me about them in one of her letters. I'm happy for Anna. Are the two of them still at Pine Ridge?"

"Yeah, I don't think they'll ever leave for good. Michael's made great progress on the reservation. Not only is he the head physician, but he's accepted the position as Indian Agent. He's a good and fair man and will always step forward to do what's best for the Sioux."

Trevor sank into a seat opposite his brother. He leaned forward, rested his elbows on the arms of the chair, and clasped his fingers together, thinking about the many twists and turns in Cole's life. "Do you ever miss the freedom of leaving this place? I know you were one to always feel comfortable here when you were younger, but now you have no choice in the matter. You can't leave."

Cole's response was immediate. "And where would I go?

Everything I love is here. Well, it is now that you're here," he teased to lighten the moment.

"Ha! Trying to make me feel guilty will get you nowhere."

Cole raised his hands in mock defense. "All right, point taken." The glimmer of humor in his hazel eyes disappeared as he thought about the past. "You know the hell August and I went through to be together. If the price of loving her is to remain dead in the eyes of the government, then it's worth every damn minute. I've got two kids who turn me inside out every time I look at them, and another on the way. I'm happy, Trevor. I never knew what that truly was until I found August." A wry smile appeared on his face. "It just hit me that I must resemble our older brother."

Trevor raised an eyebrow in question.

Cole continued with a chuckle. "You know, we both walk around like young boys in the first throes of love and lust."

"Who's in the first throes of love and lust? Christ...don't tell me someone has finally snagged Trevor?"

Trevor glanced over his shoulder when he heard his older brother's voice. "Kiss my ass, Tyler. We were just laughing about how whipped you are when it comes to Emma."

"And aren't you jealous?" Tyler crossed the room and shook hands with Trevor as the other man stood. "Glad you came so quickly. Have you had a chance to visit with Mamie?"

"She was my first stop. She's not doing too well, is she? She mentioned a lot of pain."

Tyler's broad shoulders fell with a sigh. "Steve and Carrie are doing everything possible to make her comfortable, but I don't think she'll be around too much longer. Steve thinks she's full of the cancer." Tyler perched on the bed.

Trevor settled back in the chair. "I couldn't believe how frail she is. I was warned, but it was still hard to see. As weak as she is though, she jumped on me right away because I didn't bring a wife with me."

Tyler rolled his eyes. "Plan to hear more of it. She's got lots of time now to think when she's lying in that bed. You and a future marriage is all she talks about."

Trevor leaned his head against the backrest and closed his eyes. "Christ, I'm a goner. Between her and Emma, I won't hear the end of it."

He opened his eyes again and glanced from one brother to the other, trying to decide if he should say something about Claire. The three had always shared everything. *But what if I can't find her? Then what? Better to wait...*

Cole's chuckle broke Trevor's train of thought. "I had to put up with it and look what I got in return. I wouldn't change a day with August. You're not going to let their nagging scare you away, are you? I'd love to have you around so we can catch up."

"Yup, I need to take care of some things. I'm going to take a little trip up north and check—" he paused, surprised that once again he almost blurted out Claire's story when he was not sure if he should "—check on my house and visit a few friends. I also wanted to get updated on what's going on with the property. Have you heard anymore from the Merritt brothers?"

"Not from them personally," Tyler replied, "but they've sent a representative in their stead a couple of times. Now I hear they're selling off shares and liquidating some real estate to stay afloat. John Rockefeller is sweeping them into a corner. You watch; that man's going to end up buying them out for little or nothing. He's a pretty shrewd character with millions of dollars to help him get what he wants."

Trevor shook his head. "Well, he can buy all the mines he wants, but I know a piece of property that he'll never get his hands on. Speaking of that, has anyone had a chance to check on my house?"

"August and I took a ride up there a few weeks back. You should really finish the place. It's a great location. Pretty expansive though, for a single man..." Cole left the words hanging.

Trevor pierced him with a humorous glare and rose from the chair. "All right, let's change the subject. How about the two of you show me the new foals." As he stood to follow the other two men from the room, he mused over the fact that, for now, it would be best not to discuss Claire and her family until he could discover what the future would bring.

Chapter Ten

The door slammed behind Claire as she exited the Rainy Lake lumber office. She stood a moment on the raised entryway to gather her wits before joining her children and seeing the disappointment in their eyes.

Her rushed departure from St. Paul had brought her to the city of Virginia, a booming town in northern Minnesota that was said to have employment opportunities, and to the mining office that had offered her a job by telegram. A lump in her throat grew as she returned to the rickety wagon where her children sat waiting.

"Did you get the job?" Jonah looked hopeful as he waited for her to climb up beside him.

Claire grabbed the reins from his hand and chucked them across the mule's back without looking at his expectant eyes. "They gave it to someone else," she returned in a flat tone.

Her son flopped against the backrest. A moment later, he studied the tight-lipped Claire. "What are we gonna do, Ma? Let's go back home. Trevor said he would help us."

Claire's lips thinned into an even straighter line. "I don't want to hear that man's name come out of your mouth again."

"But, he—"

"But, nothing." She struggled against the pain that welled in her chest. Trevor had given her a glimmer of hope that night in the barn when he made love to her, and then he dashed her trust to the wind by running to another woman's arms the very next day. He was a hurtful liar just like any other man.

So, why does just hearing his name weaken my knees and make my hands shake? She tried hard over the last week not to dwell on the heated tryst they shared, but to no avail. The tender moments and the gentle man left a huge void in her life. *I was so stupid to think someone like him would ever want a woman like me...* She forced his image away. It was over and there was absolutely nothing she could do about it. Her children did not need to see her mooning over a man for the first time in her life. The continuation of that sort of fantasy would not keep them warm in the winter or put food in their bellies. She finally glanced down to find Jonah staring at her. "Don't worry. I talked to the man in the office. He gave me directions to a town called Merritt somewhere east of here."

Jonah slouched against the backrest again. "I can find a job here. I don't want to keep moving."

"We don't have any choice. We're running out of the little bit of money we have. I can't even afford to rent another room for tonight. Pray that it doesn't rain again." Her back straightened with a determination she did not feel. "No, Jonah, I've made up my mind. We'll try Merritt and see what happens."

Once more, they were on the road as she headed the old wagon eastward for the town of Merritt, a supposed prospering town bulging at the seams with miners and lumberjacks. If she could not find a position with one of the logging companies, maybe one of the many small ore mines springing up one after another on what was called the Iron Range would produce some sort of living.

* * *

The town of Merritt proved fruitless. Claire pounded the dusty streets from one place of employment to another, but was turned away time and time again. She took her tired children and wearily backtracked to the expanding village of Biwabik, thankful that the weather had held out; otherwise, they all would have been in a horrible fix. All of them were weary of sleeping in the wooden bed of the wagon over the last half week, but she simply did not have any money to waste. Had Jonah not shot a passel of rabbits, they would be starving, too.

She stopped the wagon before a well-maintained building with a sign hanging over the front porch. "Biwabik Boarding House. This is it, children. This is the place I was told about. Maybe they need another cook." She maneuvered the buckboard to rest beneath a towering pine to take advantage of the shade, secured the break, and climbed down to the dirt road. "You all stay here. Do not get out of this wagon. If you're thirsty, there's water in the barrel."

The children's round eyes stared quietly at her. She pasted a smile on her lips for their benefit as her gaze moved from one to the other. Claire's fingers fluttered over the tight blonde bun at the crown of her head. "Do I look alright?"

Sofie leaned over the buckboard's side and reached out her hand. Claire took it and received a loving squeeze from her daughter. "You look pretty Ma. Don't worry. Jonah and I will watch the little ones."

Claire batted the welling tears behind her eyelids. She wished she had as much faith in herself as her children did at the moment. "Okay then. This is it. Keep your fingers crossed."

She followed the walk that led around the back of the Inn, noting the masculine clothes hanging from ropes stretched across the back yard and came to the conclusion that she would do anything; cook, clean, scrub clothes; it did not matter. She needed to find a paying job. If she did not, there was a good chance she would have to resort to doing what other widows were forced to. More than once, she had heard that, when all options were exhausted, other women gave up their children in order to survive.

Well, I won't! I refuse to let that happen. Mentally, she pulled herself up by the bootstraps, stiffened her back and, with as much gumption as she could muster, headed up steps to a screen door. Peering in, she spied an older woman who rushed about the kitchen. The smell of cabbage from the many bubbling pots wafted out past her nose. Claire ignored her growling stomach, realized in a tired part of her mind that she needed to feed the kids, and then rapped her knuckles on the wooden frame of the door.

"Well, just don't stand there," came a querulous voice. "Come in. I don't have time to be answering any calls."

Claire yanked on the door. She entered the kitchen, quelled the shaking of her hands by clutching the brim of the hat she held against her stomach, and took a hesitant step forward. "Hello. My name's Claire Holcomb. I was told that the boarding house was looking for kitchen

Keeper of the Heart

help."

The woman who busily chopped carrots on a cutting board eyed the stranger over the rim of her bent glasses. "And where did you hear that? It's news to me."

Claire stepped closer to respond, but the hissing sound of a kettle boiling over onto the stove caught her attention. Instead, she raced across the room, used the hem of her dress as a hot pad, and moved the kettle away from the heat. "I've been searching for a job," she said glancing over her shoulder. "I'll do anything. I see this place must also take in washing. I can sew, cook, scrub floors—you just tell me what you want done and I guarantee you won't be asking a second time." She turned and wiped her palms against the faded material at her hips. "I really need the work, Mrs.—" Hope rested in her blue gaze.

The solidly-built older woman laid her knife on the counter and adjusted her glasses. "My name's Norma Henderson. I run this place for the owner. You didn't hear about any offered jobs, did you? Because if you did, I'd know about it."

Claire's chin lowered for a moment, wondering if the little lie was going to cost her another employment offer. She had never wanted or needed anything so badly in her life. Rushing to the counter, she clutched the edge and met Norma's eyes. "I'm sorry. You're right. I didn't hear about anything. It's just...it's just that I'm a widow with five mouths to feed, and I've been on the road checking every place that I could, trying to find something. Please, I'm a hard worker. You won't be sorry. My children can even help out and you won't even have to pay them."

Norma's gaze scanned Claire's thin body. "You don't look very hearty. It takes a lot of strength to be lifting heavy pots and baskets of clothes."

"You saw me move that pot. I've chopped my own wood and taken care of a farm for the past two years—all on my own. I can do this. I don't care what you pay me, but I have to work."

Norma shuffled her way to one of the large stoves, picked up a wooden ladle, and stirred the bubbling contents. "So why aren't you at your farm now?"

Claire moved to the older woman's side. She would have to be honest. "Because I couldn't make my bank payment. My drunkard husband left me in debt. I couldn't make enough money to even pay the taxes after he died a few years back. I want to start a new life for my children and me. Please, give me a chance. Let me prove to you that I'm the best helper you'll ever hire. I...I just don't know what I'll do if I can't make some money to at least feed my family."

Norma warmed to the idea as she listened to Claire babble on. The older woman worked from sunup to sundown. As she watched the blonde woman wring her hands in anticipation, her thoughts moved back to a time when she was nearly in the same position—and that was with only one young son. Claire had five children. *And didn't I just complain to the boss only three days ago that I needed help? More and more mines are springing up around here...* Norma was getting too old to do it all by herself. Every room in the boarding house was rented out.

She set the ladle down and crossed back to her pile of carrots. "Where are your youngins now?"

"They're outside waiting for me in the wagon."

"Well...how about you fetch them in here for a bowl of cabbage stew and we'll talk more."

Claire rushed forward and hugged Norma. "Oh, thank you! You don't know what this means!"

"Yes, well," she said as she straightened her skewed glasses, "you most likely won't be thanking me a week from now when you're bone tired and your back is aching—that is if I give you a chance."

Claire hurried to the back door with the first light of happiness shining in her eyes in more than two weeks. "You won't be sorry." The door slammed behind her and she disappeared off the porch.

Norma shook her head, suddenly feeling good about the day. The boarding house's new owner, Mr. Stone, would just have to put out the money if he wanted to keep his rooms filled.

* * *

Claire stood on the back porch and wiped her perspiring brow with her forearm, grabbed the last bucket of tepid dishwater, and tossed it onto the ground. She trudged to a wooden bench set up beneath a tall Norway pine and sank wearily onto the half-rotted surface. The hot breeze that rustled her damp blonde tendrils did nothing to relieve the

Keeper of the Heart

horrible choking heat of late July. Jonah and the girls were inside the wooden building she had just exited, peeling potatoes for the next shift of foreign speaking ore miners. In another hour, the Biwabik Mine's whistle would blow to signal a shift change. Dirty, tired, and hungry miners would appear soon after and the rest of the afternoon would be one dirty dish after another.

Claire had yet to meet the owner who crammed as many of the workers as he could into the upper rooms. Originally, Norma informed her, the boarding house was built by a family named Merritt to provide sleeping quarters for the many miners who worked around the Biwabik Location. Running into a financial panic, however, the family was forced to sell the enterprise to concentrate more on finding the money to keep their mining interests afloat. Claire remembered selfishly thinking at the time that misery loved company—she was not the only person in the world with huge financial problems.

Under the new ownership, the little square spaces that were more like closets than rented rooms had someone sleeping in the beds at all times. As one man would leave for work, his bed was immediately taken by another who was ready to sleep the hours away until he, too, headed back to the mine that ran twenty-four hours a day. Claire and Norma worked their fingers to the bone for a mere pittance and the owner raked in double the money.

She rested her head against the rough bark of the tree and closed her eyes. Nearly a month had passed since her rushed departure from the farm and her journey to the city of Virginia in search of a new life—one where she could forget the tender touch of a dishonest man.

Don't! Don't think about him...

Claire forced herself to think about the future and how much money she could save before winter arrived. Judging by what she made, she suddenly wondered if it really was pure luck that the boarding house hired her. Thank goodness Norma Henderson quickly became a fast friend to be counted upon. If it were not for the kindly old woman, Claire would hate every moment she stood before the huge pots of boiling potatoes and the large ovens where slab after slab of meat was cooked to feed the many hungry mouths of the mineworkers. In between the kitchen work, dirty clothes needed to be scrubbed clean, bed sheets were washed, and wood needed to be hauled inside to keep the ovens going.

She forced down the growing lump of despair at her self-imposed imprisonment. Claire had no choice but to stay. A return to St. Paul would not only put her back in the possible clutches of Judd Stone, but would increase the chances of accidentally running into Trevor. She allowed one small tear to escape before she regained control of her flagging emotions, but did not have the strength any longer to force thoughts of him from her mind.

Behind closed lids, Claire allowed herself a selfish moment to relive the feel of his tender touch against her skin. Never had Frank made such beautiful love to her—not even when they were first married and he was sober.

Trevor was the one who made her heart sing with his murmured soft words of encouragement. He made her feel beautiful and loved for a short time; the middle-aged, tired mother of five with the weight of the world on her shoulders had floated away that night like a storm on the horizon. In her place came a girl ready to experience all the hopes and dreams of youth in the arms of a handsome savior.

Claire's head lolled against the tree trunk when she realized how foolish she was to think he could make a difference in her life. The final blow—seeing Trevor in another woman's arms—was what hardened her heart and gave her the courage to leave. *Never...never again will I open myself to the type of pain only a man can meet out.* She was done being a fool.

"It's about time you realize you're way past the age when any man would want you anyway," she mumbled aloud, and then, using the corner of her apron, Claire wiped the tear on her cheek, rose tiredly, and trudged back into the kitchen. Norma had left for supplies and it was up to her to assure the next meal was ready for the shift change.

* * *

Claire finished the last of the dishes after the late afternoon meal. Jonah filled the wood box and her girls stood in a row, wiping the plates and silverware dry. Norma had arrived from the store, pale and ill from the heat of the day. Claire immediately sent her home to rest. The workload was unfathomable, and she wondered how the older woman had managed to do it all herself at one time.

Keeper of the Heart

She was stacking the dishes onto the sideboard when the sound of heavy footsteps filtered into the kitchen from the hallway. A weary sigh left her throat. *Someone must be hungry...*

She turned to welcome one of the boarders, but instead her cheeks paled to a sickly ashen color as she gripped the counter behind her.

Judd Stone stood in the doorway. His mouth sagged open momentarily before he snapped it shut to replace his surprise with a slow, pleased smile that widened beneath his waxed mustache. He strode forward, pulled a chair from beneath the workbench, and settled his bulk down with his arms crossed above his bulging stomach. "Claire Holcomb. Fancy seeing you here. Norma sent me a message that she hired a widow." His head shook, and he never took his eyes from the sheen of perspiration that dampened the material down into her exposed cleavage.

Claire followed his wandering gaze and quickly buttoned the bodice closed. She struggled to keep the shock of his sudden appearance from glowing in her eyes.

"She never gave me a name. If I would've known, I'd have been here two weeks ago."

Claire's head buzzed as she gripped the counter tightly. She needed to get a hold of her emotions before Judd realized how truly upset she was. Taking a deep breath, she straightened and collected the towels from her quiet daughters, who stared at the man with fear in their eyes. "Girls? Why don't you go outside and take a break. Tell Jonah I'll be out shortly. We'll sit at the table and have some lemonade." Sofie and Sue Ellen took the hands of their younger sisters and disappeared through the door without a word. Claire finally met Judd's glowing eyes when the door teetered to a close. Chewing nervously on her bottom lip, she waited for him to say something.

"I wondered where you'd gotten yourself off to."

"I had no choice but to leave. I would have been homeless in only a matter of days."

"That's what happens when you don't honor your debts."

Anger reddened her formally pale cheeks. "I tried and you know it! Every spare penny I had was saved for the taxes." Claire did not care if he fired her on the spot. She was going to leave as soon as she could find another job anyway. Her stomach rolled at the thought. Finding other employment was going to be none too easy, but she could never stay when he was in such close proximity.

Judd heaved his bulk off the chair and strolled in her direction. Claire quickly rounded the edge of the workbench, keeping the heavy wooden surface between them. "Leave me alone, Mr. Stone. I wasn't interested before and I'm not now."

He scratched his ear and pursed his lips. "You should really rethink that decision. You know Wilkins can't protect you any longer."

Her eyes widened in surprise.

"You know, don't you, that he showed up at my office? He threatened me; warned me to keep my hands off you."

Her face turned a sickly shade of white once more.

Judd cocked his head. "No? He never told you that? You'd think he would have said something to increase the chance of getting what I tried to all along."

Claire remained silent, but her brain screamed. *It wasn't like that! Yes it was. Trevor toyed with you until he found something better...*

"I could offer you a lot, Claire."

"I have everything I need."

"Where are you living these days? In some fancy house with a nursemaid overseeing your brats? I don't think so."

Her mind darted to the rundown shack Norma had managed to help her find. For a dollar a week, it was a roof over their head and somewhere to get out of the rain. That was about it. She could find no other place to rent no matter how hard she tried. The town's buildings already bulged at the seams. "Where I live is none of your business."

"But it is. You work for me now. What if I needed to contact you?" He took a step forward. "I'm tired of playing this game. You've forced me to issue an ultimatum." His eyes narrowed.

"There isn't anything you can say that will change my mind. Just leave me alone."

Judd's hand reached up to stroke his graying goatee. His eyes pinned her to the spot where she stood just before an evil smile appeared on his face. "Those brats of yours mean quite a lot to you, don't they?"

Claire's heart banged in her chest. "You leave them out of this."

"Funny you should say that. I've got a lot of financial resources and even more connections to people at the state level. You know, I've heard that the law will come in and take children from their parents, or a widowed mother, if it's discovered she can't provide for them properly..."

Claire grabbed the edge of the table as black spots appeared before her eyes. Nothing had prepared her for the possibility that Judd Stone would do what he had just suggested simply to fulfill his baser needs. Her vision blurred with angry tears. "Why are you doing this to me? Find someone else who will give you what you want, but leave me and my children alone. Please." She was truly frightened now. If Judd managed to have her children taken away, life would not be worth living. Claire was not sure if he could really do it, but she would never give him the chance.

Judd took another step closer.

Claire took three back.

Her skirt caught on the edge of a chair. She swung her head down to yank the material free and halted the scream the crept up her throat when Judd leapt surprisingly fast across the small space that separated them. Instantly, he grabbed her arm. She tried to jerk away, but his grip tightened.

"You let me go," she ground out as she tugged against his strength.

Judd's casual demeanor of a moment earlier disappeared. "I'll let you go when I'm damn good and ready. I don't know what it is about you, Claire, but I haven't been able to get you off my mind since you disappeared." He yanked her body close. "Just remember, you work for me now. There won't be any white knight riding in to save the day. If I didn't have to get on a train and head for Duluth, you and I would be going upstairs right now. And you'd do it without a struggle. You're in my territory now, and when I decide that we're going to...spend some time together, you better agree with a smile or you'll find yourself alone. I'll make sure those brats are taken so far away that you'll never be able to find them."

"Ma? Is everything all right?" Jonah stood in the open doorway with piercing gray eyes that burned a hole in the disgusting man who clutched his mother's arm.

An angry hiss left Judd's mouth. He let go of Claire and stepped away with lips drawn into a tight line.

Claire rubbed the sore area on her upper arm and forced a smile to her lips. "Everything is fine, son. Mr. Stone was just leaving."

Judd sent a scathing glance at the ragamuffin standing in the doorway, and then swung his hateful gaze back to where Claire stood trembling. She still rubbed her quickly bruising skin. "Just don't forget what I told you. I'll be back in two weeks. We'll discuss our little agreement then."

Chapter Eleven

Trevor did not intentionally ride north. Initially, he simply wanted to enjoy the many sights of a familiar landscape. He needed to breathe the fresh pine-scented air and reconnect with the land after being gone so long from his home. As a result, he was actually surprised when Buck cantered up the lane that led to the property where his future house sat waiting to be finished.

Before he dismounted, his quiet gaze followed the slope of the new roof, the raised covered porch, and the outline of the rock fireplace—one whose stones were taken from the very foundation of the land around it. Anyone in their right mind would agree—the house was not built for a bachelor. The six-bedroom log home, complete with a large kitchen and living room, plus the outbuildings that took partial shape in the background, was definitely a home for a large family.

"What the hell was I thinking to even build something like this..."

He swung a muscled leg over the saddle and led his horse up to the porch. Securing the animal to a post, Trevor moved a few boards propped against the steps, piled them neatly to the side, and walked up the stairs. Before he knew it, he stood in the middle of the large foyer, where a staircase curved its way to the second level. Trevor wandered through the empty unfurnished rooms on the ground level, unconsciously noting the silence that surrounded him.

Soon, he found himself back in the foyer looking up the staircase again, knowing that if the house was ever to be finished, family pictures lining the curved wooden balustrades would be beautiful against the earthy tone of the logs. Slowly, he took one step at a time until he reached the open upper hallway.

Trevor meandered his way from room to room until he reached the master suite that encompassed a quarter of the second level. Enormous windows faced eastward, drawing the eye to the rising landscape. The surface of a small blue lake twinkled in the afternoon sun, just below the line of azure sky—a peaceful scene for anyone who would awaken in the room. He moved to the window and sat on the unfinished window seat and stared out.

Where was the eagerness to have his own place and enable him to shut out the noise of his brothers' families? At the moment, the house was much too quiet for his liking. *Could I really live up here in all this solitude?* After being back at home, he thoroughly enjoyed the constant commotion and excitement of having his nieces and nephews around him.

Before he knew it, as his eyes returned to the ripples traveling across the lake's surface, a picture of Jonah's smiling face formed in his mind. Trevor's broad shoulders twitched with the small snort in his throat. *The kid would love to be out there fishing. He and his sisters would sure break the silence...*

He straightened; his brow furrowed in thought. Try as he might, he could not discard the image of Claire's laughing brood playing in the yard beside a flowerbed. The fleeting thought led him on a path to their mother.

Trevor leaned against the edge of the window. She had been on his mind constantly. *Where is she?* Why did she run? His eyes rose to the where the land met the sky. She was out there somewhere. Jonah said they were going north.

Claire had touched something inside him, an emotion that Trevor had never experienced. Being close to forty, he had run the gambit with all sorts of women. But none affected him like the slender blonde whose hard life was etched into her face. No one person had evoked the feelings that niggled at him constantly. She was tough and strong one moment, and soft and womanly the next.

Making love to her was something he was not sorry about. That night in the barn, she had silently called out to him to take away her pain, and he could do nothing but answer her entreaty. Nothing was as important that night as showing her that she was beautiful in his eyes, and that he was someone to be counted upon.

Then she left without a word.

He had to find her. Claire's soul unknowingly pulled at him as no woman's ever had before. He looked around as if seeing the house for the first time, suddenly overcome by true loneliness. He needed children to fill the walls with laughter and life. He needed a woman to welcome him home—someone he could find comfort, solace and happiness with at the end of each day.

For the first time in years, Trevor admitted he was weary of his bachelor life. Claire and her brood of impish children were the reason behind the discovery—a fatherless family who really had no idea just how poor they really were.

He rose from the bench and glanced about the empty master suite one more time, imagining the sound of young voices playing on the lower level.

"Why not?" He muttered to the bare walls. "We could make it work. Neither of us is getting any younger. She needs someone who will bear some of the weight she's carrying. And the kids..." His voice echoed loudly in the silence before he fell suddenly silent. Damn, but he missed them.

Claire was not like the overly primped women of the big city. She was not born into the lap of luxury and used to being waited on daily. She had earned every line on her face and every callus on her hands—hands that had stroked the soft fur of a dead cat as tenderly as she would an upset child. Claire was real. Claire was what was missing in his life.

Trevor gritted his teeth at his own stupidity. How could he not have pursued what was right in front of him for the last month?

He hurried across the room and was down the stairs, back out in the bright afternoon sunlight, and atop his horse in a flash. Tomorrow, the last of the finishing work on his new home would start again. He would make all the necessary arrangements, and then head out to each of the small mining towns springing up in northeastern Minnesota. Jonah said Claire had a job offer. He would start with that theory and work his way back through the logging camps. Sooner or later, someone would remember seeing a lone woman with five children. He had connections and would get the help he needed to find a widow with five kids tugging at her skirt. She was out there somewhere, not too far away, and he damn well was not going to let her get away again. Claire needed him, yes, but not as badly as he suddenly yearned for her continued presence in his life.

* * *

Three days later, Trevor rode Buck down the main street of Biwabik, amazed how the small town had grown by leaps and bounds. It was said that nearly three thousand people now lived in or near the location. Dry good stores, saloons, barbershops, and a livery stable were lined up one beside the other. Townsfolk rushed to and fro from mercantile shops to lumber yards to parked wagons and back again. Dogs yapped at the constant traffic and mothers clutched the hands of their children as they went about their many errands. He remembered a time when most of the area residents thought the town of Merritt, only a mile away, would be the heart of the Iron Range. After the months went by, however, and the Biwabik Mine flourished, there was an exodus down the hill, and it looked as if the city bearing the same name was there to stay.

Trevor made his way to the city jail, excited to visit with a childhood friend who recently accepted the position of town sheriff. Dabney "Moose" Nelson was the man perfect for the job.

He dismounted quickly, nodded at a gentleman with a waxed mustache who exited the jailhouse, and slipped through the doorway to find his friend sitting behind a desk that would probably have looked bigger if not for Moose's large stature.

"Looking for any new deputies?"

Moose glanced up and slapped his knee a second later. "Trevor Wilkins, you old goat." He left the chair, rounded the corner of the desk, and stretched out an arm. "Hell, it's good to see you again." He crunched Trevor's hand in a bone-wrenching hold and shook it for all he was worth. "Come on in. I've got a little time. Sit down and let's catch up." He slapped his friend on the back and led him to a chair.

Trevor's laughter rumbled across the room. "Christ, you haven't changed." He shook his hand to get the blood flowing once more. "My hand is aching and, if I'd had something in my mouth, I probably would have choked. Still haven't learned to control that strength, have you?" He took a seat opposite the paper-covered desk and observed his old friend as the burly man returned to his worn chair.

Trevor's green eyes scanned the front office. He shook his head. The motion was accompanied by a smile. "I can't believe this is where you ended up; a village sheriff." As he said it though, Trevor concluded silently that it was the perfect place for his old friend. Even when they were children, Moose Nelson was the arbitrator through many childish quarrels. The man had an innate sense of honor when dealing with people and took that exceptional attribute into adulthood. He was a born leader, whether he understood it or not, with his high code of ethics and gentle personality.

Moose's round cheeks split with a smile. "Thanks, Trevor. I love this town. When the city elders decided to incorporate, I couldn't apply fast enough for the sheriff position. Although, I have to say, with so many people flooding into Biwabik, I don't normally have an afternoon where I can sit and shoot the bull with an old friend. So, tell me. What the hell are you doing back up here in the northland?"

"I've been gone way too long. I came back for the rest of the summer for a whole bunch of reasons—a few which I'd like to discuss with you. You know, Moose, it's been a long time since I've really felt excited about getting up in the morning. There's something miraculous about coming home to your roots. I feel more energized than I have in quite awhile."

Moose poured them each a shot of whiskey and pushed Trevor's glass across the top of the desk. "I, for one, never had the wanderlust like you. From the time I was a youngster, there was a pretty little gal that lived on the forty next to my pa's place. She always said she'd never leave northern Minnesota, so I thought, fine. I guess I'm staying here, too."

"How is Macy? I haven't seen her in quite awhile."

"Sassy as ever and still pushing me around. Cheers." Moose clinked his shot glass against Trevor's and downed the contents with ease. "And I wouldn't have it any other way. That little ball of fire makes my life complete. We've got a daughter now. Everyone says she looks just like me. Cute as a bug's ear! I'm hoping for ten more, but Macy says over her dead body. Every time I talk about it, she says I'm pushing for a gelding status." He winced at the thought, and then lifted his eyebrow as he shot Trevor a wary glance. "We fight, but then we get to make up."

Trevor's laugh finally burst out as he listened to his friend's special sense of humor. "I don't know how in hell she puts up with you."

"Well, come and find out for yourself. If she finds out you're in town and you don't come by for supper, heads will roll."

"I didn't stop by for a dinner invitation."

"I know, but we'll have it no other way." Moose leaned forward and poured two more shots of whiskey. After he slid Trevor's glass across the surface of the desk for a second time, he leaned back and casually sipped the liquor while peering closely at his friend. "I was by your place at the beginning of summer. Christ, Trevor, you've got a beautiful home in the making. Are you thinking of finishing it this fall?"

The other man shrugged. "I stopped by there this week. I've hired a crew to come out and do the finishing work. There's not much left to do, so it seems a shame to just let it sit there." He sipped at his drink.

Trevor needed the shot of liquid encouragement. The entire ride north to Biwabik, he had thought about how to approach his old friend for help. So far, his search had come up empty. Moose's position as sheriff might be the one thing he needed to get a handle on Claire's whereabouts. Finding her was not something he was ready to discuss with his brothers or their wives. He would never hear the end of it. He set his glass down and clasped his hands together. "Can I talk to you about something?"

Moose eyed him over the rim of his glass as he finished off his shot. "I was wondering when you were going to get to the real reason you came here. You got something going on?"

"Yeah, I guess I do," Trevor smiled. "I haven't discussed this with anyone else, but I need your help."

Moose waited patiently and remained silent.

"I'm looking for a woman."

"It's about time," Moose returned quickly.

The corner of Trevor's mouth turned up at his friend's smart-assed comment. "Not just any woman. I'm searching for someone in particular. Her name is Claire Holcomb. She's a widow with five kids. Very thin, curly blonde hair, and gray eyes. Probably in her late twenties or early thirties. Have you seen a woman in town that might fit that description?"

"Uh, uh, uh," Moose returned with a shake of his head. "I need more information than that before I'm going to answer your question. You've got me intrigued now. Come on, spill it."

Trevor leaned back in the chair and stared at his friend. "This is between you and me. If Emma gets a hold of this information, I'm done for."

A booming laugh erupted in Moose's throat and belted out across the room. He rubbed his large hands together with a huge smile on his face. "Oh, I can tell this is going to be good. Especially if you don't want your sister-in-law to know about it. Where did you meet this Claire?"

"Down in St. Paul. Actually, I met her son first."

"She's got a kid? You're courting a woman with a kid? You? The only lone bachelor left in northern Minnesota?"

"I'm not courting her." *I wouldn't call making love to her in the barn courting...*

"Hey!" Moose leaned forward with extreme interest lighting up his face. "Didn't you say this woman you were looking for had more than one kid?"

Trevor's eyes narrowed.

Moose waved his massive palm in the air. "All right. I'll shut up—only because I can't wait to hear more."

"I hired her son to work out at the race track where I was boarding a horse. Christ, he didn't even have a pair of boots because they're so poor. Jonah is a great kid. He's got four sisters. He, his mom, and the girls live—or rather lived there until recently—on a farm just outside the city limits. Claire's husband died a few years back, leaving her in debt and hardly able to feed any of them. To make a long story short, the bank foreclosed. I became friends with her and offered to help her out financially, but before I could finalize the offer, she lit out of town for some reason."

"So, what makes you think they're in this area?"

"Jonah said she talked about going north for a job. I've already checked out Virginia and a few other locations. They've simply disappeared. That's why I came to you. If you see them or hear anything, would you please let me know?"

Moose's head wagged back and forth. "She really got under your skin, didn't she?"

"We're just—"

"I'll tell you what your *just*." Moose leaned forward and placed the palms of his enormous hands flat on the surface of the desk. "I've known you since we were little kids. This Claire Holcomb must be a helluva woman because there's no way you would have ridden all the way up here just to see if she and her kids are doing all right." He splashed some more liquor in the two empty glasses. "Trevor Wilkins is finally going to get off his fat ass and fill up his house with a whole passel of kids. You damned well better invite me to the wedding."

* * *

Moose managed to convince Trevor to stay the night and continue their reunion after a home-cooked meal. He insisted that he and Macy had plenty of room, so Trevor ended up tagging along with the sheriff for most of the day. Wherever they went, it amazed him how respected and loved the Village of Biwabik's sheriff was.

After a long day and much reminiscing, they finally headed for Moose's home. The man lived in the center of town and, when they arrived, once again it hit Trevor how fortunate his friend was to be greeted by a loving woman and a daughter who adored him.

Macy, a tiny woman who barely came up to Trevor's mid-chest, approached him with her arms out and her dark blue eyes shining with pleasure. "It's so good to see you, Trevor. When Dabney's note came saying you were staying on for the night, I just got so excited. Come in, come in. Make yourself at home. In fact, sit at the table. I've got supper ready."

The men followed her into the dining room. As soon as they were seated and Macy set supper on the table, Trevor took one jab after another once Moose relayed to his wife that his friend was searching for a widowed woman with five children.

Trevor's head swung in his friend's direction at the man's announcement. "I thought I said this was between you and me?"

Moose worked at slicing the roast beef on the platter before him.

"One thing you gotta learn, Trevor, is that a husband and his wife never keep secrets."

Once Macy got over her initial surprise, she giggled constantly at the turn of events, agreeing with her husband that the woman must be something special for Trevor to drop everything in St. Paul and hurry north.

They had just finished the evening meal when the sound of someone pounding a fist on the front door brought the sheriff to his feet. Moose quickly crossed the cozy little living room to see who was calling at such a late hour. He opened the door to a very distressed Biwabik resident. Over the man's shoulder, the sky burned an eerie shade of orange. To the east, Moose could see that the town of Merritt was very likely on fire. He did not even need to ask what the problem was. Instead, he grabbed his hat and spun to see his wife's expression of horror. "Macy, I've got to go."

She ran to his side and wrapped her arms around him tightly. "I know, dear, I know. What do I need to do?"

He pressed a kiss to her forehead. "Keep water on the roof if you see the fire getting any closer." His big hands cupped her cheeks. "I can't stay and help you. If that fire heads in this direction, the entire town will go." She nodded and stepped away, her face a pasty shade of pale.

Trevor already had his hat on and his light jacket slipped over his vest. "I'm coming with you."

Moose nodded. "We're going to need all the help we can get."

They hurried out into the ever-brightening twilight, mounted their horses, and raced at breakneck speed to the main street where local residents quickly amassed. In a matter of fifteen minutes, Moose had the entire town mobilized. The sheriff deputized village occupants on the spot and sent them up and down the streets ordering everyone out of their homes to begin wetting their roofs. The flames burned brighter as the monstrous orange blaze charged down the hill, threatening to destroy everything in its wake.

* * *

Claire had just finished washing the supper dishes at the boarding house when the sound of panicked yelps filtered in from the side street. The door banged against the outside of the building, signaling her exit as she hurried across the porch and around the corner of the structure. The acrid odor of smoke assaulted her nostrils.

She reached the street, and a nightmare burst before her when the forest on the opposite side of the road erupted into a flaming inferno. Claire stumbled back as the explosion of flames began to devour the huge pine trees. Red hot cinders swirled in the updraft. A man grabbed her by the arm and flung her back toward the inn. "Hurry! The sheriff has ordered every man, woman, and child to wet the roofs of every building they can or this whole town's gonna burst into flame and burn to the ground!"

Claire spun in the dirt, raced for the door, and realized that the nightmare had just gotten worse. She came to a screeching halt, stood dumbfounded and stared unblinkingly at the scorching embers that plummeted onto the boarding house roof. Her brain raced when her eyes settled on her children, where they huddled near on the porch, their eyes round with fright.

Think, Claire! Her gaze darted to the ladder that leaned against the porch roof, and then to the hand pump only mere feet away. If not for the men sleeping on the upper floors, she would gladly have let Judd's building turn to ashes, but many innocent lives would be lost if she did not do something.

Spurred into action, she raced to the pump behind the Inn and grabbed three empty pails that lay on the ground. "Jonah! Fill these pails. I've got to find Ms. Henderson."

Claire hurried to the porch, raced up the steps, and found Norma frantically pulling crates of food stores through the kitchen doorway. She grabbed the older woman by the arm. "Forget those. Hurry and wake up anyone that might be sleeping. The building's going to start on fire. Go! They'll be trapped inside."

The gray-haired woman trembled in her grasp. "I'm frightened. I don't want to go up there."

"You have to, Norma! Their lives depend on it. I'm going to haul pails of water up the ladder and keep the roof wet. Now move!"

Norma shook off her fear, waddled as fast as her bulk would allow, and disappeared through the hallway door just inside the kitchen. Claire dashed back around the building and grabbed a filled pail that sat by the pump. Jonah already had two more buckets full and waiting by the ladder. Her daughters stood side-by-side, clutching one another's hands, not knowing what else to do. Claire paused to caress Sofie's soft blonde hair as her eyes encompassed all of them. "Keep the buckets coming. You girls do not come up that ladder, do you hear?"

Their heads silently nodded in unison.

"Stay together! Do not leave this yard." Claire grabbed the bucket and sloshed water across the front of her dress as she crossed the lawn. In a flash, she climbed up the wobbly rungs with a bucket in one hand, knowing that access to the top of the building was impossible. At least, she could wet down the roof of the porch, which faced the roaring fire across the road. As her head poked over the rim, a gasp left her throat. The beginnings of a small fire smoldered on the opposite edge.

Claire hiked the pail upward and placed it on the roof before she carefully stepped from the ladder and onto the wooden shakes. Grabbing the bucket, she raced across the slanted expanse, tossed the contents onto the small fire, and hurried back to where Jonah waited at the top of the ladder with another filled pail. "Hurry! Take this and fill it again."

Her son's eyes were round with fear. "The fire is too big! The whole countryside's gonna go. Come down, Ma. If the roof starts to burn, you'll never be able to put it out!"

"Move! We've got to try and keep this part wet. There are men sleeping up in the rooms. Norma's gone for them." She grabbed the second bucket and ran to the opposite edge of the roof once more. Flames shot into the air from a pine that grew in the front yard, creating a curtain of heavy smoke. Claire splashed the water across the wooden shakes, wishing there were filled pails lined in a row beside her. Raising her arm to shield her face from the horrific heat, she squinted to distinguish shadowy figures that raced around the footings of other buildings, desperately fighting the encroaching fire that threatened to engulf the entire village. Shouts of the townspeople filtered through the smoke. She could do no more. Claire needed to be off the roof and get her children to a safer location.

She turned from the edge to see Jonah struggling with another bucket on the opposite side of the roof. In the face of the thick smoke that billowed across the peak, Claire dropped to her hands and knees. Panic filled her brain as she began to crawl in the direction of the ladder.

The loud groan of splintering wood warned her of impending danger, and she leapt back just before part of the building's upper roof crashed to the porch awning in a fiery blaze sending hot sparks spewing heavenward.

"Ma! Ma, are you there!"

"Get down!" she screamed through the haze. "The roof is on fire!"

The only avenue of escape disappeared. She whirled, her frightened gaze searching for a way out of the building inferno and the sinister choking air. Her only hope was to jump off the roof on the west side of the Inn. Claire crouched down, covered her face with the hem of her wet dress, and crawled back in the direction she came from, ignoring the bite of the wooden shakes against the tender skin of her knees. Terrified, she felt her way with her hands through the thick smoke, ignoring the blistering heat beneath her palms. *Please God...please help me out of this...the children...*

She continued to crawl, desperate now to find the edge of the roof. Leaping a story and a half to the ground was better than burning to death.

"Ma!" Jonah's frightened voice filtered through the smoke from somewhere below her.

Thank god he's off the roof...

"I can see you. Keep crawling forward. You're almost there! Hurry!"

Claire never wavered. "Keep yelling, Jonah! I can't find the edge." She batted away the burning tears that blurred her vision. Thick clouds of smoke swirled around her body.

The girls took up the chorus, along with their brother. A glimmer of hope shined in Claire's brain as she crawled as fast as she could, following the beautiful sound of her children's voices. She blinked against the heavy smoke and clamped the hem of her dress tighter across her mouth and nose, craving just one second of fresh, sweet air.

Suddenly she spied her children shouting and waving their hands through the billowing smoke. Claire never wavered when her hand found the edge of the roof. She spun around and slid her body over the rim, allowing her feet to dangle above the ground and, hopefully, break her fall when she let go...

She never got the chance. One of the beams supporting the porch roof gave way, and splintered and scorched timbers rained down around her as she fell to the ground with a terrified scream.

Chapter Twelve

Trevor stood beside Moose on Biwabik's main street, surrounded by a group of thankful townsfolk. If it were not for the quick actions of the town's sheriff, most buildings would have been lost. His friend had managed to pull everyone together and, though the fire still raged through the thick forest west of town, Biwabik still stood. As far as they knew, no one suffered more than a few minor burns.

The huddled group on the street stood and watched the orange sky to the west, sharing stories of near disaster until a man's frantic voice echoed across the twilight. "Sheriff! The Boarding House just collapsed. We need help; people are hurt!"

"Dammit—I knew it was too good to be true," Moose cursed as he and Trevor leapt to the backs of their horses and raced across town to the Inn. Their hearts sank when the collapsed and still burning building came into view. Injured miners lay about the street, their moans of agony echoing in the night as their neighbors tended them. The town doctor, too, was in attendance and hurriedly assessed each individual and issued orders to those around him.

Trevor soon found himself busy putting out the sporadic fires that continually re-ignited in the smoldering rubble of the former boarding house. Once he and his fellow firefighters finally decided that the flames were not going anywhere, he headed back around to the front of the building in search of Moose. The big man stood with his arm around an older woman, comforting her with calm words.

She trembled beneath his gentle hold and dabbed at her eyes with a hanky as she shook her head. "It could have been so much worse. Thank God my kitchen girl made me wake up the miners."

Moose patted her shoulder as the woman continued to cry. "You did good, Norma. You got those men off the second floor before the whole building went down. No one was killed."

"I know," she dabbed at her tears once again, "but that poor girl was hurt. She was so brave. She went up on the roof and kept it wet so I could wake the miners, and then she nearly died when the building started on fire. Claire was trying to get off the roof when the building started to collapse. She fell."

Moose met his friend's eyes with an unspoken question. Trevor's heart thumped against his ribcage as he stepped forward. "Who did you say was on the roof?"

"My helper, Claire. Poor thing. She's pretty battered and her with all those mouths to feed..."

Trevor's stomach lurched. It had to be her. "Where is this Claire?"

Norma blew her nose into a hanky, shook her head, and tried to forget the image of Claire lying unconscious on the ground. "Doc had someone bring her to his clinic already. She's got a bad ankle for sure and burns on her hands. Oh——" her head lolled in abject misery "—I'll feel horrible if she doesn't come out of this. She was still unconscious when they left. And those poor children. Crying and wailing; they didn't know if their ma was dead or alive."

"Is her last name Holcomb?" Trevor's heart jumped at the thought of finding Claire; but, at the same time, his stomach rolled at the thought that she might be hurt.

Norma's chin lifted. "You know her? Yes! Claire Holcomb. She's just moved to town over the last month."

Moose already pointed down the avenue. "Head west at the end of the street. Just keep going in that direction. You won't miss the clinic. It's a biggest building on your left. Doc's got a sign out front."

Trevor bounded into the saddle before Mrs. Henderson had a chance to say anything further. He yanked on the reins, spun Buck around, and shot forward into the smoke-filled darkness.

* * *

Trevor pounded on the door of the clinic and waited for someone to answer. He was just about to let himself inside when an elderly woman responded to his frantic knocks. Concern darkened her eyes as she stared up at him. "Can I help you? Has someone been hurt in the fire?"

Trevor removed his Stetson. "No, Ma'am. My name is Trevor Wilkins. I'm here about a patient of yours. I was told that the doctor sent Claire Holcomb to the clinic because of injuries from the fire."

The door opened wider. "Yes. She's very lucky she wasn't hurt worse. I'm a little concerned that she hasn't fully awakened yet, but I can see she's trying. She's asked for her children more than once. That's a very good sign. It's safe to say that, even though she took quite a tumble off the roof, Mrs. Holcomb will recover."

"Are the children here?" Hope shone in Trevor's eyes. "Can I speak with Jonah?"

"Trevor?"

The doctor's wife saw instant relief flash in the big man's eyes when he looked over her shoulder.

Jonah stood in the stark white hallway looking battered and forlorn; his shoulders sagged and his soot-stained cheeks were smeared with tears. He ran forward and flung his little body into Trevor's outstretched arms as the older man dropped to one knee. The boy clung tightly to his friend's neck and sobbed against his cotton shirt. "Trevor...how did you find us?" He sniffed. "Ma is hurt bad."

Trevor rubbed Jonah's back with a gentle hand as he hugged the boy even closer. "Your ma will be okay. I promise. I'm just glad that I found you."

Jonah leaned back and used his sleeve to wipe the tears from his cheeks. "You were lookin' for us?"

"Of course I was. I didn't know where you went, but I remembered you saying you were going north. Are your sisters here with you?"

The boy's head bobbed as he battled another round of tears. "They're with Ma."

Mrs. Bjorn closed the door. "Would you like to go back and see them, Mr. Wilkins?"

"Yes, I would." Trevor stood and took Jonah's shaking hand in his.

She led them down a short hallway and stopped before a closed door. "Mrs. Holcomb is in here." She nodded and stepped aside.

Trevor found it difficult to catch his breath when he saw Claire lying in the sterile bed beneath a warm blanket. The hands lying at her sides were bandaged, blonde curls dusted with soot spread across the pillow, and the pale skin of her cheeks darkened with bruises from the fall. His gaze traveled lower then, pausing on her left ankle, which was splinted with wooden laths and strips of gauze.

Before he had a chance to go to her side, Sofie glanced up and squealed with excitement at the sight of a familiar face. A moment later, she was across the room and hugging Trevor's waist, with her sisters in tow.

He gathered them all close, but never took his eyes from the still form on the bed. The same need to totally protect and care for them all swelled inside him. Never had his heart raced with excitement or filled with the complete joy of simply gazing upon the face of another—and never had he been so scared at the thought of losing someone held dear. The emotion hit him hard, surprising his stunned mind with the intense heat that surged through his belly.

Unfortunately, Trevor was forced to take those precious thoughts and set them aside for further reflection as small hands urged him forward to sit on a chair.

As soon as he was seated, Sofie placed three-year-old Hannah on his knee. In the blink of an eye, Ruth scrambled up to perch on his opposite thigh. Her gray eyes, so much like Claire's, peeked up from beneath long lashes. She held up her chubby hand and spread her fingers. "Hi, Trevor. I'm four."

The situation was insane. Trevor scanned the five faces smiling up at him and could not help but cringe at the thought of how his brothers would have a ball with this one—St. Paul's most eligible bachelor was holding court with four of the most beautiful girls in the state—and loving every minute of it.

* * *

Claire moved her leg and winced at the pain that shot from her ankle up to her knee. Her burned fingers flinched beneath the bandages, causing a small moan to escape her lips. Something heavy encased her ankle and, even more strange, the sound of her children's excited voices met her ears. Try as she might though, she could not force her eyes open to see what had caused their enthusiasm—nor to put a face to the deep resonant tone that filtered past her ear. It was familiar, but she could not place it.

Why did she ache so? Her back and hips, her shoulder, her arms; her ankle throbbed with painful intensity. Claire struggled in earnest now to open her eyelids and escape the blackness that drifted around her. Her tongue moistened a swollen lip and another small moan escaped.

All conversation in the room died upon the sound of Claire's groan. Jonah scrambled to her side, as did Sofie and Sue Ellen. Trevor helped the two younger girls from his lap and watched quietly as they wiggled in front of their siblings to stand beside the bed. Silence reigned as they waited for their mother to open her eyes.

Long, blonde lashes fluttered against her cheeks, and Jonah took Claire's hand in his. He squeezed it. "Ma? Wake up. It's me, Jonah. Don't worry, I'm taking care of the girls."

A smile curved Trevor's mouth upon the boy's declaration. Now that the older man had arrived, Jonah was able to work through his fear and, once again, become the man of the family. *So young and so much responsibility to bear...*

Claire's head moved slightly on the pillow as she worked to focus on the faces surrounding the bed. Her gaze finally cleared, and then settled on her son's face. "Where am I?" Her voice croaked out the question.

Jonah leaned closer. "Your at Doc Bjorn's clinic. I was so scared. I didn't think you'd get out of the fire. Were you trying to jump off the roof when it caved in?"

Claire concentrated on his question. Slowly, the memory of being surrounded by flames and the close brush with death swam forward. "I fell...I was going to let myself drop over the side. That's the last thing I remember." She swallowed to wet her throat. "Is the boarding house gone? Did everyone get out?"

Jonah grinned from ear to ear and gently patted her arm, careful not to touch the bruises where the sleeve of her dress was torn. "You're a hero, Ma. Mrs. Henderson said you saved the miners by putting water on the roof."

Claire lifted her arm to pat his cheek and realized for the first time that her palms were wrapped in thick gauze. "Did I burn my hands?"

His head bobbed in response. "Doc said your ankle is sprained pretty bad, too."

Claire fought her panic. *What will we do now? How will I work? I've got to leave here before Judd finds out...* In her present state, she could not run from him...nor could she fight him if he was determined to have his way. She took a deep breath to grasp onto any courage she could muster. "I'm not the only hero. You and your sisters helped me. You're going to have to keep being a hero, Jonah. I...I don't think I can come home tonight." She winced when she lowered her arm. "Take your sisters home. And Jonah—" the tears finally won out "—I'm sorry, honey. I'm trying to keep our heads above water..."

Trevor could stand no more. He did not want to interrupt them, but Claire's tears ripped a hole in his heart. He stepped forward. "Claire?"

Her head rolled on the pillow at the sound of his voice, then her eyes rounded in wonder. "What...why are you here?"

"I was in town when the fire started. I heard that a woman named Claire was hurt earlier on the roof of the boarding house. I had to come and see if it was you."

"You shouldn't be here." She dropped her gaze from his and acknowledged the rapid beat of her heart. As injured as she was, it was still easy to remember how he had held her, made tender love to her body, and promised to help set her life straight—and it had all been a lie.

"Claire..." Trevor took one more step closer to the bed.

She turned her face away and clamped her mouth shut, refusing to say another word.

Trevor lifted Hannah from where she sat on the edge of the bed beside her mother and set the little girl gently on her feet. He glanced at Jonah. "Why don't you take your sisters out in the hall? Your ma and I need to talk."

The boy silently nodded, then his sisters shuffled out in single file. Jonah closed the door behind them.

Trevor dragged a chair across the floor and placed it near the bed. He sat down then, and could do nothing but stare quietly at the stubborn woman before him. "Is there anything I can get you?"

She sank further into the bed and kept her face turned away.

Trevor's chest expanded when he inhaled a deep breath. "Why did you leave, Claire?"

Her lids dropped over her eyes. Her jaw clenched stubbornly.

"I have to understand what happened. The last time I left your house, you were ready to let me help you out. When I came back the next evening, you were gone."

Finally, her eyes opened, but she just stared at the ceiling. She opened her mouth twice before any words came out. "I want to know why you're here."

At least she's talking... He leaned forward and rested his elbows across his knees, peering at her face for a moment before he spoke. "I came north to look for you."

"You shouldn't have."

His broad shoulders rose as he inhaled again to check his building temper, then he settled back in the chair when he expelled the breath. "It's a damn good thing I did. You've got five kids out in that waiting room who can barely take care of themselves, and now you're hurt and stuck in that bed. And, in case you've forgotten, there's still a fire raging on your back stoop. I'm going to go home with them, make sure they're fed, and spend the night."

"You'll do no such thing." Her head finally swung toward him, her eyes blazing with helpless anger. A smile touched his lips, and she yearned to slap it from his face. "Why are you grinning at me like the idiot you are?"

His anger dissipating, Trevor's smile grew wider. If she had enough spunk to flay him with her tongue, then she was going to recover from her injuries. "Because you, Claire Holcomb, have gotten yourself into a pickle, and I have the upper hand. You're stuck in that bed and, for some odd reason, you're angry as hell with me. And—" he stood and rolled his shoulders "—I don't much care. Eventually, you'll let me know what's bothering you. You always have in the past. Right now, I'm going to take your kids home and make sure they're safe and sound for the night. I'll be back tomorrow."

Claire opened her mouth to send another torrent of scathing

comments his way, but the words froze on her lips when he lifted his hand, staving off any further reprimands.

"You know what I just figured out? Your eyes turn to this steely color whenever you're ready to lambaste me. Save your breath, Claire. You're stuck in that bed and can't do a damn thing about it."

* * *

Trevor left her room and found Mrs. Bjorn in the kitchen with Claire's children. The doctor's wife had them lined up at the table drinking milk and eating cake. He had to curb the chuckle that bubbled in his throat when his gaze settled on little Hannah, whose cherubic face was covered in chocolate icing.

The elderly lady sat beside the little girl and smiled herself when she saw the humor twinkling in her visitor's eyes. "I thought that, after the horrendous evening they've had, that they all deserved a special treat. Would you like a piece of cake and a cup of coffee?"

Trevor pulled out a chair and sank onto the hard surface. "No thank you, ma'am. I think as soon as they've finished, I'll get them out of your hair."

Her white eyebrows rose in surprise. "You're taking them with you?"

Jonah immediately sat forward in his chair, but remained silent as his face lit with instant happiness.

"What else is to be done?"

"I guess—" she shrugged "—I automatically assumed I'd let them stay here until Claire was up to leaving."

From the corner of his eye, Trevor caught Jonah's expression change from a smile to an instant frown. He reached over and ruffled the boy's tousled hair. "I think everyone will do better if they're in their own beds. That way, their mom can rest well tonight. What do think, Jonah?"

The boy pushed his plate away from him. "We're ready to go anytime you are."

"Well, I guess the decision's been made then." Mrs. Bjorn rose from her chair. A moment later, she had wiped the frosting from Hannah's mouth and helped the girl off the chair.

Trevor thanked the woman one more time for everything she had done, counted heads to assure there were five, and then led Claire's children to his waiting horse. Once he had Ruth, Hannah, and Sue Ellen perched atop the saddle, he untied the reins and turned to a grinning Jonah. "You'll have to lead the way to your house." He started off on foot then, the horse with its three riders stepping along beside him. He tipped his head as he studied Jonah's carefree stride. "You look like the cat who just lapped the cream."

The boy literally hopped beside his sister, Sofie, as they moved out into the darkened, smoke-filled street. "I'm just glad you came to find us." He pointed up the lane. "We have to go this way." He would have taken Trevor's hand, but Sofie already had a tight hold on it.

"It's a darn good thing I did. I think this is one instance where your ma couldn't get herself out of trouble if she tried. What exactly happened, Jonah? How did she get hurt?"

"She was fightin' the fire," Sue Ellen spouted from the back of the horse. "Ma's a hero. We all helped."

Trevor swiveled his head and eyed the three youngest in the saddle. "You all helped?"

"Yup."

Ruth held her hand up again, her blonde locks bouncing in rhythm with the horse's gait. "I'm four, and I helped, too. How many are you?"

Trevor chuckled. "I'm more than I want to be—let's just leave it at that." He looked down at Jonah again as they continued down the dark lane. "Why was she on the roof?"

"Because a man came to the boarding house and said everyone had to keep the roofs wet. The sheriff ordered it. Ma knew some of the miners were still sleeping, so she told Norma to wake them up. The girls hauled pails of water from the pump, then I carried 'em up the ladder to Ma. She stayed on the roof to pour the water. We were workin' real hard when part of the main roof fell onto the porch. She couldn't get to the ladder anymore because of the fire. It was real smoky, and Ma couldn't see. We had to keep hollerin' so she could hear our voices. She was going to jump, but the roof caved in."

Sofie squeezed his hand. "I was scared, Trevor. I thought Ma died when she fell to the ground. Jonah made all of us help pull her away from the fire, so she wouldn't get burned. But I'm gonna try not to be

Keeper of the Heart

scared no more 'cuz you're here."

Trevor tucked her hand tighter in his. "You all did a great job. It's a good thing your mother has you."

Sofie gazed up at him, squeezed his large hand with her tiny one again, and blinked her serious and somewhat frightened looking eyes. "Are you really gonna stay with us all night? You're not leavin', are you?"

The fear she tried to hide—fear that they would be alone on a particularly scary night without an adult—pierced Trevor's heart. He bent down and scooped Sofie up and into his arms and, immediately, the little girl wrapped her arms around his neck. Adjusting her small form in his arm, he handed the reins to Jonah. "I'm not going away. We'll go home, wash the soot and ashes from behind all your ears—" he smiled when he heard her small giggle "—have something to eat, and then go to sleep so we can come back to visit your ma in the morning."

Sofie's hold on his neck tightened and she leaned forward to press her lips against his slightly whiskered cheek.

Trevor smiled. It was as if a delicate butterfly had just kissed him.

Sofie stared into his eyes. "I'm glad you're here, Trevor. I love you." She blinked once more, and then laid her head against his shoulder.

Her words stunned him—and warmed his heart. Not knowing what to say, he simply cleared his throat and glanced up at her sisters, where they rode behind them. "You girls doing all right up there?"

Three little heads nodded in response. Sue Ellen clung to the animal's mane; Hannah had her finger halfway up her nose, and Ruth lifted her hand to hold up four chubby fingers. Her little cheeks dimpled in a smile.

Chapter Thirteen

Five little chins drooped with fatigue by the time they reached the Holcomb's temporary home. Trevor's eye followed the sloping line of the dilapidated building as he helped the girls down from the back of the horse. He was not quite sure if he wanted to go inside. Even in the darkness, he could see that only one window on the front side of the house actually had an unbroken pane of glass. The door hung crooked on the hinges as Jonah wrestled to get it open and nothing but dead vines and dried up bushes dotted the ground beside a porch with missing timbers.

What the hell...

Trying to hide how appalled he actually was, Trevor made sure the four girls started for the house, again counting heads so no one was missed. It only took a second to loop the horse's reins around a garden post—the only one of the three that seemed sturdy enough to hold the animal—and he quickly followed Claire's children inside the ramshackle building.

The light from a lamp Jonah had just lit cast a glow across the cramped quarters. If Trevor was appalled by the exterior conditions, the inside of the house made him want to grab all five of his charges and rent a room for the night.

Simply put, Claire and her family had absolutely nothing except a few crates piled one on top of the other against a far wall. A rickety wooden table leaned against another wall for support. Two clean washbasins sat on the floor.

His eyes scanned the rusted stovepipe that vented out through the roof. Water stains on the wooden ceiling told him exactly why the pipe was ready to crumble into a thousand pieces. If it were winter, anyone who lived in this shack would surely freeze to death. Claire's farmhouse, even with its years of disrepair, was a castle compared to the four walls around him.

Seeing only three cots in the room, he swallowed his apprehension and turned around to peer at Jonah. "So, where does everyone sleep?"

The boy pointed at the makeshift beds, his round eyes showing his puzzlement at Trevor's question. "Right there."

"But there's six of you and only three beds."

His chin bobbed. "That's because my ma could only find three cots that were free. We don't have money to buy any more. Pretty soon though, we're going to get another paycheck and Ma says if there's any left after we buy food, we can maybe buy one more."

"So where do you all sleep?"

Before Jonah could answer, Trevor already had it partially figured out. The girls each placed a pillow on opposite ends of two cots. That only left one, however, for Trevor and Jonah to share. He turned with a skeptical eye. "So, where do I get to sleep?"

"On the last cot. That's Ma's. I sleep on the floor." He raced to one of the crates and pulled out neatly folded blankets. "Ma won't mind if you sleep in her bed. Here, you can use these blankets. They're clean. Ma always says that, if we don't give our guests clean bedding, her own ma will roll in her grave."

If Trevor had not been a grown man, he probably would have cried. The Holcomb's situation was ludicrous. The kids had nothing, absolutely nothing, yet they still followed simple rules of etiquette taught to them by a loving mother who most likely never possessed much of anything, either.

He brushed aside the ache that permeated his chest and rubbed his palms together as five pairs of eyes watched him closely. "All right, now that we've established whose beds belong to who, how about we heat up some water and get you all washed up before lights out. You're in charge of that, Jonah. I'll see about rustling us up a snack." The instant silence caught him off guard. He glanced from one child to the other. "What? You're not hungry? I didn't think a piece of cake would tide you over until breakfast."

Sofie hugged her pillow. Her gray eyes rounded. "We don't have any food. We get to eat leftovers at the boarding house until Ma gets paid again."

Trevor bit his tongue to forestall the appalled curse that almost squeaked out. He thought of the many times Mamie or Katy had scraped leftover food from his family members' plates into a slop pail, and felt more humble by the minute. "But, because of the fire, did you even get to have dinner tonight?"

Jonah stopped at the door with an empty bucket in each hand. "The doctor lady gave us milk and chocolate cake. We'll be okay. I'll go pump some wash water." He disappeared into the night.

Trevor peered down at the girls, who were still perched on the cots. Hannah had one finger pushed up her nostril past the first knuckle as she stared at him. His stomach lurched again. "You have to stop that, Hannah."

Sue Ellen pulled her sister's hand down. "Ma says you're not supposed to pick your nose."

The little girl examined her finger, and then looked up at Trevor again. "I gotta poop."

Trevor rubbed his forehead and took a deep breath, thinking of Claire sleeping peacefully in a soft hospital bed. She owed him big time. "Can you wait until tomorrow?"

Ruth slid off the cot and landed on the floor with a thud. "I gotta poop, too," she added as she stood and rubbed her butt.

Trevor breathed deeply one more time. "All right," he sighed as he looked from one set of gray eyes to another. "Who has to use the outhouse?"

Four hands shot up.

"Sofie? You and Sue Ellen are in charge of outhouse detail. Take your sisters outside and I'll help Jonah heat some water." Trevor's gaze lifted to the stovepipe as he picked up a kettle from the floor and set it on the surface of the stove. "Hopefully, we won't burn this place down, too," he muttered with another glance upward.

The girls filed out the door as he added small pieces of broken timber to the cold, charred remains of last evening's fire. By the time Jonah returned, the older man had a small blaze going. Trevor grabbed a pail, poured water into the pot, and eyed a happy Jonah making his bed on the floor.

In the few minutes he was alone in the house, Trevor had already formulated a plan. He would put up with the current conditions until morning, but that was it. By tomorrow night, the Holcomb children would have a much nicer place to live...whether their mother liked it or not. He strolled over to Claire's cot and sat down. His eyes met Jonah's. The boy grinned from ear to ear. "Is your mother planning to stay here through the winter?"

Jonah shrugged his thin shoulders. "I guess so—if she can find another job. Maybe we'll have to move on. Ma says there's lots of mines opening up and we have to just keep thinkin' good thoughts."

"Did she have a hard time finding the job at the boarding house?"

His head bobbed. "We went to a town called Virginia first, but they gave her job away to someone else. We kept looking and going from town to town until Mrs. Henderson said she would give us a try."

"Us? You mean you're all working?"

He nodded. "That was the deal. We don't get paid, but we help Ma do her duties so we can eat." He sank to the floor and crossed his legs, deep in thought for a moment. "She hates it at the boarding house. Now that it burnt, maybe she can find something better. I didn't think it was so bad before, but then Mr. Stone showed up."

Trevor's chin lifted to attention. "Judd Stone from St. Paul?"

"Uh-huh. Ma took the job cooking because she didn't know that the banker owns the boarding house. Once she found out, she said we have to be ready to leave Biwabik in case he's mean to her again."

Trevor's brain raced. *What's that bastard doing up here?* He sighed and clasped his fingers together across his bent knees. He would talk to Moose at the first opportunity. "I want to talk man to man with you about something, Jonah."

The boy's shoulders squared with importance as he waited.

"It's going to most likely take a while for your mother's ankle to heal. Even if she could work, she doesn't have a job anymore. What are you going to do then?"

Jonah's jaw hardened. "I'll find something. Maybe I can get a job at the livery stable. Or there's lots of stores in Biwabik. I could be a delivery boy."

"That's a good idea." Trevor reached across the small space between them and laid his hand on the boy's shoulder. "But what about school?"

"Ma teaches us what we need to know. Even Hannah knows her letters."

"Would you like to go to school?"

Jonah's head wagged. "Nah, I don't have time for that. I'm the man of the house now. I gotta work to help Ma out."

Trevor gave the boy's shoulder a reassuring pat, then ran a hand through his own thick hair. "You're a good son. I'm sure you could make some money, but I've got a proposition for you. Your ma's going to need a lot of rest, so she can get well." His eyes moved about the dingy shack, and he suppressed a shudder. "She's not going to like my idea, but if you and I work together, I think we could convince her."

Jonah rose to his knees and waited breathlessly to hear what Trevor had to say.

"How would you like to come and live with me for awhile until she gets better?"

The boy's eyes glittered with excitement. "With you? Really?"

Trevor's face split with a smile. "I'd like to help you through this rough time. My family doesn't live too far from here. We have a big ranch with lots of room for company. You could ride horses every day, go fishing, and even find time to go to school like other kids."

Suddenly, the bright light in the boy's eyes disappeared. His shoulders sagged as he sat back and his chin drooped to his chest.

Suddenly, having Claire's family with him was something Trevor desired more than anything. "What's the matter, Jonah? You know, we could talk about the school. You wouldn't have to start right away." The older man's smile had also vanished in the face of the boy's gloom.

"You're a nice man, Trevor, but, I can't come and live with you. Who would take care of my sisters and my ma?"

A sigh of relief whistled over Trevor's lips. "I'm not just talking about you, Jonah. I'm talking about everyone. I want you all to come. I wouldn't think of splitting you up."

Jonah launched himself through the air with such force that he knocked Trevor over backwards on the bed. He wrapped his thin arms around the older man's neck and was rewarded when Trevor hesitantly encircled his bony shoulders, providing safety and warmth and a feeling that everything would work out.

Trevor helped them both back to a sitting position as the girls returned to the house. He squeezed Jonah's shoulder. With the boy's help and Trevor's own stubbornness, Claire would not have a chance to say no.

* * *

The next morning found Trevor and all five children pulling up before the clinic in a brand new rented wagon. Trevor's horse and Claire's mule were tied to the back. The Holcomb's meager belongings were crated and loaded off to one side. A comfortable bed made from the family's many blankets was ready for Claire on the other side.

Trevor was amazed at how quickly the girls emptied everything from the house when he told them they were going to live at his home for a while. Once he loaded them into the wagon and counted heads, Jonah directed them to Norma Henderson's home so the children could say goodbye. Trevor made arrangements for any wages Claire had earned to be sent to the ranch, asked that she not inform anyone of the injured woman's whereabouts, and thanked her in Claire's stead for everything she had done.

Up to the very minute he hauled back on the reins in front of the clinic, Trevor was firm in his decision to move Claire back to the ranch where she could get the care and attention she needed. The children could be, well, just regular children for a while. The little voices had excitedly chattered the entire morning away, from the moment he stopped to buy jerky, bread, cheese, and milk for their breakfast, and they were still at it when the wagon came to a halt.

Now, however? Trevor's stomach suddenly rolled as he stared at the front door of the Bjorn's clinic. How was Claire going to take his interference in their lives? Last night, when he lay on the uncomfortable mattress, the idea to move her and her family seemed a perfect solution. Now he was not quite so sure, but what else could be done? The groundwork had been laid—it was too late to turn back now.

He set the break on the wagon and jumped down, then turned to help Jonah lift the girls to the ground. Trevor automatically set Hannah upright when she tripped and fell, and then brushed her knees off as if he had done it his entire life. He took a deep breath. This was it. Thank God Claire's ankle was splinted and she could not get out of the bed on her own. Trevor rather liked his head sitting on his shoulders.

* * *

Trevor had intended to break the news gently, but the children beat him to the punch. Claire now rested against the headboard, with straight-lined lips and glittering steel shooting from her eyes.

"Children, go sit outside on the porch. Mr. Wilkins and I need to have a discussion."

"But, Ma—"

"Please do as I say, Jonah."

Silently, all five shuffled out of the room, knowing their mother would not put up with any arguments in her present mood. Claire waited for Sue Ellen to pull the door shut before she turned her wrath on the tall, handsome man standing at the foot of the bed. "Who do you think you are?"

"Now, listen, Claire—"

"No. You listen. I can't imagine why you thought you could just pack up my belongings, thinking that I would agree to this. Just move me lock, stock, and barrel to your home?" Her bandaged hands fluttered about in agitation. "And, technically, it's not even your home. The children said they're going to a family ranch, where there's other kids to play with? You've got them all excited about something that's not going to happen. Why? Why would you do that to them?"

Trevor crossed to a chair, pulled it closer to the bed, and perched on the edge. He removed his hat and set it on the small bed stand before he met her angry gaze. "Why won't you let me help you?"

"I did. I let you take Jonah and the girls home last night—" she pushed a lock of curly hair away from her eye "—although I didn't have any choice in the matter. I know what this is. You think that just because we..." Her voice drifted off. Claire closed her eyes for a moment, then opened them to gaze at the wall above his head.

"Because we made love in the barn?" Trevor watched her face

turn to a color near purple when he stated the obvious. He nodded. "Yes. That's one of the reasons."

Her head snapped in his direction.

"Can you honestly tell me, Claire, that you haven't given what happened another thought?"

She turned her head away and refused to meet his eyes. Suddenly, her anger disappeared. At the moment, she felt absolutely nothing. No anger, no fear, nothing in the face of his question. It was easier to remain numb to the ache in her heart—an ache she had fought since seeing him wrapped in the arms of another woman. "Of...of course I have. It never should have happened. I don't know what came over me that night."

"I do. I held a courageous and strong-willed woman in my arms, one who was not lowered in my estimation just because, for a short while, she lost the strength to fight the miserable existence forced on her."

Claire's face turned a deathly shade of pale as she ducked her head.

"I'd still like to know why you ran the next day." Trevor's level gaze remained steady. "What happened? What did I do?"

The numb sensation quickly turned to the same overwhelming ache she had tried to rid herself of since the morning she stumbled home from the racetrack. How could she tell Trevor she had wakened the day after their heated tryst with renewed hope for the future? How could she explain that his tender kisses and gentle lovemaking had made her feel like a woman for the first time in years, only to discover that the emotions she felt were a sham as far as he was concerned? How does a woman describe to a man the devastation of suddenly having to close your heart for the last and final time in your life? Her head shook slowly. "I don't want to talk about it."

He sighed and dropped his chin to his chest, deep in thought. It was not long before he raised his eyes to meet hers once more. "Then lets talk about your kids. How are you going to support them until your ankle heals? Christ, Claire. I took them back to your house—if that's what you want to call it—and there wasn't even any food."

"I'm doing the best that I can." Her chin trembled along with her glistening eyes.

"Well, you're not going to be able to do it over the next few months. I don't doubt for a minute that you could pull off supporting all them, but that's only if you're healthy and uninjured. I want to help. I've told you that before. You need to make some coherent decisions and quit trying to carry the load on your own. My family's ranch is just the place for you to recuperate, and it will also provide an opportunity for your children to quit shouldering the responsibilities of an adult."

Her lips sagged open. Is that what she was doing? Allowing them to forget that they were children, because she had decided fate had something against her? Claire's fingertips covered her mouth to hold back a sob. She had never cried so much in her life as she had in the last few months.

Trevor recognized her ordeal, slid off the chair, and settled his hip on the edge of the bed. Claire's body remained stiff when he carefully took her bandaged hand in his. "I'm sorry. I didn't mean to be so blunt about it. Would you just quit fighting me for a moment and discuss this rationally?"

Her shoulders slumped back against the headboard, the proud independence finally taking leave. "What am I going to do?"

He smiled and patted her arm. "You're going to let me take you all back to the ranch. You're going to recuperate, and then we'll sit down and decide what comes next."

"You! You said let's talk about this rationally. Are you just going to dump me and the kids with total strangers?" The notion was hard for her to fathom. "How could anyone's family accept a widow with five children being dropped in their midst without any questions? I don't know how...how rich people go about their days, but where I come from, it's just not done. I have nothing. I have no future to even hope about anymore, but I still have my pride." She held out her bandaged hands. Her eyes darted about momentarily before she stumbled over her next words. "Look at me. Do you think I didn't lie here last night worried about what the future holds for the six of us? My kids are my responsibility, and I'll think of something to get by." She sent him a querulous look. "I'm never depending on anyone again, especially a man. I've gone that route and it's a dead end."

It was true. Claire had tossed and turned the night before, thinking about how she would escape Judd's clutches when the evil man returned to town. She had even thought about going to the local authorities for help, but came to the realization she could not chance it. She was nothing but a poor widow. They could take the children away in an instant, and she would never be able to get them back.

"So...marry me."

"What?" she whispered back incredulously.

"I said marry me."

Chapter Fourteen

Claire was speechless. The curtains rustled against the open window frame as the blood drained from her face. She pulled her hand back from where it lay in his palm and, still, she said nothing as his proposal swam across her brain. He simply sat there beside her and waited patiently for her to respond.

Trevor was not as calm as he appeared. He had blurted out the proposal because he could not imagine having her and the children disappear from his life again. Even with last night's outhouse calls and Hannah continually picking her nose, he had lain in her makeshift bed with just a tiny glow of light from the lantern, thinking about how precious each and every one of Claire's kids were. He lay awake most of the night trying to discover the one thing that stood out in his past that was better than having her kids around him. The only thing he could come up with was the tender moment in the barn with their mother.

The longer he studied her shocked features now, however, the more the instantaneous offer seemed to make sense. It was also at that moment that he discovered he could very well be falling in love with her.

Claire had nothing. Trevor had plenty. She lived in a rented shack. He owned a big, beautiful home that waited to be filled. She absolutely refused to give her heart away again. He would see about that. It was the perfect solution.

Hardly a breath was taken by either of them as their gazes locked.

Claire's tongue moistened her bottom lip. "You...you want me to marry you?" He had just offered her an unexpected safety net for the future—but at what cost?

Keeper of the Heart

Trevor was surer now than he was even a moment earlier. "That's what I said. It's the perfect solution."

Her bandaged hands covered her face, and he could tell she worked hard to keep her breathing at an even pace. Finally, she peeked out and stared at him for a moment. "Just like that. You're just going to hand over your life on a silver platter?"

Trevor shrugged. "It's better than my head."

Claire totally missed the humor in his response. "Why would you do that? You hardly know me. I'm past the age of being a young bride. I have five children that you would become responsible for. I—" her hands dropped to the blankets and her head shook slowly "—I can't do it anymore."

"Can't do what?"

"I can't give my heart away and be hurt. I've been through too much."

Trevor suddenly understood that he needed to keep the proposal more of a business agreement—at least for the present time. If he told her that he wanted her in his life because he thought he was falling in love, Claire would run for the hills. "It's obvious that you don't think it's right for a widow to be taken care of by a bachelor. Well, neither do I. So, by marrying me, that obstacle is overcome. Financially, I can take care of all of you. As far as giving you a home? Well, there's plenty of room where we're going." He clasped his hands in his lap. "You know, Jonah told me that, of all things, Judd Stone owns the boarding house where you worked. I'm sure he didn't tell me everything, did he?"

"What are you implying?"

"Has he given you any trouble?" Trevor grasped at anything now to sway her final decision. A bit of guilt rested in his brain, but he tossed it away. If he had to lean on her fear, then he would.

Claire lowered her chin and stared at the floor.

"Well, you just gave me my answer. Has he threatened you?"

Her eyes came up, suddenly glistening with unshed tears once more. "He said he would get the authorities to take away Jonah and the girls if I didn't...didn't give him what he wanted."

Trevor's breath hissed across his lips. "That bastard. He's not going to go away, Claire. Not unless he realizes that you're no longer available." He gently picked up her hand once more. "So, marry me.

Give yourself and your kids security for the future. I'm crazy about them."

She kept her face turned away. *And what about me? What kind of marriage are you looking for? A weathered bride to take care of your home as you while away your days with the likes of a fancier woman? But, what choice do I have?*

Claire swallowed and met his questioning eyes. "I don't want to be hurt again. I just can't go through that again."

Trevor mentally winced, realizing that Claire's married life was so tainted that she was not willing to subject herself to giving her heart away a second time. A wry smile touched his lips. "You won't be. We'll consider this a business proposition."

* * *

Moose and his wife, Macy, quickly put together the details of a small wedding after Trevor halted the wagon in front of their house and requested they stand as witnesses to the marriage.

Claire now perched on a chair in the living room of the town sheriff's home just as the clock struck noon. Her leg was propped atop a basket and Trevor stood calmly beside her. All four girls sat quietly on the sofa, their eyes round with wonder as they tried to comprehend the happenings of the day. Only Jonah looked ready to leap off the cushion with excitement after discovering that once he moved to Trevor's home, it would be permanent—and he could not be happier.

The local Justice of the Peace hurriedly opened the Bible in his hands and glanced at the soon to be married couple. To him, the situation was odd to say the least. The handsome groom calmly stood by in his tailored jacket, a man who had never been married and was close to the age of forty.

The bride was the greatest surprise, however. She looked like she should be serving the wedding meal, instead of marrying the prominent groom. A worn, but clean dress that had definitely seen better days covered her wispy body. Her bandaged hands lay quietly in her lap, resembling the calm attitude of her future husband, but it was her gray eyes that continually gave away her nervousness as they darted about the room, looking at everything and everyone except the man beside her. It was commonplace in this part of the country for a man to take a widow in wedlock, but this one possessed five ragged children. The old man's eyes jumped from the bride to the groom, a mismatched pair, to say the least.

He shrugged his stooped shoulders. *Well, it's not up to me to ask the question why.* He cleared his throat and began the service. "Dearly beloved, we are gathered here this afternoon to sanction a marriage between a man and woman..."

Claire stared at the hunched little man and did not hear a word he spoke. *Married...I'm getting married...* The thought churned her insides. She glanced around the cozy living room of Trevor's friends, feeling as if she were really on the porch simply looking in at a stranger's wedding. The sheriff stood at Trevor's side and his wife stood beside Claire's chair.

Her eyes moved to the girls on the sofa. Hannah wiggled and Sofie took her hand to keep her quiet before meeting her mother's eyes. Ruth nearly sat in Sue Ellen's lap as she eyed the Justice of the Peace with caution. Jonah simply grinned from ear to ear. *I'm doing this for them...there's nothing else to be done...*

What about you, Claire? Another silent voice resounded in her head.

There is no me in all of this, she responded. *He's made it perfectly clear that this is a business proposition... At least there'll be a roof over my children's heads. After all, I was the one who stated I couldn't give my heart away again. I'm done with love...*

She tilted her head slightly and peeked up at him. Her cheeks reddened slightly when he returned her stare a second later and winked audaciously for her benefit. Immediately, Claire snapped her head back and stared at a spot above the Justice's head. *He doesn't act like being married to me is distasteful. He's been nothing but kind and gentle since the day I met him...since the night we made love... One day at a time, Claire. For once, let someone else shoulder your responsibilities and quit worrying about the future.*

Their union might be of a business nature only, but at least life with Trevor would not be boring. Her body jumped when he bent down and whispered something in her ear.

"What?"

"The man just asked if you'd take me as your lawfully wedded husband. Haven't changed your mind, have you?"

"I—" she glanced around in a daze, realizing everyone waited for her response "—I...do."

Trevor lifted a bandaged hand and rested it in his palm before looking back at the official, who had just closed his Bible.

"Then, by the power vested in me, I pronounce you husband and wife. Congratulations."

Claire scanned the room, her brain in a bit of a fog. Was it over? Was she a married woman again? Moose shook Trevor's hand with a fair amount of vigor. Someone touched her shoulder. Before Claire knew it, Macy hugged her. Claire forced a smile to her lips as she watched her new husband over the petite woman's shoulder. She was not walking through a dream—or a nightmare. This was for real.

Macy squeezed Claire's shoulders one last time, straightened with a smile, and held her hand out to the curious girls on the sofa. "Well, I've got some lunch ready for all of us. Whoever is hungry, come with me!" The children rolled off the cushions in a flash and joined their hostess as she led them into the adjoining room. Moose followed after pressing a soft kiss to Claire's cheek.

Suddenly, she was alone with Trevor again. Flustered and not quite sure what to say, she waited silently for him to make the first move.

Trevor bent at the waist, placed both hands on the arms of Claire's chair, and lowered his face until his eyes were level with hers. "Congratulations, Mrs. Wilkins. Even though we've made an agreement of sorts, I think it's customary for the groom to kiss the bride."

Claire's heart pounded against her ribs as his mouth swam before her—just before he pressed his lips to her dry ones. His touch was warm and gentle, not demanding or frightening, but more a simple vow to seal the wedding bond. Her lids fluttered shut when she realized he was not going to let the kiss end anytime in the near future.

Trevor's belly filled with heat when Claire did not pull back from his touch but, instead, closed her eyes and returned the intimate kiss. His fingers rose hesitantly to stroke her cheek before he gently cupped her face and slanted his lips across hers. He drank in the return warmth of her mouth, instantly remembering the same sweet taste as the night they made love in the barn. Claire's slight but pleasure-filled groan met his ears just before she broke the contact.

Green eyes met gray ones.

Claire blinked. "I think—" her lungs swelled with a deep, tremulous breath "—I think your friends are probably waiting for us."

The corner of his mouth lifted as he continued to stare at her. The action sent a wave of heat right to the pit of Claire's stomach.

"I think you might be right. But, Macy and Moose are patient people. I'm sure they left us alone on purpose." His eyes silently followed the feminine plane of her cheekbones.

His intimate perusal had Claire near to shaking in her seat. "Even so, I...I think we should probably join them."

Trevor had his forearm tucked beneath her legs and his other arm around her waist before she could utter another protest. Claire was lifted against her husband's broad chest and, immediately, she squealed and grabbed at his neck, clinging to him until he adjusted her in his arms.

"I figured since I didn't have a threshold and you've got a bad ankle, I may as well help you into the dining room."

"Don't be silly. I could use the crutches...what are the children going to think?"

"That this is a day they're going to remember forever." He strolled across the room in the direction of little girls' giggles and Moose's big booming voice. "Besides, we need to get on the road. I want to be home long before it gets dark."

Instant panic replaced the quickly disappearing heat in Claire's blood. "We're heading out today?"

"There really isn't anywhere for us to stay in town. I know if I asked, Macy would insist we all bunk here for the night, but they've done enough for us. And I'll be damned if we're going back to the place you rented."

The hair rose on the back of Claire's neck. Her eyes blazed with both anger and embarrassment. The rented shack was the best thing she could find on such short notice. "I'm sorry I wasn't able to afford anything better for your sleeping enjoyment last night," she snapped.

The air of intimacy disappeared into thin air as Trevor mentally flayed himself for the thoughtless comment. One thing he had learned quickly was that Claire had an abundance of pride. "I didn't mean for that to come out the way it did."

"I know perfectly well what you meant."

"So tell me."

She turned her head away and blinked back the tears. It was not her fault that she had nothing. Claire felt more than heard his sigh as he stood in the hallway leading to Macy's cheery dining room.

"I'm sorry. Just once, Claire, accept my apology the first time around. It's our wedding day. The kids are happy, the Nelson's are loving that we asked them to be a part of all this, and I'm just excited to show you all your new home. What do you say? Can we make a pact to get through this day without exchanging barbs?"

Claire already berated herself for being so ungrateful. Trevor had given up his bachelorhood and a liberated life. In its place, he accepted her and her five children without knowing what the future would bring. She would have to pray that they could make it work, that somehow the seven of them would find neutral ground. She tipped her head to look up at him. *He's like one of my kids;* hope rested easily in his dark green eyes as he waited for her answer.

"All right. Truce."

Chapter Fifteen

Claire laid in the back of the buckboard and leaned against the side as the conveyance bounced its way southward. Her gray eyes glanced at Jonah's back, where he literally vibrated on the seat beside Trevor, asking nonstop questions about her new husband's ranch. The girls huddled in the back with her, not the least bit perturbed that, once more, they were making a move to something unfamiliar. As she adjusted herself against the sideboard, taking care not to jar her throbbing ankle, she simply wished she could be as much at ease with this new development as her children.

Her lingering gaze moved to study the man who now was her husband. Trevor laughed with her son, telling him stories from a time when he was a small boy at the ranch and the many different escapades he and his brothers shared growing up. They were stories about a life that was totally foreign to anything her children had ever experienced.

Try as she might, Claire struggled to hang onto the fact that the current situation had only come to pass because of her problem. No words of love were exchanged. It would behoove her to remember that their marriage was a business partnership only. That fact, however, did not halt one tiny tear of sadness. She had done her best and, when it was not good enough, Trevor offered an escape. She had taken it blindly.

She glanced over the edge of the wagon when it came to a halt at the top of a hill. Trevor swiveled on the buckboard seat with a gentle smile on his lips. "I thought maybe you'd like to take a look at your new home from up here."

Claire stifled her gasp. Only moments earlier, she had watched the homestead come into view, wondering about the family who was fortunate enough to live in such a fine home. The buildings looked enormous, sturdy and clean, but it was the front porch supported by beautiful log beams that grabbed her attention. To be able to sit there quietly every morning and take in the beautiful view of towering pines, to feel secure with what would most likely be a full belly, was something she could only imagine in her dreams.

She turned to Trevor and scanned his handsome, proud features as he waited for her reaction. "I can't believe how beautiful it is. Is this all yours?"

"I share ownership with my brothers." Trevor instantly decided he would not inform her about the stately home being built just north of the homestead. He planned to save that piece of information for a surprise. He cringed inwardly, trying not to think of the omission as something he would guard carefully until he needed a trump card up his sleeve.

Claire pulled her gaze from the beautiful vista below them before turning her eyes back to her husband's. She had been concerned the entire morning regarding how Trevor's family members would react to her and her brood. It was just too much—the uncertainty, the new future—everything. Her head shook, and she swallowed down a lump of fear.

Trevor had silently acknowledged her distress, which built as the afternoon hours passed. "You've gotten more quiet over the last few hours, Claire. Tell me what's wrong."

She blinked and used the tips of her fingers to brush the blonde strands from her cheeks. "What are they all going to think when you arrive married to a woman with a wagonload of children—people who aren't even in your class."

His jaw firmed. "I've told you, they're not like that. There is no difference between the people who live down there—" his dark head indicated the ranch "—and any of you. I didn't tell you before, but my youngest brother is married to a beautiful Sioux woman who means everything to us. The woman who raised me is a full-blooded Negro, and more a mother to me than a housekeeper. You'll meet both of them and see for yourself. At Lakota Pines, we don't look down on anyone."

Claire adjusted herself on her bed when he slapped the reins across the horse's backside with more vigor than usual. Even as the wagon and its stiff-backed driver lurched forward, she found the notion hard to believe.

* * *

Cole and August lounged on the front porch swing, keeping a protective eye on their son who toddled about in the late afternoon sunlight. They both sat forward at the same time when a wagon full of people crested the hill and paused at the summit.

August immediately rose from her seat and quickly stepped down the stairs to take Daniel Hawk's chubby hand in hers. The wagon on the hillside had started its descent in the direction of the house. "Come, son, let us go inside and see if Katy has any treats for us." Her worried, dark eyes met Cole's as she hurried back up the set of steps. She stopped and rested a hand on her husband's arm. "They are getting closer. We need to go inside until we know who is visiting."

Cole raised a hand and shielded his eyes. The powerful set of shoulders belonging to the man who guided the wagon was familiar—and so was the horse tied to the back. "I think it's fine, August." A smile broke out across his face. "In fact, I know it is. That's Trevor—" his grin widened "—and I can't wait to hear what's behind the wagonload of kids."

August turned to squint into the sun just as the wagon entered through the log gates, and then glanced over her shoulder when she heard the door open. Emma stepped up beside her, her brow creased with concern.

"I didn't know for sure if you knew someone was coming in."

August smiled. "It will be fine. Cole recognized Trevor."

"Trevor?" Emma placed one hand on the wooden railing and also squinted to see. "Is that a wagonload of children he's got with him?" She heard Cole's chuckle beside her.

"That it is, and I can't wait to see what's at the bottom of it."

The three watched the strange ensemble come to a halt and glanced at one another one more time in speculation before leaving the porch. Amazed, they watched Trevor jump from the buckboard and lift one child after another from the back. A small boy made his own way down the side of the buckboard to stand beside four young girls, who shuffled their feet in the dirt.

Cole's eyes scanned one child, then moved on to the next as he gently grasped August's elbow and moved down the wooden sidewalk. The children were definitely a bedraggled lot with their worn clothes and easily identifiable as siblings; each had blonde hair and round eyes that shone gray in the afternoon sunlight.

Cole nodded to his brother when he and August stopped before the line of children. "Well, Trevor, what do you have here?" He watched with even more surprise when his brother returned to the backside of the wagon and helped a petite woman to the edge.

Before Trevor could respond to Cole's question, Emma crossed to the children with a gentle smile on her lips. She stopped before Jonah and extended her hand. "Hello there. Aren't you the young man I met in St. Paul?"

Jonah wiped his hand across the front of his faded bibs first, and then held out his arm. "Yes, ma'am." He ducked his head.

Emma's gaze scanned the girls. "And are these your sisters?"

"Yes, ma'am. This is Sofie—" he pointed, and then continued down the line. "—Sue Ellen, Ruth, and the littlest one is Hannah. She's the baby." The young boy's face creased with a smile now, more at ease when the pretty lady sent a welcoming smile to all of them.

At the back of the wagon, Claire did her best to hide the trembling of her hands. It was all she could do to meet her husband's eye as she rested her wrapped palm on his arm and whispered softly. "Do I look presentable? I can't even check my hair with these bandages on."

"You're fine. This group will not be looking at your hair anyway." He stopped just short of informing her that they would be too damned interested in discovering who she was. His stomach did a small jump of its own just thinking of his family's reaction. He was really in for it... "Come on. Scoot over so I can get you in the house and out of the sun."

Claire grabbed onto his neck when he lifted her against his chest, noting how careful he was to not bump her splinted ankle. He turned to face his family. "I guess you're wondering what's going on."

"Yeah, I guess we are," replied Cole. "You didn't tell us you were bringing company. We would have been ready for...whatever we should be ready for." His hazel eyes settled on Claire's foot and hands.

Keeper of the Heart

"We could have at least made sure Steve or Carrie were here to check your...guest's medical needs. Should we send for one of them?"

Trevor nodded. "Probably wouldn't hurt."

Claire's heart pounded as she waited for him to break the news. She just wanted the marriage announcement to be over with.

Finally, her new husband opened his mouth again. "I guess we should get the introductions over with. Claire, this is my brother, Cole, and his wife, August." He nodded at Emma. "And this lady here already met Jonah when she visited St. Paul last month. This is Emma, who is married to my older brother, Tyler."

Claire's head spun as she tried to remember who was who. Earlier, on the way to the ranch, Trevor had told her about the people who resided there on a permanent basis. She tossed away her thoughts and immediately tried to catch up with Trevor's current explanation.

Her husband tightened his hold on her body. "I heard Jonah introducing his sisters, so now you all know them. This fine woman here is their mother, Claire...my wife. We were married this morning."

Trevor was not quite sure what to expect, but he thoroughly enjoyed the widening eyes and sagging jaws of the other adults. For a second, they all remained locked in surprised silence, and then everyone started to talk at once.

"Whoa, whoa, whoa. We can fill you in on the details later. I'd really like to get Claire inside. Although—" he glanced down at her reddening cheeks "—holding her isn't all the bad."

Claire gasped at his audacity before the others. As much as she and Trevor's union was going to be considered a marriage of convenience, he certainly was playing the part of a loving husband for everyone's benefit. Her flashing gray eyes settled on his face until Ruth began to hop from one foot to the other.

"I gotta go potty, Ma."

Emma immediately took the little girl's hand. "Why don't all you girls come with me and we'll go take care of business." Her emerald gaze twinkled as she finally gave in to the smile that tugged at her lips when she glanced one more time at her brother-in-law and his new wife. "Welcome, Claire. We're glad that you're here with us. Trevor can get you set up in the house. I'd be more than happy to help your children settle in until you're comfortable enough to make any changes you like."

Claire's heart warmed slightly as she glanced around in surprise. Already, Trevor's brother and his wife had invited Jonah to take a walk to the horse barns. Emma Wilkins had Hannah and Ruth each by a hand as they walked up the flower-lined wooden sidewalk, with Sofie and Sue Ellen following in their wake.

Feeling her husband's gaze on her, she tilted her chin and met his laughing gaze.

He adjusted her in his arms and winked one eye. "See, I told you. Everything's going to work out."

Claire simply remained in silent awe of the fact that he might know what he was talking about if the initial reception was any indication as to her acceptance in the future. She tightened her arms around his neck when he strode up the walk.

Trevor shouldered his way through the front entrance and felt Claire's body go slightly limp as she gazed at the interior of the rustic home. Realizing how taken she was with the beauty of the homestead, he smiled with pride and paused before taking her up the stairs. "My father built this home for my mother. Every log and most of the furniture came from the trees that used to grow on this land."

Her eyes scanned the massive wooden furniture, the shining bees-waxed floors, and the utter serenity the house exuded. Claire had never been in a home like the Wilkins'. "It's so beautiful," she breathed quietly, overwhelmed by the idea of living in such luxury.

Trevor crossed the large foyer and carried her up the massive staircase. "The house is built in a 'T'. This is the main structure and there are wings that flow both east and west. Emma and Tyler occupy the suites in the middle. Cole and his family stay in the west wing and...you and I and the kids will be in the east."

As they strode up the steps, Claire worked to overcome the instant concern his words evoked. Would they share a room? She did not know what to expect; with the quick wedding and ensuing departure from Biwabik, she had no time to dwell on what the end of the day would bring.

Trevor reached the landing at the top of the stairs and turned down a long hallway with numerous doors. Her eyes widened in amazement as she noted the chairs and small tables that lined the paneled walls. Even the corridor in the grand house was larger than the shack she

Keeper of the Heart

and children lived in when in Biwabik.

Trevor used his foot to push open a door at the end of the hall and carried Claire into a large bedroom, complete with a fireplace, sofas, and tables. He crossed to the bed and gently sat her on the edge, immediately supporting her leg, and helped her back against the fluffy pillows. Glancing up, he used the tip of his finger against the bottom of her chin to close her mouth. "You're going to catch flies if you keep that thing open."

Claire snapped her lips closed, embarrassed that she could not hide her awe at the room they occupied. "It's just that I can't get over how...enormous your home is. It's larger than the boarding house."

Trevor crossed to a window and opened the sash to allow a gentle breeze to float inside. "I don't think I told you that my sister is married to the local doctor. We'll get a wheelchair from them. That way, we can take you on a tour so you get to know where things are."

"You have a sister?"

"I was so busy telling you about everyone who lived here, that I forgot to mention Carrie. She's the baby of the family. She's got three children and helps her husband Steve with his clinic. Don't worry. When she finds out I brought a wife and five kids home, there'll be nothing but a trail of dust behind her as she races over here to get all the details." He turned and placed his hands on his narrow hips. "You'll have to get used to this entire upfront group. They've been good so far, but you can mark my words, the inquisition is coming."

Claire had to smile, despite the apprehension that roiled in her stomach. As much as Trevor tossed slightly disparaging remarks out about his family, she would be a fool to think they shared nothing but a deep love and respect for each other. "I'm trying to keep everyone straight. You all seem rather close, from what little I've noticed."

Trevor seated himself on a chair and stretched out his legs. "Guess we're lucky. We've always gotten on pretty well." Suddenly, a question stuck in his mind as he sat forward. "You know, we haven't even discussed that much about you. I don't even know if you have any siblings, or if you're parents are living."

Claire's eyes lingered on the fireplace for a moment before returning to his face. She shook her head. "It's just me and the kids. My father died years ago. My mother took ill right after I was married and

166

died shortly after." Her head tipped slightly to the side as she continued to observe him. "This is strange. We should have asked these questions before we were married."

He shrugged. "Doesn't matter—not to me anyway. I asked for your hand knowing full well what I was getting into. Past histories mean nothing. If you had siblings, they would be welcome here anytime."

A gentle knock sounded across the room, saving Claire from further comment. A middle-aged woman peeked her head around the corner of the door. "Excuse me." Her laughing eyes settled on Trevor. "Welcome back, Trevor. Emma asked me to bring up a wee bit of lunch." Without being asked in, she crossed to the bed stand and placed a filled tray on the surface. "Hello, ma'am. I'm Katy, the housekeeper. If you need anything, you just let me know and I'll be hustling it up in fine time. Emma, another of our Mrs. Wilkins, has your young ones lined up at the kitchen table. She's plying them with treats, so don't concern yourself about them. We'll all be keepin' an eye out for their welfare. A fine lot of youngsters you got there. Cute as the dickens, each and every one of them."

Claire's eyes followed the women with the Irish brogue as she hustled around pulling small feminine bottles and combs from her apron pockets. She placed them about the surfaces of various tables, talking a blue streak the entire time. "Emma and August wanted be sure you had some ladylike toiletries in this room, since a bachelor's abode it's not anymore." She paused and quickly placed a hand on her cheek as she looked around. "Ooo...there be lots of work to make this room more to the liking of a lady. I'll be seeing that your husband brings up your belongings and we'll get them put away between the two of us. Now, is there anything else you'll be needin' right off?"

Claire caught the quiet shake of Trevor's shoulders where he now stood silent by the window, and then brought her gaze back to the whirling Irish maid. "No, you've done more than enough. Thank you very much. And thank Emma and August for their kind gifts and for welcoming my children." Katy hustled from the room, and Claire immediately turned to the man who walked back in the direction of the bed. Her eyes were round with astonishment. "You have a housekeeper?"

"If that's what you want to call her. Katy's like part of the family." He sank into a nearby chair. "So is her husband, Dougan. She helps Emma and August with the day-to-day tasks. And I'm sure she was in cahoots with both of them to get up here and see what's going on."

"You mean your sister-in-laws help with the cleaning?"

"And cooking when needed. This is a big house with lots of mouths to feed. Everyone pitches in. Now, would you like me to help you with the tray?"

Claire's stomach growled, but as she glanced at the food, the emotions of the day and the trip to Trevor's home took its toll. A cloak of fatigue descended on her from nowhere, and she literally sagged deeper into the pillow. "Would it be rude if I didn't eat anything? Suddenly, I can't seem to keep my eyes open." Her bandaged hand covered her mouth when she realized her children needed to be settled in with her before she fell asleep. "Would you tell Jonah and the girls to come up? They can play quietly here in the room."

Trevor reached across the bed and pulled the covers down, waiting for Claire to roll her body onto the sheet. A moment later, he settled the quilt over her body. "Don't be worried about them. I'm sure everything's going well downstairs. Just give it up, Claire. Let someone else take on the responsibilities for a while. Take a nap. I'll bring them up later. I'm sure by that time, Carrie will be here and she can check your hands. Hopefully, those bandages can come off for good."

Claire's lids drooped and her limbs were heavy with exhaustion, but she fought the weariness for a moment more. "Trevor?"

He tucked the blanket around her chin. "Yes?"

"Thank you." She batted away the weary tears as she looked up at his smiling eyes. "No one has ever tucked me in before."

His fingers gently stroked the hair at Claire's temples as her eyes closed. "Go to sleep." Trevor watched her cheek sink into the softness of the pillow as her breathing changed to an even rhythm. He stood for a moment, staring down at his new wife, and realized that, once again, he would not change the moment for anything.

Chapter Sixteen

Trevor forced one foot in front of the other as he walked down the steps to the lower level, taking a deep breath to prepare himself for the onslaught of questions that were sure to be fired at him in a matter of minutes. Hearing voices in the library, he paused for a moment and wondered if he should run back up the stairs and hide. "Well, old man," he muttered quietly, "may as well get it over with. You know what the hell they're all like..." He squared his shoulders and headed for the lion's den.

He entered through the open mahogany doors and glanced around the room. His two brothers and their wives reclined on the sofas. His mind scanned the immediate attention his presence brought. "I suppose you're all waiting for an explanation."

"Come on in," Tyler waved with a grin that stretched from ear to ear. "After hearing about the nuptials, I poured you a splash of courage."

Trevor eyed his brother's quaking shoulders and crossed to the sidebar. Every eye in the room seemed to bore a hole through his jacket. "I said I *suppose* you're all waiting for an explanation. I didn't say you were going to get one." Someone chuckled behind him at the comment. Trevor turned with a stiff back. "You all think this is rather funny, don't you?"

The hilarity burst out of their mouths.

Tyler rose and joined his brother on the other side of the room to refill his glass. "This spoken by a man who made his two brothers' lives miserable when we brought our own wives into this house? You're only getting your due, so take it like a man." He clapped a hand on the younger man's shoulder. "What the hell is going on? You left here last

Keeper of the Heart

week a confirmed bachelor. Today, I hear tell, you were quite a sight when you pulled up in front of the house with not only a wife, but a whole passel of kids; who, by the way, are eating me out of house and home as we speak. Katy can't keep up with them."

"Yeah, well, you just hit the nail on the head. I think they've been in a constant state of hunger for years." Trevor crossed to a chair and sank onto the cushion. "Okay, where should I start?" He sat back quickly when the other adults in the room leaned forward in anticipation. His eyes narrowed as he scanned their eager faces. "You're all like a bunch of rabid dogs."

"Come on, Trevor, this is driving us crazy," Emma whined.

"You remember meeting Jonah at the race track?"

Emma nodded as she settled beneath her husband's arm when he resumed his place on the couch.

"Well, I ended up hiring him to do some menial tasks around the stable, because he wouldn't take no for an answer. His father died two years ago. Claire couldn't come up with the money to make the payments on their farm. This kid decided he would do anything to help her out. Claire has had a rough time of it. Anyway, I really enjoyed having him around. The kid's an absolute pleasure. One day, he's with me in the stall and his sister comes tearing in to say the bank collector is at their place; mind you, he's locked inside the house with their mother, against her will."

Emma and August exchanged immediate uneasy glances.

"He didn't hurt her, did he?" August clasped Cole's hand, remembering the many things she had gone through before they were married.

"No, I got there in time and literally kicked the guy out of the house. It seems he was making the rounds to every widow in the area who owed money to the bank. Need I go any further with that?"

Both Emma and August shook their heads.

"A couple of weeks later, St. Paul had a horrible storm. I went out to check on how Claire and the kids managed. The storm hit the buildings pretty hard." He was not about to fill them in completely. Claire's unsettled emotions and what happened afterwards were better left unsaid. Trevor took a sip of his drink, allowing himself a moment to bask in the memory of Claire's lips against his... "I told her I would help her figure out a way to rebuild and make the farm work, but she lit out the next day for a reason I'm still not aware of."

"So where did she go? And how did you end up marrying her? This has all happened pretty quickly," Tyler asked, struggling to follow his story.

"She ended up in Biwabik, of all places. I stopped to visit Moose and discovered her there that same night."

Emma placed her hand over her chest. "You must have been in town when the fire went through. We weren't sure what direction you had gone in."

Trevor nodded. "I was visiting with Moose and his wife when someone knocked on the door to alert us. To make a long story short, I went with him and discovered that a widow with five kids was hurt when the local boarding house caved in. I knew it had to be her. I went to the doctor's home and discovered all of them there. Claire fell from the roof and ended up with a terribly sprained ankle and burnt hands. She's lucky she wasn't injured worse."

"She fell? Why was she on top of the building?"

"Her and Jonah were trying to keep the roof wet until one of the other employees could wake up all the miners who were sleeping upstairs. When the place caught on fire, she tried to jump off the roof, but part of the building caved in, taking her with it. The kids pulled her away from the flames."

"Those poor children," Emma exclaimed. "And their poor mother."

"I still can't figure out where a wedding came into all of this." Cole watched his brother closely from across the room.

"Claire was at rock bottom. She took the job at the boarding house just to buy enough food for them to survive. Then she finds out that the same man who threatened her in St. Paul also purchased the inn from the Merritt brothers. Once again, Judd Stone started to terrorize her." He took another sip of the brandy and thoughtfully twirled the glass in his hands for a moment. Finally, Trevor looked up. "She had nowhere to send her kids when she lay injured at the clinic, so I took them back to their home. Christ—" he shook his head "—you should have seen the building they were living in. It was horrible. There was no way she could have spent the winter in that hovel."

August smiled to herself, already more or less figuring out the rest of his story in her quick mind. Trevor was a wonderful, softhearted man—much like his brothers were. She was not quite certain what led to the proposal but, after seeing the bind this Claire woman was in, there would be no way he could walk away and leave her and her children to fend for themselves.

Emma, on the other hand, was sure that Trevor kept a few details regarding Claire to himself, and she was even more certain that they were tied together because of those unspoken details. She tipped her head and studied him. Every time her brother-in-law said the woman's name or spoke of her children, his eyes softened to warm green hue. Emma was willing to bet that her brother-in-law was falling in love. She just wondered if he knew it yet.

Trevor glanced up at the members of his family, and his chest swelled with pride. Though they chuckled about his newly married status, they would stand behind him and treat Claire and her kids with kindness. "I asked her to come south with me until she recuperated. She refused, thinking it wasn't proper. Here's a woman who doesn't own a thing in the world, and she was still worried about what you all would think. So—" he drained the last of his drink "—I asked her to marry me. With a little wheedling on my part, she finally agreed and here I am, a married man with an instant family."

Silence echoed about the room. Then, once again, everyone started talking at the same time. Above the din, Trevor heard a small voice say his name. He swiveled on his chair to see Ruth standing in the doorway. Her eyes were round with hesitancy as she listened to the many voices.

Seeing that she had gotten Trevor's attention, she ran to his familiar face with her arms outstretched.

Trevor lifted the little girl onto his lap, cuddled her close, and missed the smiles that were exchanged around him. Brushing the crumbs from her mouth, he adjusted her on his lap. "What's the matter, Ruthie?"

She peeked from beneath long blonde lashes at all the strangers in the room and hugged his arm tighter. "I want my ma."

"You know what?" he crooned calmly. "Your ma's sleeping right now so her leg can get better."

"I want my ma," she whispered against his shirt with a voice that was suddenly shaky and rested her tiny head against his chest.

"How about we go outside and see all the horses? When we come back, I bet your ma will be awake and we can go visit her then. You can tell her all about the ponies you saw."

Ruth's little mouth broke into an instant grin. She slid off his lap, took his hand, and hesitantly waved goodbye to everyone else.

Trevor rose from his chair and hefted her into his arms. "Do you think the other kids will be alright or should I take them with me?"

Emma loved the fact that Trevor fit right into the role of a concerned father. "They're having fun with Katy in the kitchen. I'll keep an eye on everything until you come back." She watched the gentle man leave the room with a happy little girl in his arms.

As soon as his footsteps disappeared down the hallway, Tyler grabbed Emma's hand and gave it a squeeze. "Well, you must be just about bursting inside."

She giggled and bounced backwards against the sofa cushion. "I wouldn't have believed it if I hadn't seen it with my own eyes! Your brother is a married man after all these years of declaring how much he loved the single life. All the times August and I tried to play matchmaker and, poof, he just drives up one day with a wife and five kids, like it's no big deal." She tilted her head on the cushion and smiled up at her husband. "You do realize we're not getting the entire story?"

"Of course I do. As good-hearted as he is, Trevor wouldn't just pick someone up out of the dust and get married. I hope we don't have to wait too long for the fireworks to start. I have a feeling this is going to be good."

Emma's slender brow cocked over one eye and she nodded in agreement. Glancing at August across the room, her grin widened. "Well, I guess we can go through some boxes and find some clothes for these little ragamuffins. I don't imagine they have anything more than the clothes on their backs. Oh, and I suppose we should send someone over to Carrie and Steve's and let them know, too."

August stood with the help of Cole's hand. "I already did." She wrinkled her nose with a smile, then joined Emma as they left the room.

Cole stood and stretched his arms wide before grabbing his hat and plunking it on top of his head. Resting his hands on his hips, he eyed Tyler. "Well, what do you suppose we should do?"

Keeper of the Heart

The eldest Wilkins brother shrugged before he stood. "I don't know. Maybe kill a steer to feed those kids in there."

Cole nodded with a laugh. "Might not be a bad idea. I think they're here to stay, don't you?"

"I think you're right. And...I know what we can do. Let's head down to the barn and see how Trevor's doing at playing daddy. He abused the hell out of me when Emma first came. I think it's a good opportunity for a little payback, don't you?"

* * *

Trevor checked on Claire more than once as the day progressed, but she continued to sleep right through the dinner hour. After letting each of the children peek inside the bedroom to assure themselves that their mother was in the house, he, August, and Emma cleaned them up, found nightclothes for them to wear, and tucked their weary bodies into bed. Temporarily, they used two guest rooms, putting Jonah by himself and the four girls together.

Trevor smiled to himself now, thinking about how little Hannah had finally succumbed to sleep with her head on his shoulder as he carried her to bed. Her sweet-smelling hair pressed against his cheek had given him a feeling of completeness like never before.

He approached his own bed now, tucked the blanket around Claire's shoulders, and sat quietly in the chair to observe her. He was at a bit of loss, trying to decide where he was going to sleep. That decision was the one important thing the two of them had not yet talked about. If she did not wake soon, it looked like the chair was going to be his bed for the night.

He leaned back, closed his tired eyes, and relived the long day. That morning, he had wakened in Claire's makeshift bed after finally falling asleep for a few hours, never imagining that he would be a married man by noon.

So, how do you feel about it? He waited for an inner voice to laugh uncontrollably and tell him he had made a huge mistake. *You hardly know the woman...*

Silence. Absolutely nothing. Instead, the idea of spending the next month really getting to know her warmed the stillness. Trevor decided then and there that he would gently and slowly force Claire to open her bruised heart and see what was waiting for her in the future. And what would happen then? Maybe she would remember the security he offered when he held her in the barn for the very first time. Maybe she would see what a good father he could be to her children.

Trevor smiled. He had immensely enjoyed his time with them that night. Bath time was filled with laughter and squeals of joy, because, for once, they were not hungry, they had new clothes to wear in the morning, and they would fall asleep with excited thoughts of the day to follow. He had promised to take them all swimming. For his efforts, he received one precious hug after another from the girls.

Even Jonah, after assuring that his sisters were safe, had finally succumbed and hugged his new father good night. Trevor smiled just thinking about the boy. Emma had whispered to him earlier that Jonah, while stuffing food into his mouth, talked nonstop about everything Trevor had ever done or said. The lad had a hero and it felt damn good to be the man of choice.

I'll make this work even if she fights it. He shifted in the chair and tried to find a more comfortable position. *You might have smiled and said thank you to me, Claire, but I know well enough that one day you won't be tired and your leg will be healed, and then I'm in for it.* Well, fine. He might knock heads with her more than once, but he would come out the victor. No matter what, there was no way she was going to get away. Claire and the kids were there to stay.

He wiggled again, opened his eyes, and finally sat forward to stare with longing at the empty space beside her in the bed.

"Hell," he breathed quietly, "this is my bed." He kicked off his boots, eased his long torso across the top of the blankets, and pulled a soft pillow under his head. She could holler like a banshee and put up a hell of a fuss if she wanted. Trevor did not care; he was bone tired.

* * *

Claire snuggled deeper beneath the quilt, vaguely aware that something lay across her waist. Her body flinched in the state of partial sleepiness, but the weight remained constant. She breathed in the fresh scent of clean sheets, trying to remember where she was as she floated in the gray semi-consciousness.

Her lids fluttered open to the moonlit room, and she stared across the curve of her pillow at a shock of dark, tousled hair. With the small bit of light that streamed through the window, she could just make out the shadow of a beard that covered Trevor's square jaw; one that, up to now, had always been neatly shaved. Claire almost reached out to feel the whiskery texture but, in doing so, he might awaken and she would lose her chance to watch him.

She studied the arc of his eyebrows, which were neither too bushy nor too sparse. Dark, feathered hairs swept gently to each side over closed eyelids. Thick lashes lay against his sun-darkened skin. Her sleepy gaze followed the curve of his muscular bicep beneath the wrinkled shirt, then skittered past his bent elbow. Suddenly she realized that it was his lower arm and hand that lay over her hip.

The weight offered a strange sense of security and, along with it, an odd sense of belonging. Frank had never touched her while they slept. He took only what he needed to gratify himself, and then rolled away to snore away the rest of the night.

Claire's eyes slowly moved back up the length of his comforting arm to study his face. Her heart jumped when she looked into the dark depths that stared back.

"Hello," he whispered gently against the pillow. "I hope you don't mind, but the chair was really uncomfortable."

Surprisingly, Claire found that she did not mind in the least. Even though he was fully clothed and lying on top of the blankets, she was experiencing one of the most intimate moments of her life. Their heads lay only inches apart, and they shared the same pillow. "It's your bed. And, besides, you don't look too dangerous. Better you on the bed than me on the floor." For some reason, she could not help but smile back at him with the silly utterance.

Trevor's hand tightened slightly on her hip. "The lady does have a sense of humor. It's nice to see you smile, Claire." He propped his head up on his other hand and looked down at her. "How are you feeling? Do you need anything?"

She stopped just short of telling him she had everything she needed at that very moment. No matter what, Trevor offered her security; the one thing she had searched for her entire lifetime. Her head moved slightly against the white pillowcase. "I'm fine. I can't believe I slept so long. It must be the middle of the night."

"Well, go back to sleep. I sure plan to. Your kids tuckered me out tonight." A sleepy smile curved his lips. "You can have the next shift. And you'll be happy to know they went to bed with silly grins on their faces and their bellies full. Christ, can they eat." He covered her shoulder with the blanket, sighed softly, and closed his eyes.

Claire stared at the angular planes of his masculine face, finding it hard to believe that she lay on a bed with the handsomest man she had ever met, that they whispered in the dark about nothing, and that he had just covered her to assure she was warm.

A small jolt of satisfaction threaded its way through Claire's body when he rested his arm across her hip again. When his hand left her to find the edge of the blanket, she immediately missed its warmth. She sighed contentedly, closed her eyes, and fell into a peaceful sleep.

Chapter Seventeen

Claire awoke the next morning, rose to an elbow, and sleepily scanned the room. Trevor was nowhere to be found. The only evidence that he had even been beside her the night before was the slight dent where his head had laid on the pillow. She stared longingly at the spot, and then lifted the fluffy cushion to her nose as she thought about the moonlit conversation. She had easily fallen back to sleep afterward, knowing his comforting presence was close at hand if she should need anything.

A slight rustle of clothes in the hallway captured her attention. She waited breathlessly for Trevor to step through the doorway, but instead, two small blonde heads poked around the jamb a second later.

Claire held out her arms and waited for Hannah and Ruth to run across the room for a hug. Sofie and Sue Ellen tumbled onto the bed behind them, careful not to jostle their mother's still-swollen ankle.

"Ma!" they exclaimed in unison and all began to talk at once. Claire heard bits and pieces about the new clothes they wore, about the different foods they had eaten, and the new friends they made over the course of one day. In the face of their childish exuberance, she had to laugh along with them.

That was how Trevor found her. Claire's gray eye's sparkled brightly in the face of her family's excitement. Her complexion had lost the pallor of the day before, evidenced by the glow from the restful sleep of the night.

He stepped into the room, holding a breakfast tray with Jonah by his side. "If this is what happens when you get a good night's sleep, then I'm going to have to let you sleep in every morning."

Her cheeks reddened as her bandaged hands smoothed her unruly curls, which had loosened during the night. "I must look a mess." Her eyes darted away in embarrassment.

Trevor strolled to the bed stand and set the tray down, unable to take his eyes from her flushed cheeks. "On the contrary. You almost look like the picture of health." He glanced down at the small shadow beside him. "What do you think, Jonah? Have you heard your mother laugh like that before?" His gaze swung back to the woman who stared at him from beneath the rumpled bedspread. "I know this is the first time I've ever heard it."

Claire dragged her eyes from her husband's when Jonah bounced up onto the bed to join his sisters. She concentrated on the boy to keep her mind from dwelling on the man. "So, what have you been up to? Are you behaving yourself, young man?"

Her son squirreled a piece of toast from her tray and crossed his legs as he rested against Trevor's pillow. "It's so fun here! Last night I went out to the barn with Trevor's brother, Cole. He's a nice man. This morning, Trevor and I went to help feed all the horses. Trevor let me pick out a pony to ride and, this afternoon, we're goin' for a ride. Just us men. Ma, did you know that Trevor is my pa now? I didn't know that." He gobbled down the rest of the toast in his hand. Jonah literally glowed. "I didn't know that when you marry someone, then that someone becomes your pa. Did you know that?"

Claire darted a quick glance at the man sitting in a nearby chair with Hannah perched on his lap.

Trevor's grin disappeared when their eyes met. He had simply explained to Jonah what being married to their mother entailed as far as the boy and his sisters were concerned. Now he was not too sure he should have broached the subject, because suddenly the happy glow disappeared from Claire's face. "It's all right that I tried to give him an explanation, isn't it? Jonah didn't realize that he was here for good."

She simply continued to stare at her husband. Were they? It was hard to imagine that she would never have to take her children and leave his home—if that was the course the future held for all of them.

Claire smoothed the blanket across her midriff, fighting off a niggling fear that the current nirvana would never have a chance to last. What about her relationship with Trevor? What did he expect? Last night, lying beside him had seemed the most natural thing in the world, but she was in his bed and he most likely was tired—therefore he had climbed in beside her to sleep. What about after her ankle healed? Now that they were married, would he expect more from her?

Claire's mind swirled back to the night in the barn. Being held by him and making love with him was the most wonderful thing she had ever experienced. She had informed him afterward that he saved her from drowning. But was that momentary fleeting experience something to build a solid husband/wife relationship on? She did not think so. Trevor's gaze pierced her with the contemplation she could see resting in his eyes.

"You didn't answer me. I hope I didn't step over the line by trying to explain." He waited hopefully for the woman of the night before to appear.

She finally nodded her head. "It's fine, Trevor. I can't thank you enough for all that you've done so far." Her fingers drifted to Ruth's soft head of hair. The tips tucked her daughter's wispy curls behind one small ear as the girl giggled with her sisters and picked at the tray of food.

Trevor's shoulders visibly fell with a contented sigh. A moment later, he clapped his hands and garnered the children's attention. "I'll tell you what, kids. Why don't we let your ma get herself ready for the day? In a little while, we'll bring her downstairs and give her a little tour of the place. Right now, we can all go down to the kitchen and see what kind of treats Katy's baking."

Squeals of delight echoed in the room as the girls scrambled from their mother's side and filed quickly out the doorway, with Jonah following. Claire shook her head, aiming a leery eye at her husband. "I spent years getting them to listen to me—usually having to repeat myself over and over. With one little snap of the finger, you've got them acting like puppets."

Trevor's head fell back as he chuckled at her observation. "I might be impressing you with what you think is expertise, but I'll fill you in on a little secret. It didn't take long to figure out that you can get those five to do anything if you offer them a treat." He strolled to the open door, hesitated for a moment, and sent her a grin over his shoulder. "But if this place ever runs out of food, we're in for it."

* * *

Claire balanced on the edge of the mattress, clutching one of the four posters on the bed. Slowly, she rose to her feet, testing the strength of her bruised ankle. An instant flash of pain streaked halfway up her calf. She plopped back down, eyeing the crutches across the room. She would have to hop on one foot to retrieve them. Her head came up when someone knocked lightly on the door. "Come in."

Trevor's sister-in-laws appeared a second later with another woman in tow. Instantly, Claire knew the newcomer had to be Trevor's sister. She was a feminine version of Cole. Both possessed hazel eyes and sandy-colored hair. Claire wracked her brain trying to remember her name. Carrie!

Emma crossed the room with two pails of steaming water and entered a small alcove on one side of the room. August and Carrie followed suit. "Good morning, Claire. We thought you might like to take a bath. We picked through some drawers and think we've found some clean clothes that look like they just might fit. How did you sleep last night?"

"Very well, thank you." Leaning slightly on the bed, her gray eyes watched the women fill a tub that sat just on the other side of the small open doorway. A slim eyebrow dipped in consternation.

Cole's sister handed her pail to August, and then crossed to her newest sister-in-law. Her slender palm came out to squeeze Claire's shoulder as she sank to the edge of the bed beside her. "Hi, I'm Trevor's sister, Carrie."

Claire flashed her a quick smile, but never had a chance to say anything else; Carrie already inspected her bandaged palms.

"I'm sure Trevor told you that I'm married to the local doctor. He told me about your brush with the fire and wanted me to take a look at your hands. I'm not my husband, Steve, but I've dealt with a lot of injuries." Very gently, she unwrapped the gauze as she talked. "Trevor sent a messenger over last night. I brought a wheelchair with me, so you can stay off that foot. Is your ankle pretty sore?"

Claire met her caring gaze. "It's nothing I can't tolerate, but I still can't put any weight on it."

"I expect not. It's best to give it a few days to heal before you do that anyway." The bandages were finally off. Claire's hands were red, but the small blisters were already healing. "Ouch, that must have hurt a few days back. Well, it doesn't look like there's any infection and that's good. I think we'll leave them unwrapped. After you've bathed, I'll put some salve on them and have you fixed up in no time." Carrie gathered the soiled gauze and stuffed the pieces into a pocket of her dress. She looked up again to see Claire studying Cole's wife, August, as she hauled more buckets of water into the alcove. "Were you injured anywhere else?"

The woman on the bed shrugged her shoulders. "No, just some aching muscles because of the fall. Really, I'm fine. I feel rather silly. I don't need to be waited on. I would rather help you all." Once again, her eyes shifted to the dark-skinned woman who giggled with Emma.

"Well, there'll be plenty of time for that." Carrie patted her hand. "I'll take the splint off. When you're done with your bath, I'll come back up and wrap the ankle again."

It was not long before Carrie inspected Claire's bare and swollen ankle with a practiced eye. She sat on the chair next to the bed when she was finished.

"Now, first off, I personally want to say welcome. I'm really going to enjoy getting to know you. We've all waited a long time for our brother to find a wife." Carrie's gaze skittered about the room for a second—just before she inhaled deeply. "All right, at the risk of you thinking the three of us are gossip mongers, I'm going to speak for all of us. We're absolutely dying to get the whole story about how your marriage happened. Trevor is being his usual obstinate self and dropping only tidbits of information."

Claire observed Emma and August instantly appear from behind the alcove screen. Surprisingly, she did not feel intimidated by any one of them; so far, she had been treated wonderfully. *But,* she wondered, *how will they look at me after discovering I come from absolutely nothing?*

It was easy to see how Emma and Carrie fit into the role of well-bred society. But what about August, the Indian woman? She looked out of place with her dark skin and exotic eyes, yet seemed to fit in perfectly with the other women. The one common denominator between all three was their class and beauty. Claire blinked absently when Carrie blurted out a question.

"How long have you known Trevor? We're just trying to figure out how long he hid you from us."

Claire's cheeks turned a light pink. "He really didn't hide me from any of you. I met him in June." She spied the quick glances the other's darted at one another. "I can see you're all calculating the short amount of time. Please understand. This marriage was not planned."

Carrie belted out a loud cackle, accompanied by smiling eyes, then waved her hand in the air. "Excuse me for laughing, but I have a feeling this is going to be a better story than I thought." She watched as Emma and August took seats, with eager grins splitting their faces. "You've got all of us hooked now. You've got to give us the entire story."

Claire was stunned. These women, who were her new family, were totally different from any other people of consequence that she had ever met—and she was completely at ease with them. She still would not take the chance of making her husband look like the cuckold for their enjoyment, however. "There isn't a whole lot to tell. I met Trevor through Jonah. Your brother-in-law was kind and wanted to help me out. My husband died two years ago, and I was trying to find a way to keep my home from foreclosure. Knowing that there wasn't any chance of that happening any longer, I took my children north and ended up in Biwabik."

"Did he know that's where you were going?" Emma's mind spun. Trevor never mentioned anything about Claire before he left to visit Moose and his wife.

Claire's head shook. "No. It was a coincidence that he discovered I was at a local clinic. He came there the night of the fire, took the kids, and brought them back to a place I was renting, because I couldn't take them home myself."

Emma's lips pursed and her feminine brow furrowed. "But that was only a few days ago."

Claire nodded. "He came back the next morning with everything I owned packed in the back of a wagon—and informed me that we were all coming here to stay until I recuperated."

"I have to ask—" Carrie wondered out loud. "When did you two decide to get married? If I've got the days figured out here, you had to have married Trevor after he picked you up. That was yesterday morning."

Claire's eyes moved from one woman to the other. "I know I'm not the sort of person you're used to associating with. I've never had anything that amounted to much." Now her gaze moved, taking in the beauty of the room. "I've never even been inside a home such as this one. But I still know what's right and what's wrong. I told Trevor that it wasn't proper for a widow with five children to move in with a bachelor. It's simply not done. That's when he insisted I marry him." Her reply was not quite fact, but not a mistruth either. She shrugged, waiting for the other shoe to fall. "Honestly, I wasn't looking to be married again. He simply pointed out that I had no other choice."

Carrie stood with a sigh. "I agree with him. You made the right decision."

"But how can you all accept it so easily?" Claire had to know. "You don't even know me."

The other woman bent to pick up an empty pail with each hand. "Because I know my brother, and his decision is good enough for me. You're welcome here, Claire, and so are your children. I speak for all of us."

Emma rose from the chair, her chin nodding in agreement. "We'll leave you alone so you can bathe. Do you think you'll be able to manage the tub by yourself?"

"Oh, yes. If you'll just bring the crutches over here."

August retrieved the walking aides and brought them to Claire, then turned as the other women were on their way out. "I will be down shortly," she told them. "I would like to visit with Claire for a few more minutes." She had felt the other woman's eyes on her earlier and knew that, most likely, the perusal came because August was so different than the others. The Sioux woman waited until the door closed before taking a seat once more. A gentle smile rested on her lips. "Do you mind?"

Claire's head shook as she waited to see what August wanted to say.

The Indian woman's dark brown eyes moved about the room. "This is a beautiful house, isn't it?"

"I've never seen such a lovely home."

"I remember the first time I saw it. In fact, that was the first time

I was in a white man's home. The idea was unacceptable to me, especially when my people were on the run from soldiers. This family welcomed me and has stayed true to our friendship and love ever since. My husband could not love me more. The wisest thing I ever did in my life was to believe his promises when he said he would take care of me forever. I have lived as you, Claire—differently maybe, but still the same. Being on the outside is difficult at times. I understand that you think you will not be wanted here, but you should put your fears to rest."

Claire pressed her palms to her cheeks. "Is it that apparent? I was so frightened when I arrived yesterday. I'm not like them. I've never had money. I'm not beautiful, nor can I pass as a true lady."

August leaned forward and studied her new sister-in-law. "Every person has beauty. Because you have lived differently means nothing. You must remember that." She sat back again. "May I ask you a question?" She did not wait for Claire's permission. "How do you feel about Trevor? I ask only because it is easy to see that he has many feelings for you. And, I think he is very happy to have your children here, also."

"What do you mean—he has feelings for me?" Claire felt a small bit of excitement jump in her chest. Maybe Trevor had said something to August. Suddenly, she wished it were true.

"Trevor is a fine man—much like his brothers are. For some reason, you have captured his attention and most likely a portion of his heart. I saw it in his eyes when we spoke yesterday—and in yours only a short while ago."

Claire's gaze fell to her lap. "I don't know what you're talking about."

"I suspect there is more to your story, but it is for you to decide if and when to tell it. We all have secrets that we hold close. You must give this new arrangement a chance to work. When the time comes, open your heart—you will be amazed at what you will find."

August rose. "Think on my words, Claire. I will come and check on you later. I, too, am happy that Trevor has finally found a wife. It is good to have another sister." Without further words, August turned and left Claire thinking quietly about the strange conversation.

* * *

Claire lay in the hip tub, hardly daring to believe the luxury of the caressing, bubble-laden water that heated her body to a near state of oblivion. The final fears of the morning floated away, along with the small billows of steam that dissipated into the air. Having added the last pails of hot water to the bath, she tipped her head back to enjoy the short time left to herself.

She raised a slender arm and extended it upwards as she scrubbed the length with a soft sponge. She did not even try to stifle the satisfied groan in her throat when warm droplets trickled down her skin. The idea that it was close to noon and she lounged about with no thoughts of work for the day was absolutely sinful and wicked—but a contented smile curved her lips anyway as her lids fluttered shut with a sigh.

Claire continued to bask in the warm, soapy liquid until the soft click of the bedroom door caused her to tilt her head. She glanced at the edge of the privacy screen. *Hmmm...must have been my imagination...*

* * *

Trevor stood outside the door to his master suite, listening for any sound from within. August had left Claire over an hour earlier and, still, she had not appeared. With a frown furrowing his brow, he made the decision to check on his wife.

Quietly, he opened the door and stepped into the room. She was not in the bed or sitting anywhere in the room. He eyed the privacy screen that sat on one side of the room and silently crossed the carpeted floor to check behind it.

The breath left Trevor's lungs when he found Claire relaxing in the tub. His appreciative gaze took in the lashes spiked above her shining cheekbones and the curly blonde hair piled into ringlets atop her head. Only her shoulders and the rise of her breasts could be seen above the foaming bubbles. His stomach flipped at the warmth that suffused his blood. Trevor allowed himself a moment to study the picture of his wife's contentment before he spoke her name. "Claire?"

Instantly, her eyes flew open, a squeal of fright jumped from her throat, and she sank lower into the water. Her frightened gaze immediately scanned the area for something to cover her nakedness.

Seeing nothing, she submerged her body even further beneath the water's surface until the warm, sudsy liquid caressed her rounded chin. Claire pierced her husband with a querulous frown when a smile creased his clean-shaven face. The absence of whiskers gave way to a strong angular jaw and sparkling green eyes. Her angered mind was forced to acknowledge that he was one of the finest specimens of a man she had ever seen. "I'm trying to finish my bath. I'll thank you to leave."

"Finish your bath? It looked to me like you were sleeping. If you're not done though, I'd be more than willing to help you finish."

Claire gasped at his audacity. "I am quite able to wash myself."

One corner of his mouth turned up. "But in a business relationship, one partner always helps the other."

A flash of callused fingers against her naked skin shot through her brain, but she shoved the memory away. "Well, this partner is telling you to go away now!" She was instantly terrified, but not of the man. It was the unknown brazen shivers crawling down her spine that she feared most. "Please, Trevor...I know you're my husband, but..."

"I'll wait outside. Just holler when you're ready. I've got the wheelchair, so you don't have to use the crutches." He turned and disappeared from sight.

A moment later, Claire heard the click of the doorknob. She let her head drop to the edge of the tub, waiting for the pounding of her heart to subside.

* * *

Trevor closed the door behind him and ran two shaky hands through the thick waves at his temples. Closing his eyes for a moment, he expelled the air from his lungs. The vision of Claire in the tub and imagining her wet body beneath the bubbles had him tottering on the edge of restraint. Rubbing his palms over his face, he plopped into the wheelchair and stared at the empty hall around him.

He would start today. When Claire was finished behind the closed door, Trevor would begin his assault. *To hell with the so-called business arrangement.* He wanted a real wife, as well as a partner, just as his brothers had. He would pursue her relentlessly and make it absolutely impossible for Claire not to fall in love with him...as deeply in love as he was with her.

    His shook his head, leaned it against the back of the chair, and stared at the ceiling. It was nothing short of amazing how one tiny, willowy woman with five kids had set his heart on fire for the first time in his life.

Chapter Eighteen

Emma and Carrie observed the small faces seated about the butcher-block table in the kitchen as the children enjoyed their lunch. August and Katy hurried from one child to another as they poured fresh milk into emptied glasses.

The addition of Claire's children to the Wilkins' descendents lent an air of upheaval as high-pitched giggles erupted, filled glasses tipped, and crumbs from the countless sandwiches scattered beneath the wooden chairs and stools.

Emma pinched the bridge of her nose when yet another overturned glass sent milk spraying across the surface of the table; she watched silently as August quickly sopped up the liquid. She sent a sidelong glance at Carrie. "I really thought this would be easy. Instead, I feel like a schoolmarm on the last day of school."

A snort sounded in Carrie's throat just before she leapt forward to straighten Hannah on her chair before the little girl hit the floor. "I think this is a hoot."

"Sure you do," returned Emma as she sectioned apples at the counter. "You get to leave and go home."

Carrie patted Hannah's back and returned to the counter. "Has Trevor said anything about moving into his house?"

Emma nodded. "He's hired someone to finish up the inside. We're not supposed to say anything to Claire yet. He wants it to be a surprise." She piled apple wedges onto a plate, keeping an eye on how August managed the wild group, then swung her gaze back to Carrie. "What do you expect is going on between the two of them? We'd all be fools to think either one of them has told us the full story."

"I don't know," Carrie replied. "What's obvious is that there's more emotion there than they're portraying. Claire, I think, is holding back and Trevor gives himself away every time he speaks of her."

Emma leaned against the counter and crossed her arms, deep in thought. "Your right, and you haven't seen them together yet. He's like a puppy when he looks at her. In all the years I've known him, his attitude has always been rather cavalier when it came to discussing marriage. But, here he is, finishing up the house for a surprise with the enthusiasm of a child waiting for Christmas. I, for one, couldn't be happier that Claire is here."

August crossed from the table to the counter and lifted the plate of apples from the surface. She looked from one woman to the other. "I heard bits of your conversation. I am happy Trevor has found someone, also. I tried to speak to Claire after you left about letting the future happen as it will. She feels out of place here, because of her past. I tried to reassure her that she is welcome and that one's history does not play a part in this family's acceptance. I know that to be true."

Emma lovingly squeezed August's arm.

"I also think we should plan a gathering here at the ranch to introduce Claire to Trevor's friends. It will be a way for her to feel more at ease knowing that he is proud to announce his marriage. She is very insecure about how she will be received."

Emma shrugged a slender shoulder. "It's a good idea, but we really can't take the chance. I don't want to jeopardize your and Cole's safety. We've worked hard to assure no one knows you and Cole lived through the battle at Wounded Knee. If someone discovers you two are here..." She shook her head. "No, I just don't think it's worth the risk."

August smiled. "There is no other way. With all these children to care for, it would be too hard to hold the party somewhere else. Do not worry about Cole and myself. We will take our son and daughter to stay at one of the logging cabins." Her eyes twinkled with instant humor. "I will have no problem filling the day when I have my husband to myself."

Carrie laughed uproariously when August's eyes widened slightly and her slender eyebrows bounced over dark lashes just before she returned to the children. "I imagine not," she called after her. "You've sure changed your tune since you first arrived."

August raised a sassy chin. "I have learned from the best. And we need to make Claire feel comfortable."

"All right." Emma smiled at August's earlier wit. "Let's talk to Trevor about it and see what he thinks. It would be fun. We haven't had a party here in quite awhile."

* * *

Claire appeared in the open doorway of the suite. She balanced on the crutches, and her darting eyes were everywhere but on her husband. Though her hair was pulled back into the tight bun and her bodice was buttoned up to beneath her chin, Trevor observed his wife in a different light than earlier. He knew now that her pale skin flushed in the heat of warm water and that her blonde ringlets framed high cheekbones when she pulled them atop her head to keep the curly length dry. Already her features had lost the weary look born of constant worry after receiving a much-needed rest.

Without a word, he shot out of the wheelchair and helped Claire to sit. Leaning the crutches against the wall, he flashed her a smile. "Now that you're seated safely in your chariot, I'd like you to meet someone. Remember when I told you about Mamie?"

Claire nodded silently.

"She's waiting to meet you. I told her we'd visit this afternoon." Trevor dropped his hands to the handles on the back of the chair and wheeled Claire down the hallway.

They paused at the top of the stairs, and her eyes widened slightly before she glanced up at him. "You're not going to push me down the stairs in this thing, are you?"

He raised a dark brow and pretended to give her words some thought.

"Trevor!"

A good-humored chuckle sounded in her ear as he bent to whisk her body into his arms. Claire automatically clamped her arms around his neck when he took the first step downward, then took a moment to eye his masculine features. "I think I've discovered something about you."

"And what would that be?"

"That you love to tease."

A smile curved his mouth. "I think I've discovered something about you, too."

She tipped her chin and waited silently for his conclusion.

"You've got a fun, yet womanly side that you don't let people see very often." They reached the bottom of the staircase. Trevor placed Claire gently on a bench and, before he turned to retrieve the wheelchair, he hesitated with his hand on the railing. "I plan to nurture that side until I never see you scowl again."

Claire watched his broad back when he paused with a foot on the bottom step before returning to the second floor for her chair. Her cheeks instantly turned pink when he sent her an impish wink before heading back up. Wringing her hands, she wondered what the future really would bring, still finding it hard to believe how quickly her life had changed because of one handsome man.

* * *

Trevor wheeled Claire around the main floor of the ranch house until they had collected all of her children. From the last stop in the kitchen, the entire group headed for Mamie's room at the far end of an adjoining hallway.

Trevor stopped before the old woman's door and looked at the small faces around him. "Okay, everyone. Mamie's expecting us all to behave. She's been waiting to meet each and every one of you, but we're not going to make too much noise because she's been sick. Do we have a deal that we'll all be on our best behavior?"

The children all nodded their heads in agreement, but their mother began to doubt the idea of hauling them all into a sickroom. "Maybe they should meet her later. If she's ill..."

"Mamie will have a fit if she doesn't get to meet all of the children. Just this morning, she went on a tirade because they haven't been in to see her. And she's also chomping at the bit to meet you."

Claire's trembling hands smoothed her already tidy hair. "But what if she doesn't like us?"

Trevor reached for the doorknob. "Believe me. You're going to pass with flying colors."

The door opened and Claire's eyes immediately flew to the old woman who lay in the bed. Trevor wheeled her in, and her entourage followed. Mamie's skin was as black as the night; her contrasting curly hair had turned white, confirming the woman's extended years.

Mamie's eyes opened and her ebony cheeks rounded above her smile. "Oh, lordy...finally I gets to meet the woman of my boy's dreams." She lifted her hands and motioned for everyone to move closer to the bed. "Come! Come so as I can see your angel faces!"

Trevor positioned Claire's wheelchair beside the bed, hiked Hannah into his arms, and gathered the other awestruck children around him. Settling his hand on his wife's shoulder, he tipped his head in her direction. "Mamie, this is Claire."

The old woman's body shook in the bed as she cackled with glee. "I knows who she is. Tsk, tsk." Her head wagged. "My, but you is a handsome woman. My Trevor knows how to pick 'em."

Claire immediately held out her arm and shook the dark fingers. "It's very nice to meet you, Mamie." She took Jonah's hand next and gently pulled her son to her side. "This is my oldest child and only son, Jonah."

Mamie's arms came out again. "Come here, boy, and gives Mamie a hug."

He stepped forward with round, uncertain eyes and let the old woman squeeze him, but his worried gaze never left Trevor.

Mamie watched as the boy took a quick step back to his mother's side, then rested her hand across her heavy bosom. "Lordy...this be a fine day in the makin'. I can go to my grave knowin' all my boys will be taken care of! Yessiree. Now, who are these beautiful lil' girls lined up here?"

Trevor suppressed a chuckle at the little one's stunned expressions. He settled Hannah more securely in his embrace. "This here is Hannah, the youngest. Her sisters are Sofie, Ruth, and Sue Ellen," he added as he indicated each one.

Mamie studied each girl over the rim of her spectacles. "Beautiful, just beautiful." Her gaze swung to Claire. "And it be easy to see why when their ma is so handsome. Aint she, Trevor? I bet you be thinkin' she's the prettiest thing around."

"Yup," he answered as his gaze slipped to his wife. "I'd have to agree with you on that one."

Claire's cheeks flushed, realizing that she was the object of her husband's perusal once again.

"Ha! You gots her to blushin' now, boy," Mamie hooted when she observed the younger woman once more. "New brides will be blushin' a time or two, now won't they? Yessiree, that's what they does sometimes." She leaned forward and patted Claire's hand. "Trevor, why don't you take these young tots for a walk in the sunshine while I have a little visit with their ma?"

Claire's eyes widened in instant panic. She did not want to be left alone with anyone but her husband. *Why does this old woman want to speak with me?* She did not dare, however, challenge the request as Trevor directed the children to the door. Her worried eyes met his before he left the room.

Trevor gave her a thumbs-up. "I won't be too long. When you're ready, just wheel yourself to the kitchen. Katy can come and get me outside." He allowed the children to file out before him, then disappeared.

The room became suddenly silent. Claire peeked up to see Mamie's scrutinizing eyes and instinctively squared her shoulders while she waited for some condescending comment to leave the woman's lips. Why else would she want to speak with her alone?

"You can settle down, child. I'm thinkin' you be ready to leap out of that ol' chair."

Claire's eyes widened at Mamie's intuitive comment.

"I wanted to talk to you alone without any pryin' ears. I never know if I'll live to the next minute, so gotta say my stuff now. Girl, I couldna be happier 'bout you and my boy, Trevor. You is exactly what I bin wishin' for."

"Excuse me?" Claire was mystified at the direction of the conversation.

"You heard me. It does my ol' heart good to know he'll be lovin' someone like you after I'm gone. I don't care what I bin hearin'. You two are tied, that for sure enough, fast courtship or not."

"Miss Mamie...I want to be honest with you. Trevor married me just to help me out."

"You mean so *you* can be helpin' *him* out."

"What?" Claire had a difficult time following Mamie's strange way of stating things.

Mamie chuckled, then puckered her thick lips for a moment. "You don't see what's happenin', do ya, girl?" She did not wait for an answer. "That boy had me goin' for years, tellin' me he would neva marry because he liked his lonely life. Lordy, it just took him longer than his brothers to smarten up that beefcake head o' his. It just took some years 'til he found you. I tolds him you were out there." The old woman leaned deeper into her pillow, suddenly worn from the visit even though not much time had passed. "I don't know what you runnin' from, but I can see ya is scared. You just have ta figure it out in your head—'til then, you let that boy keep your heart for you. You'll be findin' your way back to it once and agin. Yessiree, I seen this before in this household. Mamie knows."

* * *

That night, Claire worked her way down the upstairs hallway to the bedroom suite. A smile tugged at the corners of her lips as she turned the wheels of the chair, thinking about her daughters' tired excitement as they relayed the news of the second day in their new home. Now, after tucking them all into bed and not knowing where Trevor had gotten himself off too, she decided to head for her own room.

Just my room, or Trevor's, too? That single thought had Claire on edge. She tried to discuss the subject with her new husband earlier, but someone always seemed to be around. Claire wheeled inside the suite, then turned back and eyed the door. *What should I do? Leave it open or close it? Is he coming in or not? Where is he going to sleep? If I close the door, I might not have a chance to speak with him in private. If I keep it open, he might think...*

Claire decided to stay on middle ground; she positioned the door half-closed, then wheeled across the room and stared at the massive bed that sat against the east wall. What did she want? She spun the chair away from the tempting sight and headed behind the screen, finding it easier to concentrate on something other than the coming night.

Maneuvering the chair as best she could for privacy, Claire rose and gingerly put a small bit of weight on her ankle as she hurriedly undressed and donned a nightgown; she was not willing to chance another unexpected appearance by Trevor. She folded her clothes neatly over the seat of a wooden chair, threaded her arms into the sleeve of a robe, and managed to get back into the wheelchair without it shooting out from beneath her. A sigh of relief escaped into the small space. "Thank goodness I don't have to do anything else," she muttered to no one. Just undressing on one tottering leg had been a workout. She swiveled the chair and headed back around the screen.

"And just what else were you planning to do?"

A squeak of fright left Claire's throat when her eyes darted up to where Trevor lounged in an overstuffed chair before the unlit fireplace. Her hand fluttered over her chest. "You scared me. I didn't hear you come in."

"That's because you were busy talking to yourself—or someone. I almost looked behind the screen to see who was with you."

"If you..." The words died in her throat. "You're making fun of me again, aren't you? Paybacks aren't fun, Trevor. Better watch over your shoulder."

The dark brows danced over his gleaming eyes upon her attempt at humor. He was happy that she seemed more relaxed in his company. Trevor watched as she wheeled across the planked floor toward a pitcher of water sitting on a small table. Claire silently poured herself a glass, and then turned to stare at him. "Can I talk to you about something?"

"Shoot."

"Yesterday, I fell asleep in the afternoon and didn't wake up until the middle of the night. There was nothing else to be done, considering what time it was. This is your room, however."

Here it comes, old man...

"I just don't know how all this is supposed to work, Trevor. I feel...I feel awkward asking you this, but...where are you going to sleep tonight? We never had a chance to discuss it today."

He sat forward in his chair, but before he could say anything, Claire beat him to the punch.

"I also don't know how much you've told your family about us. Carrie, Emma, and August did their best today to get all the details."

"Don't feel bad. My brothers dogged me all afternoon, too."

Claire smoothed the cotton robe over her thighs, instinctively felt his gaze on her, and peeked up. "What have you told them? Do they know the reasons I'm here? Do they know about..."

"If you're talking about the night of the storm, your secret is safe, Claire. I would never tell anyone about what happened between us, unless you wished them to know." He watched her shoulders drop with a sigh of relief at his answer. "I didn't realize that you were so worried about that little fact getting out. I could have set your mind at ease this morning. They also don't know that we've got a business arrangement of sorts. I figured the less they knew, the less they'd harp on both of us."

"Thank you for that. I felt the same way today. I wasn't about to say anything that would make them ask you even more questions the next time I wasn't around."

He chuckled quietly. "Well, thank you. Looks like we're partners in crime. They can be an overbearing bunch when they want to."

She smiled at his observation. "I don't know if overbearing is the right word. I guess, being the newcomer, I can see how close you all are. Familiarity breeds intrusion, Trevor, whether it's intentional or not. It must have been nice growing up that way; to have people in your life who will always step forward to assure your best interests, and also having brothers and a sister to share things with at the end of the day." Claire mused over that fact, lost in gentle thoughts as she became quiet and stared at the dark sky outside the window.

"That's what we're doing now, and I like how it feels."

She turned her head. "Hmmm?"

"We're sharing our thoughts of the day." He hesitated. "That's what married people are supposed to do. If one has a problem, the other helps to find an answer."

"I never had that with Frank," she stated quietly. "He made fun of my thoughts. I was told that dreams are only for the lucky and the rich. After a time, I discovered it was better to simply keep everything to myself, rather than have my hopes dashed to the ground."

Trevor rose and crossed to where his wife sat in the wheelchair. He would give anything to wipe away the years of uncertainty. *But hasn't the past shaped the woman of the present?* He reached out to lightly brush her soft cheek with his fingertips. He felt more than saw her swallow. "I would never do that to you. You know that, don't you?"

Their eyes locked as she sifted his words in her mind. Slowly, her head nodded. "I know you wouldn't. You've more than proven that. It's just rather hard for me to trust anyone at times."

The room was silent until Trevor cleared his throat. "Do you need help getting into bed?"

"No, I can do it." She wheeled the chair closer to the bed and used her arms to lever her body, struggling a bit when the chair refused to remain stationary. A moment later, Claire was hauled upward into her husband's arms. He set her gently on the quilt.

"Thank you," she stated timidly.

"You're welcome. Now, let's get back to the original question."

She nodded in agreement.

"Where do you want me to sleep tonight? The kids have the guest rooms. Last night the chair just didn't seem an option when I was so tired, but it's your call tonight. Just bear in mind that, if we have separate rooms, we'll be harassed on a daily basis." A tiny smile tugged at his mouth as he watched the hesitancy grow in her eyes. "I promise I'll stay on top of the covers if you'll give me one side of the bed. I can be trusted. Honestly."

Claire eyed him from beneath slanted brows as she slid to the other side of the bed and disappeared beneath the quilt. "It's your bed, and I don't feel like being under the microscope. Just remember, you're the one who said you could be trusted."

He waited until she shoved a pillow closer to his side of the mattress. Turning the lamp down until only a small glow flickered across the wall, he climbed onto the bed.

Claire missed his surprise in the darkened room when she sat up and leaned down to drag a spare quilt from the bottom of the bed and into her arms. She handed it to him. "Take it. I'll sleep better without the guilt of knowing you'll be cold once morning gets here." She plopped back down and rolled onto her side, facing away from the center of the bed.

Trevor lay on his back and stared at the shadows on the ceiling, totally amazed that she had so easily let him share the same bed—even though they had at least a foot of space and layers of bunched blankets between them. Sleeping in the same room would give him many opportunities to be alone in her company.

He did not want to go to sleep. He wanted to whisper with his wife in the dark; he wanted to recapture the air of intimacy they shared the night before; he wanted to bask in the warmth of belonging to someone, no matter what the conditions. Remembering how comfortable the middle of the night conversation actually was, he decided to tell her something now, rather than waiting until morning. "Say, Claire?"

"Yes?" She hoped her response was not too eager. She had tried to come up with something to talk to him about, but fell short of a plausible excuse.

"Emma and Carrie spoke to me today. They want to have a small wedding reception for us. How do you feel about that?" He heard Claire's sigh before she rolled onto her back and silently stared at the ceiling.

Finally, she responded. "What did you tell them?"

"That I needed to discuss it with you."

She smiled. That was nice. "Do you really feel it's necessary? Your family has done so much for me and the kids already."

"They're not the type to keep a tally. A wedding reception is rather standard in these parts. I think they're looking for an excuse to show you off."

A tiny snort rattled in Claire's throat. "I hardly think so. More like they want to parade you around. There's one thing I've learned since we arrived yesterday. Everyone absolutely loves the fact that you're married. I could have been a monkey and their reaction would have been the same."

"Doesn't say much for me, now does it?"

Claire giggled, took a chance on what his response might be, and rolled onto her hip to face him. "Doesn't say much for me, you mean."

Trevor bunched the pillow beneath his head and settled himself on his side. "I'm not following you."

"Think about it." She folded her hands and tucked them between her cheek and the soft pillowcase. "They all wanted you married. Is that one of the reasons you asked me?"

"Claire, don't even..."

"No, I want you to answer me honestly. This whole marriage thing happened so fast. The last forty-eight hours has rolled by like a dream. I'm just waiting to wake up and face the future."

"The future is you and the kids, here...with me."

Claire nibbled her bottom lip for a moment with indecision. "Is it really? What kind of marriage do you envision over the years?"

His brow furrowed.

"See? You can't even answer that, but I can. You never planned to marry—at least that's what I've heard from everyone. It's like a big joke that you brought home a wife and a bunch of kids in a package deal. We're not young adults just starting out, Trevor. Most people our age have ten to fifteen years of marriage behind them already. They're settled and know where they're going. I don't. I don't know what to expect. I'm contrary to everything you're accustomed to in a woman. I'm not young, I'm not rich, and I'm certainly not beautiful."

Trevor reached out until his fingertips brushed her cheek once more.

The slight touch made Claire long to lay her head on his shoulder and try to find some semblance of hope for the future. She stayed where she was, however. What would he think?

"Don't say that, Claire. From the first time I saw you, I was intrigued. I saw a totally different person than how you see yourself. I saw a mother who worked tirelessly to beat the odds—a willowy blonde who would take on the world to protect her family. I admire you and, despite the horrible years you've had, I'm almost glad they happened, because they brought me to you."

Claire's chin quivered with emotion, but she pressed her face tightly against the back of her hand. *Tell him what you want!...I can't! The future is too uncertain...*

Trevor's warm breath whispered across her cheek as he sighed. "So, here we are. Two people tossed together because of fate. I, for one, am not sorry, so don't ever think that I am. When I asked you to marry me, I meant it. So quit worrying about the future. I plan to look after all of you."

But do you plan to love all of us? Do you think you ever could? Claire's eyes followed the line of his masculine jaw until her gaze rested on the wavy hair against the stark white pillow. Her heart pounded and the force of her emotions made the breath catch in her throat. Sometime between the day she admonished him on the street and the very short moment ago when he promised to take care of her, Claire discovered a warm love for the man beside her. Her fingers curled tightly around the pillow as she battled to keep her hand where it was.

All you would have to do is reach out. You're not a young girl.

You're a mature woman who needs to take the first step if you ever want to have what you've always dreamed of...

"So, what about the reception? Should we let Emma know to start planning?"

Claire shrugged her shoulder. "I guess."

"Is there anything you need before we go to sleep?"

Claire bit the inside of her cheek momentarily. "No, I'm fine."

Trevor dragged the quilt over her shoulder. "Well, just let me know. Goodnight—and don't worry about the future." He rolled to his other side, his teeth clenched in frustration. For a moment, he had almost broken his own promise to take their new relationship slowly.

Imagine what she'd have thought if I had pulled her into my arms...

Chapter Nineteen

Claire and Trevor gathered around the oak dining room table with the rest of the family to finalize plans for the reception that would be held in their honor in only one week. As much as the new Mrs. Wilkins was apprehensive about the party that had quickly escalated to something far larger than she imagined, Claire kept her feelings to herself.

Originally, she had imagined a small, intimate gathering of close family friends, but somewhere in the shuffle the reception had become the biggest party of the summer. Over the past three weeks, she had found a measure of contentment while building solid friendships with the ranch's womenfolk. Her sisters-in-law made it easy for Claire to find a niche in the daily workings of the home, sharing small tasks as her ankle and hands healed.

How could she step forward with enthusiasm when the thought of being surrounded by cultured society woman made her shake in her shoes? She acknowledged the current sick feeling in the pit of her stomach, and then struggled to push it aside when her husband laughed beside her. Trevor's arm rested on the back of her chair now, and he gave her shoulders a squeeze.

"I think that's a great idea, don't you, Claire?"

She glanced around the table when she heard her name and noticed everyone's eyes on her. "I'm sorry, my mind was somewhere else."

Trevor chuckled. "This is all a little overwhelming, isn't it? Emma just suggested that you and she head for Duluth to find a new dress for the party."

"I...I hadn't even thought about that. How far away is Duluth?"

"It's about a four hour ride from the ranch," Emma replied. "I think we'll have to stay overnight so we're not rushed. I wouldn't have suggested it, but seeing that you're walking around now, it would be fun to spend some time together."

Claire panicked. "What about the children? I can't just leave them. In fact, except for that one night I spent at the clinic, I've never been away from them overnight." Trevor took her hand in his—something he had been doing on a regular basis over the last four weeks. Every time he touched her, Claire's heart thumped in response—just as it did now.

"Don't worry about them. I'll keep them so busy they won't even know you're gone."

"But—"

"No buts. You go with Emma and don't worry about a thing."

Again, Claire felt that she was being railroaded, but there was nothing she could do about it in the face of everyone's enthusiasm.

* * *

The next morning, Trevor escorted his wife to the waiting coach after she had said a teary goodbye to Jonah and the girls in the kitchen. The children handled the idea of their mother leaving for an overnight stay far better than she did. Trevor finally had to force her from the room as Katy smiled at the other woman's resistance and continued to fill breakfast plates with the August's help.

As the couple stepped onto the porch, Claire adjusted the beautiful hat Emma had loaned her for the trip. In fact, everything she wore was on loan—including the clothes packed in the valise strapped to the back of the coach. Claire had never worn such fine garments in her life and struggled not to feel out of place because of them.

She glanced up to see Dougan in the driver's seat. Emma was already inside the carriage, leaning out the window and giving Tyler one last kiss goodbye. Seeing the intimate display, Claire's cheeks suddenly paled as she waited to see what her own husband would do in the company of the others. The last time he kissed her was at their wedding a month ago. As much as she looked forward to lying in the dark and laughing with her husband every night, not once did he make an attempt to make love to her or even kiss her goodnight.

The pressure of his fingers at her elbow halted Claire as they strolled down the wooden walkway. She turned to face him, finding comfort in the fact that he gently placed a hand on each of her shoulders.

"Now, you have the list of shops where you can charge under my name?"

"I have it, but I won't be needing all those names. I just plan to buy a simple dress, Trevor. I really don't have to go to Duluth. Emma has plenty of material in the sewing room. I could easily make myself something to wear. It will be far cheaper than spending money on a store bought dress."

"And how many times have I told you that this little trip will be good for you? Have you ever had a chance to just go shopping for the thrill of it?"

Claire rolled her eyes beneath the starched brim of her hat. "I hardly think so."

"Then have a wonderful time—and don't come back until you have a new wardrobe and clothes for all the kids. I mean it. I can see by the set of your jaw that you're just putting up with me for the moment and plan to be frugal once you're there. I'll have none of that. If I have to, I'll have a little talk with Emma before you leave."

"This is so ridiculous. I'm worried about leaving the kids, Trevor. It's so foolish to go and spend all this money—"

The words died in her throat when Trevor unexpectedly lowered his mouth and captured her lips. His mouth feathered across hers and a soft moan escaped her throat as he pulled her gently against his broad chest.

Claire's knees nearly buckled beneath her. Totally taken aback at his intimate goodbye, she could do nothing but cling to him and wait for the kiss to end. It did not, and a small part of Claire's brain registered the sound of Tyler's laughter as it floated across the yard.

Trevor finally lifted his head. Green eyes smoldered for an instant before he blinked his driving passion away. "I guess you should get going. I'm going to miss you tonight."

Claire's tongue moistened her lips as she panted to regain her equilibrium. Her round gray eyes stared up at him. "Why did you do that?"

Trevor used one finger to lift her chin until her mouth closed shut. "Isn't it customary for a husband to kiss his wife goodbye?"

"I...I guess." *But that was more than a simple goodbye kiss...*

He clasped her hand with a twinkle in his eye and led his red-cheeked wife the rest of the way to the carriage. Carefully, he handed her up the single step, moved back to stand beside his brother and latch the door closed.

* * *

Claire's gaze continually flitted about the interior of the hotel restaurant, hardly believing that she sat in the center of such opulence as her fork pushed the food around her plate. She was too excited to eat. At first, she did her best to pretend the high-class women draped with sparkling jewels and the unfamiliar elegance of the building did not affect her, but she finally gave into the childlike enthusiasm of feeling liberated for the first time in her life. There were no children to tuck in, no decisions to be made, and no one harassing her about overdue payments. A flash of Trevor's handsome face filled her mind for a second. She wished he was by her side to enjoy the evening with her.

Emma sipped her wine across the table, noticing how her sister-in-law's eyes glittered like brushed silver. The heightened color of Claire's face complemented the newly-coiffed hairdo that resembled golden strands of the sun. The woman's curls literally bounced as she swiveled her head constantly to take in everything around her. Emma's eyes followed the modest neckline of a new dark blue dress she insisted Claire purchase earlier that day. *I wish Trevor was here to see the change...*

Carefully setting her goblet on the linen tablecloth, Emma rested her hands beneath her chin and had to comment on Claire's transformation. "You are absolutely turning heads in here tonight."

The other woman instantly ducked her chin and fiddled with her silver fork. "Don't be silly, Emma. Who would be looking at me?"

"Just about every man in this restaurant."

"You're mistaken. They must be watching you." To Claire, her sister-in-law was one of the most beautiful ladies she had ever known.

"Don't you realize that you are utterly stunning?" Emma returned. "I'm so glad we decided to stop at a salon and treat ourselves today. I never realized how curly your hair was." Emma tipped her head, further studying her sister-in-law. "I think I'll have the hairdresser come up to the ranch and do your hair before the reception."

"That's not necessary. I can do something with it."

Emma nodded her head slowly as she continued to observe the woman across from her. "Yes, that's exactly what I'm going to do. Not that I think it's necessary; but, since it's a special occasion, we're going to knock Trevor's socks off on the day of that party."

Claire's head snapped up at the other woman's comment, immediately interested when Trevor's name was mentioned. To cover her reaction, she latched onto the subject at hand. "What do you mean by 'it's not necessary'?"

Crossing her arms, Emma leaned back against the padded chair, not quite ready to answer her yet. "How are things going between you and Trevor?"

"Fine." Claire nearly knocked her wineglass over when she reached for it.

Emma did not believe the other woman's words for a second. Even though the two were together constantly at the ranch, whether it was a solitary walk most nights after dinner, or a game in the yard with her children, Claire was always careful not to touch her husband. Except for that morning's kiss before leaving for Duluth, they never acted like newlyweds.

Emma and Tyler had more than one discussion about the fact. Trevor and Claire seemed more like best friends than husband and wife. The only glances the two shared were during discussions about the kids, and those looks were very non-committal. *Yet, when Claire's not looking, Trevor devours her with his eyes...and she always manages to appear prim and proper. Well, tonight I'm getting some answers.* "Are the two of you planning to have any more children?"

Claire snorted her wine into the goblet in a very unladylike manner, clapped her hand over her mouth to cover the sound of her choking, and finally wiped her tearing eyes with a napkin.

Emma hid a smile. "Pregnancy happens—sometimes there's nothing one can do about it."

Claire dropped her napkin to the surface of the table, folded her hands in her lap, and lifted her eyes. She had to talk to someone about her relationship with her husband. Who better than Emma? She had welcomed Claire with open arms and the two were actually quite close. Struggling with the pregnancy comment, she decided to ignore it for the moment. "You've been so good to me since I arrived. I can't thank you enough for that. For the first time in my life, I'm sleeping not because I'm bone tired, but because I can't wait for the next day to arrive."

Emma remained silent, instinctively knowing that Claire, being such a private person, was trying to get around to something that was difficult for her to speak about.

"I can't wait for the next day to come, because I can spend it in my husband's company. He's kind, generous to a fault, and has given my children security when I could barely keep our heads above water."

"It's not that you didn't try, Claire. You realize that, don't you?"

Her blonde head nodded. "In retrospect, I'm proud of what I was able to accomplish on my own. But things were very bad when I first met Trevor. To me, he was a rich man who most likely thought of me as white trash."

Emma reached across the table and waited for Claire to offer her hand. When she did, her fingers were given an encouraging squeeze. "Don't ever think of yourself in that vein. Trevor has always spoken of you with great respect. He admires your courage. He loves you."

The three words made Claire lightheaded just thinking about the possibility. That was not how their relationship was, however. A sad smile curved her mouth. "He doesn't, Emma. I found myself with no money, I was injured from the fall, and I had no job to return to even if I could go back to work. I had finally hit rock bottom. When he proposed to me, I refused at first because the only reason he asked was to help me out of a horrible bind. There was no love involved on his part."

"You're wrong, Claire. He might not have felt as strongly as he does now, but Trevor would never step into a marriage if he wasn't sure that his feelings were sturdy enough to carry him into the future. He does love you. I can see it in his eyes every time you step into a room."

Claire wished that Emma's observation was truth, but how could that be? Not once had he held her as tenderly as the night they made love for the first and only time. No, Trevor had offered her a business relationship and that was the way of things. Everything else, like sharing the same bedroom, the wedding reception, all of it was simply for the sake of appearance.

Claire withdrew her hand and stared at her wineglass, momentarily lost in thought. Emma's question about future children still rattled her brain as she slowly brought her eyes back to her sister-in-law's. "We haven't discussed children because there's no chance there will be any more."

Emma's hand fluttered over her chest. Sympathy rested in her green eyes. "I'm sorry, Claire. I didn't realize that you couldn't have any more babies."

"That's not the reason." She spied Emma's instant confusion. "In order for me to become pregnant, Trevor and I would have to be...intimate. Our marriage isn't like that."

"But..." Emma's words died in her throat. She simply stared at Claire's sad eyes as she put the facts together. Once again, one of the Wilkins brothers was making the same old mistake. Misunderstandings had haunted them all at one time or another. Her mind sifted through the past to a time before she and Tyler discovered that they truly loved one another. It was not until Emma found the courage to go to him that her marriage became the blessed union it now was. The hidden love that Claire and Trevor carried with them throughout the day was easily seen by everyone else in the family. Why was it that they could not glimpse it themselves?

Claire sipped her wine, and then swirled the small bit of liquid left in her glass before she glanced at Emma again. "There's not much left to say after knowing that, is there? Just one time in my life, I wish things would follow the proper course. You know, Emma? I would give anything to have a marriage like yours—one where I would never doubt how much my husband desires me."

Emma could remain silent no longer. "It wasn't always like that. Nothing is truly as it appears on the surface. I take it you think I've done everything correctly in my life. That notion is so far from the truth. I had only known Tyler for a month. He came to New York, where I lived back then, to set up a partnership with my father. At the end of four weeks, he returned to Minnesota—and left me heartbroken...and pregnant." She heard Claire's tiny gasp from across the table. "After discovering that I carried his child, I refused to tell him, but my father insisted differently. He shipped me west on the first train and demanded that Tyler marry me."

"I don't imagine he took that too well."

"No, he didn't. He detested me and didn't believe the baby was his."

"But you're both so happy now. How did that come about?"

"There were lots of reasons, but mostly because I had the nerve to go to him one night. Once we stopped being so angry with one another, we quickly discovered all the misconceptions that had kept us apart." Emma leaned back with a heavy sigh. "Everyone has skeletons in their closet, Claire. You need to bury yours and go after what you want. And I know what you want is your husband—in the fullest sense. Don't worry about the outcome. Trevor will be there waiting for you."

"Excuse me, ladies."

Claire and Emma glanced up in unison to see a tall, handsome man standing beside the table.

Silver hair colored his temples, blending into thick brown waves. His dark eyes flashed as the masculine full lips curved upward in delight at the two beauties before him. "I hope I'm not intruding, but I was sitting across the room and couldn't resist coming over to say hello. My name is Charles Goodsworth, and I'm in Duluth on business. I would be honored if you two fine ladies would let me purchase you a glass of sherry to finish off the night."

Emma darted a meaningful glance at Claire, grabbed her small purse from the table, and rose to her feet. Her sister-in-law followed her up. "Why thank you for the nice gesture, but we have just decided to retire for the evening."

"Are you quite sure? Nothing would please me more than to be in the company of two beautiful ladies."

Emma adjusted her shawl across her shoulders. "As delightful as that sounds, Mr. Goodsworth, we are both happily married women." She nodded her head to the man. "Good evening, sir." Her gaze swung to the blonde beside her. "Are you ready, Claire?"

The other woman nodded, rounded the table to join her sister-in-law, and the two strolled from the dining room.

***

Charles Goodsworth stood by the empty chair until the two women disappeared into the lobby. Turning on his heel, he worked his way back between the many patrons until he returned to a table against the back wall.

His dining partner smiled beneath his thin mustache. "What did you do, scare them away? You were supposed to get some information for me. You must be losing your touch."

Charles yanked out his chair and sank to the surface in a huff. "That damned redhead wasn't biting. She immediately said that they were planning to retire for the evening, and then hauled the blonde away with her."

Judd Stone lifted his expensive cigar to his lips and took a drag. Expelling the smoke from his lungs, he watched the blue cloud float across the table before he replied. "I know you were cut off at the knees, but did you manage to find out anything?"

"The redhead said they were both happily married."

Judd stubbed out his cigar, reached for his wallet, and tossed some bills onto the table. "Well, now my interest is rather piqued. I can't believe Claire Holcomb landed on her feet. We'll just see about that."

Charles slugged down his fancy drink. He had the looks and the cloths to match, but high society manners were something that had passed him by. "So what's the deal with this Claire person?"

Judd stood, the legs of his chair scraping across the marbled floor. "In due time, Charlie. Are you sure you didn't get any other information? Who was the redhead?"

The other man shrugged. "Don't know."

Judd shot him a glare. "Well, you had damn well better find out." He turned, glanced once at the empty table across the room, and headed for the door.

Chapter Twenty

Regina Simpson marched through the front entrance of her elaborate home and slammed the door behind her. She picked off her gloves finger by finger and tossed the expensive leather onto a burnished table in the foyer. Her feathered hat followed. Stomping into the library, she crossed to the sidebar and flung open the heavy door. Regina ignored the rattle of glass against glass as she pushed about ornate bottles in search of the cognac. Not finding it, she turned, took a deep breath, and bellowed out to her butler.

"Breton! Come to the library immediately!" Regina flounced across the floor and dropped onto a soft-cushioned sofa to wait. "Breton!" Her fingertips tapped angrily against the expensive brocade. "Breton! I need you now!"

The sound of the butler's quick footsteps resounded on the tiled floors of the outer hallway. A moment later, the frazzled man appeared in the doorway. Regina never gave him a chance to respond to her call. "How many times do I have to tell you to keep the bar stocked with cognac? There are plenty of other butlers in the city that would love to have your job. What do I pay you for anyway? Now, I better have that bottle in here in a matter of minutes or they'll be hell to pay!"

The man's jaw tightened to control his anger as he backed from the room. "Right away, ma'am. It'll only take me a moment to retrieve a bottle from our kitchen stock." He disappeared in a flash before his employer could subject him anymore to her irrational behavior.

Alone again, Regina whirled off the sofa and stalked to a large window that overlooked a manicured courtyard. Her glittering eyes and pinched mouth evidenced her building anger as her toe tapped against the carpeted floor. She had just come from afternoon tea with a select group of wealthy St. Paul dowagers. Regina had been forced to smile and act as if the gossip she heard that afternoon did not bother her in the slightest. "That son of a bitch..." she mumbled aloud and patted her hair for the lack of something better to do until she had a drink in her hand.

Trevor Wilkins had secretly married and invitations for a wedding reception were now being received by a select few in St. Paul. Most recipients had the notes in their possession for over a week already—all except Regina. She took the omission as a slap in the face. "And so did those old cronies today," she finished her thoughts aloud.

Regina paced the room and finally returned to the sofa, plopped down again, and picked at a few bits of lint that clung to the front of her expensive dress, calming herself as her thoughts returned to the tea party. More than one sarcastic remark was sent her way under the guise of laughter as the women commented time after time about Trevor's unavailability. They all knew that, at one point, the handsome middle Wilkins' son escorted Regina about the city and most expected what was true. She had fed his ego, played the feminine fatale, and managed to coax him into her bed for more than one delightful afternoon. *And for what?* So a group of old bags could laugh about it? The one thing Regina hated most in her life was being made the butt of a joke.

"Mrs. Simpson?"

Her head snapped around to see Breton with a bottle of cognac in one hand and a filled glass in the other. "You can put everything right here on the table." She eyed the nervous man as he hurried across the room and carried out her directive. When the feat was accomplished, Regina's head nodded to the hallway. "You can go now. Close the door behind you."

"Yes, ma'am." Breton scuttled away. The click of the latch sounded a second later.

She reached for the snifter and gulped a large draught of the liquor, her mind refusing to acknowledge the fact that she had been passed over for another woman. She had spent tireless weeks cultivating her relationship with Trevor, offering her residence, her money—what little she had left—and even her body in hopes of receiving a marriage proposal. After the day she had driven downtown to the racetrack to find him, however, he had disappeared from the city and her life without a word. Try as she might to discover his whereabouts, Regina had not heard a single thing about the missing man until that very afternoon—and then had to cover her surprise in the face of her tormentors.

"Married..." Her fingers tightened around the stem of the glass. "You bastard." A deep, tremulous sigh raised her shoulders as she stared across the silent room. She had counted on snagging the handsome bachelor, along with his bank account. Now, she would have to settle for one of the many flabby widowers in the city if she was to continue her accustomed lifestyle.

A knock sounded on the door, bringing her attention back to the present. "Come in," she snapped.

Breton appeared again, albeit hesitantly, his back straight and his eyes not quite meeting his employer's.

"This better be good."

"You have a visitor, ma'am. Your cousin has come calling for you. Shall I bring him in?"

Regina's hand fluttered in silent affirmation as she nonchalantly sipped the fine liquor once more. She listened to the butler's voice in the hallway and kept her glittering eyes on the doorway.

Judd Stone strolled into the room and waited for Breton to leave before he greeted the woman who sat dejectedly on the sofa. "Cousin Regina, why the long face on such a beautiful day?"

Her slim eyebrows arched. "Well, look what the cat dragged in. Don't expect me to get up and get you a drink. Pour one yourself if you're thirsty." She eyed him as he crossed to a leather chair instead.

"Rather early to be drinking, isn't it," he noted as he sank down onto the soft surface.

She ignored his remark and took another sip. "Where have you been off to? I haven't heard from you in weeks."

Judd removed his fedora and placed it on his lap as he crossed one knee over the other and relaxed into the chair. "I've been hard at work. Something you should think about doing if you want to remain in this mausoleum you live in." His eyes skittered about the room, noting the flamboyant opulence of her library.

"What are you talking about?"

"I *have* been managing your accounts, Regina, since Sydney died. You've been spending an awful lot of money this past year. Keep it up and you'll be in the streets."

Trevor's recent marriage crossed her brain, restoring the anger that had disappeared with Judd's appearance, but she swallowed the resentment down. "You're creative. Figure something out." She set the near-empty snifter on the table, clasped her hands in her lap, and studied the man across from her.

Judd was Regina's first cousin. She had grown up with him, but that did not mean she had to like him. Regina more or less became accustomed to him in her life and put up with man like she would a pesky fly. "So what brings you out visiting today? You could have easily sent a fiscal report from the bank if my financial state of affairs is the reason you're here. What are you up to now?"

"Ah, Regina—" he chuckled "—you do know me now, don't you. I came to collect you and your baggage. I want you to come north to Biwabik with me."

"Biwabik? What's there for me? It's nothing but a small mining town full of ignorant peasants who dig in the dirt. I've got far better things to do in St. Paul." *Like finding a new husband...* "I never could understand why you purchased a home up there anyway."

"Business, my dear, business. With the natural ore that's been discovered in the northern part of the state, I'd be a fool to let the chance of a financial windfall slip through my fingers. Have you heard of the Merritt brothers?"

She shrugged. "Who hasn't? I heard they're not long for the good life, though..." In fact, Regina had once entertained the idea of snagging one of the brothers, but soon discovered that their financial empire was on shaky ground. "Isn't John Rockefeller from out east breathing down their necks?" *I wish he'd breathe down mine. I could use his money...*

"Exactly. And when they topple, I'm going to be there to cash in; hence, a temporary residence to stay close and keep my eye on things. I also purchased a boarding house in Biwabik this past summer. My receipts for three months were very impressive, to say the least. I lost the building though, in the wildfire I'm sure you read about. Or do you even read the posts?"

"Get to the point."

"I've just come from Duluth after discussing some insurance I took out on that property. I've got a bundle of money from the settlement just waiting to be spent." Now he had Regina's full attention.

She straightened against the back of the sofa and struggled to maintain an air of disinterest. "You're leading up to something, Judd. Just spit it out. Where do I come in?"

"I heard that Trevor Wilkins has finally been taken off the market."

She could not prevent the flush that stained her cheeks at the reference to her former lover. "So? What does his marital status have to do with your insurance?"

Judd examined a fingernail after noting her heightened color. "Patience, my dear. I heard some gossip over the last few days. I didn't realize it was Wilkins you were after. You never mentioned the man's name. Didn't you plan to have him in your clutches on a permanent basis?"

"At one time, but I lost interest."

Judd belted out a laugh at her flippant return. "The hell you did. Don't play games with me, Regina. I also know how your mind works. I've heard people talking about how jilted you must feel after working the man so hard. Even bedding him didn't do the trick, did it?"

Her blue eye's flashed. "Go to hell, Judd."

"Only if you come with me, my dear." He chuckled again. "I fear my stay there would be much too boring if I didn't have you around." His balding head tipped as he watched her. "You and I are cut from the same mold. I need you to help me with something. In fact, you're going to go to Wilkins' wedding reception on a little spy mission for me."

"What are you talking about? I never even received an invitation."

"So? Just show up at the door with some excuse about knowing you were inadvertently left out and understand that it happens sometimes. In fact, I bet I could procure an escort if that would make you more comfortable."

Regina rolled his idea around in her brain. Being seen at the reception would stop the gossip of how she was purposely overlooked by the wealthy family. Maybe she could even start a little trouble for Trevor for replacing her with someone else. She began to warm to the idea. "So, who am I spying on—if I decide to help you?"

"Wilkins' new wife, Claire. She used to be Claire Holcomb, from right outside St. Paul. I won't go into details now, but I've got something to settle with her. As far as Wilkins...I have plans for him already. A little bit of a repayment of sorts."

Regina glanced at the ceiling, deep in thought. "Claire Holcomb." Her eyes finally dropped back to her cousin's. "I don't seem to recall that name around the city. Is she from some family out east?"

"East of town, maybe. Claire was a poor dirt farmer's widower who was down on her luck and, at one time, at risk of losing her rundown property to my bank. She wasn't a very good bargainer. She lost everything."

Regina bounded from the couch, angry because Trevor chose an ill-bred woman over her and elated as her sharp mind quickly put together the correct facts. The manicured finger on one hand pointed at her cousin as she reached for her goblet once more. "And I bet before she lost everything, you were going to ride in and save the day—and the farm—as long as you were granted some special favors!"

Judd's brow rose in surprise at her intuitiveness.

"That's it!" Regina squealed with glee. "But she got one over on you by marrying a rich, handsome man so she wouldn't have to put up with the likes of you!"

Judd's lips thinned into a straight line as his eyes narrowed. "Be careful, Regina. I could ruin you in a second," he threatened.

"Oh, get off your high horse. All right, if I help you, what's in it for me?" Regina would be damned if she let on that she did not much care what her payment would be. To get her revenge for being dumped by Trevor and to see what he married would be worth the trip north. She may as well profit from it, however.

"I'll set up a bank account with some of the insurance money. You won't have to pay out a penny for your lunches and wardrobe for the next year. That way, you can continue your lifestyle as it is, until you snag some rich old goat to pay your expenses after that."

Regina yearned to slap the condescending smirk from his face. Knowing the type of man he was, however, Judd would probably smack her back. She poured a splash of cognac into a clean snifter and refreshed her own before crossing to her cousin. Handing him the drink, she raised her glass and pasted a smile on her lips. "Cheers. To revenge."

Judd's eyes narrowed further as he clinked his glass against hers. "To revenge."

* * *

Claire wiggled on the padded seat and strained her neck to see out the carriage window. She and Emma would be back at the ranch just in time for the evening meal.

She missed her children dreadfully, but could not discount the fact that the last two days spent in her sister-in-law's company had cemented a permanent bond of friendship and love. Emma had opened her eyes to a new world, one filled with a whirlwind of shopping, exquisite dining, and the chance to be a woman without care and responsibilities.

The top of the carriage was loaded down with packages of personal items that Claire never expected to own. She had argued repeatedly that to splurge so unnecessarily was foolish. At Emma's insistence, she had finally given in and let the woman fill her arms with the trappings of the rich. Silken nightgowns, shoes for every occasion, and five new day dresses waited to be unpacked, along with presents for her children. A special dress to celebrate the occasion of her wedding was packed separately in thick layers of tissue.

And, during the continual rush from one mercantile to another, they had discussed Claire's relationship with her new husband. Trevor was also the topic for most of the ride home. Emma repeatedly told Claire that she must be the one to reach for what she desired.

Can I do it? Claire's heart jumped with the memory of the smothering pain she felt the morning she spied Trevor in another woman's arms. Her entire life had been one disappoint after another, except for the kids. Leaving Duluth earlier that day, she was firm in her determination to simply let the future happen as it would. Now though, only four hours later, she had decided to put aside her fear and, for once, let down her guard and take a chance at real love.

Claire looked out the window again as the carriage began its descent down the hillside road to the ranch. *I'll never be able to do it...*

Find the courage and see this thing through...

Can I even compete with his past dalliances?

Her hand smoothed the crisp material of her new skirt first, then fluttered to the lacy collar that adorned her new white blouse. Even in the simple attire, Claire felt like a queen as her gaze skittered out the carriage window once more. Was dressing the part enough to capture his attention?

Her stomach rolled when she thought about her husband. Had he missed her? The night before was one of the loneliest she had ever experienced. Not having Trevor's warm comfort beside her in the dark had left her huddling in the middle of the bed, picturing his dark head against the pillow.

She inhaled a deep breath to ease the pounding of her heart, but she could not keep her eyes from straying to the house and the possibility of a complete life that loomed before her. The memory of his ardent kiss the morning before still burned her mouth. Would her return home warrant another one?

Her hand grasped the edge of the window as the carriage entered the yard. Trevor strolled out onto the porch as her children streamed through the doorway behind him, their arms waving in the air.

As the buggy halted at the end of the walkway, Emma reached across the seat and clasped Claire's free hand in a show of encouragement before Dougan opened the carriage door. "I'm going to keep one of your dress boxes in my room until tomorrow. I don't want Trevor to get a glimpse of that gown until you come down the steps. Don't waste any more of your marriage living in fear. Remember what I told you; he'll be there waiting."

* * *

Trevor leaned against a support beam at the top of the steps and watched the carriage come to a halt. Over the course of the long day, he had constantly checked the top of the hill in search of Claire's arrival. The past two days were the longest he had experienced in quite some time, but the night was the worst.

Their suite echoed with Claire's absence. Trevor tarried overlong in the leather chair the evening before, purposely avoiding the loneliness he knew he would find in the bed. Giving in, he finally crawled on top of the quilt to surrender to sleeplessness and simply stared longingly at her pillow. He missed Claire's late night whispers as they laughed quietly about something one of the kids did or something that Mamie spouted from her sick bed.

Now, as she alighted from the buggy and the children crowded around her, he could not hide the grin that creased his face. *You missed her all right...you missed her quiet presence beside you in the bed and the soft sound of her breathing...*

Claire glanced up with a glowing smile on her face, took a small hand in each of hers, and headed up the walk. Trevor tipped his head and studied her graceful stride as he moved down the steps to greet his wife. The late evening sun glinted off her blonde curls—curls that were not pulled atop her head in the usual tight bun. Instead, escaping ringlets fluttered in the late afternoon breeze. A frilly white blouse was neatly tucked into the soft leather skirt that wrapped around her trim hips. Claire's forgotten youth shined out for everyone to see. Gray eyes sparkled into his as she stopped before him and tilted her head up.

As the children scooted back to the carriage to help with packages, Trevor grasped his wife's hands, suddenly realizing how much softer they were than the first time he held them. The only way to describe Claire at that moment was to say that she literally glowed. "I don't know what you did in Duluth, but I've never seen you looking so happy...and beautiful."

Her breath caught in her throat with his compliment. "Emma was a wonderful hostess. I should be exhausted, but there wasn't enough time to be tired. I had so much fun!" She giggled like an adolescent.

Trevor's heart flipped at the tinkling sound as it disappeared on the wind. *To hell with it...* He wanted her in his arms. "I missed you." He pulled her gently into his embrace, tightened his arms around her slender waist, and kissed her warm temple. "I'm glad you had a good time, but I'm even happier that you're home."

Claire wanted to stay right where she was forever, but finally pulled away to study his smiling eyes. "Did they all behave?"

"Who? Oh, you mean the little hellions?"

"What?" she gasped. "Were they horrible?"

Trevor's head fell back when he laughed—just before he placed an arm around her waist and urged her up the steps and into the house.

"I'm teasing you. They were perfect. They always are. Although, Hannah wasn't too sure she wanted to go to bed without you tucking her in. I finally managed to rock her to sleep early enough."

Before Claire thought on it, she placed her palm against his chest as they entered the house. "You're always so good with all of them. Where is Hannah now?"

Trevor clasped her hand before she pulled it away, enjoying the feel of completeness when his wife was near. "We were up pretty early today. She fell asleep on the swing waiting for you, so I put her in her bed. The sight of you is going to make her one happy little girl when she wakes up."

"Ma!"

Trevor reluctantly dropped Claire's hand when Jonah burst through the open doorway. "Emma says these packages are for us!" His sisters poured into the foyer behind their brother.

"Can we open them? Please?" Sofie hopped elatedly from one foot to the other.

Claire laughed at their excitement. "Of course you can. Let's go up to your rooms and try everything on. But remember. When we're done, we'll hang up your new clothes so they stay clean and pressed for the party tomorrow." She watched them race up the steps, lugging the wrapped packages, and turned to her husband. "I forgot to have them thank you, so I'll do it. They've never had anything new from the store—most of their clothes are used or I made them."

"Apparently, you haven't either by the smile on your face. You're pretty as a picture in your new clothes."

Claire's cheeks instantly turned pink with the second compliment—a malady she seemed to be suffering on a regular basis when she was in her husband's presence. Trevor's reaction was exactly what she had wished for earlier. To break the silence and his close perusal, she headed for the staircase. "I suppose I should go help them before they have things strewn all over the floor." She took the first step, hesitated with a hand on the balustrade, and then turned. "Why don't you come up with me? It'll be fun to hear what they have to say."

Trevor's step was as light as a young boy's as he moved to her side, took her hand in his, and led her to the second floor.

***

Later that evening, with supper finished, Claire and Trevor sat with the other adults around the dining table. As they discussed the events of the coming day over the din of children playing about the room, Trevor could not take his eyes from his wife's excited smile and shining eyes. She was a different person since returning from Duluth. When he had the chance, he planned to speak to Emma to see what spurred the change.

Claire could feel her husband's eyes watching her every move. More than once when she turned, his immediate smile warmed her blood and, as the evening progressed, he took every opportunity to squeeze her hand or touch her arm. She lifted her eyes and caught Emma's gaze. Her sister-in-law had the audacity to secretly wink at her across the table, which produced another flush across Claire's cheeks.

August yawned, and then rose from her chair. A moment later, she rounded the table and clasped Claire's shoulders. "I want to wish you a happy day tomorrow and say goodbye now. We plan to leave before sunup. It would not be wise for us to meet anyone on the road."

Claire clasped August's hand with a sigh on her lips and turned on her chair. "I wish you could be here to celebrate with us. We'll miss you." August was someone special in her life. The Indian woman was the first to extend the hand of friendship when Claire arrived at the ranch, and she would never forget how she was put at ease with August's kind words.

"I will be thinking of you. We will be back home the day after next and you can tell me all about the fine time you had." August touched her cheek to Claire's, and then moved on to hug Trevor as Cole stepped up.

He pressed a soft kiss to Claire's cheek. "Don't feel bad that we have to leave for a couple of days. I'm looking forward to having my wife all to myself."

Claire ducked her chin, knowing exactly what Cole spoke about. The couple's love shone brightly for everyone to see—as did Emma and Tyler's. *If only Trevor felt the same...but, tonight, he has been different...* She sighed. *I'd best wait. Tomorrow, after the party, we'll sit down and discuss this. I want more. I want him...*

Keeper of the Heart

Claire watched as Cole hunched down to gather his young son. Placing the child in his wife's arms, he gently lifted his sleeping daughter from a nearby cradle. Taking August's hand in his, they left the room with one last wave.

Claire's gaze lingered on the closed door after the couple left. *They're so in love. No matter all they've been through, it's easy to see how strong they are when together...* Claire sighed again and turned to her husband. "We should've had the party somewhere else. That way, they wouldn't have to hide out somewhere."

He patted her hand. "They don't mind in the least. You heard Cole. He's looking forward to the bit of privacy."

Claire ignored the quick rapping of her heart at Trevor's slight innuendo. "Where are they going?"

"There's a logger's cabin west of the ranch in a very secluded area. The place is set up for them with all the comforts of home."

Claire sat back. "Still, I wish they could be here."

Before she could say anything further, a small argument erupted across the room between Ruth and Sue Ellen over a doll. Claire started to get up, but Trevor's hand stayed her. "I'll take care of it."

He endlessly surprised her. Trevor took to fatherhood as if he had done it his entire life. Within seconds, he broke up the small battle, laid on the floor, and wrestled gently with all kids.

As she watched the antics across the room and listened to the high-pitched squeals of happiness, Claire turned her eyes to Emma's. Once again, her sister-in-law closed one eye in a devilish wink.

Chapter Twenty-One

Claire stood before the mirror and looked unbelievably at the woman who stared back at her. Her slender hand reverently touched the gown where the bodice rested against her collarbone. Her sister-in-law stood behind her. A smile widened across Claire's face when her eyes found Emma's. "I can't believe it's me..."

"Why not? You're a beautiful woman," Emma returned as she checked the tiny row of pearled buttons at Claire's back. "I think this shade of blue is perfect for you. It makes your gray eyes resemble the color of the sky. I'm so glad you decided to go with this style. Trevor is going to think you're absolutely gorgeous."

Claire's gaze returned to the mass of blonde curls pulled high atop her head. As Emma promised, the same hairdresser from the trip to Duluth had shown up at the ranch early that morning. "I'm nervous about meeting everyone today, but I'm actually excited, too. Thank you so much, Emma. I never thought I could look like this." Claire turned and, following an impulse, hugged her friend's shoulders, careful not to muss Emma's exquisitely coiffed hair.

The other woman squeezed her sister-in-law back. "It's not me, Claire. I just dressed up what was already there."

"Ma?" a tiny muffled voice sounded from the hallway. "Can we come in?"

"I'll get the door." Emma swept across the floor, holding the front of her gown gingerly in both hands.

Every move the woman made was carried out with extreme grace and femininity. Claire would have to follow her example and remember to walk slowly with her head held high. For now, though, she needed to find a brush to fix her daughters' hair.

As the door swung open, Emma gasped at the sight of Claire's girls lined up in the hallway. "Oh, my goodness. Look at how beautiful you all are. Come in so your mother can see you!"

Sofie entered first, holding Hannah by the hand. Sue Ellen followed with Ruth. They were clothed in matching yellow dresses, reminding Claire of a field of buttercups. New white tights covered their chubby legs, and black shoes with straps shined in the late morning sun that streamed through the windows. The sight of their happy faces nearly brought a tear to their mother's eye.

Claire's arms spread wide as she leaned over to encompass them into one big hug when they ran across the room. "Emma's right. I've never seen you four looking so pretty." Leaning back, Claire's eyes darted from one to the other. "Who did your hair for you. And, oh! You have matching ribbons!"

Sofie turned her head slowly, afraid that if she moved too quickly, her ribbons would spring to the floor. "Katy did our hair. She said the ribbons were a present for some of her favorite girls. Ma, we're beautiful as pots of gold at the end of a rainbow. That's what Katy said."

Emma and Claire giggled at the comment as Ruth stepped forward and took her mother by the hand. Her eyes held a solemn look of worship as she studied Claire in the new gown. Her little hand reached out to touch the blue gossamer material before her round eyes raised to the curls that coiled around Claire's head. "'Member the princess you told us about that lives in a gold castle with servants and all kinds of white kitties? You're her, Ma. You look as pretty as a princess."

Claire did not care if her dress wrinkled or not. She sank down and enveloped Ruth in her arms. Closing her eyes, she laid her cheek against the softly braided hair with a yellow ribbon tying the strands at the end. "Thank you, Ruthie. I feel like a princess. You're so sweet." Claire glanced up at the other girls. "You all are. I think Katy is right. You're my pots of gold at the end of the rainbow." She eyed the door for a moment, the unshed tears glistening in the gray depths. "So, where is Jonah? I haven't seen him in his finery yet."

Ruth's nose crinkled in dislike before she spoke up. "He's with Trevor. He's being nasty, Ma."

Claire's eyes widened as she stood. "Nasty?"

Sofie's head bobbed, and she answered before her sister did. "He says we all look like dumb old ladies going to church. He wouldn't let us go with him to find Trevor, because he said only guys can be together in the library."

"He thinks he's so smart because he has a new suit," Sue Ellen piped up with a serious tone to her lilting voice. "But I told him that us girls were prettier, because he looks like a chicken in his tight pants."

Claire and Emma burst out laughing at the same time. The girls looked at one another, and suddenly they smiled in unison. It was so good to hear their mother laugh, instead of receiving the usual reprimand to get along with their sibling.

"Well—" Claire sighed happily and held out her hands to the two youngest "—why don't we go downstairs and let me make the decision if your brother looks like he's going to lay an egg or not."

Sofie rolled her eyes, thoroughly enjoying her mother's high spirits. "Oh, Ma, you're so silly!"

Emma picked up the box that earlier held Claire's dress and headed for the door. "You go ahead. I'm going to go check on Tyler and the kids to see if they're ready. I'm sure our guests will be arriving soon."

Claire was surprised that her apprehension had disappeared; her stomach never even rolled at Emma's announcement. Feeling suddenly more excited by the moment and, with her girls by her side, they left the suite to meet the day. This was the moment she had waited for; Claire could not wait to see her husband's reaction.

* * *

Trevor paced at the bottom of the steps, his eyes constantly darting up the staircase as he waited for Claire. Emma had given him strict orders to stay out of the bedroom while she helped his wife prepare for the day.

Jonah slumped in a chair with his chin propped on his fist over a bent elbow, silently watching his new father with an exasperated pout on his lips. Now that his sisters had disappeared, Sue Ellen's retort about her brother resembling a chicken had him worried that he was not as sporty looking as he had originally thought. A skinny finger yanked on the collar of his shirt to allow more breathing room. Suddenly, he was not all that enthused about the coming party. The loud sigh that escaped his mouth brought Trevor's head around to check on the boy.

"What's wrong, bud?" The older man crossed the hall and lowered himself onto a bench.

Jonah slumped forward, clasped his hands together, and buried them between his knees as his legs swung to and fro from the edge of the chair. "Is the party gonna last all day?"

Trevor smiled to himself as he spied the boy's dejection. "Most likely. We've got a lot of people coming to wish your mother and me well. I don't imagine they'll go home right away." His eyes darted up the empty stairwell again. *What's taking her so long?* He crossed his arms over his chest and leaned back against the wall with a heartfelt sigh of his own.

Jonah wiggled until his thin shoulders sagged against the back of the chair again. "I 'spose we can't help with the horses tonight, can we?" His last words held a hopeful note.

"Not tonight." Trevor eyed Jonah as the boy continued to squirm on his seat. "How would you like to ride some fence lines with me in a couple of days? We can head out early. Just you and me."

Jonah straightened in the chair, the woeful look in his eyes gone. "Sure! Just us men."

Trevor shook his head, laughing on the inside about how Jonah's demeanor changed immediately with the 'boys only' invitation. "Until then, let's have a fun day. Katy made lots of treats for all of us." *There...the promise of food ought to send his thoughts in another direction.*

Trevor glanced once more up the staircase and immediately bounded to his feet. As he walked to the bottom step, his eyes darkened with appreciation at the sight of his wife where she carefully descended the steps, holding Hannah and Ruth's hands. Sofie and Sue Ellen followed behind.

Witnessing the gorgeous vision in light blue made him weak in the knees. His eyes lingered on blonde ringlets that framed a wide smile, and then moved to the slight bit of cleavage that disappeared into the rounded bodice of her dress. Claire's nipped waist accented the gentle line of curved hips, and silver slippers peeked out from beneath the flounced hem of the skirt. His wife was absolutely stunning and stole the breath from his lungs.

Claire carefully stepped down, maintaining the smile on her face. The sensual look in Trevor's eyes as he stared upward from the foot of the steps set her formerly calm stomach into motion. No man had ever gazed at her with such blatant desire. As she reached the last step, she was even more overwhelmed by the veiled yearning that sparked his eyes to a deep hue of emerald green. Claire placed her palm over her satin-encased abdomen in an effort to control the sudden return of a rolling stomach. If not for the children, she wondered if Trevor would have swept her into his arms.

"Ma looks like a princess, don't she?" Ruth broke the thrilled silence with her pronouncement as she peeked up at her stepfather.

Trevor clasped his wife's hand, lifted it to his lips, and pressed a tender kiss to the soft skin. "You couldn't be more right, Ruthie. She's absolutely beautiful." His eyes smoldered when he met Claire's stunned gaze. "I think I'm about the luckiest man around to be married to such a lovely lady."

Even Jonah slid from his bench when his sisters giggled, and he approached the small group to get a closer look. His mother resembled someone who had stepped out of a fairytale.

Trevor glanced down at the boy for a second, then his eyes darted immediately back to his wife. "What do you think, Jonah? Did you ever think your ma could look so pretty?"

The boy's head nodded with enthusiastic agreement. "You could be one of them fancy ladies in the store windows down in St. Paul, Ma."

A tiny laugh bubbled in Claire's throat. It was easier to respond to her son's observation than to worry about her heated cheeks. "Why thank you, Jonah, but I think I'd just rather be a rancher's wife." She took a chance and peeked at Trevor.

A wide grin appeared on his clean-shaven face. "A very good choice on your part, Mrs. Wilkins. And speaking of that—" He reached a hand inside the lapel of his jacket and withdrew a small wrapped package. Placing it in his wife's palm, his eyes continued to smolder. "A wedding gift for my lovely bride."

"But...I didn't know we were exchanging gifts." Her hand shook. "I didn't get you anything."

"I didn't expect anything, Claire, so don't you dare worry about it. This is something I felt you should have—something I should have taken care of already. Go ahead—open it."

Her children crowded around as she slipped off the satin ribbon and slowly lifted the lid of the box. Nestled inside an embroidered piece of silk was a shiny gold wedding band.

Claire's smile instantly disappeared as she met her husband's gaze. Overwhelmed by the sheer beauty of the diamond that twinkled from the band's center, she swallowed and shook her head slowly. "I...I don't know what to say. This is the most beautiful piece of jewelry I've ever owned. It's too much, Trevor."

He took the ring from her shaking hand and easily slipped it over the knuckle of her third finger. "It's not too much. I need to apologize for waiting so long to give this to you. It hit me one night when we were planning the reception that I never gave you a ring." His head tilted as he studied her hand. "It seems like it fits."

She stared at her finger momentarily before she raised her eyes again. "Thank you. It's perfect."

Trevor raised a bent elbow and offered it to his wife. "Should we wait for the others outside on the porch? It's a beautiful day." He could hardly wait to get Claire on the swing beside him where he could hold her hand and thank his lucky stars.

* * *

The newlyweds stood in the early afternoon sun, greeting their guests at the door as one carriage after another drew to a halt before the house. Claire's head whirled with the many introductions to not only family friends from the surrounding area but, also, business associates from across the state. As each group filed by, her confidence grew. She was accepted warmly by one and all, but that was not the main reason for the sudden change in her self-assurance. It was the pressure of Trevor's comforting hand against the small of her back and his constant attention that kept the smile on her lips. He was proud of her and made certain that his guests were aware of it.

And through all of the many introductions, Claire's mind persistently contemplated what the end of the day would bring. She and her husband would make their way to the second floor suite, where a new silk nightgown waited. She would don the beautiful garment and go to him. That night, Claire's marriage would truly begin. She would take Trevor in her arms and declare her love. Just the thought of feeling his warm skin beneath her hands caused her heart to beat wildly. She sent a prayer of thanks heavenward that fate had brought him into her life.

A soft smile tugged at the corners of her mouth as she mentally shook her wandering thoughts away and glanced up to take in Trevor's handsome features. Claire was taken aback when she saw the livid tick that tightened his jaw. A streak of anger also flashed in his eyes. She laid her palm against his arm to garner his attention. "Trevor? Is something wrong?" She watched his eyes close for a second, then open again to look down at her as he tried to shake off whatever bothered him. His eyes darted away.

Claire followed the line of his gaze. Instantly, a shudder ran through her limbs and the blood drained from her face. The woman who shared an intimate embrace with her husband only a few short months ago alighted from a fancy carriage on the arm of a handsome gentleman. As the couple walked toward them, the dark-haired beauty never took her eyes from Trevor's masculine form.

A rush of nausea raced through Trevor when he saw Regina Simpson strolling toward him on the arm of Leonidas Merritt. *What the hell is she doing here? I saw Emma's list...she wasn't on it...*

Regina held her head high as she stepped up to the porch. Refusing to acknowledge the willowy blonde bride, she fixed an even wider smile on her red lips when Trevor finally met her gaze. Her hand dropped from her escort's arm as she rushed forward to greet her old lover. "Why, Trevor! It's so good to see you!" She kissed the air by his cheek and curled her fingers around his hand. "All your friends from St. Paul have missed you terribly! You've been all the talk with this secret little marriage of yours. Shame on you," she pouted as she flicked his chest gently with her leather gloves.

If I handle this right, I can get her out of sight and deal with this later on... Trevor forced his clenched jaw to relax and glanced down at his wife. Claire stood silent and white-faced beside him. His brow furrowed in concern, sure she might be faint from standing so long in the receiving line. "Claire? Is something wrong?" He wrapped his arm around her waist, offering his own body as support. "Do you need to sit down?"

Regina's blood boiled. Trevor had never looked at her that way. She yanked Leonidas forward, drawing the groom's attention back to her. "You remember Mr. Merritt, don't you? He said he met you in St. Paul."

Trevor shook the man's hand as he continued to watch Claire from the corner of his eye. "Yes I do. Mr. Merritt has had some business dealings with Tyler. I hope things are going well with your company." He tipped his head toward the woman beside him. "I'd like you to meet my wife, Claire."

Leonidas dipped his head in acknowledgment. "My pleasure, Mrs. Wilkins."

Regina jumped forward and clasped Claire's cold hand. "Shame on you, Trevor, for not introducing this quiet little woman to me." She affected a warm smile and swung her eyes back to Trevor's pale wife. "My name is Regina Simpson. Trevor and I are...old friends. I would love to sit with you later on and hear all about how you captured this handsome bachelor, halted his terribly wild ways, and forced him to settle down."

Trevor pulled Claire closer to his side and answered for her. "Claire didn't force me to do anything, and I'm not quite sure that I'm going to give her up for even one minute today. In fact, I hear the fiddles starting, so I think we'll go inside and join the others. My wife has had enough of the sun today. If you'll excuse us?" He took Claire's hand and quickly led her through the open doorway and into the house.

Claire had no choice but to follow. Trevor had her hand in a death grip. As they worked their way through the crowded room, it was all she could do to keep her tears at bay. How dare he approve an invitation for a former lover and flaunt the woman beneath her nose? Claire was no fool. Regina gave herself away immediately with the cool look in her flashing eyes. The woman was none to happy to be meeting Trevor's wife, no matter how much she cooed and smiled.

A roar of approval shook the rafters when the newlyweds finally made their way to the middle of the enormous living room. One voice after another urged them to begin the dancing. As the first strains of the fiddles commenced, Trevor took Claire's hand and led her to the middle of the room. Gently placing his other palm on the small of her back, he moved them around the floor, becoming acutely aware of her silence for the first time.

"Do you realize that we've never danced together?"

"I'm sure you did a lot of it in St. Paul," she replied with a flat tone that belied the warmth of the forced smile on her face.

Trevor leaned back slightly and stared down at her. "Is something wrong? Are you not feeling well? You did look a little pale when we were outside."

His hand was firm and warm against her satin-covered back, creating an indefinable emotion that went straight to her heart. Claire struggled to hold onto her anger, though. If she did not, the terrible ache of betrayal would take over. *Tonight will never happen. I was a fool to think it would...*

Heat radiated from the spot on her back where he touched her, and her breath suddenly came in disjointed rasps. She breathed deeply to calm her jangled nerves. "I'm fine Trevor." As she said the words, she wanted to tear herself from his arms and race upstairs, where she could be alone.

Trevor's brow furrowed. Something was missing in her tone. The earlier happiness and excitement was gone, and he wanted to know why. "So, why the sudden change in attitude?"

"I don't know what you're talking about." As he turned her on the floor, Claire's eye caught sight of Regina Simpson; the woman's eyes were narrowed into pointed daggers. No matter how hurt she was by the appearance of Trevor's former lover, the as yet undiscovered catty side of Claire emerged out of nowhere. *He's my husband, and I'm damn well not going to just hand him over.* One slender arm snaked upward to wrap around her husband's neck, and she let her body sway closer until her breasts brushed innocently against his chest.

Trevor instantly pulled her against him, and the sudden contact with his hard, firm chest weakened Claire's knees. He whirled her again to the subtle beat and, this time, her eyes met Regina's directly.

Resting her cheek against her husband's chest, she allowed the sound of her husband's heartbeat to calm her frazzled nerves. Her eyes fluttered shut, blocking the view of the other woman. *I can't worry about her. I have to accept the fact that Trevor had a life before me. She's here and there's nothing I can do about it, so...*

Trevor felt her chest rise and fall against him in a contented sigh and cursed silently as his gaze scanned the crowded room. He wanted to be alone with his wife. The feel of her soft breasts as they brushed his chest, the curve of her tiny waist beneath his hand, and the light scent of her perfume all combined to affect him in ways he had not experienced in a long time. It felt so good just to hold her...

Trevor gripped his emotions in a fierce hold and vowed silently that, tonight, his wife would not have the chance to crawl alone beneath the quilts. Tonight, he would celebrate his marriage by loving the woman in his arms.

Claire blinked and gradually became aware that the airy strains of the fiddle had quieted. The applause of the guests filtered into her mind, forcing her back to the present. Stepping back from her husband, she could still feel the warmth of his strong arms around her. She tipped her head and met his glittering eyes. The same desire that she had witnessed in his eyes at the bottom of the staircase blazed even brighter across his rugged features.

Her anger at Regina Simpson's presence disappeared. Claire would not waste anymore of her life. She loved him, and that was all she needed to think about. "Thank you for the dance."

Chapter Twenty-Two

Leonidas Merritt sat by himself at an outside table beneath a large umbrella. He had no clue where Regina had gotten herself to, but no matter. He would be a fool to think he was anymore than her escort. Earlier, when the music stopped, he insisted she join the rest of the guests for a light luncheon, instead of following Trevor Wilkins' every move. He did not know the man well, but no groom deserved to have an old lover around making trouble for him. Regina finally agreed, not wanting to create a scene when Leonidas firmly clenched her arm. She sat with him for a matter of ten minutes before making some trivial excuse to leave.

His eyes moved to where the Wilkins brothers sat at another table laughing among themselves. The groom had his arm draped across his new wife's shoulders. The man's fingers automatically caressed the smooth silkiness of her bare upper arm as Tyler and his wife, Emma, conversed casually with the couple.

Leonidas picked up his drink and studied the bride. Watching the willowy blonde, he found it hard to believe that Trevor Wilkins would ever have had a dalliance with the likes of Regina Simpson. The two women were from opposite spectrums. Claire Wilkins, despite everything he had heard from Regina's spiteful mouth on the way down from Biwabik, exuded an honest, earthy persona for everyone to see. His gaze moved to the children, who tumbled on the grass within their mother's eyesight. For Wilkins to take on a passal of kids that did not even belong to him, the mother must be one helluva woman.

"Don't tell me your mooning after the bride."

He glanced up when Regina settled in a chair beside him. She leaned across the table to reach for a dainty sandwich and brushed her breasts across his arm in the process. Leonidas cringed at her vulgarity. If he were not looking for a chance to speak with the Wilkins men one more time about the proposition that still hung in the air, he would leave and let Regina figure out her own way back to Biwabik and her cousin's home. "Not mooning. Just admiring. It seems her husband has an extreme fondness for the woman. I don't blame him. She's quite attractive."

Regina bristled at the response. She was sick of hearing what a wonderful wife and ready-made family Trevor had found for himself. "Oh, come now. She comes from absolutely nothing. The wedding was a pity marriage, that's all. I've been talking to some of the guests. Did you know that no one here really knows her background?"

He sipped his drink and set the glass on the table. "I'm sure you made certain they were all well-informed." A mental shake of the head accompanied his thoughts as to why he had allowed Judd Stone, Regina's cousin, to convince him to let her attend the wedding on his invitation.

"Well, honestly, Lonny. As guests, they have a right to know that she isn't even in their social class. She shows it by sticking to Trevor's side like some milkmaid, rather than making her guest feel comfortable."

"Haven't had a chance to get him alone yet?"

"No, but when the music starts again, you can bet—" She stopped short, realizing that she had given her feelings away as far as Trevor was concerned. Regina settled back in her chair and patted her shiny brunette hair. "I just think she's being rather rude in not sharing the groom with his friends." She leaned over and rested a hand on his arm. "Lonny, will you get me another glass of sherry? It's so warm out today."

Regina unwittingly gave him the excuse he needed to be away from her. "I'll be back shortly." He rose and headed in the direction of the small family group. Regina could wait for her damned drink. It looked like Tyler and his wife were about to leave the table. He needed to speak to both the brothers before he lost the opportunity.

* * *

Tyler turned his head and glanced at his brother. "Don't look now, but I think Mr. Merritt is on his way over."

Trevor handed a dandelion to a tired Hannah, who sat on his lap, and then shrugged. "I was wondering if he was going to approach us today. It's been awhile, hasn't it? I don't hear anything good out there as far as his investments go. He just can't seem to gather enough capital to get the creditors off his back. I still feel the same about that piece of property. What about you?"

"I haven't changed my mind. Cole feels the same," replied Tyler. "Do we stop the conversation immediately, or let the man say his piece?"

"I guess we let him talk. May as well sit down and get it over with."

Claire stood and gathered Hannah into her arms. "I'll take Hannah upstairs for a nap and leave you to talk among yourselves."

Trevor followed her up, laid his hand on the sleepy girl's head and kissed her cheek. "Be a good girl for your ma." His eyes met Claire's. Without thought, he bent slightly and brushed his lips against hers. "Are you sure you couldn't use some help?" He had not come across the chance to speak to her privately, to understand why she had become increasingly quiet as the day wore on. He could not put his finger on it, but had known her long enough to understand that something was not quite right.

"I'll be fine. I think I'll take all the girls upstairs for a small rest. It looks to be a long night yet." Claire refused to meet his eyes directly before she quickly turned her back to him.

Trevor's brow dipped in a frown as he watched her head for the house with her four daughters and Emma in tow. *What the hell is going on with her?* He turned on his heel, slumped into his chair just as Leonidas reached the table, and watched Tyler take the man's offered hand in his.

"Mr. Merritt. Sit down and make yourself comfortable." Tyler waited until his guest was settled in the chair and joined him a second later. "Sorry that I haven't had a chance to seek you out. It's rather crazy around here with all the people."

Leonidas waved his hand. "No problem. I thought I'd take a walk over, since you weren't occupied with any other guests." His gaze encompassed both brothers. "I didn't chase your wives away, did I?"

"It was time for the kids to take a rest," Trevor replied, who was still slightly perturbed at his inability to stay in step with his wife. "What can we do for you?"

A wry smile curved Leonidas' mouth. "I think I've laid that answer at your feet already. You haven't, by any chance, given any more thought to the sale of your northern property?"

Trevor leaned forward and clasped his hands on the table's surface. "I wish I could help you out, Mr. Merritt. We all do. The bottom line, however, is that we've decided to stay firm in our decision. If it were any other piece of property, I would probably be negotiating right now. As it is, I have a home up in that area that is almost completed. I'll be moving my family there sometime in the near future." He watched the other man's shoulders fall along with the air he expelled from his lungs. "I have to be honest. What I've been hearing is not good. This financial panic that's spreading across the country does not bode good things for the future. A number of banks are closing. How is your company's fiscal status, if you don't mind me asking?"

"Not good—the banks that are still open don't want to loan money. I won't lie to you." Leonidas shook his head with a deep sigh. "At the beginning of the year, things were going well. We pushed hard and the Merritt name was one to be reckoned with. Our company remained viable. But now we find it necessary to pour quite a bit of money into our mines—money that is tied up in the rail line from Duluth. I'm sure you've heard that our creditors are breathing down our necks." He paused and looked from Trevor's concerned expression to his brother's. "My family members are waiting to hear from me. If I can't persuade you to sell, then we will have no choice but to go to John Rockefeller and accept his proposal for a buy-out."

Trevor's chin came up. "You're making a mistake. There must be some other avenue. If that man has his way, he will eventually control everything he can get his hands on."

Leonidas shrugged helplessly. "We have no other choice. No matter how some investors look at him, John is a smart man and continues to amass his fortune."

"My, my. Are you gentlemen going to talk business the entire afternoon?" Regina sauntered closer to the table, twirling her sun umbrella with pouting red lips. "I'm feeling a little put out with no one paying attention to me."

Both Tyler and Leonidas rose to their feet, as manners dictated, but Trevor continued to sip his drink and eye the woman over the rim of his glass. Finally, he pushed himself away from the table and rose in gentlemanly fashion.

After casting a curious glance at his brother, Tyler pulled out an empty chair between him and Trevor. "Please, have a seat. Mrs. Simpson, isn't it?" He waited for her to sit down before he returned to his own chair, as did the other men.

Regina set her open umbrella on end beside her chair. "Widow Simpson. My husband, bless his soul, succumbed a year and a half ago. I've just recently come out of mourning."

Tyler's brain worked furiously to try and think of something to say. The other males at the table had suddenly become mute. "I'm sorry for your loss."

Trevor's jaw clenched. *Mourning, my ass.* Regina had dogged him even before her husband, Sydney, died. He was instantly ashamed to think that, even though he refused to have anything to do with the woman when her husband was alive, he had easily given into his baser needs once the man lay cold in the ground.

Regina leaned across the short space between her chair and Trevor's and rested her hand on his arm. "I haven't had a chance to speak to you all day." Her lashes fluttered as she spoke again to Tyler. "You see, Trevor and I were old friends when he lived in St. Paul."

The unspoken facts instantly meshed inside Tyler's head. *Ah, hell...someone from Trevor's past. No wonder he looks ready to explode. Think!* "I know a lot of people from the city miss him, but we're very happy that he's come north on a permanent basis. You must have had a chance to meet his new wife, Claire? We're all quite taken with her and very happy for him. She's a wonderful lady." The music struck up inside the house once more, providing a means to get he and his brother away from the table. "In fact, I'm sure she'll be down soon, so her groom can take her for a spin on the dance floor."

Tyler hid a smile when he noticed Regina's back stiffen in response to his babbling. *There...that ought to save Trevor's ass for the time being...*

A sudden smile appeared on her red lips, stopping Tyler's

thoughts dead. "Yes, I have met her. And, speaking of the music—" she popped up from the chair and tugged on the groom's arm "—I insist, Trevor, that you share one little dance with me before your wife returns. If we don't do it now, I may never get my turn."

Trevor was trapped. He flashed his brother a woeful look and could do nothing but rise and offer his arm to his insistent guest. "I was going to go up to the house anyway. One dance, Regina, then I'll be leaving to find Claire."

Regina clasped his bent arm tightly, twisted to snatch her umbrella off the ground, and held the twirling sunshade over her head with a smile. "We'll just see about that. I'm sure I can persuade you to give me more than just one little spin around the floor."

Trevor's lips drew in a tight line as he led the woman into the house.

* * *

Claire stood behind the curtain in the girls' room, clutching the heavy material until her knuckles turned white as she watched Regina Simpson slither across the lawn in the direction of Trevor's table. Her heart sank a moment later when all three men stood. Tyler pulled out a chair, and then waited until Regina seated herself beside Trevor before he joined them again.

Her chin trembled as she gripped the curtain even tighter. *I should have known...she wouldn't be here if he didn't want her to be... But how can I blame him when she's so beautiful? She's the type of woman he might have spent his life with—if it wasn't for his generosity when we had nowhere else to go...* Claire's former insecurities reared inside her brain. Even with as complimentary as her husband was earlier, and even the gift of the wedding ring, did not belie the fact that Trevor once possessed a different life—one filled with stunning women who had breeding and aristocracy coursing through their veins.

Claire's mind struggled with the pain of watching Regina lean in Trevor's direction and place a hand on his arm. Only a few minutes passed before he rose and offered her his arm. The woman sidled up beside him, lifted her fancy umbrella, and smiled up into his eyes.

Claire whirled from the sight of the two of them headed for the house, arm in arm. Her knees shook as she sank onto a chair and clamped a hand over her mouth; she did not want the coming sob to awaken the sleeping girls.

Her panicked, tearing eyes darted about the quiet room. She would need to pull herself together for the many hours ahead. Claire gave herself a few moments to control the aching need that gripped her body and forced it away—just as she had done with many other desires in her life. Trevor would never completely belong to her.

She rose a bit unsteadily and inhaled deeply. As much as she would like to haul Regina from the house by her own two hands, Claire would not demonstrate her lack of breeding by acting like the dirt farmer's wife she would always be.

* * *

Trevor and Regina entered through the open door to the living room. The widow pasted a wide smile on her face for everyone to see and hugged her escort's arm against her breast, ignoring his concealed attempt to pull away.

Glancing up, her eyes hid the fact that she wanted to slap his handsome face for his lack of responses to her silly observations as they strolled to the house. Regina gathered her wits about her, however, and pulled him to the center of the room before he managed to bolt from her sight. She lifted her hand and waited for him to take it. He hesitated. "Oh, come on, Trevor. Just one dance for old time's sake."

He sighed heavily and glanced at the entrance into the living room. He did not see Claire, but he *did* notice how the guests kept an eye on them. He took Regina's hand, placed his palm on her slim waist, and began to move about the room. "Everyone is watching us," he stated quietly. "Why is that? Regina, how many people know that we were seeing each other at one time?"

She was thrilled to be back in his arms. "I imagine some have speculated. After all, Trevor, St. Paul's society always kept an eye on you. You're wealthy, handsome, and *was,* at one time, very much available. Let them gawk. I've missed you so much, and it feels so good to be with you again."

Trevor's eyes widened when he looked down at her. "You're not *with* me, Regina. I'm simply dancing with a guest at my wedding."

"Haven't you missed me even a little?" she pouted.

Trevor sighed visibly and made the decision to gently end any misconceptions the woman had as far as the two of them and their past were concerned. "Listen, Regina. I'm sorry if I led you to believe that there might be a future for us. That was not my intention. I'm a married man now. I...I love my wife dearly." A slight gasp escaped her mouth and, again, Trevor sighed. *How ironic that she's the one who gets to hear those words the first time I speak them aloud.*

Trevor's declaration was enough to make Regina forget she was in his home and at his wedding reception. "I would like to know just one thing. Were you seeing her when you were *bedding* me?" Regina clutched at his hand and pushed closer until her breasts flattened against his chest.

"Stop that—" Trevor growled, totally shocked that Regina would act the way she was before all his guests.

"Why, Trevor; why did you marry another woman? I love you." Regina was desperate. "We could still continue to see one another..."

"This is neither the time nor the place, Regina. Besides, things just happened..." He paled slightly when he glanced up to see Claire standing in the doorway clutching the back of a nearby chair in a death grip. Her wide, gray eyes never left his face. Trevor grabbed the widow's arm and, trying to keep the anger at himself in check for taking what she had offered in the past, he hauled her as inconspicuously as possible to the divan that was pushed against the wall. He lowered his head and spoke for her ears alone. "My wife is waiting for me. I'm sorry, Regina—"

He turned on his heel then, and headed for the doorway. His heart pounded. Claire had seen Regina's little stunt on the dance floor. He was sure of it—and he was just as sure that there would be hell to pay because of it. He could not blame his wife, however. This was supposed to be Claire's day, and he felt like the biggest oaf in northern Minnesota.

Claire stepped forward when he reached her. A gentle smile curved her mouth, belying the ashen color of her cheeks. Instead of the anger Trevor fully expected her to heap upon his shoulders, she surprised him by reaching out a hand. Her eyes were slightly swollen though, as if she had been crying.

"Claire..." he spoke quietly, feeling horrible that he was the cause of her distress, "...I need to explain something to you right now."

"Can it wait?" She read the instant confusion in his eyes and continued. "I just thought that this would be a good time to dance, since the girls are sleeping. I won't have to keep such a close eye on them." She had come down from her daughters' bedroom with every intention of accepting Trevor's past. Seeing him with Regina in his arms, however, and the way the woman pressed her body to his had caused uninvited anger to flare brightly in her heart—just before the physical ache in her chest threatened to suffocate her once again. Even with the many contrary emotions prodding at her insides, Claire still refused to react in front of her husband's guests. She had seen most of them eyeing the woman in Trevor's arms, and then searching her own face as she entered the room.

Claire tucked her hand beneath Trevor's elbow and led him straight to Regina, instead of directly to the dance area. His eyes widened when she stopped before the woman who had literally been gnashing her teeth only seconds before glancing up in surprise.

Claire held out her hand expectantly. Regina stood warily and pressed her manicured fingers into the bride's palm. She had no choice when so many others kept their eyes glued to the trio, waiting to see what would unfold.

Claire forced another soft smile to curve her lips. "I didn't have the chance when we first met to thank you for coming to celebrate the day with us. I'm afraid I was a little overwhelmed by all the guests that were arriving. I hope you're having a good time and that you enjoyed the dance with my husband."

Regina was speechless.

"I hope we'll have a chance to chat later on," Claire continued. "I'm so excited to meet all of Trevor's friends. But, for now, I think I'll take the opportunity to dance with him, since our children are napping. Good day."

Regina's fingers dropped to her side when Claire led a silent Trevor in the direction of the fiddles.

Son of a bitch... Claire's reaction proved without a doubt that she saw Regina's antics. There would be no other reason to have approached the woman. "Let's go outside, Claire. I want to talk to you in private," he stated as he began to move her around the floor.

"Why in private, Trevor? It seems that everyone here witnessed your dance with that woman." There—it was out in the open. She smiled as she glanced around the room. "I'm upset, yes, but I refuse to make a scene in front of all these people."

"I'm sorry, Claire. I didn't mean for you to see that."

Claire nearly burst into tears with his honesty. He most likely planned to keep the widow and his relationship with the woman a secret. But now? Everyone was aware of it. As they continued to dance, Claire's head began to pound. As much as she loved the man in her arms and would continue to do so, she could not accept him flaunting his past beneath her nose. Claire's back stiffened. *I don't deserve that—no wife does, whether the marriage is a business partnership or not.*

"You're angry with me."

Her cheeks were starting to ache with the bogus smile still in place. "No woman desires being made the fool..." She hung on the precipice of losing complete control and racing from the room, sobbing into her hands before their guests.

"Claire—"

She scratched her way toward composure. The only way to maintain it was to hold onto her anger. "Shut up, Trevor. Everyone is watching us."

His eyebrows rose in disbelief. He had never, even in the earlier days when she lambasted him at every turn, heard Claire use those two words with such fervor.

They continued the dance in silence, looking like a loving couple who were having the time of their life.

* * *

Claire quietly closed the door to Hannah and Ruth's room and her thoughts turned to earlier that evening when she and Trevor carried the two heavy-lidded little girls to their beds. The quickly deteriorating day hung over both their heads, and they had ended up snapping at one another with every turn of the conversation. Claire was angry at Regina's presence, and Trevor fumed because his wife dug in her heels and refused to discuss it with him.

Her heart pounded even now with the memory of how he had

clutched her arm in the upper hallway, demanding to be heard. He had quite eloquently stated that he would be "goddamned" if he was going to wait another minute to fully explain what had happened on the dance floor.

In turn, Claire stated that it looked to her like he was definitely headed for hell. She had raised her nose arrogantly in the air then, and left him standing with his jaw hanging. He finally recovered and caught up to her on the steps as she returned to the party to bid goodnight to their guests.

Now, as she walked slowly down the hallway, Claire was all too aware of the fact that he waited in their suite for her to arrive. She had made every excuse possible to draw out the evening, using the time to prepare the things she wanted to say to him. Doing so was the only way to cling to her anger; she had to, or risk crumbling from the hurt evoked every time she thought of Regina Simpson—and risk being used by a man once again.

Claire paused before a family portrait of her husband and his siblings that hung in the hallway. Crossing her arms, she leaned in and studied the picture; she did not possess a single portrait of herself as a small child. Nor did she have any of Jonah and the girls. Eyeing the chair that sat only a few feet away, she sank onto the surface and glanced at her surroundings.

Gaslights, encased in beautiful brass votives, flickered in a line as far as the eye could see. Her hand followed the edge of the smooth wooden arm of her seat. Her gaze dropped to the blue satin that covered her body. The chair and the dress had probably cost more than what she would have needed to pay her taxes in order to keep the farm.

Her shoulders fell with the weary sigh that escaped her lips. There she was, basking in the lap of luxury; something she had dreamed about her entire life. Only now did she realize that the dream, now *her* reality, held no substance whatsoever. Claire could easily take her children, leave the house right at that very moment, and walk back to the rented shack in Biwabik. For this newest dream to work though, Trevor would have to follow, for no other reason than that there was no other place he would rather be.

Claire leaned against the backrest and closed her eyes. She loved him; plain and simple. The mere thought turned up the corner of her mouth in a wry smile. *Plain and simple—just like me...* Therein lay the problem. No matter how she tried, Claire would never measure up to the high standards her husband was accustomed to. To just walk away, as she had planned earlier, was not the answer either. Better to see his handsome face on the pillow than to spend her life in misery, wondering if she would ever set eyes on him again.

A small streak of pain pierced her heart when she thought of how this night should have ended. She should be in his arms right now, rather than mooning over the fact that it would never happen.

Anger, Claire. Hang on to the anger or you'll forgive him for anything...even another woman. Think about Regina Simpson and go in swinging. Remember your pride...

She rose from the chair and continued down the hall until she came to the open door of their room. Peeking in, she spied Trevor lounging in one of the chairs before the fireplace. He looked more relaxed than he had the entire afternoon. Claire flexed her shoulders, lifted her chin, took a deep breath, and sauntered into the room. She closed the door behind her.

She could see him out of the corner of her eye as she crossed to the bureau and pulled a plain cotton nightdress from a drawer. She paused when her troubled eyes caught sight of the beautiful, ultra sheer nightgown that she had originally planned to where that evening. Her blood began to boil as she wondered how many times Regina had pranced before her husband in the same. She slammed the drawer.

Ignoring the man who watched her every move, Claire stomped across the room and stepped behind the privacy screen to change. She heard him clear his throat; *I hope he chokes on whatever he's trying to get rid of...*

"Are you finally ready to talk to me?" His voice floated over the top of the screen.

"Go ahead. No one's stopping you." Claire jerked her arms from the sleeves of the dress and tossed the garment to the floor.

"I want to apologize for today."

"What did you do?" Claire listened to his sharp intake of breath as she eyed her discarded gown. *Besides making me look stupid in front of everyone?* She had always taken excellent care of the few things she owned. Now was not the time to change things. She bent down, scooped up the dress, and neatly hung it on a peg—anything to occupy herself so she did not tear around the edge of the screen and punch the son of a bitch.

"I didn't do anything." Trevor tilted his head when he heard a muffled snort from somewhere behind the screen. "What was that for?"

He almost blurted out the fact that the only thing he did was confess to Regina how much he loved his wife. But admitting his feelings to Claire in the middle of what looked to be a heated argument ready to happen was not how Trevor imagined his wife should hear the words for the first time.

"If you didn't do anything, then why are you apologizing?" Claire plopped down on a chair and stripped off a silk stocking in one smooth movement.

Trevor's fingers tightened into a fist. "You're really making me pay for dancing with Regina, aren't you?" Nothing. Absolute silence. "Claire?" He rose from the chair.

She heard him stand up. In one quick jerk, her other sock was off and floating to the floor. Yanking her old nightgown from a second peg, she slipped it over her head and waited with a pounding heart to see what he would do next. His silence gave her a quick second to think. *Why can't you just say you love me?* Her lids drooped as she leaned against the wall.

"Claire?" He took another step.

"I hope you're not thinking about coming back here," she warned. "I'm trying to change."

He stopped short. "Well, hurry up, or I will. Dammit, Claire, I want to get this straightened out."

Good...he sounds frazzled. I'm not the only one having a horrible night. She stood, wiggled her butt until the nightgown flounced around her ankles, and hurriedly tied the ribbons tight at the bodice—all the way up to her chin. Stepping from behind the screen, Claire shot Trevor an angry glare, marched past where he stood, and climbed into the bed.

His hands spread wide in amazement as he watched his wife yank the quilt up to her chin. A puzzled look flashed in his eyes. "I thought we were going to have a discussion?"

"I'm tired. I really hoped you were done yapping." The hair

stood up on the back of her neck when he rolled his eyes heavenward and stomped back to the chair. Claire's anger instantly seeped to the surface. "All right. Do you want to know why I'm so angry?"

"What the hell do you think?" he spouted back as he crossed his ankle over one knee. Trevor wrenched his boot off, tossed it onto the floor and proceeded to do the same with the other one. "I've only been trying to get it out of you all goddamned day."

"You don't have to cuss!"

He swung his head in Claire's direction. "Lady, I haven't even begun to cuss. Would you just spill it?"

Claire's chest heaved. "I'm angry because you had the nerve to invite your past lover to *our* wedding reception and parade her under *my* nose. You know what, Trevor? If she's the kind of woman who can give you what you're looking for in life, then be my guest. I'm done crying about it."

He bounded from the chair in his stocking feet, his face reddening by the second; his green eyes shot sparks of fire. "I didn't invite her here. I don't even remember her name being on the guest list." He paused and his eyes narrowed with suspicion. "Wait a minute. What makes you think I have any kind of past with her anyway? That's a huge assumption when we only shared a dance."

Claire sank into the pillow, her anger suddenly replaced by the strangling hurt she had struggled to keep at bay over the past weeks. "Because I saw you with her in St. Paul—and because I'm not a fool."

"When?" His mind raced to put Claire and Regina in the same room. It had never happened.

Claire's fingers curled around the edge of the blanket as she stared at him. "When I walked to town the morning after the storm." Her voice lowered. "I saw you with Regina at the stable—she was in your arms. You kissed her and said you'd probably see her sometime that week."

Trevor ran a hand through his tousled hair, trying to remember. "Claire, I don't know what..." The words died in his throat. Regina had visited him at the racetrack the morning after the storm. The memory of how badly he wanted to rid himself of the woman so he could get to Claire's house—and hold her in his arms again—roared in his brain.

She watched the memory of that morning dawn in his eyes. "I

see that it's all coming back. How do you think I felt when I saw the two of you?"

Trevor dropped into the chair again, as if the wind had been knocked from his lungs. His head came up and he stared at Claire's trembling chin. "Is that why you left St. Paul without a word?"

"What was I supposed to do? You left my house the night before with a promise to come back. I actually believed that you wanted to help me." She ducked her head momentarily before meeting his gaze once more. "I actually believed, Trevor, that sharing what we did in the barn meant something to you. I hurried to town on my own that next morning, determined to find you and discuss the future—if we had one. Instead, I came out the fool again. I should have known that some poor dirt farmer's widow could never keep your attention."

"It wasn't like that at all. Yes, Regina is someone from my past, but..." He lowered his head for a moment and ran a hand through his hair before meeting her eyes again. "Christ, Claire, I didn't even know you existed before I met Jonah and the rest of you on the street that first day. Until then, yes; Regina was a part of my life—a very minimal part of my life. But she means absolutely nothing to me now. I have you and the kids, and I couldn't be happier." He rose and took a step toward the bed.

She lifted her palm to stave off his advance. The memory of Regina clinging to his arm, and the intimate dance Trevor shared with the woman soon after, still prodded at her heart. Claire was drained. "I'm done discussing it." She sank into the pillow and rolled to face the wall.

Trevor's heart sank as he studied the slim line of her back. He wanted to tell her he loved her—he wanted to hold her in his arms. "Well, then, let's talk about—"

"Not another word or I'll go make my bed with the girls tonight. What will your family have to say about that?" She instantly winced, wondering when she had become such a shrew. Claire instantly hated herself. She wanted him beside her—even if he did not want to make love to her. It was her insecurity, after all, that had caused the turmoil of the day. *You fool! If you want him, then fight for him!*

She sat up in the bed and turned to face him, then her eyes flew to the door as it closed. He was gone. Claire stared in disbelief. Trevor had made his choice—and she could not blame him. She was the one who ultimately sent him into the comforting arms of another woman.

Keeper of the Heart

Chapter Twenty-Three

Claire entered the kitchen the following morning after hustling herself from the suite. Trevor had finally returned to spend the night in the chair. The man had tossed and turned until the wee hours, then finally, his breathing changed to a deep, regular rhythm as the sun crested the hoizon. Claire quickly took the opportunity to make good her escape. The smell of frying bacon atop the woodstove floated on the air as the swinging door closed behind her.

Katy glanced up to, looking to see who was entering the kitchen at such an early hour. "Well, good morning to you, Claire. Let me stoke this fire, and I'll be pourin' you a cup of coffee. You're up early after the big day."

Claire waved a hand, picked through Katy's many aprons that hung on a peg near the door, and donned one that had definitely seen better days. She crossed to a cabinet and grabbed a cup. "No, just keep doing what you're doing. I'm perfectly able to take care of myself. In fact, I'm going to help you with breakfast today." *And every day...*

"Oh, no need," the housekeeper replied as she closed the cast iron fire door. "I've got everything under control. I told Emma that I would take care of breakfast today. If no one comes down, then I'll be hustlin' trays up the stairs. My treat after the wedding party."

Claire hesitated, momentarily wondering what the Irish woman would think when she was informed that one of the 'Mrs. Wilkins' planned to become a servant in the household. Deciding to say nothing yet, she quickly poured herself some coffee, set the mug on the worktable, and bent to retrieve a stack of clean plates. "I'll set the table in the other room just in case anyone comes down." She bent over the worktable to count out the correct number of forks.

Katy watched Claire beneath a furrowed brow, slightly surprised that the 'bride' was in the kitchen so early in the day. After a quick glance at the woman's faded dress, the housekeeper's curiosity got the best of her. "I see you're wearing the dress you arrived in."

Here it comes... Claire piled cloth napkins on the stack of dishes and remained closed-mouthed.

Once more, Katy's gaze scanned the washed out garment. "If you be needin' a clean dress, Claire, I'd be happy to do washing today."

"Oh, my clothes are clean. I've decided to earn my keep, starting here in the kitchen, but didn't want to ruin a new dress in the process. Now, what else would you like me to do when I'm done setting the table?"

The Irish woman leaned forward and placed her hands on each of her slim hips. "What are you talking about, Claire? Just what do you mean by 'earning your keep'? You labor as hard as Emma and August when it comes to this house."

Claire picked up the dishes and cradled them in her arms, finally finding the courage to meet Katy's questioning eyes. "I'm more like you than I am the other ladies in this house, Katy, and I have come to the decision that my place is here, in the kitchen, and not sitting at the main table acting as if I were some grand dame. I...I discovered yesterday that I can never compete in the world of the rich."

Katy smacked her forehead with an open palm, shook her head, and leaned against the counter. "Have you discussed this new notion with your husband...who just happens to be *Mr.* Trevor Wilkins?"

Claire shrugged. "I'm sure he'll figure it out eventually when he comes down for breakfast."

"And I'm sure you be knowin' that he will not take this lightly?"

"Why should he care?"

"Ha! Because you're his wife!"

"Well, one never would have known that yesterday afternoon." Claire studied the ceiling above her head until she regained the control of her swarming emotions. "The women Trevor is used to are far more beautiful and intelligent. I just don't fit inside that mold."

"What are you talking about? How can you even say that?"

"Because it's true."

Katy immediately pointed at a chair; her demeanor brooked no resistance. "Sit down, Claire."

"Katy, I—"

"Sit!" the housekeeper admonished, and then nodded her chin when Claire finally relented, set the dishes on the table, and plopped down on the seat.

Katy crossed to a stool and perched on the flat surface. "All righty, then. We'll discuss what brought on this new attitude of yours in a minute. But, first, I've got something to say. Have you stopped to really look at the other women in this house? Yes, Emma is a blueblood through and through, but has she ever treated you at a lesser status because of it? No—" her hand sliced through the air "—that woman has one of the biggest hearts I know—just like her sister-in-law, who only a short time ago was a fugitive Sioux. That one doesn't even know how to read, yet Cole loves her just the same—just as your man loves you."

Claire's head snapped up and her eyes turned to steel. "He doesn't, Katy. He plays the game, but I'm not the woman he wants to spend the rest of his life with. His actions yesterday showed me that."

"What are you spoutin' about now?" The woman crossed her arms over her chest. "Tell me about yesterday."

"Let's just say that it didn't take long for my husband to end up with a rich widow from St. Paul on his arm. She reminded me of a cat in heat, rubbing herself against him every chance she got, and he didn't seem to mind in the least. Katy, Trevor is accustomed to cultured, beautiful women. I'll never be able to compete with that."

"Ah, go on. Trevor is too much of a gentleman to make a scene in public by sending a shrew like that away. Listen, girlie; the man's in love—with you! If he wasn't, you wouldn't be here. And he loves your children."

Claire had to agree with Katy's last statement. She had no doubt that her husband had deep feelings for all five of her kids. His constant worry was that something would happen to one of them. They, in turn, loved him back.

Claire rose from the chair and scooped up the stack of dishes. On her way out to the dining room, she hesitated by the door and glanced back at Katy. "I agree with you that he does love my children. That's probably the reason I'm still here; not once has he even mentioned the word 'love' in reference to me, Katy. And...as embarrassing as this is, I ruined my chances last night to ever have him say those words to me. I was so angry and hurt that I never gave him the opportunity to explain. Instead, I turned my back on him. He left our suite for God knows where. Hours later, he came back and slept in the chair. He doesn't want anything to do with me and it's no one's fault but my own." Her shoulder leaned heavily against the door as she prepared to exit the kitchen.

"Wait just one minute!" Katy heaved herself from the stool and rested a hip against the counter. "I won't even be askin' you if you love that man. It's as clear as the nose on my face. But I never took you for a quitter, Claire. Not once. So, if you're of a mind to act as a servant in this house, then make it work to your advantage. Then we'll be done with this foolishness once and for all."

Claire retraced her steps, however hesitantly. Katy had piqued her interest. "What are you talking about?"

"Aha! I was right—you aren't a quitter. I've seen many strange things around this ranch, Claire, since me and my Dougan arrived. One thing though, I've learned for certain. The Wilkins men may strut about and act like the world owes them a favor at times, but their women can change that attitude with a snap of their fingers." She smiled and reached out to squeeze the younger woman's arm. "I'm thinking that if you start to act like a servant around here, instead of his wife, it could be the one thing that will push that husband of yours into 'fessing up to his feelings."

The woman's observations swirled in Claire's brain. As depressed as she had been the entire night, Claire still berated herself for not continuing the late night conversation. Instead, she ignored her husband, rolled to face the wall, and stubbornly refused to talk. Maybe Katy had a point. Maybe it was time to take the bull by the horns. Claire stood on a ledge; it was time to take the leap. Her eyes met Katy's sparkling ones. "Are you sure know what you're talking about?"

The housekeeper grinned from ear to ear and raised her palm. "God's word. Not one of the men in this household has ever been swayed by money in a pocket or fancy fluff in expensive walking shoes. They go straight to a person's heart to find their worth. You mark my words. Besides, *Mrs.* Wilkins, what do you have to lose?"

A hesitant—and hopeful—smile spread across Claire's face. Her eyes twinkled. "Katy? I think I'll be working along side of you this morning.

* * *

Claire strode through the kitchen door with the stack of plates in her hands. Her eyes widened when she discovered Emma pouring coffee for Tyler, who was seated at the table.

Her sister-in-law glanced over her shoulder. "Good morning, Claire. We didn't think you and Trevor were down yet. I was just going to get Tyler a cup of coffee, and then inform Katy that we're here. Since she promised to treat us this morning, we decided to sneak down early and have a quiet breakfast before the kids wake up." Her hand stopped in midair, with the pot handle clutched in her fingers. Her green eyes scanned Claire's faded dress and Katy's old apron. "Why are you dressed like that? You've got an entire closet full of new clothes."

Claire's gray eyes darted from one to the other. Chewing nervously on her bottom lip, she finally decided to come clean. After all, it was Emma who once stated that she had been forced to go after what she wanted. "I'm taking your advice, Emma. After yesterday, my husband needs a push in the right direction. This morning, I plan to shove him good."

Tyler leaned forward, rested his elbows on the table, and rubbed his forehead with his hands. "Ah, shit," he murmured.

Emma hooked another cup with her little finger, crossed to the table, and took a chair beside her silent and suddenly nervous husband. Calmly, she filled the mugs and placed the pot on the table. "I thought something was going on yesterday. What happened?"

Claire set the plates on the table and smoothed the front of the worn apron. "That's neither here nor there. Just follow my lead after he comes in and don't say a word. I've got to get back in the kitchen before he shows up." Her chin rose as her startled eyes darted in the direction of the living room. "I think I hear him coming down the steps. Please, you won't say anything, will you?"

Emma's smile flashed, letting Claire know she was in agreement.

"Tyler?"

Claire's brother-in-law finally raised his twinkling eyes. "You know, to hell with it. I wouldn't miss this for all the tea in China."

* * *

Trevor came down the front staircase after searching the second floor for his wife. The kids were still sleeping, so the next best possibility was the kitchen.

At daybreak, he had sprawled in the chair, angry with Claire because of her stubborn humility. He was sorry now that he had lost his temper and left her to herself. Through the long night, he came to understand Claire's unreasonable stance. She had experienced nothing but hard knocks her entire life and trusting anyone—even a husband that professed to be by her side always—was not something that came easy for her. Thinking further on it, that prickly pride of hers was one of the reasons that drew him to Claire in the first place. *Well, that's going to end today. She can spout off and act like a shrew, but I'm going to have my say. I love those kids and I love her—the partnership ends today if I have to tie her to a chair.*

A wry smile curved his lips. Some people might think he was crazy to even try, but that's what he was—crazy in love with Claire.

Trevor strolled into the dining room looking rumpled and slightly weary. Looking around, his shoulders fell with a sigh when he discovered his wife was still missing. "Have any of you seen Claire?"

Emma busied herself with a string springing from her lacy cuff. "Not this morning." She glanced up. "Have you seen her, Tyler?"

He mutely shook his head and sipped his coffee.

Trevor dragged out a chair and sank to the surface. "Well, I wonder where she went. She wasn't in our room when I woke up. I'll have to check with Katy and see if Claire's been through the kitchen. Pass the coffee, will you? I'm in dire need of a cup."

Emma bit the inside of her cheek and did as requested. After darting a quick glance at her husband, where he sat beside her, she settled back and waited for the show.

She did not have long to wait.

The hinges of the swinging door creaked when Claire whirled through with a dish of scrambled eggs in one hand and a platter of fried ham in the other. She nodded her head at Emma and Tyler. "Good morning. You two are up bright and early." Ignoring Trevor, she proceeded to the sideboard.

Trevor's speculating green eyes followed her. *What the hell is she wearing...* He stood, pulled out the chair beside him, and waited to help Claire be seated for the early breakfast.

After assuring a serving spoon was laid beside the ceramic dish filled with eggs, Claire turned and scanned the table. "Oh, I see there's no pitcher of water out here and you need some warm muffins. I'll get them immediately." She disappeared back inside the kitchen in a flash.

One of Trevor's dark eyebrows lifted quizzically as he watched the door swing to a stop. He shifted where he stood, his mind dwelling on the fact that Claire wore one of Katy's aprons. His scrutinizing gaze swung to Tyler and Emma's expressions. Neither seemed to notice that his wife not only looked like a maid, but was acting like one, too. His fingers tapped the back of the chair. *Maybe I'm imagining it...*

Claire returned with a glass pitcher of water and the promised muffins and carefully placed both on the table before Emma. Once again, she ignored Trevor where he stood behind her chair. She hid a smile. *Sorry dear, but I won't be sitting in it this morning...*

Tyler's eyes swept downward when his brother's gaze narrowed even further; he ignored Emma's gentle kick beneath the table.

The newest Mrs. Wilkins turned on the heel of her old shoes and surveyed the table. If was difficult to miss Tyler's expression; the man leaned over his bent elbows once again, rubbed his forehead, and hid a wry smile from his brother. "Is there anything else I can do for all of you before I start the dishes?" She tipped her head and smiled. "Well, just let me know. I'll let you eat in peace now. Have a good morning." Claire lifted her chin, rounded the table, and headed for the kitchen door.

"What's going on, Claire?" Trevor ground out. He had had enough. Whatever his wife was up to, he damned well was going to put a halt to it.

Claire's first mistake was actually letting her gaze touch her husband's reddening face. His glittering eyes pinned her to the spot where she stood. She nervously cleared her throat. *Stay calm...* "Why nothing. Is there a problem?"

He glowered at her. "The breakfast on the sidebar is getting cold." His head nodded at the chair before him; his tense hands rested on the back. "If you'll sit, I'll get you a plate and we can all enjoy our meal together." Trevor absolutely refused to meet his brothers' eyes, more angry than embarrassed that Tyler and Emma were forced to witness Claire's strange behavior.

"No, thank you. I've got quite a bit of work to do today in the kitchen. Maybe you'd like to invite someone of a...a higher class to sit beside you. I'm sure the conversation would be so much more stimulating." Claire lifted her nose in the air and sashayed from the room.

From the corner of her eye, Emma spotted Tyler's shaking shoulders. She did not dare look directly at him or all would be lost. Claire's performance was much more entertaining than she expected. Emma controlled the laughter that was a hair away from bursting from her throat, and peeked up to check her brother-in-law's reaction.

Trevor literally seethed with anger where he still stood behind the chair. His jaw clenched tightly and his eyes smoldered. She watched his fingers clasp and unclasp the wooden backrest; all hell was about to break loose.

Trevor took a deep breath and marched after his wife.

* * *

Katy nearly jumped out of her skin when the swinging door banged loudly against the interior wall of the kitchen. Claire whirled to see her husband's large frame filling the doorway. Controlling her inner turmoil at the site of him, she crossed her arms beneath her breasts, cocked her head to the side, and raised a slim eyebrow in question. "Is that really necessary, Trevor? If you'd like something, you don't need to be slamming doors to get my attention. Ring the serving bell—I'll be sure to come running."

Trevor's eyes narrowed dangerously. "Come back in the dining room right now and eat your breakfast," he seethed through a still-clenched jaw.

"I'm sorry, but right now, I've got work to do."

Trevor inhaled a deep, calming breath, then strolled leisurely into the kitchen, allowing the door to swing closed behind him. He never took his glittering gaze from her face.

Claire felt strangely like a mouse being stalked by an angry tomcat as he approached. Quickly, she stepped behind the workbench, putting the large slab of wood between her and the man whose face was getting redder by the second. "What are you doing?" she asked suspiciously.

Trevor reached the end of the workbench and continued around the corner, noting how white Claire's face became when she realized she really had nowhere to run. "I'm collecting *my* wife, so I can enjoy breakfast with her by *my* side." His words were stilted with anger, despite his composed features.

Claire sidestepped around the opposite end of the butcher-block table, beginning to doubt her earlier idea of moving from the position of wife to that of a family servant. "I'm not hungry. I ate this morning with the farmhands."

Katy's eyes bulged at Claire's outright lie and, in a flash, her hand completed the sign of the cross over her chest. Maybe she should not have pushed Claire into the confrontation. The housekeeper cautiously glanced at Trevor to gage his reaction. Seeing the masculine jaw tick with anger, she hustled across the kitchen and raced through the swinging door.

Trevor ignored the woman's departure and continued to circle the table, never taking his eyes from Claire's face.

She kept moving, to stay one step ahead of him.

"We're going to go into the next room and visit with my brother and his wife. If you don't want to eat—fine. You can have a cup of coffee," he churned out through clenched teeth.

Claire decided to put an end to it. "I wouldn't sit next to you if you were the last man on earth. Go find yourself a rich floozy—I know where you can find one."

Trevor launched himself across the surface of the workbench and, sliding on his buttocks, sent pots and pans crashing to the floor in all directions. Before Claire could gather her wits and run, his hands had snaked firmly around her waist. He held her in place until he was able to slide his feet to the floor beside her. A second later, he dragged his kicking and screaming wife through the doorway and into the dining room.

Claire was mortified to think of the spectacle they created in front of her in-laws and a cringing Katy, but the fact did not stop her from struggling against his hold. "Let go of me!"

Trevor tightened one arm around her waist and hefted her body off the floor and against his hip. "Not until you've had your morning cup of coffee."

Emma and Tyler sat frozen, stunned by Trevor's reaction to Claire's snub. There was reason to no longer wonder where all the noise came from; they were seeing it first hand. Trevor firmly held his squirming wife with one arm and yanked the apron from her body with the other. Pulling a chair further out from the table, he forced her to sit. His breath came in harsh pants as he stared down at the rosy hue of embarrassment that stained her cheeks. Keeping a firm hold on her shoulder, he dragged the coffee urn across the table, splashing hot liquid into her cup and all over the wooden surface. "Now...would you care for any cream with that coffee?"

Claire's lips snapped shut in stubborn refusal. She would not answer him.

"I guess that's a no." Trevor straightened behind her, breathed deeply while he flexed his taxed muscles, and pulled out his own chair. He could not look across the table at Tyler and Emma. The back of his pants had barely brushed the flat seat when Claire popped up from her chair and bounded around the opposite side of the table. She ran for the kitchen.

The back of Trevor's chair crashed against the wooden floor a split second later. He was only a step behind her. Claire failed to make it even halfway across the room before she was scooped into the air and tossed over her angry husband's shoulder.

"Put me down!" she bellowed.

Trevor tightened his grip on her flailing legs. "Not on your life. We're going to have this out right now whether you like it or not. And if you don't quit kicking, I'm going to spank your ass like one of the kids."

Claire hung from the waist over his broad shoulder and beat against his back. "You wouldn't dare!" she panted.

"Keep that up and you'll find out if I'd dare to or not." He spun and finally met the laughing eyes of his brother and sister-in-law. "If you'll excuse us, I'm going to take my wife for a little leisurely stroll

Don't wait supper if we're not back."

* * *

Trevor stomped out the front door, across the porch, and down the steps. Claire's muffled plea begged for him to put her down, but her appeal went unheard.

Ruth and Sue Ellen, early birds that they were, already played in the front yard. The little girls let a ball roll aimlessly across the grass, watched their stepfather tramp past them with their mother slung like a sack of potatoes over his shoulder, and instantly fell into step beside him.

"What ya doing?" Ruth asked as she skipped to keep up.

Claire brushed the hair from her eyes and strained her neck to see her daughter. "Tell Emma to come out here right now!"

"Never you mind, Ruthie," Trevor spouted. "Your ma wants to go for a horseback ride and that's what we're going to do. You just stay here and listen to the rules. Understood?" He smiled and sent the little girl a wink as his long legs ate up the ground beneath him.

Ruthie stopped and locked her fingers with Sue Ellen's when the girl paused beside her. "Okay. Have a fun time."

Claire groaned and hung her head in defeat. "You're not going to get away with this."

"Get away with what? All I'm doing is taking my wife for a morning ride."

He shoved her atop the first saddled horse he came upon and bounded up behind her a second later. A deep breath filled his lungs, then he locked an arm around her slender waist, and dug in his heels. "Now, shut up and enjoy the scenery."

* * *

Claire sat stiffly in the saddle, struggling to keep her backside from resting too tightly against her husband's thighs—the ones that circled her body intimately as they rode north. Neither of them had said a word since they passed through the ranch's gate. At present, Claire did not have the courage to glance over her shoulder and discover if the set of his jaw was relaxed or if it still possessed the angry tick of only an hour before. She continued to hold her silence when he turned off the main road to follow a well-trodden wide path.

As they rounded a small bend at the top of a hill, Claire's eyes widened in surprise. Nestled in the valley below was a magnificent log home with a good-sized barn and fenced pastures that filled in the backdrop.

Claire nervously batted at the wisps of curls that floated about her forehead and took a deep breath. "I don't want to go in, Trevor. You've proven over the last hour that you don't care to talk to me, but you can at least listen. I'm not presentable to be meeting anyone. Please, turn around and bring me home."

His only response was to dig his heels into the sides of the horse and urge the animal into a trot as he reined the animal in the direction of the house.

Claire mouth set in an angry line, and she curled her fingers around the horse's windblown mane in order to keep her backside from bouncing against her husband.

Trevor finally reined the animal to a walk as they approached the front of the house. Now that they were in the yard, Claire easily recognized the signs indicating that the home was new; the freshly whitewashed gate, the mounds of dirt with only bits of grass breaking through the packed surface of the ground, and no sign of any animals in the back pastures.

"Where are we?" Claire had to ask, hoping she would get some sort of amiable response.

Trevor dismounted and tied the horse to a hitching post. At last he met her eyes. She was infinitely thankful that the angry blaze was gone.

"Would you like to see the inside of the place?"

At least he's talking to me again. "Will the owners mind?"

Trevor shrugged. "I don't think so. They haven't moved in yet." Without another word, he lifted his arms and waited for Claire to reach out to him. Rather than fight him, she leaned into his arms. His hand wrapped around her tiny waist and, immediately, a jolt of heat raced through her body. *If only he could feel the same way when I touch him...*

Trevor lowered her to the ground and, with a gentle hold on her elbow, led her across the expansive covered porch, then opened the door and guided her into the foyer. He dropped his hand to his side and waited for her reaction.

Claire's curious eyes took in the beauty of the main hall; burnished oak panels lined the interior walls, reaching to the high ceiling that supported the second floor. Slowly she turned to glance up the stairway, her gaze pausing momentarily on an open sitting space beneath the heavy balustrade. A short walk brought her across the foyer, and she peeked into a lavishly furnished living room to her right and a dining room to the left. When she turned back to face her husband, relief washed through her at the total absence of the anger he had carried with him the entire ride. "It's so beautiful. Can we keep looking?"

He nodded. "I don't think the owners will mind. Why don't you tag along with me? We'll take a look upstairs."

Her eyes returned to the upper hall as she followed him up one step at a time. The smooth, sturdy feel of the banister beneath her hand and the absolute beauty of the second floor completely stunned her. A large grandfather clock ticked quietly at the end of the wide hallway, welcoming her as she glanced into one bedroom after another.

Without a word, Trevor disappeared into a room at the end of the corridor without a word. Claire hesitated because of his earlier silence, but decided to follow. She stepped into one of the biggest bedrooms yet. Her gaze scanned the massive furniture, but her main interest was drawn to the windows. Sunlight spilled in where Trevor stood in the warm rays.

"I don't think I've ever seen such a lovely home," she breathed quietly. She stopped beside him and stared at the lake in the distance. "Whoever is fortunate to live in this house will be a very lucky family." She turned, tilted her chin, and glanced up at him. "I feel...happiness in the air for some odd reason. It's peaceful beyond belief. Why did you bring me here?"

"Because I wanted to know your thoughts." His finger tenderly brushed her chin before it rested lightly on her shoulder. "You just said you could feel the peacefulness inside these walls. But you also mentioned the word happy? Could you be happy here?"

She shrugged beneath the weight of his hand. "Who wouldn't be? This is like the home I've always dreamed about."

The corner of Trevor's mouth turned up. "Well, then, it's yours."

Confusion whisked through her brain. "What do you mean,

mine?"

"This is my home, Claire. Since we're husband and wife, then it also becomes yours."

Her lips parted, and she shook her head slowly. "I don't understand. This looks like a new home."

"It is. I started it about five years ago, but only recently commissioned workers to get it completely finished. I was hoping to move my wife and our children in here before the weather turned too cold."

Overwhelmed, instant tears trickled down Claire's cheeks. "But, what about..."

"What about how much I love you?" He watched her fingers cover her trembling lips. "What about the joy you and the kids have brought me? I don't want to continue the way we've been, Claire. I know you're angry with me because of what you think I feel for Regina. I feel nothing; you've got to believe that. Absolutely nothing compared to the emotions I experience every time I look at you."

Claire was still frightened. What she wanted most in life was the love of the dear man standing before her, but her own low self-esteem would not allow the reality. "I'm not special, though." Heavy tears slid down her cheeks. "I'll never be like her. I'm plain and I don't—"

Trevor lowered his mouth, stopping any further words. His lips whispered across her moist ones and traveled to the side of her neck.

Claire's lids drooped and she wondered if he could hear the pounding of her heart.

"How can you say you're a plain woman?" He nuzzled her ear and slowly pulled her against him as he breathed the scent of her clean hair. "Right now, your cheeks are flushed and your beautiful eyes are sparkling with tears, making them turn to a soft gray that reminds me of a piece of silver." He pulled back, cupped his hands on either side of her face, and used his thumbs to brush away her tears. "We're not kids, Claire, and I don't expect you to look like one. When I look at you, all I see is a courageous woman who would never give up the good fight. I see someone who would walk through fire for the lives of her children. And, I see the woman I have come to love more than life itself. I'm sorry that it's taken me so long to tell you. I want you in my life always, because you're already in my heart."

Claire's fingers lifted to wrap around his hands as the tears flowed harder.

"I need to hear it, Claire. I need to hear that you feel the same. This house will be nothing if you're not here to share it with me."

"Trevor..." she whispered, one hand swiping the happy tears away. "I do...I do love you—with all my heart. I've been so miserable because I love you so much but...but I didn't think you could ever feel the same."

He lowered his lips to hers. Claire's palms slid up his broad chest and around his neck. His comforting embrace, coupled with the lips that pressed soft kisses against her temple, became a silent vow to always love her and to forever keep her safe from the world; a warm promise that Claire would never have to fear anything again.

A muffled groan left her throat as his mouth moved back to devour hers; his hands urged her body firmly against his chest. "I need you, Claire," he rasped against her seeking lips. "I've needed you my entire life, but I could never find you...stay with me—now..."

Her fingers slid tentatively to the buttons on his shirt, signaling Trevor that she needed to feel his naked skin beneath her palms. She needed his heat against her. She needed him.

His hands left her body for only as long as it took to shrug off his shirt and unbutton his pants. The first garment found the floor as he dropped to one knee, lifted her slender foot, and removed a shoe. The other followed the same path as Claire's exploring fingers delighted in the feel of his thick wavy hair.

Trevor stood before her again then, his chest expanding with each quick breath as his fingers moved to free the buttons at the back of her dress. He groaned softly when his mouth discovered the hollow beneath her ear, and Claire's head lolled to allow him easier access to the soft skin. Eager hands found the edges of the gaping bodice of her dress. He slid the cotton material over her shoulders, following the same path with light, feathery kisses. The faded gown slipped to the floor as his mouth moved on to the crest of her naked breast. Trevor's heart thudded wildly against his ribcage.

He wanted her, and reveled in the fact that she felt the same burning desire. He had never known the joy of making love to a woman whom he cherished with his whole being; with his entire heart. And,

Trevor knew, he would never forget the feeling for as long as he lived. Claire set him on fire.

He swept her into his arms, kissed her long and hard and, in three long strides, placed her gently on the bed. He removed his pants with anxious, shaking hands and kicked them away as he joined her atop the soft downy quilt.

Claire stared up at him through shuttered, passion-filled eyes when his body gently covered hers. A tremulous smile played about her parted lips as she ran her fingers through his thick hair once more, her heart bursting with the complete freedom to love him fully. The realization that she had finally found the love of her life after so many lonely years clogged her throat.

His hands moved over her body with an exquisite slowness as he slid her pantaloons down slender legs. Wherever his palms touched, a tender trail of heat was left to scorch her skin. Soon, her entire body smoldered beneath his fingertips. Claire yearned to feel his heat once more—the same heat that had licked her soul during the weeks since he saved her from drowning in her own fear on a stormy night in the barn.

"Now, Trevor..." she breathed quietly. "Make me feel safe. Make me understand one of the ways I can love you..."

His palm left her breast and traveled lower, over the flat silkiness of her stomach, then slipped between velvet thighs. Claire urged him on with eager lips and clutching hands until he could no longer stave off his own surging emotions.

Trevor poised himself on strong arms and stared into the smoldering gray eyes beneath him. His lips searched for hers and, as his tongue delved into her mouth, Claire surged beneath him and clasped his shoulders tightly. He entered her with slow, rhythmic movements and was rewarded by the tightening of her muscles around him and the sensual rise and fall of her body.

Claire held her breath as Trevor took her upwards. His tender loving whispers of desire and need echoed inside her body. A flicker of heat filled her with love and security as it intensified into a flame that took her breath away. Only this wonderful, caring man had the ability to carry her away as no other ever had.

Trevor heard her groans, and then her cries of fulfillment somewhere in the recesses of his mind. A feeling of total completeness overwhelmed him as he pulled Claire even tighter against him. It was the turning point for him; he stroked harder, seeking his own release now, and spilled his seed into her depths. His own rapturous groans of fulfillment echoed in the room.

Claire's breath came in cleansing gasps as she floated back to reality; gasps that mingled with the heat of his kiss and whispered words of love.

Trevor rolled onto his side, gathered a quilt over their naked, entwined limbs, and tucked Claire's head against his shoulder. His arms held her body with a gentle protectiveness. No words were needed as they drifted into a contented slumber in the warm rays that spilled through the window.

Chapter Twenty-Four

The quiet presence of the house surrounded them. Trevor cuddled Claire's warm body in his muscular arm as he lay beside her in the waning light of day. Her head nestled against his shoulder; her breath warmed his naked skin. "I love you, Claire," he whispered into the darkening room.

She smiled sleepily and tucked her arm across his broad chest. "How did you know I was awake?" She felt his shrug beneath her cheek.

They lay quietly until Trevor broke the comforting silence. "I want to move all of us here and be a family." His fingers gently brushed her upper arm. "You know, I started building this house years ago, but I never felt any excitement to complete it—not until I came north after you disappeared from St. Paul. I walked through this house one day and it suddenly hit me why. It was because I had no one to share it with; no woman in my life to love until I met you."

Claire ran her fingers across his lightly furred chest and smiled against his skin. "I think I fell in love with you that night in the barn. No one had ever put me first—until you."

He raised himself up onto one elbow and brushed a strand of curly hair from her cheek as he stared down into her eyes. "I'm sorry you were so hurt the next day."

She sighed, clasped the masculine hand that rested across her hip, and laced her fingers with his. "I never want to feel that way again. I woke up that morning, filled with hope that maybe I wouldn't have to move the children away from everything that was familiar. And I was full of hope that maybe, just maybe, I had found someone who would not judge me by what I possessed, but by what was inside me." She paused for a moment. "I remember putting on my best clothes—which weren't much, but I felt beautiful in them. When I reached the racetrack and saw Regina in your arms, I wanted to die."

"God, I'm so sorry. I was trying to get rid of her, so I could get back to the farm."

"I know that now. But, at the time, I felt that a life with you was simply a childish dream. I lost all faith in myself. I raced home, packed what we would need, and headed north so I could forget." Claire pressed her fingers against his lips to feel the satiny texture as she gazed up at him. "It was horrible, Trevor. I was so frightened."

His fingers again brushed away curly, blonde strands of hair, this time to expose the silky skin of Claire's shoulder. "You'll never have to be frightened again. You'll always have this house to live in and me to protect you. I love you, Claire. I love Jonah and the fact that I have a son now—" his mouth dipped to brush a kiss against her collarbone "—and Sue Ellen and Sofie with all their little mothering skills—" Trevor's lips moved on to his wife's slender neck "—and Ruthie with her simple joy at just being four years old—" Claire smiled silently when his mouth hovered above her own. "And how can someone not love Hannah with her butterfly kisses? I'm the luckiest man in the world to have all of you."

Claire's heart fluttered crazily with the knowledge that now his love encompassed not just her, but all of them. Suddenly, she gasped and heaved herself to a sitting position. The quilt floated past her bare breasts and bunched gently onto her lap. "The children!" Her gaze flew to the window. "Oh, my goodness, we've been here most of the day! It'll be well past supper time before we reach home." Her hands flew to her heated cheeks as she gasped again. "What is everyone going to think?"

Claire tossed the quilt aside, ready to leap from the comfort of the bed. Her progress was halted, however, when Trevor dragged her body back onto the wrinkled sheets and used a muscular thigh to pin her to the mattress. "I'll tell you what they're going to think." His head dipped to steal a kiss from her warm lips, then his mouth nuzzled the tender spot below her ear. "That I knew what I was talking about when I said not to wait supper." He heard the intake of her breath beside his ear as she remembered the earlier episode. "They're going to wish they were us. No kids, no worries; just the feel of naked skin—" he kissed the tip of a velvety breast "—against naked skin..."

"Trevor..." she whispered lightly. Her lids fluttered shut as a roughened palm slid sensuously over the slight curve of her hip and lower. Claire groaned when a flame inside her belly ignited once more. "We should go..." Trevor's mouth lifted from her breast, and Claire searched his face in the fading light. The desire in his eyes reached out to her heart.

"Not yet. Stay forever with me." He slid over her body and entered her gently, his gaze lingering when her eyes instantly darkened with matching desire. He waited for her answer, knowing already how she would respond.

Claire reached up to cup his whiskered cheek. "Forever..."

* * *

Another hour passed before Trevor gave in to Claire's sense of responsibility and finally hefted himself from the mattress to join her as she searched for her stocking. They would travel to the ranch by moonlight, slip into the house quietly, and be home in the morning when the children awoke.

Trevor's eyes searched the floor for his boots in the flickering candlelight as he buttoned the back of his wife's dress. The intimate gesture warmed his heart.

So many things about Claire had changed over the course of the day. Her sparkling gray eyes met his at every turn. She took the opportunity to touch him repeatedly and, more than once, initiated the passionate kisses that ended up with her in his arms. The tense set of her slim shoulders and the weariness etched across her face were gone for what he hoped would be forever. Trevor vowed silently that he would do his best to make sure the two never returned.

His fingers slid from the last button at the neckline to her narrow hips. Locking his fingers around her waist, Trevor pulled Claire against his long torso and his lips tortured the satiny dip where her slender neck met her shoulders. Claire tilted her head back and sighed contentedly; his palms slid over her midriff to cup her breasts. "Are you sure you really want to go home?"

She smiled and covered his hands with her own. "Don't be silly

Knowing your family, they'd all be here in the morning anyway."

A deep chuckle rumbled in her ear.

"You do have them figured out, don't you? I suppose if we stay any longer, they'll show up with supper and five extra kids in the back of the wagon."

Claire turned in his arms and linked her hands behind his neck. "I love you. I'll remember this day forever." A tiny giggle escaped past her lips.

"What?"

"Can you imagine what Tyler and Emma thought when you hauled me out of the house?"

His head fell back as an even louder chuckle burst out before his eyes squinted to accompany a whining groan. "I'm never going to hear the end of it. I'm sure by now that Cole and August have returned home and my younger brother is dying to flay me with his comments."

She laughed with him, and then the humor in her eyes floated away. "They're all so wonderful, aren't they? Everyone—Tyler and Emma, Cole, August—they treated me like family from the first day you carried me into the house. Carrie also arrived with her arms open. They never made me feel out of place—and I was too stubborn to see what was right in front of me." Her gaze scanned the room as she clung to his shoulders. "And now...now you've told me that this beautiful house is for me and my children." Her eyes returned to his. "You've given me so much. I love you, Trevor, but not because of everything I just stated. Mamie told me something when I first met her. She said that, if I let you keep my heart until I wasn't frightened anymore, that I eventually would find my way back to it again. She was so right."

Trevor was so overwhelmed by Claire's heartfelt words that he pulled her close and clung tightly to her willowy body, amazed that simple fate had brought such happiness into his life. He breathed in the scent of her hair, knowing that no other woman would ever be able to take her place in his heart.

"We should really be on our way, Trevor."

"I know..." He sighed happily.

Claire finally stepped from his arms and stumbled on a lone boot whose toe stuck out from beneath a chair. She bent, picked up the footwear, and shook it at her husband, who was in the process of stuffing his shirttails into his pants. "Do you know much I hated the sight of these things every time I saw you in St. Paul?"

"My boots? Why would you hate them?"

"Remember that first day we met? Jonah had stolen an apple from the General Store."

"How could I forget? I had a kid that could have doubled for a rat terrier clinging to my leg."

Claire snorted at his comparison with a shake of her head. "These boots signified how poor I was. I couldn't even afford to spend five cents on an apple. I constantly wondered how much you paid to keep these things shiny. I had a name for you because of them."

He eyed her suspiciously.

"You were 'Mr. Shiny Boots'."

"That's it? Hell, I figured it'd be much worse, considering how you felt about me a few months back."

Claire rolled her eyes. "Put your boots on. We really have to get going."

He reached out with a crooked grin on his face and snatched the boot where it dangled from her fingertips. Sitting down on the edge of the bed, he slid it easily over his foot, and then grabbed its mate from the floor beside him. He stood a moment later and snuffed out the candle. The lovers left the dark room hand in hand.

* * *

"Shhh...stop that, Trevor, or we'll never get in the house without being seen!" Claire playfully slapped at her husband's hand where it rested on her left buttock.

Seeing that the gas lanterns still burned brightly in the living room and library windows when they approached the ranch, they had stabled the horse and snuck to the back of the house. They huddled outside the kitchen door in the dark now, planning to use the kitchen staircase to make their way to the second floor undetected.

"I don't want to stop," he whispered as he gently pressed her body backward and pinned her dainty form against the side of the house. "I've got twenty years to make up for." His head lowered as he stole a kiss from her smiling mouth, reveling in the playful wife he had discovered over the course of the day. Trevor's thoughts quickly drifted into oblivion, however, when Claire molded herself to the front of his body and returned his kiss passionately.

Moments later, he lifted his swimming head and reached for the doorknob. "I've changed my mind. I want to get upstairs as quickly as we can."

Claire giggled when he pulled her through the entrance to the kitchen, then fell silent when Trevor lifted a finger to his lips. The sound of muffled adult voices drifted to them from the other side of the house. Claire closed the door carefully, wincing when the click of the lock echoed in the room. They tiptoed across the floor like two thieves in the night.

Trevor clasped Claire's hand when they reached the staircase. He pulled her up behind him, his mind preoccupied with how enjoyable the next few hours would be, wrapped in her loving arms. He held his breath when they reached the landing on the second floor and glanced in both directions. The slight giggle behind him was enough to make him turn; his wife stood only inches from him, her hand clamped over her mouth. Her shoulders shook. "What are you laughing about?" He whispered as he pulled her down the hallway to their room.

"You!" she hissed back. "You should see what you look like, sneaking around in your own house."

"Well, I'll be damned if I want to put up with Cole and Tyler tonight. Those two have been after me on a steady basis ever since I brought you into this house. Payback—that's what they call it." He stopped his hurried flight down the corridor as they approached their room, then whisked Claire into his arms and kissed her quickly to stifle her surprised squeak. His green eyes glowed when he lifted his head. "I want one more night of you all to myself."

Claire sighed softly and tightened her arms about his neck as he entered the dimly lit room. Someone had left a lamp burning low. Once inside, Trevor basked in the feel of her body sliding sensuously down the front of his as he closed the door with his heel and sought her swollen lips once more.

"Mommy?"

Claire hid a smile at her husband's groan and tipped her head to see Hannah sitting in the middle of the bed. The little girl's sleepy eyes looked around as she clutched a ragged blanket. Sending a wry smile in the direction of Trevor's pouting lips, Claire crossed to the bed and perched on the edge. Hannah scuttled across the quilt and crawled into her mother's arms.

Claire cuddled her soft, warm body close and pressed a kiss against Hannah's sweet-smelling hair. "Hi, Baby. What are you doing in Mommy's room?"

The little girl tucked her blanket beneath her chin. "I missed you." Hannah's round gray eyes moved to Trevor's when he joined them on the bed. "Hi, Trevor."

"Hi, sweet thing. Do you want me to tuck you in your bed?"

"No."

His eyebrow rose. "No? You're not tired?"

Hannah rolled from her mother's arms, scuttled back to the middle of the bed and disappeared beneath the quilt. "Hannah sleep here."

Trevor's hesitant gaze swung to his wife's.

Claire simply shrugged with an amused smile curving her mouth and waited to see what he would do next. It was Trevor's call.

"Are you sure?" he questioned Hannah. "Me and your ma are...tired."

Hannah patted the pillow beside her. "You sleep here." She yawned and clutched the blanket tighter, the picture of heavenly innocence.

Trevor's shoulders slumped instantly when he realized that sleep was going to be the only thing he would do in the bed that evening. His lips pursed when he eyed his wife's twinkling eyes. "All right, Hannah," he said without looking at the girl. "It looks like you're going to be the only one that gets what she wants tonight. Climb in, Mrs. Wilkins. I'll turn out the lamp."

Claire reached for a quilt folded at the end of the bed and drew it over her body as she settled beside her daughter. Trevor joined her a second later, climbing beneath the quilt with a sigh. Reaching out, he tucked his wife's body close and stretched out his arm until he had both her and Hannah in his embrace.

"I love you, ladies. Good night."

Claire heard his smile in the dark. "Love you, too," she returned

quietly.
"I love everybody," a small voice giggled.

Kim Mattson

Chapter Twenty-Five

Regina paced about the living room of Judd's home in Biwabik like a caged tigress, waiting for her cousin's return. As soon as the man entered the house, she would demand to be taken back to St. Paul. She had had her fill of small town mentality and its men—including Trevor Wilkins.

Shaking her head in disgust, she crossed to the window and checked for any sign of Judd. Try as she might, however, thoughts of the one-time handsome bachelor and his recent marriage came racing back to taunt her. How was it that a poor dirt farmer's wife could snag the affluent Wilkins brother, and she, Regina Simpson, was turned away? *That damn wife of his...* Claire Wilkins had done her best to thwart Regina's every attempt to speak to her husband at the party. There was nothing left to do but leave Biwabik and head for St. Paul as quickly as she could.

Regina's mind floated even further back, to a few days before the reception. Never one to let a chance go by when it came to a potential mate, she had soon discovered during her short stay at Judd's that Trevor was her only prospect. None of the ill-mannered oafs in the town possessed the proper decorum or the finances to be considered even close to the level of respectability she searched for in a new husband. Yes, she was definitely ready to get back to the big city and begin spending some of Judd's promised money.

Not that I can trust him to keep his word. Judd will have a fit when I inform him that there's not much to tell, except that Claire seems to be deeply in love with her husband. And Trevor, that idiot, acts like he feels the same way. Regina's back stiffened. *Well, Judd's going to pay up no matter what—this was his idea. It's not my fault that a homely widow ended up with the luck of the draw...*

With a nervous toss of the chin, she flounced down onto the soft cushions of Judd's sofa and stared angrily across the room. *I need money. I'm going to have to come up with something...*

She had damn well better. Lately, Regina had begun to feel the sting of rejection by more men than she could count. Once, she was the bell of the ball, loving the fact that most women were threatened by her beauty and financial status. Over the course of the last year or so though—especially since Sydney died—a subtle change had occurred. Regina refused to believe the difference was due to the fact that her husband was so well respected when he was alive and she, at the same time, was so detested.

A strangling finger of fear abruptly prodded at her mind, sending an odd shiver of the unknown down her spine. *What will happen to me? I'm going to end up beneath some grunting old man, hoping the entire time that he'll die and not have spent all his riches...*

Regina rubbed her sudden aching forehead and sank back into the cushion. Trevor really was her only hope if she did not want to be miserable the rest of her life. The man might never have loved her, and maybe never would, but Regina found it hard to swallow that he could so easily toss away the passion they had discovered together. She sat forward, her brow furrowed deep in thought.

That's it! That's why I couldn't put a finger on why he was so unapproachable. Regina was surprised the reason did not hit her sooner. Trevor had felt the need to treat her the way he did at the reception for only one reason. He could not give away his true feelings before friends and family—and certainly not with his plain wife at his side. Somehow, the poor man must have been forced into the marriage. After all, who in their right mind would take on a widow with five children when he could have a woman like Regina?

She tilted her head and rested her gaze on the darkening sky outside the window. Her slim fingers tapped out a beat against the arm of the sofa. Maybe she would not insist on heading back to St. Paul after all. Maybe she would enjoy the comforts of Judd's home for a while more. Her cousin employed a cook and a butler who, so far, had taken care of her every demanding whim. The so-called gentry living in Biwabik made her scoff at their attempts to become true high society. For the chance to bed Trevor again, however, their mundane attempts to befriend Judd Stone's cousin would be just the entertainment she needed to while away her days until she could formulate a plan.

Glancing at the clock, she rose from the settee, donned an expensive silk wrap, and picked up her reticule. For the second night in a row since Leonidas left her on the doorstep, it looked as if Judd might not get home until well into the evening. He was out the door that morning before she awakened and had a chance to speak to him. Fine. Regina knew where to find her cousin. Tonight, she would begin to set her future in motion.

* * *

Regina entered Biwabik's only upscale tavern, situated on the end of the main street. The building was purposely erected away from the more distasteful saloons patronized by the many foreign speaking miners and loggers who frequented both the front rooms and the back.

She regally lifted her powdered nose, ignored the leering stares of the many men who filled the smoky room, and scanned the tavern until she spotted Judd at a corner table. Regina stepped from the landing and sauntered around the numerous tables in his direction. She was halfway across the room when she realized Leonidas Merritt and his brother Cassius, were in a deep conversation with her cousin.

Judd glared when she came to a stop beside the table. The Merritt brothers immediately rose to their feet, but the other man simply continued to stare angrily as he settled his body against the back of the chair.

Regina batted her thick lashes at the older Merritt brother. "Well hello, Lonny."

Leonidas cringed inwardly; he hated the nickname she had dubbed him with, but nodded anyway. "Regina..."

"It's nice to see you so soon after yesterday's pleasant outing."

"What are you doing here, Regina?" Judd barked at her.

Regina nodded with an air of self-importance when Cassius procured a chair for her. She daintily sat on the edge. "Thank you, Mr. Merritt." She turned her stony gaze on Judd. "It's nice to see there are gentlemen still left in this wicked little city." Her cousin simply puffed on his expensive cigar, unmindful when ashes fluttered to the table near where Regina's white-gloved hand lay on the surface. She pursed her lips and withdrew her fingers, tucking them into her lap. The Merritt brothers returned rather hesitantly to their seats.

Judd tossed her another glare. "What brings you out at this hour?"

"I needed to speak to you. I haven't seen you at your house since I returned there last night."

His eyes shot across the table. "I've been working. I'm sorry that you came down here to find me, but I'm rather busy at the moment. You can return home, and I'll speak with you when I get back."

Regina was just about ready to spout back at him for ordering her about as if she were a child, but Leonidas broke the crackling silence.

He shuffled on his chair. "We should call it a night, Mr. Stone. I don't know how much more there is to discuss anyway. We've given you our bottom line, which is that our decision is final. I'm sorry that we couldn't wait for you."

Judd kept a tight check on his irritation and forced a smile to his lips. "All I need is another month or so. If you wait, you can make even more money, plus retain your company."

Leonidas scooped up his gloves from the table. "You don't seem to understand, Mr. Stone. We can't wait any longer." He rose, with his brother following him up, and turned to the woman who had joined them. "Regina? It was a pleasure to escort you yesterday to the Wilkins'. Have a nice evening—what's left of it." He tipped his hat, turned on his heel, and left the table with Cassius in tow.

Regina watched them go before turning her surprised gaze back to Judd. She sat back in a huff. "Pleasure, indeed. The man could have cared less if I was by his side yesterday. I thought he was rather rude when he dropped me off last night."

"You had no business showing up here. I was trying to conduct business."

Regina leaned forward with a condescending gleam in her eyes, but maintained a smile on her lips. "Get rid of the angry look, Judd. What are people going to think? I was tired of sitting around and waiting for you. There's absolutely nothing to do in this godforsaken town. So, what was this meeting all about? Why are those men sorry they couldn't wait? And for what?" Her dark eyes flitted to a clean glass. "Pour me a drink, please."

Judd took another toke of his stogie, ignoring her request to be waited on. "Why would you think I'd share my business dealings with you?"

"Because I have information for you in regard to the party yesterday."

"Save your breath, Regina. I managed to get enough details about the newlyweds from Leonidas to know that Trevor Wilkins is deeply in love with his wife. It doesn't look like Claire is going to be tossed into the streets anytime soon. I guess I didn't even need to have you go. Besides, I have bigger problems."

Regina's mind raced. If she did not come up with something quick, Judd would most likely withdraw his funding over the next year—and she needed the money to sustain her extravagant ways. Besides, now that she had made the decision to get Trevor back into her clutches, Regina was not about to let opportunity pass her by. She needed to buy some time. "What kind of problems?"

Judd shook his head. "You're tenacious, aren't you?" His fingers smoothed the thin mustache above his lip. "All right. It's rather evident to the Merritt brothers that they are chasing a dream—one that is coming to a quick demise. They've done well in the past, but can no longer afford to meet their mining payrolls or many other liabilities. No one will extend credit for the materials they need to stay solvent and creditors are pounding on their doors as it is. They've decided to sell their stock in the company to John Rockefeller at a ridiculously low price."

"So why does that present a problem for you?"

Regina jumped in her chair when his fist came down hard on the surface of the table; she quickly recovered. "Stop it!" Her flashing eyes darted about. "You're making a spectacle out of both of us," she hissed.

Judd waited for the many pairs of patrons' questioning eyes to look away before he answered. "I'll tell you why it's become a problem for me. I wanted to buy those stocks. All I needed was another six weeks and I would have had all the financing to accomplish it. They refuse to wait for me. Dammit, Regina, this was going to be my big chance to become wealthier than I could ever dream."

She watched his anger build as his eyes darkened. His finger pointed at her a second later. "And do you know whose fault I can lay most of the blame on? Trevor Wilkins and that bitch of a wife of his."

"Trevor?" she gasped. "What does he have to do with this? Or, for that matter, his white-trash wife?"

Judd's fingers tightened around his drink glass as he angrily tamped out his cigar. He shot Regina a glare. "Because Wilkins has a piece of property just south of here that sits on top of a huge ore deposit. The Merritt family has been after him to sell. They even offered him a piece of the pie, as far as all the timber growing there. He could profit greatly from the venture, but refuses to do so because he built a home there—for his new wife and the brats she brought with her." He leaned forward and his voice lowered. "That chunk of land was the Merritt's last chance. What they would have profited from the initial ore loads would have paid their bills and kept them in control. But, because that arrogant son of a bitch refused to sell, Rockefeller will step in, take over ownership, and do it without any outside investors."

Judd's thoughts immediately flashed to the day Trevor threw him out of Claire's house. If Wilkins had kept his nose out of the widow's business—and her life—the Merritts would most likely have gained ownership of the property. The former lumberman would have stayed in St. Paul—most likely playing his days away with the woman who sat across the table. Rather than scrambling for capital to buy the total sum of stock options in the mining venture, Judd could have invested, reaped a great profit, and not had the hassle of managing the operation.

What he was left with was absolutely nothing; no chance of getting the Merritts to wait the month out; no chance to buy in with Rockefeller; and no chance for wealth beyond his wildest dreams. No matter how Judd looked at it, all dead ends led back to Trevor Wilkins. And, to add insult to insult, even the lowly widow was out of his clutches because of her so-called happy marriage.

Regina listened to the man's rantings; her brain worked furiously to keep up with the details. She would wager her last dollar that she could convince Judd to do anything to exact revenge on the man she wanted for her own.

She sat back in her chair and studied the angry features before her. *In doing so, however, I might run the risk that he would go after Trevor first, and leave Claire for last. Where does that leave me in all of this? No, I've got to approach this from a different angle...*

Regina reached across the table, dragged the fine bottle of whiskey closer to where she sat, and poured herself a hefty splash rather than wait for Judd to do it. "So, let me get this straight," she mused out loud, then took a sip. The whiskey burned her throat, but the warm afterglow of the fine liquor in the pit of her stomach helped to clear her head. "To make a rather long story short, if Claire had given in to your proposal in St. Paul, she most likely would never have ended up with Trevor. Consequently, he would have cared less about the property because he would have had no one to share it with."

"Go on," Judd returned. "I can see the wheels turning in that head of yours."

Regina leaned her elbows on the table and swirled her drink beneath her nose. "And there is absolutely nothing you can do to change the Merritts' minds."

His eyes narrowed. "Don't remind me."

"So, why not put your energy into something else? Why bemoan the fact that you feel cheated?"

"Because I was."

"Well, the situation won't change, Judd. So, after having said that, let's put the other facts out on the table. You asked me to come north with you, because you had a score to settle with Trevor Wilkins. Really, when you think about it, what would settling that score accomplish—especially now?" Regina could see Judd was ready to listen by the subtle change of his previously tense jaw. She smiled inwardly. She just might get what she desired in the end. "You know that I want him. If he didn't have a wife hanging on his coattails, I don't think it would be too hard to sway him back in my direction. Forget about him and exacting revenge. Concentrate, instead, on his wife."

A single eyebrow rose over Judd's eye. "You're that sure Wilkins would come running if Claire was out of his life?"

Regina shrugged, remembering the heated sensation of Trevor's skin against hers. "It might take him some time but, yes; eventually, if I draw on our past experiences, I think I could convince him that I'm the one he needs to be with." She picked up the flask of whiskey and freshened her drink. Holding the bottle up, she waited for Judd to hold out his glass. When he did, she poured him a shot. "So now that leaves us with one more question. What do we do about Claire?" Regina's red smile widened when she met Judd's glowing eyes.

Yes, things just might turn out after all. Regina clinked her glass against Judd's. "Cousin dear, you and I have to do some planning. Take me home and I'll fill you in on all the lovely little details."

Chapter Twenty-Six

Claire's eyes fluttered opened. Feeling the warmth of Trevor's body against her back, she sighed with contentment; she was happier than she had ever been. She would have hugged her sleeping husband if not for the fact that she did not want to miss seeing the sunrise one last time from their room.

Careful not to rouse Trevor, she slid carefully from beneath the weight of his arm and scooted slowly to the edge of the bed, feeling like a child waking on Christmas morning. One last glance at his prone body almost made her jiggle the mattress just to see what he would do, but she decided against it. Trevor had worked so hard over the last few days that she swallowed back the urge to be in his arms. Instead, she grabbed her robe and covered her nude body.

Claire tiptoed to the window as she tightened the sash around her tiny waist. Moving the curtain aside, her gray eyes scanned the horizon. The already changing hue of the predawn sky outlined the towering pines at the hilltop's summit.

It was moving day. The new house, an hour's ride north of the ranch, sat ready and waiting for the few personal belongings they had left to haul. Hence, Trevor's exhaustion. New furniture was in place, food stores stocked, and even livestock dotted the pastures. Now the only thing left was to gather the children after breakfast, say their goodbyes and head north.

Claire leaned against the window jamb with a soft smile curving her mouth, closed her eyes, and thought about how much her life had changed since Trevor reached into his pocket, pulled out a nickel, and offered to pay for a rotten apple. Her luck had finally changed that day.

and she had not even realized it at the time.

How could I have not known? He gives us so much love...

Claire's heart nearly burst with the emotions he touched within her daily. Whether it was a smile and a loving pat on the back for one of the kids or a smoldering look of desire from across the room, he was always there; always ready to make her world a better place to live in—just as Emma had said he would.

Claire turned to study her husband's sleeping form. Trevor lay with a pillow bunched beneath his tousled head of hair, making her want to return to the bed and run her fingers through the thick length. Her gaze rested on his naked upper torso. She now knew the strength of the broad, tanned shoulders, which contrasted deeply against the stark white sheets. Her eyes followed the length of a muscular arm—one that could hold her tenderly or glisten in the afternoon sun with the tight cords flexing as he worked around the ranch. The memory of his callused hands against her sensitive skin made her heart leap in her chest. Trevor was always there—always ready to give her more.

Her eyes moved to his face. The warmth of his loving gaze filled her.

"Claire?" The soft sound of her name whispered from his lips.

She tucked her hands behind her, leaned against the window jamb, and tilted her head silently with the smile still in place.

The muscles in his arms bunched when he rose to a sitting position. "What are you doing up so early? Is something wrong?"

She shook her head slowly. "What could be wrong? I have you and I have the most exciting day of my life ahead of me."

She watched a grin break out across his whiskered cheeks as he tossed the blanket from his naked body, slid his feet over the edge of the bed, and crossed silently to where she stood by the window. Claire wondered if she would ever tire of the sight of his sleek muscles and powerful body.

"So, what are you doing?"

"I wanted to watch the sun come up one more time from this window." Her eyes scanned the room and returned to his. "I'm going to miss this place and the people who live here, but I can't tell you how happy I am to be moving to the new house. Thank you for everything, Trevor." She straightened and clasped his hand. "Want to watch with me?"

He nodded, and she turned to face the horizon. Trevor pulled her back against his body, locked his fingers over her belly, and rested his cheek against the tumbling mass of blonde hair.

They stood quietly as streaks of pink and yellow shot across the sky like lazy fingers relaxing on the autumn horizon. The shifting colors of billowy clouds heralded the return of another day as a bright orange orb rose slowly over the pines, turning the dark treetops to a luminous shade of green.

Claire sighed happily.

Trevor dipped his head and nuzzled his wife's slender neck. Her eyes closed to the glory of the sunrise as she reveled in feel of his warm breath against her skin.

"Come back to bed with me," he whispered huskily against her ear. His hands slid to her waist and slowly untied the sash.

Claire's heart pounded; she would never tire of her husband's gentle touch.

His nimble fingers opened the robe and traveled slowly across her silky stomach as he continued to kiss the soft spot below her ear. One hand traveled upward until a firm breast lay cupped in his palm. "Hmmm," he sighed quietly. "I love how you feel in my arms."

Claire turned to face him, and Trevor slipped the robe from her shoulders. He lifted her into his arms then, and she clung tightly to him relishing the soft kisses he pressed against her mouth and the love that rested freely in her heart.

He returned to the bed.

* * *

The buckboard, laden with items from their last minute packing came to a halt in front of the new house. The children scattered like ants from the back of the wagon. Claire giggled at their squeals of joy when they raced for the house. Trevor jumped down from the seat and held his arms out to help his wife down.

"Aren't you going to come inside?" he asked when she continued to stare at the house.

Finally, her sparkling gaze met his. "I can't believe this place is ours. I just want to sit here and look at it all day."

"No way." He chuckled. "I'll be damned if I'm going to do all the work. I'm still holding you to the partnership; fifty-fifty on all duties. Well, all except one. Hannah's bathroom detail is all yours."

Claire reached for his shoulders with another laugh. Instead of being swung to the ground as expected, Trevor let her body slide slowly down the front of his, refusing to let her step from his embrace.

"Welcome home, Mrs. Wilkins."

She flung her arms about his neck and pulled his mouth closer. "I couldn't be happier to be here, Mr. Wilkins," she whispered before she cupped his face with her hands. Her eyes suddenly darkened with emotion. "Thank you, Trevor, for coming into my life and saving me from myself. Thank you for loving my children the way you do." Her fingers played over his firm jaw and rested against his full lips. "I love you so much."

He lowered his lips across the few inches that separated their mouths, pulled Claire closer, and slanted his mouth across hers.

* * *

Jonah reached the top step of the porch and turned to see what held up his mother and Trevor. Seeing the two locked in an intimate embrace at the side of the wagon, he flopped down onto his butt with a pout and crossed his arms. "Ah, geez, there they go again," he stated rather testily when Sofie sat down beside him. "They're always swappin' spit lately. What's the matter with them anyway?"

"They're kissin," Sofie giggled. "That's what people do when they're married."

Sue Ellen exited the house again, with Hannah and Ruth by her side. Her chubby cheeks creased with a happy grin as she cuddled her doll. "Ma says she loves Trevor. She gets all silly when she talks about him."

"Well, that's stupid," Jonah returned and sent the embracing couple another querulous look. "Trevor used to be more fun before they started this kissin' stuff."

Sofie belted him once across the arm. "It ain't stupid."

Jonah lifted his fist and clenched his teeth. "Quit hittin, Sofie, or you're gonna get it."

"Then you quit sayin' it's stupid!"

"I won't! I can say anything I want, and I think kissin' is stupid!"

Ruth scurried across the porch and rapped her knuckles on the back of her brother's head. He spun around on his butt, sending her jumping back to hide behind Sue Ellen with a giggle.

"Knock it off, Ruth."

The little girl stuck her tongue out with a devilish grin, then ducked back behind her sister for protection. "Kisses are fun. Ma says so."

Jonah sent all his sisters a scathing look. "Things are gonna change around here once we're moved in. Me and Trevor will have men things to do."

"What are ya gonna do, Jonah?" Hannah asked and would have stumbled if Sofie had not caught her. The older girl held the little one's hand until she was settled safely on the top step.

"All kinds of things that boys do with their pa's. Were gonna go fishing and hunting and work together around the farm." His heart warmed to the idea. Having Trevor in his life on a permanent basis was about the best thing he could imagine. He still did not like the idea though, that having his hero around meant that 'hero' would be kissing his ma all the time.

Ruth scuttled across the porch and plopped down on the other side of Hannah to stay out of her brother's reach. She spread her fingers in her lap and quietly counted to four.

Sue Ellen moved to the edge of the porch, hiked her elbows over the railing, and swung her feet as she watched Claire and Trevor cuddle by the wagon. "Do you think they're gonna kiss all day? When I'm as old as ma, I'm gonna kiss my kids' pa all day."

Jonah snorted. "Who'd want to kiss you, Sue Ellen?"

"Shut up, Jonah, or I'm gonna tell ma. Lot's of people will want to kiss me."

"Kissin's stupid."

Sofie belted him again. "It is not!" She took one look at her brother's face and lit off the porch, one step ahead of him. The chase was on.

"Run, Sofie!" the other girls squealed in unison.

Sofie managed to stay ahead of Jonah as they raced around the corner of the building and disappeared. A moment later, Sue Ellen, Hannah, and Ruth headed after them to give their sister a hand if needed.

* * *

Trevor's lips lingered against his wife's mouth, then he lifted his head when he heard the girls squealing. He grinned when Sofie and Jonah raced across the yard and rounded the corner of the house. Their three younger sisters soon followed, Hannah being the last to disappear because of her short legs. Their excited shrieks floated on the breeze.

He wrapped his arm around Claire's waist as they headed to the back of the wagon to begin unloading. "I can't believe how well they all get on. Looks like they're going to love being here, don't you think?"

Claire smiled and held out her arms to accept a light crate of linens. "You should have heard them last night. All they could talk about was how wonderful it would be to have their own rooms. Then Hannah suddenly wasn't too sure about being alone. I think her and Ruth will probably be bunking together for awhile."

Trevor dragged a heavier crate from the wagon and hefted it atop his shoulder. "Well, better Hannah with Ruthie than snuggled between us. I hope they run circles around the house all day and tire themselves out."

Claire fell into step beside him. "Why is that?"

"Because I plan to keep their mother up most of the night without any interruptions." He winked down at her.

Claire lifted her pert nose in the air. "Funny, I was planning to do the same to you."

A hearty laugh burst from Trevor's throat as they approached the steps. "My wife, the wanton. It's a good thing I got you away from Emma and August. Who knows what would have happened to you in their company."

Claire just shook her head, climbed the steps with Trevor following behind, and balanced the crate on her hip to open the screened door for her husband. Hearing a thud behind her, she turned to see him straighten from where he had just dropped his crated load on the wooden planking. Silently, he took the box from her hands and set it down, also.

A moment later, he scooped her high into his arms and spun her in a circle.

"Trevor! What on earth—" She clung tightly to his neck.

The next thing she knew, his lips covered hers. He finally lifted his mouth, and she gazed lovingly up into his face. "What are you doing?"

"I've been thinking about this for weeks. There's no damn way I'm going to let you walk over that threshold. I know you've been here countless times, setting things up, but this is for real, Claire. We're finally moving in and today is the first day of many wonderful years in this house. I want to carry you across. I want to grow old with you by my side. I want to raise these kids and give them every opportunity possible. And, I want to love you more than I do now—even though I don't know if that's possible."

Claire reached up with tears sparkling in her eyes. She drew his mouth to hers and brushed her lips against them—softly, sweetly—letting the intimate embrace express her emotions.

Trevor sighed contentedly when their gazes locked. "Now I know where Hannah learned to give butterfly kisses."

Claire tenderly rubbed her thumb over his lips. "I love you."

"Are you ready to go in, Mrs. Wilkins?"

"Of course, Mr. Wilkins."

* * *

"Listen..." Trevor tugged on Claire's hand and stopped in the upper hallway. His head tilted as his eyes darted about the long corridor.

Claire glanced around in confusion. "What?"

"Do you hear it?" he whispered.

Her voice lowered in instant conspiracy. "What? I don't hear anything."

A mischievous grin creased his face. "Nothing. Absolutely nothing. Total silence."

Claire giggled, took a swat at his arm, and then grabbed his hand. "By now, you should be able to tune them out. I do it all the time. Come on, let's go to bed."

"Ha, that's exactly what I was planning to do..." he returned suggestively.

As they entered the room, Claire sighed happily. "I think today will go down as one of my favorites." She sank to a chair placed before a mirror and began to remove the pins holding her hair in place at the crown of her head. Her eyes followed her husband's reflection as he puttered about the room. "All afternoon, I had to keep opening doors and looking into the rooms. I've never had so much space to just call my own." She eyed Trevor in the mirror as he turned away from the corner of the room with a box in his hand. "Did I forget to put something away?" Claire fluffed her blonde curls around her shoulders, picked up a tortoise-shell brush and ran the soft bristles through her heavy locks.

Trevor set the box on the bed. "No, just a box I found downstairs." He leaned forward and reached inside. "Now, what do we have here? Claire—" he motioned without turning "—come here and see this."

She rose with the brush in her hand, continued to smooth out her curls, and crossed to the bed. A surprised gasp left her mouth when Trevor lift a small bundle of white and turned to face her.

"What...where did that come from?" She tossed the brush onto the bed and reached for the small kitten with a smile. "Oh, isn't he cute." The tiny animal cuddled against her neck, reminding Claire of another white cat that she had loved so dearly.

Trevor's fingers stroked the kitten. "He's a house warming gift just for you."

Her eyes lifted slowly. Tears sparkled brightly as she suddenly realized the significance of his gift. "Trevor..."

"He's your white kitten; the one you can sit with on the porch."

Claire took a deep breath to halt the trembling of her chin. "How did you know? I've never said anything."

He smiled when the kitten nudged his head against Claire's hand, urging her to scratch his tiny ears. "Jonah told me one night when we were sitting out by the lake. We were talking about the farm. He said he didn't miss living there, but was sure you did—especially since you left Snowball buried there. He mentioned something about some elderly woman who had a cat and how she used to sit on her porch with it on her lap. He said the cat was always so important to you."

Claire sank to the edge of the bed and continued to cuddle the furry animal in her arms.

Trevor sat beside her and slung an arm around her shoulders. "You look like you're going to cry. Do you think you could tell me why?"

She shrugged, and then sniffed. "If I do, you're going to tease me."

Trevor held up his palm. "I promise to be good. I know he means something important."

Claire gazed down for a moment, expelling a sigh from her lungs. "I used to pass this house on my way to town when I was first married. There I was with a small basket of eggs and some milk from the cow, hoping to sell it all so I could at least purchase some flour with the money I received. This old woman would sit on her porch with her fluffy white cat and just watch people go by. No cares, no worries. She was always dressed neatly, every white hair on her head in place, and she would happily wave and wish me a good day." Claire sighed, clearly seeing the past in her mind. "I guess that cat represented security to me. wanted so to be just like that woman. One day, she offered me a kitten from a litter playing on the porch." Claire glanced up to see his reaction to her story. "Since then, except for the last few months, I've always had one."

Trevor gave her shoulder a small squeeze. "Well, now you have one again. If you want, I'll get you ten more."

Claire wiped her eye and giggled. "I think one is enough for now."

"I knew there was something about you having a white cat, but couldn't quite figure out what Jonah tried so hard to explain. So, do we have a new Snowball, or does this guy get his own name?"

Claire set the kitten on the bed, reached up, and pushed Trevor backwards on the mattress. A second later, she straddled his waist and began to unbutton his shirt. "I'm not thinking about names right now I'm thinking how much I want to hold my husband in my arms. I'm thinking what a wonderful man he is, simply because he'll do anything— including a surprise gift of a kitten—just because he can't tell me enough times how he will always care for me." Claire whisked her finger through the wiry hair that furred his exposed chest. Leaning over, she kissed his lips lightly while relishing the feel of his hands lightly skimming her back. "And I want to tell him again how much I love him."

Trevor nuzzled her mouth, wrapped his arms more securely around her body, and murmured quietly. "So tell him."

"I love you."

Chapter Twenty-Seven

Three weeks later, after an early Sunday meal, Trevor was with the kids in the living room, stretched out on his back and breathing hard from a playful tussle with Jonah. The boy's sisters, all except Hannah who curled up on the sofa, tumbled about the floor around them.

Claire strolled through the doorway and stopped short as her eyes glanced about. The sight of a spacious living room, the smiling faces of her neatly-clothed children, and Trevor's obvious desire in every glance he sent her way, still combined to overwhelm her to near tears. Claire wondered if she would ever lose the notion that she walked through a wonderful dream.

She rested her hands on her hips and winked at Jonah when he glanced up with a grin. "Are you wearing Trevor out?"

"Nah, he keeps winning."

Ruth spun on her butt and used the back of her hand to brush strands of blonde hair from her eyes. She sent her mother a crooked smile. "I got a ride on Trevor's back."

Claire moved across the room to join Hannah on the sofa. "And you didn't get bucked off?"

Ruth's head wagged. "Nope."

Trevor rolled to his side and propped his head over a bent elbow. "Don't believe anything they tell you. They're killing me, Claire."

She laughed as she plopped down on a soft cushion beside her youngest daughter. "Whose fault is that? Keep egging them on, and you'll be old before your time." She cringed though, when a loud grunt burst from his mouth as Sue Ellen and Sofie double-teamed their stepfather.

Claire laughed at their antics, then turned her head and studied her youngest for a moment. Hannah clung to her blanket. Her round cheeks were colored with a rosy hue as she glanced listlessly around the room, disinterested in the joyful hoots that came from her siblings.

"Don't you feel good, baby?" Claire reached out and pressed the back of her hand against the little girl's forehead. "Oh, my goodness. You've got a fever." She lifted Hannah into her lap, already going over the day's events in her head. Only that morning, her youngest raced about the house, seeming to be in perfect health. She had even eaten her dinner with as much gusto as the other children.

"I don't feel good," Hannah whispered into the crook of her mother's neck.

Claire cuddled her closer. "I don't imagine you do when you've got a fever." She glanced up to catch her husband's attention. "Trevor? Has Hannah been on the sofa since you've been in here?"

He sat up with Ruth clinging to his back. "Yeah, I guess so. Is something wrong?"

"She's got a fever. I think I'll take her upstairs where it's quieter and see if I can get her to lie down."

She rose with the little girl in her arms and headed up the steps. Once in Hannah's room, Claire gave her a drink of water and tucked her in.

"Mommy?"

Claire brushed the hair from Hannah's forehead. "Yes, baby?"

"Sleep here." Hannah patted the bed.

Claire almost said no, thinking about some afternoon projects that needed to be completed, then decided differently. "Okay. I'll lay down with you if you promise to sleep for a while. You'll feel better when you wake up." She climbed onto the bed, pulled the little girl close, and before too much time passed, they both fell asleep to the sounds of muffled laughter below.

* * *

"Claire...wake up."

Someone patted her shoulder. She rolled away from the heat in her arms and blinked to awareness. Trevor leaned over the bed. "I must have fallen asleep."

"How's Hannah?"

Claire's hand immediately reached for her daughter's forehead. "She's even warmer than earlier." She slid her legs over the edge of the bed and let Trevor help her stand. She turned back to comfort Hannah when the girl whimpered and opened her eyes. "Stay here, Hannah. Mommy's going to get some water and we'll cool you down." She straightened again and turned back to her husband. Immediately, she spied his troubled eyes. "What's wrong?"

"Dougan rode over from the ranch. He just left."

Claire waited silently, knowing that whatever he had to say, it was not going to be good.

Trevor's shoulders rose as he inhaled a deep breath. "Mamie passed away a few hours ago."

Claire's fingertips rose to her lips. "Oh, Trevor, I'm so sorry."

He went into her outstretched arms and pulled his wife against him. "I can't believe it finally happened," he murmured beside her ear. "She's been with us my entire life. It'll be so strange going to the ranch and knowing she's not there anymore."

Claire felt his defeated sigh beneath her hands.

"I told the kids to get ready to head on over to the ranch. Steve and Carrie are already on their way. Jonah's hooking up the wagon now. But if Hannah's sick, maybe we shouldn't drag her out."

Claire reached up to cup his cheek. "You have to go, Trevor. I'll stay behind. In fact, if it would be easier, just leave the kids here. That way you can ride over on horseback and it won't take so long."

Trevor kissed her forehead with a sad smile curving his mouth. He sank to the edge of the bed and rubbed Hannah's arm as the little girl stared up at him. "Not feeling so good, hey? Your ma will fix you up. Pretty soon, you'll be feeling better."

"Okay," Hannah breathed.

Trevor bent and pressed a kiss to her warm cheek. Reaching for Claire once more, he hugged her close. "I shouldn't be gone too late." He shook his head, at a loss as what else to say in the face of Mamie's death.

Claire wrapped her arm about his waist as they left the room. "Just do what you have to do. Give everyone my love. Tell Emma and August that Hannah should be well enough by tomorrow. I'll ride over and help with whatever needs to be done." She turned to face her husband. "I know how much Mamie meant to all of you. I know how I felt about her, and I haven't even known her very long. She was a wonderful woman."

His head hung as he nodded, then he clasped Claire's hand. "She was. You sure you'll be all right with Hannah being sick? Do you need anything before I leave?"

"Just go. Ride safely. I'll see you tonight."

* * *

Two hours later, Claire prepared a light supper for herself and the kids. Sofie and Sue Ellen played in Hannah's room to keep an eye on the young girl for their mother.

As Claire sliced pieces of bread and stacked them onto a plate, her eyes lifted to a clock on the shelf. She wondered how Trevor and the rest of his family were handling Mamie's death. A sad smile lifted the corners of her mouth, remembering the faith the old woman had possessed that Claire and Trevor would eventually find their way to one another. *Thank goodness she died happy, knowing her boys would be taken care of...I'm going to miss her...* With a heartfelt sigh, she placed the platter of bread on the table and turned back to retrieve silverware from a drawer.

"Ma! Ma, come quick!"

Sofie's voice echoed from across the house as Claire dropped the forks in her hand onto the counter and rushed through the kitchen door.

"Ma!"

Claire raced across the living room as Sofie hurried down the steps. "Sofie! What is it?"

Her daughter skidded to a halt on the bottom step, grabbed her mother's hand, and pulled her up the staircase. "It's Hannah! She won't wake up! Sue Ellen even shook her, but she won't answer."

Claire bounded around Sofie and took the steps two at a time. Her mind registered the fact that Jonah and Ruth came running behind Sofie. She raced the short distance to Hannah's room, her heart pounding in fear.

Sue Ellen looked up with tears streaming down her cheeks as she held her little sister across her lap. "She won't wake up, Ma. I'm sorry...I thought she was sleeping."

Claire lifted Hannah's limp body into her arms as one hand whisked over the soft, heated skin of her daughter's face. "Hush, Sue Ellen, it's all right. You didn't do anything." Ruth, Sofie, and Jonah stood silently in the doorway and watched fearfully.

Hannah's skin was on fire. Claire lightly slapped a soft, hot cheek. "Hannah, come on baby. Wake up. Mommy's here. Hannah, please..."

Claire dipped her head and placed an ear beside the child's face, listening for the sounds of the child's shallow breaths, and trying at the same time to think what needed to be done next.

"Jonah. Hook up the wagon. We've got to get to the ranch. Steve and Carrie are there."

Jonah whirled from the doorway without question.

Sue Ellen swiped at the tears on her cheek as she scampered off the bed. "Is Hannah gonna be all right?" she asked fearfully.

"She'll be fine, honey. We just can't wait the time it'll take to send for someone. Girls. Grab your coats. Get mine from my room and bring along blankets and a container of water. Bring some towels in case we need to sponge her down on the road."

Trevor...please be on your way home...

Claire hurried out of the room with Hannah's body pressed tightly against her heart. She battled the terror clawing at her insides as the sinking sun approached the horizon outside the window.

* * *

Claire got Hannah situated on a makeshift bed behind the seat of the wagon with the help of the girls. By the time she crawled over the rail onto the driver's bench, Jonah scrambled up beside her. Grabbing the heavy leather reins, she slapped them across the horse's flanks and headed onto the road.

The next half-hour passed quietly, except for Claire's worried questions to the older girls in back. She continually glanced over her shoulder. The answers she received from her daughters were always the same. Hannah remained limp on the bundle of blankets, unaware that they raced through the darkening landscape. Claire watched the lane before them as the wagon wheels rolled over the miles that brought them closer to the ranch. She prayed that Trevor would appear, swallowing back the lump of fear in her throat as each corner twisted to a barren, open road.

Rounding another turn, she hauled back on the reins slightly as a carriage approached, guided the wagon closer to the side of the road to allow passage for both conveyances, and then frantically slapped the reins across the horse's backside again to urge the animal into a gallop. Claire never even glanced at the couple who passed them by.

* * *

Judd Stone and his cousin were on their way back to Biwabik from the city of Duluth. Weeks had passed since the Wilkins reception, and Regina began to whine incessantly about her forced imprisonment in a small city. Judd, having had enough of her caterwauling, finally took her south for three days. The result of the excursion was a much lighter pocketbook after her constant shopping and dining out at expensive restaurants. But, at least, her bitchiness had taken leave.

Seeing a wagon that raced headlong in their direction, Judd reined toward the edge of the road and let the farm wagon go by. His eyes rounded when he recognized Claire and her children in the waning light of day.

Regina clutched at Judd's arm. "Was that who I think it was?" She swiveled on the seat and stared around the edge of the canopy as her cousin brought the carriage to a quick halt.

Judd's gaze searched the road in both directions. "What the hell is she doing out at this time of the day—and without Wilkins at her side?" He swiveled on the seat and again looked about.

"This is our chance, Judd. Let's go after her."

His eyes narrowed as his fingers gripped the reins. "This isn't how we planned it. It would be too much of a risk grabbing her off a main road where anyone can witness it. And she's got her brats with her. No, this isn't the time. We need to wait for another opportunity."

Regina clutched his arm tighter. Her teeth clenched at his resistance. "What are you talking about? This is the perfect time. We've been trying to figure out how to kidnap her from her house. Now you won't have to. Turn this damn buggy around and get going!"

"Regina..."

"Don't you 'Regina' me. I want that woman out of Trevor's life!"

"What about the kids?"

"Give me those reins if you're just going to sit there." She made a grab for the leather straps in his hands, but Judd held them away. Regina hissed with exasperation; her lips thinned ominously. "As far as the kids go, leave them on the road. By the time someone discovers them, we'll be long gone."

"Those kids will recognize me, and I'll have Wilkins and his brother on my heels."

Regina leaned over the seat and rummaged through various boxes of clothing. "Here. Put this scarf around your face," she stated as she folded a piece of silk for herself. "Now, move!"

***

"Ma, that buggy is coming back!" Sofie hollered as she bounced against the side of the wagon. "They're coming fast. They must know us!"

Claire slowed the horse to a trot and glanced over her shoulder. Did the buggy belong to an acquaintance of Trevor's? Whoever it was waved an arm. Claire brought the wagon to a complete halt and looped the reins around a wooden post. She swiveled on the seat and squinted her eyes, but in the near darkness it was too difficult to make out any familiar features. The only thing she could discern was that a man and woman sat on the seat. Maybe it was someone who could ride ahead and find Trevor.

Climbing over the seat, she sank beside Hannah and felt the little girl's cheeks; she was still unconscious. Claire wanted to weep with frustration and dread. She feared, however, that if she started now, she would unable to get back any semblance of control. She gently lifted Hannah into her lap, needing the comfort of holding the child in her arms, and then leaned against the side of the wagon to wait.

The buggy passed them and stopped a short distance ahead, it riders' faces turned away in the dim light. Claire straightened—a finger of apprehension weaved its way down her spine. Jonah stood, ready to jump to the ground from his former seat beside his mother. "Jonah!" Claire's sharp tone stopped the boy in his tracks. "Stay where you are." Her son slowly sat, keeping a puzzled eye on his mother.

Claire leaned slightly forward and automatically tightened her hold on Hannah. The woman stayed in the buggy while the man stepped to the ground. He turned then, and Claire saw the scarf wrapped around his face and the hat pulled low across his brow. Her first instinct was to have Jonah whip their horse into motion. When he drew a pistol from his pocket, she knew it was too late.

He approached the wagon with the gun steady in his hand.

"Ma..."

"Hush, Jonah." Claire swallowed her panic as her frightened gaze followed the stranger; he walked to the back of the wagon. "Stay where you are." Sue Ellen and Ruth sidled across the buckboard and pressed their bodies close to their mother.

The man stopped. He pointed the metal barrel directly at Claire. "Get out," his muffled, gravelly voice ordered from behind the scarf.

"I don't know what you want, but I don't have any money on me." Her hands shook as they clutched Hannah. "Please, I'm trying to get my sick daughter to a doctor."

"Shut up!"

Claire felt Sue Ellen's body jerk beside her as the girl clutched at her arm. Ruth began to whimper softly. "What...what do you want?"

"I want you to get out of the wagon—now."

"Please, my daughter needs a—"

"Get out now!"

Ruth cried louder.

Claire's heart pounded. "If you'll just—"

The stranger leapt forward, dragged a screaming Ruth across the wagon bed, and placed the barrel against the little girl's head.

"No!" Claire choked out as she hurriedly placed Hannah in Sue Ellen's shaking arms; her eyes never left Ruth's quaking body. The frightened girl sobbed as she struggled to be free. "Don't hurt her! I'm doing as you say. Please, please don't hurt my little girl..." Claire scrambled toward the back of the wagon, and a sob caught in her throat when the gun swung up to point at Jonah.

"Tell that brat to sit and stay put."

Claire spun to her son. "Sit down, Jonah. Please...it'll be all right if you just do as he says."

Claire's body trembled so fiercely that she could barely slide over the edge of the wagon to a standing position. She held out her arms for Ruth, but the stranger yanked the little girl further from her reach. The back of Claire's hand floated to her lips to keep the terrified sobs from tumbling out. "Please don't hurt her." Frightened tears, not for herself but for her children, rolled down her cheeks. "I'll do anything you want. Just let her get back in the wagon."

"Ma...Ma..." Ruth sobbed as she flailed to reach Claire's hand.

The stranger yanked the girl closer to his body. The gun returned to Ruth's temple.

Claire froze with helplessness. "Don't cry, Ruthie. Please, don't cry. Just stand still and everything will be fine." She swung her watery gaze toward the demon who held her child. "She's just a little girl. Please don't hurt her. I beg you. I'll do anything you want. Just let her go—"

"Shut up!" he screeched. The slits of his eyes darted about them.

Claire's shoulders shook with the silent sobs in her throat. Her hands flew to her mouth to keep her fear inside. "Please..." she gasped quietly as her brain raced to discover a way from the nightmare thrust upon them.

"Walk away from the wagon."

Claire raced to the middle of the dark road. "I...I did as you asked. Let her go." She helplessly watched the gun waver beside Ruth's tightly squeezed eyes. The girl wept silently as she shuddered in the stranger's grip. Spots of black appeared before Claire's eyes. She took a deep breath to clear her head and tried to keep the man's attention on herself, instead of her child. "My husband can give you money. Lots of money. If you let my children leave, I'll go with you. He'll give you anything you want..."

Judd lifted the pistol away from Ruth's head and pointed it directly at Claire's chest.

Claire waited to feel the sting of a bullet tearing into her body as the words died in her throat. *I don't care!* her brain screamed. *Just don't shoot my babies...*

Judd's gaze slithered to the bawling girls in the wagon. The boy sat rooted to the seat. The banker was in a horrible quandary as he tried to decide what to do next. The boy looked capable of driving the wagon down the road for help. Most likely, Claire was on her way to the Wilkins homestead in search of help for the sick kid in back.

Judd calculated the time it would take for them to reach the ranch. They could get there within thirty minutes. The lead-time would not be enough for him and Regina to reach the abandoned mine where he planned to hide Claire.

He would have to shoot and kill all of her brats in order to keep Wilkins guessing as to the disappearance of his wife. After a time, Regina would be able to sweep in and console the grieving widower. The irritating woman would then persuade Wilkins to head south to St. Paul and sell his property in the north—to Judd. The natural ore lying beneath that land would make the banker wealthy beyond his wildest dreams.

The pistol swung toward the wagonload of wailing children.

Claire screamed. "No!" She took three running steps and skidded to a halt when the man quickly trained the barrel of the pistol on her chest once more. Sinking weakly to her knees, she began to plead. "You want me. You don't want them. Please, let them go. I'll do anything you want. Just...just don't hurt them."

Regina rounded the horse hitched to Judd's carriage. "What are you doing? If we don't get out of here, someone is going to come along and we'll both be in jail. Get her in the buggy and let's go."

Claire's eyes swung to the woman who had scarves tied around her face. Her hair was covered completely and a velvet robe concealed her body. Claire prayed desperately that the man would pay heed to his accomplice's suggestion.

"They'll bring help if we let them go."

"We'll be long gone by then. If you don't get her in the buggy now, I'll do it myself and leave you here."

Judd's fingers tightened around the pistol and, for a fleeting moment, he considered disposing of his cousin along with the Holcomb children. No, he could not. He needed Regina as a means to an end. A frustrated sigh left his mouth just before he shoved Ruth roughly toward the back of the wagon. She stumbled and pitched to the ground.

Claire's breath tumbled from her mouth in silent relief, then her gaze moved to where her sobbing daughter sprawled on the ground and stared up at her. "Get in the wagon, Ruthie. Everything's going to be all right."

"Ma..."

"I'll hold you again, baby, but right now you have to get in the wagon," Claire replied softly. "Just be a good girl and do as mommy says."

The girl stared blankly.

"Honey...do this for mommy." Claire could barely get the words out as her eyes continued to dart toward the pistol. "Sofie will help you up. Get in the wagon."

Ruth rose slowly, took two shaky steps, and clutched Sofie's outstretched hand in a death grip. A moment later, both her sisters hauled her into the back.

Judd stalked to Claire and yanked her to her feet. "Tell them to head south."

Thanking God silently, Claire ignored the pain elicited by the man's tight grip on her arm and nodded her head at Jonah. "Take the wagon and go, son. You're in charge of your sisters. Get Hannah to a doctor as quickly as you can. Go to the doctor immediately." Claire stared at her son, praying that he would not argue and that he would understand he needed to get to the ranch for help. She wanted them gone. She needed to know that they were safe from the pistol in her captor's grip.

Jonah nodded, sank to the wooden seat, and unwound the reins. With a snap of his wrists, the wagon lurched forward.

* * *

Jonah fought his tears as the wagon rounded the next bend. He continually glanced over his shoulder until his mother disappeared from sight. He had never been so frightened in his life. The sound of his sobbing sisters echoed in the near darkness around them. Ruth lurched to the edge of the buckboard and started to vomit over the side.

Jonah yanked hard on the reins and brought the wagon to a stop. Scrambling to see into the back, he saw Hannah still sprawled on top of the blankets. Sue Ellen held Ruth's heaving shoulders as Sofie poured water onto a towel and wiped her sister's mouth.

He jumped down and hurried to the horse. As fast as his fingers could fly, he unbuckled the harness.

"What are doing, Jonah?" Sofie sniffed as she grabbed another wet rag and dampened her little sister's forehead. "Hannah's burnin' up. We gotta get help for ma." A quiet sob gurgled in her throat.

"That's what I'm doing. I'm going back after that carriage."

"You can't...we gotta get Trevor. It's dark, Jonah. I don't want to stay here without you. You can't leave us. Ma said you were in charge."

His fingers worked furiously at the buckles. "There's a lantern in the box. Light it and you'll be fine. Trevor said he wasn't gonna be late comin' home. He should be here soon. If I don't follow ma now, we'll never know where that man is takin' her." The harness poles fell to the ground. He tossed the thick straps of leather over the horse and raced to the animal's head. Looping the long reins in his shaking hands, Jonah led the animal to the back of the wagon and hopped into the bed. A moment later, he pulled the horse closer, stretched his leg over the broad back, and slid on top of the animal. "Don't be scared, Sofie."

"What if that man shoots you? What if he shoots ma?" Sofie's voice trembled along with her hands as she lit the lantern.

"He won't see me, I promise. I'll stay far enough behind. When Trevor comes, tell him I'll meet him at the junction to Biwabik after I know where ma is. There's no turns in the road until then. Those people must have headed north with ma, cuz they ain't comin' back this way. It'll be all right, just like ma said. Just stay in the wagon and wait for Trevor."

He yanked on the reins and dug his heels into the horse's sides.

Sofie slumped against the seat, wiped the tears from her cheek, and listened to the retreat of galloping hooves. Soon, the only sound to be heard was that of Ruth being sick over the side of the wagon.

Chapter Twenty-Eight

Trevor's body rocked gently with the tempo of the horse's cantering gait. His eyes automatically watched the road before him as his mind wandered over the events of the last hours. He was grateful beyond words that he had been able to sit beside Mamie's bed before her cold body was taken away. Memorizing her familiar features, he had almost felt that the old, beloved woman would open her eyes at any moment and smile up at him. As he kissed her leathery cold cheek one last time, he had silently thanked her for the many loving years she bestowed on not only him, but his family, too. His only wish was that she could have lived longer to enjoy Claire and the children's company.

A sudden picture of Claire's soft eyes floated through his mind. Trevor still wondered what he had done right in the past to be so blessed by having her in his life now. He was anxious to be home and to be welcomed into her comforting arms.

Rounding a corner, Trevor's attention was drawn to the glow of a lantern flickering ahead on the road. *Someone must be having some troubles...* The last thing he wanted to do was to delay his arrival home as he helped a neighbor or friend make needed repairs. Tightening the grip on his reins, he urged the horse to a quicker gait.

As he approached the abandoned wagon, his brow furrowed at the sight of the harness poles resting on the ground. His puzzled gaze skittered about for only a second—then his heart skipped a beat when he realized the wagon belonged to him.

Trevor hauled back on the reins and leapt from the saddle. "Claire!" He bounded forward when a small blonde head peeked over the edge.

"Trevor?"

"Sofie? What the hell happened?"

The little girl launched over the side of the buckboard and into his arms. She clung tightly to his neck, sobbing as he cradled her quaking body. A streak of fear pierced his chest. Trevor strode to the back of the wagon. His troubled gaze settled on Ruth, who lay on a blanket with Hannah clasped in her embrace. Sue Ellen huddled close by.

"Where's your mother? Sofie, you've got to tell me what happened."

"Hannah's sick," she hiccupped against his neck. "I was so scared. We couldn't wake her up at home, so Ma put us all in the wagon to find Steve and Carrie. She needs a doctor, Trevor." The girl continued to tremble as she clutched him tightly.

Where in hell is Claire? Trevor set Sofie on the edge of the wagon bed, gently forced her arms from around his neck, and jumped inside. He scrambled to Hannah's side. Ruth cried quietly and stared up at him from the blanket.

Sue Ellen stared at him with round eyes. "I wanna go home. Don't make us stay here."

Trevor reached out to pat her shoulder. "It's okay, Sue Ellen. I promise, I won't leave you here. Sofie, where's your mother and Jonah?" he questioned again over his shoulder as his hands skimmed across Hannah's brow.

"A...a man took her away. We stopped on the road and he got out of his buggy with a gun."

Trevor's heart slammed in his chest.

"Jonah unhitched the horse and went after them. He said for you to wait at the junction. He's gonna see where they're taking ma. Don't leave us here, Trevor," she pleaded.

His head snapped up. "They? There was more than one man?" His stomach rolled as bile bubbled in his throat.

"A lady was with him."

Trevor pulled Ruth into his embrace when she sat up and reached for him. The girl whimpered quietly against his chest. Gently, he rubbed her back. "It's all right, Ruthie. Don't be scared," he crooned.

"Ruth won't say anything." Sue Ellen's voice trembled with fear. "She's been throwin' up, Trevor. That mean man took her out of the wagon and put his gun against her head. I can't get her to talk to me."

Trevor's chin sagged to his chest, overwhelmed by the terror he felt. He tightened his hold on Ruth. *Jesus Christ...* "Come here, Sofie." He waited until the girl crawled to his side, then placed a comforting arm around her thin shoulders. "How long ago did this happen?"

Her blonde head shook slowly as she swiped at her tears. "I don't know. It's been so scary waiting for you to come. Jonah said you would. It was dark when he left."

"Here, you hold Ruth's hand for a minute while I get Hannah. Go wait by Buck." The ride back to the ranch would take longer with all four girls on the horse with him, but it was quicker than fighting his mount hitched to an unfamiliar harness. There was no way in hell he would leave them alone any longer—and Hannah needed Steve and Carrie. It took some convincing but, finally, Ruth clutched Sofie's fingers and between the older girl and Sue Ellen, they persuaded her to get out of the wagon.

Trevor tenderly wrapped Hannah in a blanket and lifted her limp body until her tiny head rested against his shoulder. He scooted back to the edge, lowered his feet to the ground, and hurried to his mount. Ruth stood beside Sofie and gripped her sister's hand; her eyes were tightly squeezed shut. Sue Ellen was perched on top of Buck.

"She won't get on without me," Sofie stated quietly.

Trevor held out the unconscious girl and placed her in Sofie's arms. "Hold your sister." Once his arms were free, he hunkered down and forced a smile to his lips. "Ruthie, can I help you up?" Trevor was not sure how far he could push the fragile state the girl floated in. Her head slowly wagged. The vacant stare in her eyes frightened Trevor beyond belief. "If you let me help you up, I promise that Sofie will be right beside you. You can hold her hand all the way to the ranch. Honey, Hannah is really sick. We have to get going. Then I'm going to go get your ma. Please, Ruthie, let me help you."

Her round eyes blinked once, and then she tentatively held out her trembling hand. Trevor quickly lifted her from the ground but, before he set her on the horse, he hugged her tenderly and kissed her cheek. "I love you, Ruthie. Everything's going to be okay. Do you know that I love you?" Her tiny chin nodded. "You're a good girl. You're a brave girl. We'll get back to the ranch, and you can stay with Emma and

August. You're safe now."

He placed her gently atop the horse as Sue Ellen scooted back in the saddle. Taking Hannah from her sister, he held out his arm. Sofie hooked her hands around it and climbed up with her stepfather's help. Trevor was right behind her, settling Hannah more securely against his chest as he sat on Buck's rump. Only seconds passed before he reined in the direction of the ranch.

* * *

Jonah finally caught up to the careening buggy as it raced away with his mother inside. The horse strained beneath him as he clung tightly with one hand to the long reins. The fingers of the other entwined in the flowing mane. He had no idea where he was but, as long as there were not too many forks in the road and with the dim light from the small slice of moon, he felt confident he could get back to find Trevor.

Another mile passed before the carriage slowed and leaned precariously on one wheel as it turned sharply off the main road onto a mere trail, heavy with scraggly brush on both sides of the wheel tracks. Jonah urged his horse forward, straining to see into the darkness, listening to the sounds around him. Every so often, he heard the scrape of a metal wheel rim against a boulder. He continued on, praying his ma was alive and not hurt. The boy just wanted the buggy to stop. He wanted to see his mother alive—and he wanted Trevor by his side.

Another ten minutes went by until the carriage passed beneath a wooden train trestle and turned toward a bank of tin-covered buildings. Jonah urged his mount behind the cover of brush and squinted into the darkness. He heard the carriage door open, and then the sweet sound of his mother's voice floated back to him. He could not see her, but at least Jonah knew she was alive.

He waited quietly as the sound of footsteps on wooden planks told him that Claire and her captors were most likely entering one of the buildings. Rusty door hinges groaned in the dark and, only moments later, a light flickered in a window as a lantern was lit. The horse beneath him whickered softly, sending a streak of fear down the boy' spine. Jonah held his breath; his heart thudded in his ears.

A door slammed, blocking out the little bit of light that shined onto the porch.

The air left his lungs in a whoosh. Jonah slid from his mount's back, quickly looped the reins around a tree, and moved stealthily across the yard. His eyes darted about when he reached the building. Hearing muffled, angry voices come from within the abandoned structure, the boy hunkered down, crawled onto the porch, and crept quietly to the window.

Jonah's heartbeat continued to pound inside his head as he slowly rose to peek inside. He wanted to scream in anger when he spied his mother being forced into a chair. Claire's abductor stood with his back to the window. Jonah's knuckles turned white as he gripped the rotted windowsill.

A woman moved into his line of vision. Jonah ducked slightly but continued to peer through the dirty glass; his mouth sagged open when he recognized her from the day of the party. As she turned to walk toward the window, Jonah dropped out of sight. If the door opened, he would run like the devil chased him. He waited, hardly daring to breathe. Nothing.

Snaking his body upward once more, he gripped the sill again until he was eye level with the bottom of the window.

Mr. Stone!

He whirled from the window, crawled back across the porch, and raced to his horse. Once he felt he was far enough away to be undetected, he dug his heels in and headed for the junction.

* * *

Tyler, with Katy's help, hurriedly shoved supplies into saddlebags lined up on the workbench in the kitchen. He glanced at the woman when he heard her sniffle. "We'll find them, Katy."

She hurried to the counter with her head shaking, grabbed two filled canteens of water, and raced back to drop them into the leather sack. "I just keep seeing the two of them..." She swiped at the wetness on her cheek. "If that horrible man felt no compunction against holding a gun to a four-year-old's head, what is Claire going through? And Jonah...he's just a little boy..." She shook her head again as she checked the contents in one of the saddlebags once more. "God take that man from this earth..."

Keeper of the Heart

Tyler dared not even think about Claire in the clutches of a madman. The sick feeling in the pit of his stomach returned—the same feeling he experienced when Trevor tore through the front door just a short time earlier. Hannah hung lifelessly in his arms and his brother's face was white with terror. Claire's other three daughters followed him in, their pale cheeks streaked with tears. Little Ruthie was in shock. Steve hurriedly carried the child up the stairs behind Trevor, listening to the explanation of what transpired on the road. Sue Ellen and Sofie sobbed and clung tightly to Emma and August.

Katy pulled a hanky from her pocket and wiped her tears. "I think you're all set. I've got to go up and see how the girls are doing." She hurried from the kitchen.

As the door swung behind her, Tyler grabbed a strap and began to buckle the bag in front of him. He paused when he heard Trevor's booming voice coming from the dining room. His brother had just given him five minutes to prepare for the road or he would be left behind.

The door swung open again and Trevor's large frame stormed into the kitchen. His troubled, angry eyes met his brothers. "Tell him he's not coming."

Tyler glanced up. "Who?"

Cole stepped into the room with a heavy jacket in his hands, a saddlebag slung over his shoulder, and a rifle resting in the crook of his arm.

Tyler grabbed his own jacket and slipped his arms into the sleeves. "What do you want me to say?"

Trevor's fist slammed against the surface of the table. "He can't take the chance. We've spent the last few years keeping Cole hidden. I'll be goddamned if I'm going to visit him in a prison somewhere if he's found out." Getting no response from his older brother, Trevor swung his gaze to where Cole waited by the back door. "I can't stand here and argue with you. I have to go."

"Then you can argue with me when we're on the road, because I'm not staying behind."

Trevor snatched a saddlebag from the table and headed across the kitchen to the outside door. Before he stepped into the night, he hesitated, glanced up to meet Cole's compassionate gaze, and reached out to clamp a grateful hand on his brother's shoulder.

***

The three brothers raced into the night; through the gate, past Trevor's abandoned wagon twenty minutes later, and on to the junction in the hope that Jonah would be there. Trevor prayed the entire way that the boy was safe and awaiting his help. And Claire—he could not even contemplate what life would be like without her by his side. As they neared the crossing, however, only the moon's rays shimmered across the empty space. Hauling back on the reins, the three looked at one another.

"Now what," Tyler asked.

Trevor glanced about as his mount pranced beneath him. "Goddammit, we have no idea which way he might have gone. We have to give him some time to come back. Christ..." He struggled against the terror that burgeoned in his chest and ran a hand across his bristled cheek. "He's only a kid out there, trying to do a man's job. I can' believe he took off after them."

"He's the only hope we've got right now," Cole stated rationally. "We need to bring the law into this, Trevor. Why don't you and I stay here—Tyler can go on to Biwabik and bring Moose back with him."

Trevor snapped his head in Cole's direction. "Moose thinks you're dead. No. You might have talked your way into coming this far tonight, but you won't talk me into putting the noose around your neck."

"It's a chance we need to take. It's a chance I'm willing to take."

"Well, that's too goddamned bad! I'm not!"

Cole's eyes flashed in response, but the man remained silent. Trevor shook his head helplessly and glanced around again, trying to decide what to do. Having Moose involved in the search, would up their chances of finding Claire; the man knew the area. But at the same time could he be trusted to forget his oath of office? Would he report to the authorities that Cole did not die at Wounded Knee?

Cole saw Trevor's hesitation and pressed him further. "Trevor, this is Moose we're talking about. This is the guy who considers you good friend. He used to mine, too."

Trevor struggled with the decision, wishing Jonah would appear so he would not have to choose. He stared at a Cole for another moment. A defeated sigh left his mouth seconds later when his gaze met Tyler's.

"It's only five more minutes to Biwabik. No matter what, Tyler, you be back within twenty minutes—either with the man or without. I'm not waiting any longer than that. Cole, you head up the fork. I know we can use Moose's help, but you're going to keep out of sight." His harried gaze swung back to his older brother. "Twenty minutes, Tyler. If you're not here and Jonah hasn't shown up by then, Cole and I are heading north. You'll just have to catch up."

Tyler nodded, reined his horse around, and raced for Biwabik.

* * *

Trevor paced in the darkness. His eyes watched both lanes leading to the junction. He wanted to pound his fists against the ground; he wanted to hold Claire in his arms; he wanted to wrap his fingers around someone's neck until he choked the life from their body; he wanted the nightmare to end.

He whirled to rest his forehead against Buck's massive neck and inhaled a deep breath to settle his roiling stomach. The three breaths that followed finally accomplished his goal, but he was powerless to rid himself of the terrifying ache in his chest. The helplessness of the situation ate at his gut. *Five minutes... If Tyler's not back in five minutes, I'm leaving...*

Suddenly, Trevor's chin jerked up. He pressed a calming hand against Buck's neck and tightened his grip around the reins, urging the horse to stand still. Cocking his head, he held his breath and listened intently.

He launched himself into the saddle and spun the horse around at the sound of hooves pounding against the packed dirt road—and waited for the unknown rider.

Jonah skidded to a halt beside Trevor. The older man yanked the boy from the foam-covered horse and clutched him to his chest, fighting the tears that burned behind his lids. "Jonah..." His large hands skimmed the boy's head, then moved on to his back and arms to assure himself that he was not injured.

The boy clung to his shoulders, feeling safe for the first time that night.

"Where is she?"

"There's a mining place about three miles up the road that has buildings." The boy's voice caught in his throat. "It's Mr. Stone, Trevor. I saw him! And a lady that was at the party is there, too."

"Is your ma hurt?" Trevor's mind scurried. He pictured Stone's face in his mind and tried to figure out who the woman could be.

"I...I don't think so. They made her sit on a chair. She looks scared, Trevor."

Trevor hugged the boy close one last time and kneed Buck until the animal sidled up beside Jonah's mount. He put the boy back on the horse. "Tyler went into Biwabik to get the sheriff. Stay here and tell him I've headed out. Did you see Cole on the road?"

Jonah's head nodded as he swiped at the tears on his cheek. "He caught up to me when I was going by. I told him where ma is. He said you were here. Cole headed north already. Mr. Stone's got a gun, Trevor. I want to go back with you." A tiny sob burst from his mouth.

Trevor reached out and clutched the boy's arm. "You did right by following your ma, Jonah, but someone's got to let Tyler know where she is. If we don't do this right, I might not make it to the mine in time. Now listen to me. If Tyler has the sheriff with him, you can't say anything about Cole being with me. Can you do that?"

Jonah sniffed and nodded his head. "I promise..."

"As soon as you tell Tyler where I went, I want you to head for the ranch. Your sister's are there. I swear I'll bring your mother back."

Jonah nodded again as Buck and his frantic rider shot forward into the darkness.

* * *

Claire pressed herself against the back of the chair and turned her face away from Judd's wavering hand. Her lids closed so she would not have to stare at the cold metal of the gun he clutched in his hand. Breathing deeply, the odor of rotting wood, musty burlap sacks, and a strange metallic scent assaulted her nostrils. If she lived to see another day, Claire would never forget the foreboding scent of imminent death. Pain ripped through her shoulder a second later when Judd suddenly grasped her, commanding her attention.

"Look at me, Claire."

She struggled against her fear and slowly opened her eyes. Regina stood to her right, pointing a small derringer. Her red lips curled in a scornful sneer. Refusing to meet the woman's eyes, Claire straightened in the chair and met Judd's withering stare. The barrel of the pistol still wavered directly in front of her. "Why are you doing this? If it's money you want, my husband can make arrangements."

Judd leaned back and let the fingers that gripped the butt of the gun hang at his side.

Claire let out a breath of relief, but her hands continued to shake where they lay were clutched in her lap.

Judd snorted. "Oh, your husband will make arrangements all right—funeral arrangements." His feral gaze locked with hers. "I'm still amazed that you landed on your feet like a cat, Claire. If Wilkins hadn't come riding in on the proverbial white horse that day at your farm, we wouldn't be here now. You'd still be residing in that run-down place of yours in St. Paul." He leaned forward and traced the line of her tense cheek with his finger. "All you would have had to do is spend just a little time with me."

Claire jerked her head away from his touch. "You're not going to get away with this. Trevor will hunt you down."

Judd's mouth turned up. "How? He doesn't have a clue who took you. He'll never find you—not right away at least. When you and I are through here, we're going to take a little walk across this compound. There's an empty mine shaft..." His gaze left hers and moved to a crate shoved against the wall. "There's dynamite stored in that little box there. Maybe we'll even blow up the entrance to the mine. Need I say anymore?"

Claire battled her threatening tears. She would not give the monster a chance to see how truly frightened she was. Judd was right. Trevor would never find her in time. *At least the children are safe...* A flash of Ruth, cringing in the man's arms, helped her recapture a bit of courage. Judd might end her life tonight, but she would die knowing that Trevor would always keep them safe.

Regina sauntered closer. Her calculating gaze rested on Claire momentarily before she sent a sidelong glance to her cousin. "Why don't you do whatever you're going to do with her, Judd? I want to get out of here—and start consoling Trevor over his wife's death."

Claire's eyes widened. She looked from one to the other, still trying to reason why they were together. Her eyes returned to bore through the smug woman. "Trevor will never be consoled by the likes of you." A split second later, her head reeled from a vicious slap.

"Don't you dare speak my future husband's name again! You'll be gone from this world soon enough," Regina seethed as her finger twitched against the trigger. Her anger evaporated, however, when the woman on the chair gasped repeatedly and brought a shaking hand to her cheek. "He would have married me if you hadn't figured out a way to snag him."

"Don't damage the goods, Regina, or you'll be sitting along side her in the mine shaft."

Regina spun to face her cousin. "Shut up, Judd—and don't be threatening me. Remember, I'm the one who will coax Trevor into selling that piece of property. If it wasn't for me, you wouldn't even be this close to getting your hands on it."

Claire's brain still spun as she tried to follow the conversation. She blinked back the stinging tears in her eyes and fearfully watched her captors. The nightmare she had walked in would not disappear. They were both insane. She did conclude one thing though, from the screaming spat that continued on—her abduction had been planned. They may not have intended to take her from the road, but, at some point, they would have spirited her away. Claire's demise, in their minds, would allow access to the man Regina so desperately desired. In return, Judd would become wealthier than he had ever imagined by gaining control of some of the Wilkins' land.

Claire's chin sank slowly. She huddled in the chair and tried not to move. The longer they argued, the longer she would live. Enough time had passed that Trevor had to be searching for her by now. She was more certain of that by the second. *But, will he find me in time?* She clung to the fact that he would.

A silent sob welled in her throat. At least her children were not injured, and they were not in the clutches of Judd Stone. The fact that she did exactly as Judd asked of her earlier, had spared their lives. If she could keep him and Regina arguing—if she could keep Judd from taking what he wanted—her chances of leaving the storage shed alive would increase tenfold.

If not? Her soul wept. Never again would she be able to hold a precious little body in her arms as she crooned her love. And she would never...never hold the man she loved again.

A frightened scream burst from her mouth when Judd grabbed her by the arm and wrenched Claire from the chair. "Don't do this!" she pleaded as she struggled against his tight grip.

An evil smile played about Regina's mouth in the face of Claire's terror-filled eyes. "Get her out of here. Have your way with her, and then kill her. We have to leave before someone happens to stumble across this place."

Claire struggled in Judd's arms. "Don't be a fool, Judd! Trevor's family can make you rich without the property. You don't have to kill me to get what you want. Don't listen to her..."

He fought her flailing arms. Claire scratched and kicked wildly—and received the back of his hand as a reward for her efforts. Her body spun, pitched forward and skidded across the dirty floor. Stunned, she slowly clutched the side of her face, and then rolled onto her side. Raising herself up slowly on one arm, she looked up and stared into the barrel of Regina's small derringer.

"Get up."

Claire tried. The ground tilted beneath her.

Regina leapt forward and pressed the short barrel against Claire's temple. "I said get up!" she screeched. Claire tried again. A moment later, the other woman jumped back, her captive forgotten. She lifted her eyes to the roof—and to where Judd already stared upward. "What the hell was that?"

Chapter Twenty-Nine

Cole quickly looped his mount's leather reins around a thick tree branch a good distance from the buildings in the abandoned mine yard. Studying the open expanse between where he stood and the one structure with light spilling out the window, his narrowed eyes silently mapped out a route—one that would keep him hidden in the shadows created by the light of the moon. Clenching the rifle tightly in his grip, he moved swiftly, every sense sharpened by the muffled voices that filtered into the night.

Reaching the ramshackle building, Cole eased himself onto the porch at the corner of the structure. Pressing his body against the front outer wall, he waited a moment to assure no one had been alerted to his presence, then slithered to the window. Slowly, he twisted his head until he was able to see inside.

Cole's heart skipped a beat. Claire sat pressed against the back of a chair; her abductor brandished a pistol before her face. The woman in the room unexpectedly turned in his direction; she also wielded a small derringer. Cole ducked away and hugged the wall at his back.

His jaw clenched tightly. *Son of a bitch...where are you, Trevor?* Two guns were drawn inside; the situation was worse than expected. He needed to get Claire out of the building.

He drew in a cleansing breath. Inching his way back to the window, his gaze darted about the interior, searching for another exit or window. His heart sank when the situation worsened by the second. Stacked against the walls were crates marked 'Dynamite'.

Suddenly, the man grabbed Claire by the shoulder. Cole's stomach lurched at the fear in his sister-in-law's eyes. He continued to peer into the cabin while his brain scrambled to put together a plan. Rushing the door was not an option. Though the mine location was abandoned months earlier, it was possible that there were still sticks of dynamite in the crates. The rescue would most definitely turn into a gun battle and a stray bullet could blow up the building. No, Claire's tormentors would have to be drawn outdoors—and he could not do it alone.

He barely breathed as he listened to the heated conversation going on inside—something about the Wilkins' property. He strained to hear. His eyes narrowed when the woman sauntered across the room. She called the man "Judd." Cole's lips parted in surprise. *Judd? Judd Stone, the banker? The man who Trevor spoke about—the one who terrorized Claire in St. Paul...*

Cole nearly leapt through the dirty window when the woman's fierce slap sent Claire's head spinning. Judd turned. Cole caught a quick glance of the man's face before he jerked back for a second time. He hugged the exterior wall again; his lids slammed shut with the helplessness that roared through his blood; his fingers clenched the rifle. *I'm sorry, Claire. I have to wait. This has to be done right or you'll be hurt...*

A scream pierced the air, and the hair stood on the back of Cole's neck. His eyes flew open and, once again, he swung his head to peek inside.

Claire struggled fiercely against Judd's hold, ignoring the woman's small derringer that hovered menacingly nearby. Suddenly, Judd backhanded Claire and she pitched to the floor. The woman leapt forward then, and her shriek met Cole's ear. "Get up!" She pressed her gun to Claire's head.

Without thinking, Cole furiously dug inside his jacket pocket and pulled out a bullet. Backing off the porch and out from the cover of the metal overhang, he tossed the bullet onto the tin roof. It bounced off the pitch, rolled down the length and dropped to the ground. Another quick glance inside the building told him that the distraction was enough to draw the attention away from Claire. Judd turned toward the door and took a step.

"Cole!"

Trevor's whispered hiss was music to Cole's ears. He raced

silently to the end of the porch and leapt into the darkness just as Judd approached the door.

Another scream rent the air, and Cole's hand flew out to forcibly hold his brother back. "You can't just go charging in there," he whispered frantically. "There's a man and a woman, and they both have guns. Christ, I think the guy's Judd Stone."

Trevor's chin dropped to his chest as he struggled to stay where he was.

"The place is full of old dynamite crates. Lord knows what's inside of them. We can't take the chance, Trevor. We need to draw Judd and the woman outside. If a stray bullet were to hit one of those crates, the place would blow sky high with Claire in the middle of it."

* * *

Regina pressed the derringer against Claire's neck. Scorn burned in her gaze as she stared down at the other woman's white face. "I should just shoot you and be done with this." She glanced over her shoulder at where her cousin reached for the door. "What are you doing?"

"I'm going to check on that noise."

"Get back here," she ordered. "That scratching was just an animal of some sort." Regina tipped her chin toward Claire, who trembled violently beneath the pressure of the small derringer. "I've just about had my fill of this smelly, rotting building. Take her in the other room and do what you've been waiting for, so we can get the hell out of here."

Judd immediately forgot about the door and crossed back to Claire. He yanked her to her feet.

Claire shrieked her terror, and waves of blackness washed through her head. She thrashed feebly, but the half-hearted attempt served only to make Judd tighten his hold as he dragged her across the floor. He glanced over his shoulder at Regina, who stood in the middle of the floor with her arms crossed over her chest. "I prefer to do this without an audience. Go outside. When I'm through with her, I'll let you know."

"This is your last chance," Regina stated with conviction. "If she's not dead within fifteen minutes, I'll do the deed myself."

"No!" Claire cried.

Judd turned, forced Claire into the next room, and slammed the door behind him.

Regina's lips were still drawn in a tight line of disgust as she headed for the porch.

* * *

Trevor and Cole dove silently to the ground when the door opened and light spilled onto the porch. They eyed one another as quick, agitated footsteps crossed to the railing. When all was silent, they carefully lifted their heads eyelevel with the wooden planking.

Cole heard Trevor's slight intake of breath just before anger blazed in his brother's eyes. Together, they watched as Regina Simpson strolled down the rickety stairs.

Cole ignored Trevor's obvious anger—and the reasons behind it; he pointed to himself, and then nodded to Regina.

Trevor tipped his head in understanding, then drew his pistol and trained the barrel in the direction of the open doorway as Cole crawled across the grass to the edge of the porch. The younger brother waited until Regina walked toward the carriage, then he laid his rifle on the ground and swung his gaze to the open doorway one last time to check Trevor's status. Then, with the stealth of a cat, he rose to his feet and padded after Regina. A split-second later, his brother jumped onto the surface of the porch and tread softly to the entrance.

Regina stopped halfway to the buggy and glanced up at the moon. Her thoughts wandered back to what was going on inside the building; she only hoped that Judd would finish grunting atop Trevor's wife quickly. Her cousin wanted to leave Claire's body in the mineshaft; Regina did not agree. She wanted Trevor to discover Claire's dead body as soon as possible, therefore bringing an end to this entire escapade. Only then could Regina sweep in, comfort the grieving widower, and reclaim what she had worked so diligently to acquire over the last year.

From out of nowhere, a hand clamped over her mouth and an arm simultaneously tightened around her body. Regina's muffled scream was a mere squeak as she struggled crazily against the brute strength that pinned her arms to her sides. Helplessly, she was dragged into the darkness.

* * *

The sound of tearing material bounced off the dank walls of the small room. Claire lay on the dirty wooden floor, her sobs and her struggles muted by Judd's weight as he kept her pinned firmly beneath him; one hand pawed at her heaving breasts while the other dragged the hem of her skirt up past her knees. His fingernails scraped the tender skin of an inner thigh as the hand worked its way to her waistline. Claire felt nothing other than the utter terror that burned inside her brain as his mouth ravaged her neck and his fingers worked their way into her underclothes. Claire's flailing hand grabbed at the hair on the side of his head and pulled.

He cursed beside her ear, struggled to capture her wrists, and pinned her arms above her head. "It's useless to fight, Claire. In the end I'll win out." He chuckled lewdly, then stared at her parted lips. "I've waited far too long for this."

Claire blinked back the unbidden tears that glistened in her eyes. "Let me go. Please, don't do this."

Judd's smile only widened as he secured his hold on her wrists with one hand, then allowed the other to snake downward and cup a full breast that was barely covered by the shredded material.

"I hate you!" Claire choked out. "I hate you for what you're going to do to me, and I hate you for what you did to my children!"

He simply chuckled again and lowered his head; his mouth chased after her bruised lips. He captured them a moment later, then he ground his hard length against her and brutally squeezed her tender mounded flesh.

Claire screamed in pain as the room spun around her.

The door crashed against the wall.

Light spilled into the room, framing the large form that filled the doorway. Trevor bounded forward an instant later, yanked Judd from his wife's body, and dragged the man upward. Hauling back his fist, he smashed it against the banker's face. The force of the blow sent Claire's attacker flying back against the wall. Trevor's raging mind registered a loud grunt as a dazed Judd slipped to the floor. The man stared up at his assailant in disbelief as he tried to slide his body back up the wall. Trevor never gave him the chance. He lunged again, this time using the toe of his boot to deliver a blow to the other man's abdomen. Judd sank to the floor for a second time.

"Trevor!" Claire choked out.

He whirled and sank to his knees, gathering Claire into his arms. She was alive, and his heart burst with the knowledge.

"He's got a gun..."

Trevor's gaze swung back to Judd just as the other man's hand slid toward his pocket. "Get out of here, Claire!"

She scrambled across the floor to the open doorway as Trevor charged her attacker. His fingers twisted around the material of the man's shirt as he jerked him upward once more. "You're going to pay this time, you bastard—" His fist connected with Judd's stomach.

The man's grunt ended in a wheeze as his knees buckled beneath him; Trevor tightened his grip and sent another grueling punch into Judd's midsection.

The cowardly man gasped for air and weakly lifted a hand to ward off any further blows. "Stop..."

"Stop?" Trevor returned through clenched teeth as he twisted the man's shirt even tighter around his throat, cutting off his air supply. "Did you stop when Claire begged you to? It sure as hell didn't sound like it, you son of a bitch." He slammed his fist into Judd's stomach once more. The man would have buckled forward, but Trevor shoved him roughly against the wall. Hauling back his clenched fist, he went after the banker's face.

Bones crunched beneath the blow. Blood splattered from a broken nose. Trevor's own knuckles split open as, time after time, his fist met the battered skull, fueling the red haze of fury that burned in his brain. The blows continued until Judd slipped unconscious to the floor— and until the sound of Trevor's name on Claire's lips pulled him from the utter depths of an all-consuming rage.

Trevor stepped back and his hands dropped to his thighs; his head hung in exhaustion. His chest heaved; his breath rasped from his lungs. Finally, he straightened and nudged the fallen man with the toe of his boot. Still breathing deeply, he turned to search his wife's pale features. Claire huddled in the doorway, one hand reaching out to him as the other clutched the torn shreds of her bodice. Thick tears coursed down her cheeks. He hurried to her, welcomed her trembling body into his arms, and pulled her tightly against his chest. Silently, he thanked the heavens above that she was still alive.

Trevor's heart ached over what Judd had put Claire through in the last hours. A past promise to always keep her safe filtered through his brain. He had failed. *Never again...I'll never give anyone the chance again...* "I'm so sorry, Claire. I'm sorry that it took me so long to get here."

She clung to him, too frightened to let go. Her body shuddered against his. "Take me out of here," she choked out. "Trevor, please. Just take me to my children."

Trevor glanced at where Judd's body sprawled lifelessly across the floor. He hoped the man was dead. If not, then Trevor would make sure that he swung by the neck. As soon as Tyler and Moose arrived, he would drag the son of a bitch outside and hand him over.

Trevor crossed to where the battered Judd lay on his back. He dug his hand into a torn pocket, yanked out a pistol and, with one last hate-filled glare, returned to Claire's side. He wrapped an arm around her waist then, and led her outside.

Not until they reached the porch did Claire suddenly realize that Regina was missing. "Oh, my God! Regina! She was with Judd. She was going to kill me...after Judd..." Claire could not finish the sentence. She clutched her husband's arm, terrified that the woman would return.

"It's all right, Claire. Cole is with me." His eyes searched the darkness. "He's got her out there somewhere."

"The children..." A sob escaped Claire's throat, and Trevor tightened his arm about her waist.

He helped her down the steps. "They're at the ranch with Steve and Carrie. I brought them there when I found them on the road."

Claire's chin trembled. "Hannah...I couldn't wake her up." Her shaking hand covered her mouth. "I didn't know what to do Hannah...my baby..." Her sorrowful gaze met his. "I...I thought she would die in my arms. Is she..."

"I'm sure Carrie and Steve managed to get the fever down. I couldn't wait to find out. I had to find you. She's in good hands—they all are."

Claire rested her head against his chest. "And, Ruthie...that monster pulled her from the wagon—" Another sob caught in her throat as she remembered the horror of watching one of children almost die before her eyes.

Trevor kissed the top of her head. "She's okay, Claire." He would accomplish nothing now by telling her the emotional state Ruth was in when he left the ranch.

"I want to go to them now. I need to see them..."

"We'll go. It's going to be all right—I promise."

Claire wrapped her arm tighter around his waist as they crossed the dark compound to Trevor's horse, battling the fear that still consumed her.

Trevor's gaze searched the circumference of the yard for Cole. Only the sound of crickets could be heard as he headed to where Buck was tied to a tree under the cover of brush. "I've got Claire! Are you out there?" He did not dare call out to his brother by name. Somehow, he would figure out a way to cover Cole's presence when needed.

Nothing. Silence.

* * *

Judd's head lolled and his eyes flickered open. A painful groan escaped his throat as he rolled onto his side and struggled for air. Rising to an elbow, he waited for his head to quit spinning, then used the wall to support himself as he rose shakily to his feet.

He staggered to the doorway of the small room, leaned heavily against the jamb, and scanned the empty mine office through the swollen slits of his eyes. Where was Regina? *The bitch must have escaped before Wilkins showed up...*

If not? Hope burned in his chest that Trevor had killed her. The plan had gone horribly awry. He closed his eyes until the floor quit titling, then held his aching gut and staggered toward a case of dynamite. Muffled voices filtered into the room from outside, and he froze. It would be only a matter of time before he was hauled away to face charges that would put him in prison for the rest of his life, or worse.

Judd grunted with the effort it took to push aside the lid on one of the boxes. The crate held only a few tools. He crawled to the next box and worked the top off. Three small sticks of dynamite nestled atop dirty sawdust. Judd reached in.

* * *

Cole lifted his head where he crouched beside Regina when Trevor's voice echoed across the night. Claire was safe and they were out of the building. His scathing eyes flickered toward the face of the gagged woman before he gripped her arm and hauled Regina to her feet. "Let's go."

Regina mumbled incoherently behind the handkerchief. Her wide eyes displayed her fear as she attempted to yank her arm free of his hold.

"Knock it off lady," he responded to her effort and tightened his grip. "I don't know why the two of you did what you did, but I'm damn well going to find out. I hope both of you hang." He reached up, pushed the tangled brush aside and gave her a light shove. "Now, move!"

* * *

Claire and Trevor continued across the compound until they reached the tree line. He stopped and glanced at their surroundings again before entering the thick brush. "Cole's out there somewhere with Regina. Tyler went to Biwabik to get Moose. They should be here shortly." He pulled his wife close once more and brushed his hand over the loose curls that hung to Claire's shoulders. "You're all right, aren't you? Judd didn't..."

"No," she replied softly as she wrapped her arms around his waist.

"Can you tell me why Regina was with him? I can't figure out the connection. Why did they kidnap you?"

She clung to him tightly; the fear in her heart ebbed as the nightmare receded from her brain. "They're cousins. Regina wanted you—enough so that my life meant nothing. If they hadn't pulled me out of the wagon on the road, they would have found some other way. They were going to kill me..." She rested her forehead against his chest and suppressed a shudder. "Regina saw herself comforting you; eventually she felt the two of you would be together. She was going to talk you into selling our property to Judd, so he could mine it in the future."

Trevor rested his cheek on the top of her head and closed his eyes. It was hard to imagine such insatiable greed that would allow a woman's life to have no meaning. Judd would pay dearly. If the man did not swing by the neck, Trevor would assure that he lived behind bars the rest of his life.

"Wilkins!"

Trevor spun, yanking Claire's body behind him. Judd Stone leaned heavily against a railing on the porch. He held a lantern in one hand. Something rested in the other as the man finally found the strength to straighten and hold up both arms.

"You think you've won, you bastard!" Judd's insane voice echoed across the dark compound. "You can have the bitch, but you'll never get me. I won't rot in jail." His head lolled momentarily as he blinked to clear his whirling brain. "See this?" he bellowed and held his hand higher. "It's dynamite. Can you see? Come on, you goddamned coward! Come out of the dark...maybe you'll die with me."

Goosebumps rose on Claire's arm as she listened to his insane laughter. She leaned closer against the comfort of Trevor's body, thankful the man could not see them.

Trevor's eyes widened with incredulous understanding when Judd lifted the lantern closer to the dynamite. Suddenly, he spun, grabbed Claire's arm and dragged her into the thick brush. "Run! He's going to blow up the building!"

Claire raced alongside of him, her feet tripping over jutting roots and fallen branches in their frenzied flight toward questionable safety. Trevor's eyes darted frantically for heavier cover, then he jerked his wife's body toward a stand of thick Norway pines that were cloaked in the darkness. Yanking her to her knees, he pressed her body against the backside of a massive trunk just as a huge blast shook the ground. The explosion illuminated the forest around them.

The concussion's ferocious thunder sent them sprawling onto their backs and, an instant later, Trevor scrambled to shield Claire's body with his as huge tree limbs snapped like tinder wood around them.

Claire huddled beneath her husband's body as one massive explosion after another rocked the ground. The forest lit with the brightness of a false sun, and her ears rang, drowning out the frantic thud of her heart. The sudden jerk of her husband's body atop hers was followed an instant later by a pain-filled groan.

"Trevor!" Her eyes flew open and she turned her head. A large branch lay across his lower back. She struggled beneath him.

"I'm okay!" he hollered beside her ear. "Just stay down!" His arms tightened about her shoulders as they waited for the blasts to end.

Trees continued to rain down around them until the illumination finally dimmed and small eruptions replaced the massive ones. Trevor rolled from Claire's body then, and, together, they crawled from beneath the heavy branch. He rose stiffly and helped his wife to her feet. His palms skimmed her face and shoulders, searching for injuries. "Are you hurt?"

She shook her head and flung herself into his outstretched arms. "He killed himself..."

Trevor nodded as his chin rested against the crook of her neck. "It's over, Claire."

"I'm glad...I'm glad that monster is dead..."

Trevor stepped from her arms and grasped her fingers. "Come on. We've got to check on Cole. Christ, I hope he wasn't near the explosion." They retraced their steps, carefully stepping over the fallen trees—then froze when they stepped into the yard. Every building had been leveled to little more than rubble. The piles of debris still burned brightly.

Trevor's gaze searched the compound, but Cole was nowhere to be seen. They skirted the far side of the mine yard, avoiding the fallen structures. Judd's carriage and the horse had been blown across the compound and now lay in a dead heap. He was sure if he searched long enough, he would find bits of Judd's body in the rubble. Trevor would not waste his time. "Are you out there!" he hollered to Cole as he clutched Claire's hand tightly and waited for a response.

"I'm here!" a voice answered from somewhere in the distance. "I'm fine!"

They waited until he emerged from the opposite tree line. Regina's arm was clutched in his grip. He forced the woman to walk in front of him as they headed toward the other couple.

Trevor's gaze bored into the disheveled woman's eyes. "Let her talk," he sneered when they reached him and Claire. He waited silently as Cole pulled the handkerchief from between her lips. His wife moved closer to him.

As soon as Regina lips were free from the gag, she took a deep breath, ignoring Cole's painful grip on her arm. "Trevor, this isn't what it looks like—" she pleaded.

"What the hell did you think you were you doing? I want the truth—now!"

"He made me do it, Trevor. Judd forced me to help him kidnap Claire. You've got to believe me."

His wife stepped forward and leveled her gaze on the beseeching woman. "She's lying. She was the one who masterminded the whole thing."

Regina's eyes registered instant panic. "I did not! I told Judd it was a stupid prank! I love you, Trevor. I would never do anything to hurt you or anyone around you. Please, you've got to believe me!"

Trevor's already hard jaw clenched even tighter. "Gag her again. I won't listen to her lies."

"No!"

Cole managed to get the handkerchief back between Regina's lips and silence her deception.

Trevor took the gun from his holster and handed it to Claire as his gaze continued to bore into Regina's. "Here. You can have the pleasure of pulling the trigger if she tries to run. Get on the ground, Regina—and stay there." The woman's head shook fitfully until Cole forced her down. "Now you can see what it feels like to have someone hold a gun to your head. It's up to Claire whether you live or die."

Regina's eyes snapped shut as she choked behind the restraint.

Trevor's gaze swung back to Cole's laughing eyes. "Get the hell out of here before Tyler and Moose show up. With that blast, this place is going to be crawling with people."

He nodded, but before he turned to leave, he reached out to lay his palm on Claire's shoulder. Unable to find the words to express his relief, he simply gave her a tender hug.

The sound of pounding hooves reached the clearing. Cole smiled. "I guess that's Tyler with the cavalry. I'll see you on the road." He turned and sprinted to the trees. Cole's body melted into the darkness as Tyler and Moose charged into the yard.

The two riders reined their mounts to a skidding halt. Tyler vaulted from the saddle when he spotted Claire standing beside her husband. His instant smile disappeared a second later when he recognized Regina huddled on the ground—and saw the pistol Claire pointed at her head.

"What the hell happened? We were only a couple of miles away when all hell broke loose. God, I was certain you were all killed."

Trevor ran a hand through his thick hair. "If Regina would've had her way, the feat would have been accomplished."

Tyler stared at the cowering woman. "What the hell is she doing mixed up in all of this?"

Moose dismounted and approached the small group. His eyes settled on the woman in the dirt. "I imagine this is where I come in."

Claire continued to hold the pistol in a death grip until Trevor removed it from her trembling hand. "It's a long story, Moose. Judd Stone was also involved."

"Judd? Judd Stone, the banker?"

Trevor nodded. "He blew himself up, along with buildings." His gaze turned to Regina. "Her name is Regina Simpson. She helped to kidnap Claire. Just keep her behind bars until I get to Biwabik sometime in the next few days. I'll fill you in on all the details then. Right now, my wife needs to go home and see her children." He took one step with Claire beneath his arm, and hesitated. Turning back, he watched Moose help Regina to her feet. The woman mumbled repeatedly behind the gag. As Moose removed the binding, Trevor met his brother's questioning gaze. "We'll *all* see you at the ranch, Tyler."

The eldest Wilkins brother nodded his understanding.

Regina waited for the gag to disappear. Who was the other man? For some reason, Trevor wanted his presence hidden. If she was going down, it would not be alone. The words tumbled from her mouth when she was free to speak. "Don't let them walk away!" she urged the sheriff as she glared at her former lover. "He's hiding something—they're all hiding something!"

Moose stopped short and glanced around.

Trevor shrugged when the sheriff's eyes rested on him—just before he turned a quizzical gaze on Regina. "Now what lies are you spouting?"

"Don't give me that. There was another man here helping you. I should know. Sheriff, whoever it was, he manhandled me into the woods while Trevor rushed to get Claire."

Trevor's eyes narrowed. "So where is he now? You know, Regina, I've had just about enough of you. I think the blast rattled your brain. I almost didn't get to Claire in time because I was trying to get you out of the way first. I wish I would've had some help. Maybe my wife wouldn't be standing here with her dress torn open. Quit stalling the inevitable. You're going to jail and there's nothing you can do or say that will change that." His gaze swung to Moose. "Get her out of my sight."

* * *

Claire and Trevor reclined against soft pillows in the bed in their old room at the ranch. They spoke quietly, so as not to wake the children. The comforting light of a gas lantern turned low flickered across the room.

Trevor cuddled Hannah's cool body against his broad chest. The little girl squirmed in her sleep, and her tiny hand floated about until she found her stepfather's bandaged knuckles. A second later, Trevor tucked her chubby fingers into his palm. It was amazing how the little girl's state of restful slumber felt so different than the comatose state she was in earlier. He kissed the top of her soft head and grinned at his wife.

Claire continually ran her fingers through Ruth's soft hair as the girl slumbered beside her; she smiled back. Her gaze moved to Sofie and Sue Ellen, who were sprawled beneath a quilt at the end of the bed, and then crossed to her son. Jonah's even breaths drifted to them from where he slept on the window seat.

Claire peeked up at her husband and felt the loving warmth of his gaze. She reached out a hand and rested it upon the muscular arm that held her youngest so protectively. "I'm glad we decided to stay here and not head home. They're exhausted after this horrifying day—and thank you for suggesting they stay with us in this room. I needed to have them close by."

The corner of Trevor's mouth turned up. "I couldn't agree with you more. I was so concerned about Ruthie. Seeing you though, really seemed to help her out. Emma told me that she didn't say a word until she saw you come in the door. We'll take it slow and eventually she'll understand that there's nothing to be frightened of anymore." He pressed another kiss against Hannah's hair. "And this one. Thank God the fever broke. Christ, Claire, when I found them alone—" He shook his head, overwhelmed by the knowledge that everything he held so dear could have been snatched away forever.

Her hand traveled up to cup his whiskered cheek. "I refuse to dwell on it, Trevor. As horrible as this day could have turned out, it didn't. It's over. We're here together and that's what really matters when all is said and done." Tenderly, she brushed the back of her fingers across his jaw. "I'll never be able express how much I love you and how thankful I am that you walked into all our lives. From this day forward the past is no more. I will never look back—only forward. Always forward." Her gray eyes glowed, echoing the power of her conviction.

Trevor reached up and placed his hand over hers, then tilted his head and kissed the inside of her soft palm. "That's a deal I'm going to hold you to. I love you, Claire. And I love these five kids with all my heart."

She sighed happily. "Six—"

His brow furrowed for an instant—until his gaze settled on her widening smile. His heart thundered in his chest as her one word response sank in. "Six?"

Her head nodded against the pillow.

Epilogue

July 4, 1919

"Enjoying the peace and quiet?" Claire's lilting voice floated to him on the breeze.

Trevor grinned up at his wife. "It's a beautiful morning. Want to sit with me for a few minutes?"

She leaned over and tenderly lifted the white cat from his lap. A moment later, the animal strolled to the top of the steps and plopped down in the warm sun.

Trevor pulled his wife onto his lap. Claire automatically tilted her head to enjoy the whisper of a kiss he pressed against the sweet-smelling expanse of her neck. A shiver raced through her in response to her husband's nearness. Once again, she offered up a silent prayer of thanks for his presence in her life during the past years.

"Mmmm, you smell good." Trevor tucked her head against his shoulder and absently brushed his fingers across a slender arm as he stared out into the yard. "I've been sitting here listening to the loons. I don't think I'll ever get tired of hearing them sing across the lake."

"I know. I hear them and they remind me of all the good things in my life."

Trevor gave Claire's arm a squeeze. "How are you doing?"

He missed the sad smile that touched her lips because her head was tucked close beneath his chin. "Good. I think everything is ready for the party."

He adjusted her on his lap, moved his free arm to clasp her near, and locked his fingers around her slender body. "That's not what I'm talking about."

Her soft sigh whispered past his ear. "I'm so happy that everyone will be here today. I spoke with Emma yesterday. She and Tyler are so excited that the children have all arrived home—except for Thomas. After fretting for three weeks, she and Tyler finally received word that he'll be home this morning. They're picking him up at the train station as we speak." She hesitated for a moment, struggled against the ache in her chest, and finally acknowledged his last comment. "Why can't they find him, Trevor?"

He knew she did not mean his nephew, Thomas. Claire spoke about their son, Jonah, who disappeared weeks before peace was declared and the war finally ended. His fingers moved again across her arm. "We just have to keep believing he's out there somewhere."

Her hand crept down his arm to find his hand, and she laced her fingers through his. "I should know where he is. I should feel it in my heart, but there's nothing." Claire blinked away the instant tears that burned behind her lids. The day was supposed to be a day of happiness. She had promised herself she would not cry. "There's just this horrible emptiness that I have to push away in order to get through every minute."

Trevor understood the emotion. He had lived it every day since the telegram from the War Department arrived. Jonah was not his blood child, but no man could be prouder to call such a fine boy his son. The flash of a small urchin standing warily on the street with a rotten apple in his hand settled in his mind. *How many years has it been since fate brought Claire and the kids into my life?*

The vision slowly changed to a proud young man in a lieutenant's uniform standing on a railroad platform, struggling to remain strong as he bid his family goodbye. That was four years ago. Trevor fought the lump in his throat as he continued to rub her upper arm. "We'll get through this, Claire."

Her head dipped further into the crook of his neck. "I know. As long as we're together, I know I can be strong." She brushed her lips below his ear. "I love you." The last three words were barely a breath.

Trevor sighed, closed his eyes, and rested his weathered cheek against the softness of his wife's hair. "Hmmm, I don't think I'll ever get tired of hearing you say that."

They sat clinging to one another, drawing strength from the

many years of love they had shared, and thinking about the time that had passed so quickly and the many smiles of their missing son.

Claire turned her head and searched the road when the sound of a whirring motor reached her ears. She glanced back to her husband's sad eyes and pressed another kiss against his lips. "Well, that must be the first of the guests arriving. Promise that you'll meet me here tonight. When everyone's gone, I just want to sit and finish the night out here on the porch."

The corners of her husband's lips turned up. "You've got a date, Mrs. Wilkins." His gaze moved from her beautiful gray eyes to where Cole parked his vehicle in the driveway. Trevor chuckled when he helped Claire from his lap. "I can't believe he talked August into taking the car. She hates that thing." He placed the flat of his palm against his wife's back and they strolled across the yard to greet the two as more vehicles rounded the bend in the road.

Soon, Cole and August's entire clan poured into the driveway from the many autos. Sons, daughters, and grandchildren spilled across the manicured lawns after laughing hugs were exchanged. Trevor welcomed them all, happy that he and Claire had decided to host the party. There had been too many nights of sadness as they waited to hear word about Jonah.

The many members of the Wilkins' clan gathered beneath awnings that had been erected for the Fourth of July party. They munched on delicacies Claire had labored over for the last week, and waited excitedly for the rest of their large group to arrive. Within the next half-hour, Tyler and Emma's grown children crested the hill, mounted atop the beautiful horses raised at the ranch. Carrie and Steve drove in next, with their children and grandchildren in tow. It was not long before they, too, reclined beneath the awnings and quickly updated their lives with cousins and siblings, happy to be together after the turmoil of war.

Trevor eyed the commotion as he stood beside his younger brother and shook his gray head. "I can't believe how many of us there are. Claire has fretted all week that there wouldn't be enough food." As he said it, he watched his wife take Hannah's little son by the hand. Together, she and her daughter led the toddler up the stairs. A moment later, the three disappeared into the house.

Cole followed the line of Trevor's gaze, took a sip of his cold beer, and sighed heavily. "How are the two of you holding up?"

Trevor squinted into the sun and took a second to gather his wits about him. "We're doing okay. I'm glad Claire had this party to worry about. I think it's helped to keep her mind off of Jonah, at least for a while. We were just discussing his disappearance again when you and August drove up. Damn, I wish we'd hear something. Even if it was a telegram saying he was..." Trevor could not finish the sentence out loud. Jonah, gone from their lives forever, would be unfathomable. He nodded his head with a sad smile when Cole patted his shoulder for encouragement. "Claire refuses to even talk about the possibility."

Cole poured them both another beer and turned to look over his shoulder when he heard another car slowing to turn into the driveway. Tyler and Emma sat in the front seat. Thomas hung out the back window and waved wildly to everyone. As the car came to a halt, he shoved the door open, his eyes searching the faces of his many relatives. The one he sought was not in the crowd. Tyler walked around the vehicle as Thomas leaned back into the car and handed his father a pair of crutches.

Trevor sidestepped beneath the canvas awning to get a better view, wondering what took the group so long to hustle across the yard. He watched as Thomas carefully placed his arm around a man and helped him from the back seat. Suddenly, the earlier mayhem of excited voices quieted.

Trevor's glass fell from his shaking hand as he rushed around the table; his chest burned with joy. His long legs gobbled up the small distance between where he stood and the parked vehicle. Jonah leaned heavily against the side of the car as Tyler and Thomas placed the crutches beneath his arms, supporting his body over the one remaining leg.

Tears blurred Trevor's vision as he stopped before his son and silently wrapped the thin body in his trembling embrace. His son's shoulders heaved within his grasp.

"Pa...I'm home," he managed to breath out as the comfort of his father's arms rocked him close. Four long years had passed since he left for Italy; four long years of craving the sight of his parents' faces. The only thing that had kept him from going mad amid all the killing and the following months of imprisonment was the thought of being held in the arms of the wonderful man who had walked into his world one day, and the woman who had given him life.

"Jonah..." Trevor sobbed as he clutched the young man to his chest. His tears flowed freely for all to see.

Tyler wrapped his arm around Emma, blinking back his own tears as his wife wiped the wetness from her cheeks with a dainty hanky.

August and Cole hurried across the lawn and into the dusty driveway through the swinging gate. The rest of the party flooded through the gate behind them. Hoots of joy echoed as they crowded around, their eyes tearing, too, as Trevor and Jonah clung to one another.

Cole stopped beside Tyler, his heart filled with happiness for his brother—for all of them. He swiped at the wetness on his cheeks, squeezed August's shaking hand, and met Emma's sparkling green eyes. "Did you know?"

She shook her head as she dabbed at her tears. "I almost fainted when I saw Thomas helping him from the train. That's why he didn't come home when expected. He'd been searching for Jonah for the last three months and finally discovered him when a Prisoner of War camp opened their gates."

Trevor finally stepped back and cupped his son's thin face. His watery gaze lowered to where Jonah's trousers were pinned closed just below a swollen knee. "Son...Jonah...I'm so sorry." Trevor struggled for breath once more, at a loss as what to say.

Jonah's weak smile broadened, even though heavy tears flowed down his face. "I...I made it home, Pa. That's what counts." His eyes moved to the house. "Where's Ma?"

Trevor stepped to his son's side and wrapped a supportive arm around his waist. "She's in the kitchen. We'll just..." The words died in his throat when his gaze settled on his wife as she stepped through the doorway and onto the porch with a bowl in her hands.

Claire stared at the cluster of people, assuming that Tyler and Emma must have finally arrived with Thomas.

The mob in the driveway slowly parted, and Claire's gaze focused on her husband and the tall, thin man whose waist Trevor's arm encircled.

The bowl crashed to the surface of the porch, sending fresh fruit rolling across the planks. Claire hiked up her skirt as she raced down the steps, never taking her eyes from the person who was an answer to her prayers. "Jonah!" she choked out his name through instant tears. "Oh, my God, Jonah..."

His name repeatedly left her lips as she raced across the yard through the gate, and over the gravel with a hand clamped over her mouth. "Jonah...Jonah..."

"Ma!"

Claire's vision blurred with tears as she centered on his outstretched hand; she refused to acknowledge his partially amputated leg. Her chest burned with pain as she skidded to a stop and saw his tears of joy.

Her baby...her little boy, who toddled bravely across a fallen log, shinnied up a tree or scrambled down a barn ladder with the extreme grace of youth...

Tears of sadness for what the war had stolen from her son mixed with the joyful ones. She reached with shaking hands to tenderly touch the weariness that etched his thin cheeks.

The war had taken his youth, but not his life. For that she would always be thankful. His once boyish face now held the wisdom of age and life's sufferings. Whether he was whole did not matter, though. She and Trevor would help him face the days ahead—they all would.

Jonah's hands trembled as he reached out to his mother. Claire pulled him to her breast, closed her eyes, and gently swayed with him in her arms. Memories of holding a small boy in her arms filtered through her mind; the reality of the broken man pierced her heart, but they would look forward—always forward.

"Come," she said gently, then placed her hand in the crook of his elbow. "Walk with me to the house." Her tearful gaze met Trevor's.

He saw the suffocating pain in her eyes—and he saw how she struggled to push it away. Her face glowed, despite the sob that threatened to choke off her next words. "As Mamie used to say, this one fine day in the making."

She held Jonah's arm gently as he swayed above the crutches, lifted his chin proudly, and slowly escorted his mother to the chairs set beneath an awning. Trevor walked beside them with tears still glistening in his eyes. The many family members followed, clasping Thomas' hand and pulling him along within their midst.

Claire waited for Jonah to pull a chair out for her from beneath the table before she sat down. Trevor quickly placed another beside his wife and struggled not to help his son as Jonah's breath rasped over his lips. Finally, the young man managed to lower himself onto the surface. His pale face smiled up at his father for allowing him the dignity of completing the process on his own.

Everyone dragged chairs or benches close, anxious to speak with Jonah—and to hear what he had to say. He sat with Claire's hand clutched in his, still finding it hard to believe he was back in Minnesota. As he listened to the many questions swirling around him, he breathed deeply of the fragrant lavender growing in the yard and the pine-scented air floating on the breeze. They were scents that had always given him comfort; they were scents of home.

"Uncle Trevor!" someone called. "It's time for a toast."

Trevor shook his head where he flanked Jonah's other side. He was too overwhelmed by the events of the day, too besieged with gratitude to a higher power. They would expect his typical humor—something he could not accomplish on such a day as this.

"Oh, come on! What would a family get-together be if we didn't hear from you?" His many nieces and nephews urged him on as he continued to shake his head. No, he would rather sit quietly and continue to count his blessings.

"Pa?" Jonah leaned heavily on the arm of the chair. "I used to lie on my cot when I was a prisoner. I would hear the sound of your voice and...and it got me through the night. Could you say something for me?"

"Way to go, Jonah!" Someone laughed again. "Make him talk. Speech! Speech!"

Trevor rose hesitantly from his chair amidst the excited whistles and applause. Drinks were quickly replenished and passed around. Cole shoved a beer into his brother's hand and, with a pat on his shoulder, moved to stand beside August and take her hand in his. Tyler wrapped one arm around Emma's waist and rested his cheek against her soft hair. Trevor moved to stand behind Claire. A hush descended across the yard.

Trevor cleared his throat, his mind suddenly blank. Being the storyteller of the group, he tried to conjure up something from past years, but all he could think about was the fact that Jonah was sitting in front of him.

Claire recognized his predicament and, reaching up a hand, waited for her husband to clasp her fingers. "Just speak from your heart," she breathed out. "You'll find the words."

Trevor ducked his chin momentarily and closed his eyes. The trill of a loon echoed from the nearby lake as if lending him courage to find the right words. He raised his head again and scanned the many familiar smiles. They waited—the people whom he had loved for many years.

Claire squeezed his hand, and he filled his lungs with fresh, sweet-smelling air.

"Before we toast, I'd like to say something first..." He breathed deeply. "We have been blessed. All of us. We've had the strength of our families, ever ready to lend support when we falter—" his gaze moved to his nephew, Thomas "— ever ready to sacrifice and go the extra step without thinking of one's self." He set his glass on the picnic table suddenly finding it hard to breathe. "Thank you, Thomas, for the gift you gave us all today." His free hand dropped to Jonah's shoulder. His son immediately reached up and covered his father's shaking fingers to lend him courage.

Trevor swallowed, his gaze encompassing the group once more. "The world is changing. As I look at all your faces, I wonder about the journey that lies ahead for each and every one of you. I want to tell you something about what I've learned from mine." He cleared his throat before turning his gaze on Tyler, Cole, and Carrie. "Hold the love of your family close. Because the four of us have been able to do just that we've discovered together that life cannot rob the soul of its spirit. Life might sometimes dash our hopes to the ground but, from those ashes dreams arise."

Emma pressed her fingers to her lips with a teary smile and sent him a silent kiss. Cole placed an arm around August's shoulders. Carrie leaned her head against Steve; tears sparkled in her eyes.

"So I'm telling you, fate will take you on your own amazing journey. Don't be afraid of it. Let it lead you where you need to go. Life is sometimes so fragile, but you can make it strong." The only sound to be heard was the gentle flapping of the awning above them as it lifted in the light breeze.

Trevor cleared his throat again, reached for his glass, and lifted it high. "Now, a toast to all of us." He was infinitely thankful that the lump in his throat began to recede.

"Here, here!" was the spirited reply as glasses were raised.

"First, to the older generations among us—"

"Oh, come on, Uncle Trevor!" someone shouted. Hoots of laughter followed, but Trevor's eyes twinkled with glee.

"May we all continue to live to a ripe old age and show these youngsters what tough stock they come from!"

"Here, here!" Tyler and Cole shouted in unison. They both laughed along with Trevor at the friendly jeers elicited by his declaration.

Trevor raised his hand for silence, enjoying the shift of everyone's mood. "Now, a toast for the rest of you. Go after life with an open mind. Find what you want and don't be afraid to grab it." He squeezed Claire's hand as her mouth curved in a knowing smile. He winked at her and swung his gaze to his nephew. "Thomas, you wouldn't by any chance have your harmonica with you?"

Thomas smiled with a nod of his head, reached into his breast pocket, and pulled out the instrument. He brought it to his lips, and soft mellow strains floated on the wind.

Trevor pulled Claire to her feet, and her happy smile illuminated her face when her gaze met his.

Trevor bowed at the waist; the twinkle in his eyes brightened. "Would you share this dance with me?"

Claire stepped into his arms—the gentle arms of a husband who had vowed to love her always; the man who held her heart in the palm of his hand.

As they danced across the grass, she laughed up into his glowing eyes. Every day was the beginning of a new journey with Trevor by her side.

Kim Mattson

Kim Mattson was born and raised in northern Minnesota and has lived there her entire life, spending a lot of her childhood fishing and camping with her sisters, father, and grandfather. To this day, she still loves being close to her roots. She thanks her many friends and family who have supported her desire to write. Being captivated with it, she doesn't plan to stop any time soon. In fact, she is now writing full time!

NORMANDALE COMMUNITY COLLEGE
LIBRARY
9700 FRANCE AVENUE SOUTH
BLOOMINGTON, MN 55431-4399